SAN ANTONE

V. J. BANIS

ARBOR HOUSE / NEW YORK

Designed by Richard Oriolo

Manufactured in the United States of America
10 9 8 7 6 5 4 3 2 1

Library of Congress Cataloging in Publication Data
Banis, Victor J.
San Antone.
I. Title.

PS3552.A476S2 1985 813'.54 85–6164
ISBN 0-87795-683-9 (alk. paper)

To Roby Karl and Russ La Fazia,
for shining me through that dark night

I am particularly grateful to Karen Nelson of the Big Bear Lake Branch of the San Bernardino County (California) Public Library, not the least for remaining cheerful while facing that barrage of questions attendant upon writing a historical novel.

PROLOGUE

"Bother the doctor's orders."

It was impossible to sleep. The closed windows, the shutters fastened over them, could no more shut out the maddeningly repetitious sound of gunfire, the terrified bawling of cattle, than they could hold at bay the fine, gritty Texas sand that forever seeped into the house—into food and drink, and bed linen, and undergarments, and even, she sometimes shocked people by mentioning, the very crevices and openings of the body.

She struggled unavailingly to sit up, surrendered to necessity, and reached resentfully for the cane kept now at bedside.

The room was dark, the motionless air hot and weighted. She crossed to the French doors, trying to muffle the sound of the cane on the tiled floor; someone was likely to hear and come to badger her.

After the gloom inside, the afternoon sun was blinding, and scorchingly hot. Farther along the wooden balcony, a curtain of vines provided little dappled pools of shade, you could almost smell the cool, but there was none here, directly outside her room. She liked the sun, and the Texas heat—as thick as molasses, sometimes you had to push your way through it. She never minded that. After all, that was what she'd built the balcony for in the first place; that, and the entirely private satisfaction of surveying her domain, if she felt the whim.

Not that she could, of course, not literally. A million acres now to the Folly; no, closer to a million and a half. Even from the airborne view of that hawk—or was it, yes, a buzzard, and she knew what he was after, damn him to hell, it wasn't just the wind stirring up those mountains of dust across the plains, there—even from his soaring heights, it would be impossible, the eye could not take it all in. Sometimes even her mind's eye could not.

It *was* her domain, though, there was no question of that.

At least for the moment, though the time was fast approaching when the reins must pass into other hands. No easy choice, either: Into whose hands? She'd made her choice, and she was content with it; but others, she well knew, would not be. There would be challenges, battles. Those reins would not be so easy to hold.

Unconsciously she smacked her lips at the thought. She wished she could be here to see—oh, well, not that she wanted to live forever. The truth was, she often found herself admiring those old Indians who, feeling the end approach, had ridden out alone into the wilderness to wait for death in dignified privacy. If it weren't for the concern, the bother that it would cause others . . . or maybe she simply lacked the courage.

Though to her thinking, it took no small courage to face that day-to-day dwindling of one's strength, one's resources. Never knowing when or how you were going to make a fool of yourself again—the stumble on the stairs, the food spilled on dressfront, the train of thought slipping from the mind in midsentence. When you got down to it, in the end, living was a swindle.

No, she'd be glad to be done with that; she looked forward with a sort of hopeful dread. Who could say, maybe there'd be challenges wherever she ended up, and she wasn't going to take any bets just where that would be; it would be awfully dull otherwise, wouldn't it?

But, she couldn't help wondering what her successor would do with all the responsibility she was handing over. Yes, and all that power as well. You played that down with others, but there was no need to pretend to herself; she had amassed power, too, along with all the rest.

Well, if you wanted to sum it all up, *she* hadn't done so badly with it, if she did say so herself. When she thought back, to South Carolina—to that simpering southern belle...

Her thoughts drifted. South Carolina. Eaton Hall. She suddenly found herself remembering Ellen Goodman.

Good heavens, forty years or more since she had seen that woman. It was odd, sometimes she could not summon up in her mind the faces of her children, her husband, people she saw every day. And yet she had but to close her eyes and there was Ellen Goodman, in the dining room at Eaton Hall, her eyes wide, her mouth agape, for they had both just heard, for the first time, those words that would come to mean so much....

PART I

JOURNEY HOME

ONE

"San Antonio?" Ellen Goodman's plump cheeks quivered
on the words. "But that's out west someplace, isn't it?"

"Texas," Lewis Harte said curtly.

"Texas? I don't think I—"

"Our new state," Mr. Mallory said. "Our twenty-eighth, I believe."

"But, still, a wilderness...Aren't there Indians, and things like
that?"

"Horsefeathers," Lewis said, and drained his glass of claret. The
black man standing just behind his chair moved swiftly, silently, to
refill it. Lewis's wife, Joanna, counted mentally: his fifth glass.

"And you've actually been there, Mr. Mallory?" Ellen's aunt Sarah
turned her astonished gaze on that gentleman. "To this Santa—
Santa..."

"Well," Mr. Mallory said, "I haven't exactly been to San Antonio,
but I have seen Texas. Our ship stopped at the port of Galveston
on the way here. I found it quite a civilized city, actually."

7

"Perfect rice-growing country, he tells me," Lewis emphasized. "Isn't that right, Mallory?"

"As to that, I can't really say, not being a grower myself. What I saw, however, seemed not unlike what I see hereabouts. Lowlands. Galveston sits on an island, but the mainland looks wet and marshy. The climate is hot, dampish. I can say this, it's a booming port, and likely to become more so. Easy sea access. I should think that would be useful to a planter." He directed this last remark to Joanna, in a conciliatory tone, as if to apologize for encouraging her husband's scheme.

"Damned useful," Lewis said. He shot his wife a glance and banged the table with his fist, causing his wine to spill over the rim of his glass. Joanna watched the crimson stain spread across the tablecloth.

Papa John, the slave at Lewis's elbow, saw it, too, and made a move as if to clean up the spill. Lewis waved him away.

"Leave it," he snapped. He looked at his wife with wine-clouded eyes, his expression stubborn and angry. "Well," he demanded, "haven't you anything to say?"

She knew that it was a mistake to argue with her husband when he'd been drinking as he had all evening; but she could not help feeling alarmed at the proposal he had just so unexpectedly made.

"Surely you can't mean you've already made up your mind," she said, attempting to placate him with a smile. "Such a big move. Couldn't we talk this over, tomorrow, perhaps?"

Lewis turned to Mr. Mallory. "Unfortunately, as you can see, my wife is inclined to value her own opinions rather highly. Higher, sometimes, than those of her husband. That is what comes of permitting a woman to read and write."

"But it's not a question of reading," Joanna said, knowing even as she spoke that she was inviting trouble. "To uproot your family, to carry your wife and children to some far-off wilderness, about which we know next to nothing..."

"I know enough," Lewis said, his color darkening ominously. "I know that the new state has agreed, after lengthy negotiations, to honor that old land grant my father held from the Spanish—for a fee, of course, but the payment is a modest one, considering the amount of land involved: five hundred thousand acres. A half-million acres, I tell you, you'd think a woman would take pride— why, it's a hundred times what we've got here. Yes, and what we've got here we're not likely to have for long, the way things are headed.

That damned fool, Lincoln, he wants war, there's not a doubt of it, he wants to bring the South to her knees. And this talk of freeing the slaves, that alone spells our ruination. You couldn't run Eaton Hall without slaves, no, nor any other plantation either. I ask you, Mallory, man to man"—he emphasized the matter of gender—"is that the truth or is it not?"

"I'm bound to say you're right about that," Mr. Mallory said, avoiding Joanna's glance.

"You see? You see? If you were half as smart as you think…" Lewis turned on his wife, his arms flailing the air.

"But surely," Joanna said, "if the president frees the slaves, they will be freed in Texas as well as South Carolina?"

"Texas is a far cry from here. Your Great Emancipator may march his armies into Dixie, but Texas is not so easy a matter— the distance alone would give him pause."

"And, this is my home—"

"Do not say 'my,'" Lewis shouted, standing up so abruptly that his chair toppled over backward. Papa John made an attempt at catching it, unsuccessfully. It hit the floor with a crash that made Ellen Goodman squeak with alarm.

"Do not be impertinent with me, madam. What was yours became mine the day we wed. I am master in this household, and I remind you, a wife owes her husband obedience, as I'm sure either of these fine ladies—neither of whom, I'm convinced, has been tainted by your so-called educational pursuits—will agree with me." He glanced expectantly in the direction of their female guests.

"A woman's place, certainly, is with her husband," Sarah Goodman said, adding with perhaps a lack of conviction, "wherever that may be."

"Exactly," Lewis said, pacing rapidly to and fro; Papa John, trying to retrieve the fallen chair, was forced to dance an eccentric jig, avoiding his path. "The matter is settled, my mind's made up. I've already instructed my bankers to make the transfer of funds. We'll move to Texas before the year's out. I mean to move the house, the slaves, the crops—and my family as well. No, not another word, Joanna. You try me too far." He turned and strode swiftly from the room. A moment later the chandelier rattled an accompaniment to the slamming of the door.

The silence that followed in its wake was intense. Now that he was gone, Joanna regretted pushing her husband as she had. She ought to have known that in front of others he'd be obligated to make a display of his authority. Perhaps if she had been more subtle in her arguments—oh, but that was wishful thinking, wasn't it? Lewis was not a man to be dissuaded once he had set his mind to something, even something so monumentally dangerous and foolish as this appeared to her.

Sarah Goodman rose from her chair, signaling her niece to do likewise. "Since we'll be leaving early in the morning, perhaps it is as well if Ellen and I retire," she said in a voice plainly indicating her disapproval.

More rumors, Joanna thought, watching them go. More tales carried from plantation to plantation, for the Goodmans were inveterate visitors. Half the population of South Carolina—the half who weren't already acquainted with the stories—would hear before year's end of Lewis's drinking, of his wife's odd habit of educating not only herself but those of her slaves who wanted to learn as well.

She remembered belatedly that she still had one guest at her table, and turned her eyes on him. "You're leaving tomorrow, too, I believe, Mr. Mallory."

"Necessities of business," he said. "And I can tell you I shall sorely regret my departure."

The remark, she knew, was intended to be flirtatious; she was not unmindful of the lust in the man's eyes when he looked at her. As a young girl, Joanna had looked long and hard at herself, and accepted that she would never be pretty; she had settled for beauty instead.

Perhaps if she loved her husband, his wenching and their lack of relations might have provoked her to jealousy, driven her to flirt, to welcome the attentions of men like Mr. Mallory. She had seen other marriages in which that happened.

That charge, at least, could not be leveled at her. She regarded Lewis's neglect of her as a welcome relief. They had three children, three fine children. There was no need..... Sometimes, it was true, she felt the emptiness. Surely there must be something else. She had observed couples, a few; she sensed something between them, something in the way they looked at one another, not only with love but with a desire that was warm and beautiful, that made her aware of some untouched sense of "womanness" within her, neglected, sleeping.

But her instincts told her it was not what she saw in Mr. Mallory's gaze, what she had seen in the eyes of other men.

The truth was, though she would have admitted this to no one, she had never responded the same way with her husband on those few brief occasions when he had come to her bed. It was wrong of her, she knew; a woman had no right to resent her husband's touch. She could not help herself. Even in the beginning, before he'd begun to drink so badly, it had been that way.

She pushed her chair back. Mr. Mallory leaped up to help her, and Papa John moved swiftly around the table, but she was on her feet before either could give her assistance.

"I'll leave you to your port, Mr. Mallory," she said.

"Your husband will no doubt return soon to join me," he said.

"Perhaps." She could have told him that was unlikely. By now, Lewis was with one or the other of the Negro wenches, whose company he preferred to that of his wife or his guests. It would be morning before he returned to the main house. "If you'll excuse me—Papa John will see to your needs."

With unmasked disappointment, he watched her go until she had disappeared up the stairs. Too bad, he thought, a lovely woman like that. That hair, all red and gold; there was a flower those colors that spilled over the arbor of his garden in Charleston; he must make a point of learning its name. And her eyes, green, but not cool as you'd expect; like a green fire, smoldering down deep in its ashes.

Diablerie, the French called it, that air of barely damped recklessness; she had that, all right.

And, so obviously unsatisfied. How he'd longed to lick that bead of sweat from the cleft of her breasts. It was the right man that she needed, not all that nonsense with books and learning. Her husband was right to disapprove of that; he ought to have beaten such ideas out of her long before this. *He* would make her forget such foolishness soon enough....

"Would the gentleman care for some port?"

The Negro voice startled him. He glanced at the slave waiting to hold his chair. "Yes," he said. "And one of your master's cigars."

There was a scurrying noise above her; Joanna glanced up to see three young faces peering at her through the balustrade.

"What on earth?" she said. "What are you three doing up at this hour?—as if I didn't know. Listening, where you've got no business."

They stood up as she finished climbing the stairs. It never failed to astonish her that her daughter, barely sixteen, was now as tall as she was. Gregory, at fourteen, was nearly as tall, but James was small-looking for his nine years, though apparently determined to make up for it in extra mischief.

"It's not true, is it?" Melissa demanded in a whisper. "We're not moving to that—that place, are we?"

"Will there be Indians?" James asked, looking entirely enthusiastic at the prospect. Gregory surveyed her in expectant silence.

"We'll see," Joanna said, giving each a brief hug. "Come along now, all of you, back to your beds. If your father had seen you, you'd have earned Mammy a good hiding, for no fault of her own. Scoot now, before I give you all one instead."

The children allowed themselves to be put back to bed, though James—"Jay Jay" to the family—gave every indication of being a long time awake, and Melissa's complaints continued unabated.

"It's not fair," she grumbled, barely pausing to return her mother's kiss. "I haven't even come out. And you promised me, my next birthday, my first ball..."

"I'm quite certain, my darling, wherever there are young ladies, there will be parties as well," Joanna assured her. "It's one of the verities. And I'm equally certain you've got no concept whatever of what Texas is like, no more geography than you've been willing to learn."

"Father says geography is unladylike."

"He's entirely right, but we needn't let that sway us. To sleep now, or you'll be much too haggard-looking to have birthday parties."

She looked in one final time at the boys. Gregory was already asleep—he was never any bother. James's determined pretense, eyes squinted tightly shut, was utterly unconvincing, but she did not challenge it. Little boys could be counted on to fall asleep eventually.

Her maid, Savannah, was asleep on the floor at the foot of her bed. Joanna did not trouble to waken her. She thought it silly that so many of the women of the South could not undress themselves without a slave's help. Like so many of the conventions of southern living, it was more stifling than comforting. She had once even gone so far as to insist on some other—to her way of thinking, more suitable—sleeping place for the girl, only to have Savannah come to her in tears, begging to be told what she'd done to provoke her banishment. In the end, she'd found it easier to let Savannah sleep where she was accustomed to sleeping. Savannah was a heavy sleeper; not waking her when she came in was Joanna's form of compromise.

Changing into her nightdress and a peignoir, Joanna sat at her dressing table and let down her hair for its nightly brushing. The routine was automatic; it left her thoughts free to turn where they would.

Texas. San Antonio. The truth was, she knew scarcely any more about them than her daughter did.

She'd heard of San Antonio, only because there had been that trouble there, a place called the Alamo. A sort of fort, if she remembered correctly, or a mission, maybe—she wasn't clear. Mexicans and Texans, or perhaps they were already Americans then. The Texans had gotten the worst of it. It had all been years ago, when she had been quite young. "Remember the Alamo" had been a popular battle cry in the war with Mexico, though she suspected many of the men she'd heard mouthing it were not much better supplied with details than she was.

In the end, the Americans had triumphed, as it seemed they inevitably did. Texas had become a state. A slave state; on that question, at least, southerners were always clear.

So there was some logic on Lewis's side: A slave state offered the consistency of their way of life. From his point of view, that was an argument in favor. Rice-growing land. That was, after all, what Lewis did, what he knew, what their sons were being prepared to do. And certainly he was talking of plenty of that land; she could not even imagine how much land a half-million acres represented. The acreage of Eaton Hall seemed large to her, and in comparison it was next to nothing.

Nor was Lewis the first to think of moving away from South Carolina; the talk of war and emancipation had prompted a number of others to make or consider such a move of late.

But a wilderness, the "Wild West." Indians, yes, surely. She had heard the tales of what happened to those westward-journeying pioneers: massacres, scalpings, women and children carted off by savages, used in ways that defied imagining.

If it were only the two of them; if she had more confidence in her husband's capabilities...Lewis, however, couldn't tame his thirst for whiskey—what could he hope to do with an untamed land?

Eaton Hall ran itself, or rather its slaves, its managers, its overseers ran it; ran it despite Lewis. Lewis drank and whored; or alternatively, whored and drank.

And there were the children to think of. Bad enough for the boys, but boys did, notwithstanding their mothers' fears, take to adventure. James was already agog at the prospect; and Gregory, though he would take longer to decide just how he did feel about it, might very well look forward to the move also.

Melissa was another matter. She was right to fuss. Years lost from that time of your life were never really regained.

On the other hand, what could she do? Arguing with Lewis, resisting him, would only make him more contrary, perhaps solidify what was nothing more than a whim into a real decision.

She thought then of her uncle in Charleston, Horace Hampton. He had been her guardian when she was young, he was godfather to their children. Besides, he was a successful lawyer, and a friend; his advice could be counted on.

She would go to see him tomorrow; he would know how to dissuade Lewis, or thwart his will if necessary.

Her mind made up to that, she draped her peignoir over a chairback and, extinguishing the lamps, slipped into her bed. Savannah still snored discreetly from the floor.

In her mind, Joanna began to rehearse the conversation she would have the following day with her uncle, supplying his lines as well as her own. It was a habit she had, enacting beforehand many of the major occurrences of her life, so that often it seemed when she lived them that she was only repeating something that had happened to her before. She had never been sure whether she possessed some uncanny ability to read the future, or whether she made such a strong impression upon herself that it molded the circumstances to her will; but more often than not, things turned out strikingly as she had envisioned them.

This time, however, even when she finally fell asleep, still going over the dialogue in her mind, she was aware of a tiny doubt that kept confusing her intended line of argument.

TWO

She had been a mere fifteen when her parents died, in an outbreak of cholera; first her mother, and only two weeks later her father. "He simply couldn't live without her," many had said, and Joanna had been left mistress of Eaton Hall.

Uncle Horace, her father's brother and now her guardian, had made his position clear from the very first. "You'll have to marry," he said. "Eaton Hall needs a master."

At first she had demurred, resisted. She knew more about running a plantation than most women did, more than many men, in fact.

Her upbringing had been unique. Few of the men she knew, and virtually none of the women, had what could be remotely described as an education. True, on the wealthier plantations, there were tutors who graced the young aristocrats in French and the social niceties. The men learned to hunt, and to run their plantations, often badly. The women learned to flirt, to sew and embroider, and to gossip.

For entertainment, they made house visits. They came uninvited, unannounced. Family. Friends. Sometimes actual strangers, with no more claim on hospitality than a mutual acquaintance. Wagons were packed with trunks and boxes, slaves dangled their feet over the rear or walked behind in the dust of the road. The distances and the awkwardness of travel made short visits inappropriate. They came to stay, and stay they did; for weeks, often for months. Most southerners welcomed the break in routine. Joanna, however, never minded solitude; indeed, since the death of her parents, in whose company she had delighted, she had come to prefer it.

Her father had wanted a boy, and without stinting on affection toward his only daughter, he good-naturedly chafed her for failing to match his expectations. He had raised her in many ways as he would have raised a son: She had been taught to read and write at an early age; more than that, to *think*, "Else," he said, "you might as well be gaggling about with the other women." She could ride, and she had learned much of running a place like Eaton Hall from accompanying him when he was about the business of it.

She might have turned out one of those mannish women who make others uncomfortable and look ill at ease with themselves; but her mother had been so lovely and loving, such a gay, laughing creature, that Joanna's femininity had developed unimpaired. They were considered a peculiar family, of course, but none of them had minded.

And then, Joanna had found herself an orphan, and mistress of a great plantation. Having been raised to think for herself, she had thought she would manage on her own, and had put off her uncle and his suggestions of marriage.

She had soon been dissuaded of the notion. It was not that she lacked ability; no one took her seriously. Perhaps if she had been older, a little more sure of herself... or perhaps that wouldn't have mattered, perhaps the problems she encountered were indigenous to the southern way of life.

She ordered things from stores and they did not come, or the wrong thing altogether was sent: "I thought this was probably what you really wanted" was the excuse. She issued orders to her overseer; he looked at her with a condescending smile and did exactly as he chose. She fired him; he stayed on, running things his own way in defiance of her. She went to the sheriff; he smiled, too, and suggested she consult her uncle.

Which, finally, she had to do, or see Eaton Hall fairly sink into the ground on which it stood. He uncle's position was still the same: Eaton Hall needed a master. She must marry.

Lewis Harte had been handsome; the second son of a nearby plantation, neither grand nor shabby. She had looked over the men her uncle suggested, had been looked over in return. She had married Lewis.

It was unfair to her, really, to blame Lewis. It was doubtful if marriage to any of the other swains who had sought her hand would have satisfied her any better. She had looked at them again since, wondering if she'd chosen badly; gradually it had come to seem to her that there wasn't much to choose among them.

The truth was, even if one of them had been different, the life-style common to them all, the way of life demanded of "the southern gentleman," forced them to fit a common mold. Would any of them, after all, have welcomed her early efforts to help run things, to "correct" what she saw as Lewis's mistakes?

It was doubtful. Probably any one of them would have been just as resentful as Lewis had been at being informed by a mere woman how to manage a plantation—resentful and increasingly stubborn.

Of course it had been a mistake on her part. If she had been more subtle... But she hadn't been raised that way; she had been taught all her life to value her own intelligence, her knowledge, for the special thing it was.

Even her uncle, to whom she had turned expecting support, had been unconditional in his opinion that she was in the wrong: Eaton Hall was no longer hers; it had become her husband's, to do with as he saw fit. *She* had become her husband's property, hardly more than his slave.

Against that, she had stormed, she had railed, she had wept and pouted—she had done everything a foolish and immature girl could do to spoil what might have been a good marriage.

That damage had never been repaired, though in time a sort of truce had settled over things. She tended to household matters. She educated her children as best she could and, eventually, those of her slaves who wanted to learn. Lewis ran the plantation or, more and more, let it run itself. Sometimes she suspected he let it grow shabby to spite her, but she no longer provoked him by voicing such suspicions. The distance between her bedroom and his, once only a few feet, grew longer, until it seemed an impossible journey for either of them to make.

Instead, he planned a journey to Texas.

"It's his decision to make," her uncle had informed her that morning. "There's nothing to prevent his selling Eaton Hall if he chooses."

"Aside from the fact that it is my home, what about me? What about our children? I am your niece, they are the grandchildren of your brother."

"He is the master of Eaton Hall. He is your husband. He is the father of your children."

"Then there is nothing I can do to prevent his carrying out this scheme of his?"

"Nothing."

She was thoughtful for a moment. Then, "I shall simply not go."

He looked surprised at this. "And what do you propose to do instead, with no home, no means of support, no husband? You can't imagine Lewis would divorce you, and even if he did so, what man would marry a divorced woman? You would be a fallen creature."

"You would not refuse to take us in, surely?"

"Indeed, I should be obligated to refuse, both legally and morally. Furthermore, your husband would be entirely within his rights to call me out, and I am too old to fight duels." He saw the defeated slump of her shoulders, and spoke in a more kindly tone. "I think you do your husband an injustice."

Her head snapped up. "I?"

"He's not the first to think of such a move; you yourself have admitted as much. What do you know about this Texas? I'll wager, very little. And the land grant he's certified, a half a million acres, it hardly seems he means to slight his obligations to his family."

"If we live to reach this San Antonio. You can't deny that between here and there lie grave dangers."

"I'm sure your husband has considered them."

"And in any case," she said, standing, "it is customary for men to stick together in these matters."

"Not only customary, but essential, if things are to be run rightly. I think a woman might wisely depend upon men to handle such things, as they are beyond her ken."

His disapproval of her attitude was evident, but at the moment she was too angry, and too disappointed, to be temperate.

"As my husband has handled the plantation I handed over to

him by marrying? Tell me the truth, is it not worth less today than when he began to manage it?"

His quick blush told her that her charge was true, but her own intimate knowledge of Eaton Hall had confirmed that suspicion long ago.

"It is unladylike of you to concern yourself with such questions," her uncle said, and looked away from her angry gaze.

"Well, then, uncle, I promise you, when I die on some trackless waste because of this folly, I will do so in a ladylike manner, so as to embarrass no one."

She swept from the room, ignoring even his "goodbye," but when she was on the street outside and had walked off a little of her annoyance, she was ashamed at having been so sharp with him. It was hardly her uncle's fault that society viewed women in such a light. He was more tolerant than most; another lawyer might have refused any discussion at all at the first hint of her reason for consulting him.

Back at Eaton Hall, she thought of her father. There are always choices. Her father had told her that. But he wasn't here now to enumerate them for her. Very well, then, what were her choices? So far as she could see, there was no question of whether she was to accompany her husband to Texas. In a sense, she supposed she could be grateful to her uncle for making it clear that there simply were no alternatives. So, granting that she would be taken to Texas regardless of her feelings in the matter—what choices then were left to her? She could continue to rail against it. Fight with Lewis, frighten the children, make things difficult—in short, she could go as a victim. Or, she could make the best of it. "Nothing is a complete disaster if you can learn from it, build upon it." That, too, had been her father's advice.

Build upon it. How long had she chafed at the limitations of her life here in South Carolina, the vacuity, the boredom of conventions that were an ingrained part of "the southern life-style"?

She was a misfit. She had been all her life. When her parents had been alive, it hadn't mattered particularly, but since then her life had seemed barren and without any prospect of improvement.

She found herself suddenly wondering if people were so rigidly bound, so hemmed in, in Texas. Here, in South Carolina, in a world inbred with all the wealth and trappings of genteel society, she found life empty.

What if, in that emptiness of the western wilderness, people grew to fill the space?

"Now," she chided herself, "I'm resorting to wishful thinking."

Someone—she couldn't recall who—had said that hell was anywhere one didn't belong. Well, she had long known she didn't belong here, without having the slightest notion of where she might belong. It would be funny, wouldn't it, if Lewis turned out to be right, if Texas were where she belonged after all.

She went along the marble-tiled hallway and flung open the doors that gave onto the library. She began to study the shelves thoughtfully, taking down a volume here, a volume there—any book that she thought might tell her something about this new state of Texas.

THREE

Lewis had not forgotten his scheme, nor changed his mind about it. On the contrary, he had acted with a resolution and dispatch rare for him.

Carts, drays, wagons—every possible type of vehicle that could be used for transporting their belongings—were purchased or ordered built, and an incredible herd of horses and oxen to pull them rounded up in makeshift stables at Eaton Hall.

Within a fortnight, Joanna had watched their fine china, their elegant crystal and porcelain carefully packed into barrels filled with sawdust. Chandeliers were taken down and packed, furniture was crated. Even the elaborately carved mantelpieces, the doors, the inlaid floors went, until there was nothing left but the empty shell of what had once been their splendid home.

As nearly as possible, Eaton Hall was to be lifted up from one place and set down in another, virtually intact.

Such a move was not accomplished overnight. It was nearly a year later that Joanna stood on the deck of the schooner *Nancy* and watched a cutter approaching from the port of Galveston. The city itself, on its sandy island, lay in the distance, shimmering in the afternoon heat.

The immense caravan that had been assembled to transport their home and furnishings was traveling overland under the management of their overseer, Campbell. The family, with their personal belongings and the household slaves, had made the trip by sea, sailing from Charleston through the Florida keys and up the Gulf of Mexico.

A long trip. Joanna, eager to be on land again, was impatient with the delays. The children, even the enthusiastic Jay Jay, had grown quarrelsome. The slaves, when they weren't moaning and retching from seasickness, sang hymns and prayed loudly for safe delivery.

As for Lewis, he had astonished Joanna with the industry he had displayed in arranging their move. He had remained sober for weeks at a time and, charged with the thrill of his vision, had seemed altogether a changed man.

It had made Joanna view what lay before them with more optimism. Perhaps after all a new life, a new land were the cure not only for her husband's dissolution but for their marriage as well, and she had primed herself to put the best face on things. She had begun to think perhaps she had judged him unfairly.

The transformation in him had lasted until they were at sea. Inactivity had undone it. Bored and restless, he had soon begun relieving his impatience in drink. It was no time at all before he was making nightly visits to the open deck where the slaves slept. In the past week, that had been very nearly the only effort he made to rouse himself from the hammock in which he slept and drank.

There was a bumping and scraping as the cutter came alongside. From the quarterdeck, Joanna watched a trio of men come aboard. Two of them had the air of bureaucracy about them: the harbormaster and the customs officer, she supposed; the captain had explained that they would be coming aboard.

It was the third man, however, who captured her attention, and not only because he was in the uniform of the U.S. Army.

He was tall, so tall that he dwarfed the others. He removed his hat to run his fingers through a shock of dark, wavy hair. The hat's brim had thrown his face in shadow; now Joanna could see the sharply chiseled features, high cheekbones, ridged brows.

He spoke to the ship's captain, then turned in her direction.

Even at the distance, Joanna felt the intensity of his gaze, though it was on her for only a moment.

He spoke to the captain again; then the two of them came toward her.

"Mrs. Harte, may I present Lieutenant Webb Price of the United States Army," the captain introduced them.

"Lieutenant Price," Joanna murmured. She glanced once into eyes of an astonishingly soft blue shade, and then quickly away, looking over the rail at the water below—as if she hadn't been seeing it for weeks on end.

"Is your husband about, Mrs. Harte?" the lieutenant asked.

Joanna saw the captain's lips tighten involuntarily in a gesture of disapproval. Lewis's behavior had hardly escaped the notice of the crew, and it was evident to her, if not to Lewis, what they thought of it.

"He's in our cabin," Joanna said. "I can fetch him for you, if you like."

"That won't be necessary. I'll send one of the sailors," the captain said. He barked an order that sent one of the crew scurrying below, then turned back to Joanna. "Lieutenant Price will be providing you with an escort to San Antonio."

"Really? That's very generous of you, lieutenant." She allowed herself a smile; the lieutenant did not return it.

"Your husband has influential friends," he said. His tone made it clear that the generosity of the gesture had not been his idea.

Though she had known nothing about a planned escort, Joanna was not surprised. The Hartes had been a prominent fixture in South Carolina society for several generations. With Lewis, the name had lost some of the respect in which it had once been held, but not all; even with the tensions that had mounted steadily these last few years between the North and the South, Lewis could still wield a certain amount of influence in Washington, as he had over the question of their land grant.

She wondered if that would still be true in the future. Texas was a great deal farther from Washington than South Carolina had been, and not only in miles.

It occurred to her suddenly that they had gone from being the landed gentry, the establishment, to being "settlers," newcomers. Perhaps they would be resented by the local people, as the southern aristocracy had resented and disdained the more recent arrivals to their states.

Certainly Lieutenant Price looked none too pleased with their arrival. "We shall try not to be a bother to you," Joanna said.

"I don't see how a three-hundred-mile journey through a desert infested with unfriendly savages could be anything but a bother," he replied.

Joanna blinked. "Three hundred ... but, I thought we were practically there?" None of the books she had had at Eaton Hall had contained maps, nor more than the sketchiest accounts of the new state.

"Texas," the lieutenant said, "is a large state, Mrs. Harte."

"Ah, here comes Mr. Harte now," the captain said.

Despite her feelings for her husband, Joanna could not help having a certain perverse admiration for him. Watching him now make his way along the deck, you would hardly know that when she'd last seen him, he had been in a drunken stupor. His rigidly controlled gait might have been nothing more than a landlubber's adjustment to the motion of the ship's deck.

Could the lieutenant tell? she wondered. She glanced briefly sideways at him, but it was impossible to read those expressionless features.

The captain made the introductions. "Excellent," Lewis said, shaking the other's hand. "We should be ready to leave in a day or so—no sense hanging around. I ordered a carriage before we left South Carolina. In the meantime, we'll be staying with the Montgomerys, on Broadway. Maybe you know them."

"I'm afraid you'll find a carriage ill-suited for the journey to San Antonio," Lieutenant Price said. "A wagon would be far better. A covered one, of course; you'll want protection from the elements. The trip is a rugged one, and Texas weather can be a trial for those not used to it."

"But surely it can't take that long—a day or two..."

"Two months. A little longer."

There was an awkward silence.

"I should add," the lieutenant said, "there are certain dangers as well. Though of course we'll do all we can to minimize those."

Lewis had the look of a bewildered child—a bleary-eyed child; his face looked puffy and his hands, Joanna saw now, could not quite be kept from trembling.

She realized belatedly that her husband had caught her staring at him, and she braced herself for one of his outbursts of temper.

Instead, he said in a strained voice, "I must think of my family, of course. My wife, and my children. If you could apprise me more fully of the situation—I seem to have come ill-prepared...."

His voice trailed off. Joanna felt an unexpected pang of sympathy for him. She knew he had made an effort; she could see the effort he was making now. If it weren't for his sickness—and it was a sickness, to her way of thinking, a sickness of the spirit; she felt that Lewis was genuinely unable to control his drinking for any length of time and, once he'd begun to drink, unable to control his other actions as well.

She had an uncomfortable thought: How much was she to blame for all that was wrong—with her husband, with their marriage, with their lives? She had done much that, surely, had driven him from her. Had she driven him from South Carolina as well?

"I think there's a great deal we need to discuss," Lieutenant Price was saying. "If the captain will let us use his cabin?"

"Of course," the captain said; he hesitated briefly. "Perhaps you'd care to join us, Mrs. Harte?"

It was none too subtle, and barely short of a slap at Lewis's competence. She would have liked very much to join them. The truth was, ignorant as she was of conditions in Texas, she was likely to be the one to have to cope with them. She knew what happened when Lewis faced disappointment, unexpected difficulties; she'd seen him run his tongue over his lips just then, as if they were parched.

But she'd seen something else as well, in his eyes, something unfamiliar and yet immediately recognizable; it had been a long time since her husband had asked anything without demanding it.

And a woman did owe her husband loyalty, didn't she? The more so, surely, if she could not love him.

Unbidden, an image of the lieutenant's blue eyes, like a splash of water on a warm day, came to her; she had avoided meeting them since that first, worrisome glance.

"I think not," she said aloud. "I prefer to leave those matters in my husband's hands. I'll just go get the children ready. We will be going ashore soon, won't we, captain?"

"In about an hour." His tone was curt.

Joanna watched them go, Lewis already talking in a voice a shade too hearty, clapping the lieutenant on the back as if they were old friends.

Rugged journey. Texas weather. Dangers. It occurred to her that she was going to become, after all, one of those "pioneer women" she had admired so much. Traveling by covered wagon across a harsh wilderness, with three children to worry about...

No, she amended, trying not to succumb to the despair that suddenly threatened to engulf her—four children. And one of them was a drunkard.

FOUR

Galveston had the look of a southern city—shuttered windows and long verandas; walled gardens and oleander blossoms. Joanna noticed as they drove that many of the houses were raised up off the ground—like elegant dowagers, veiled in trellises, comically standing on stilts.

"Galveston Island is subject to floods and violent storms," Lieutenant Price explained when she mentioned this fact. "Even with the stilts, the first floors are sometimes flooded."

"Is this the season for such storms?"

"Yes, but you needn't worry. Broadway, where you're going, is somewhat elevated over the rest of the island."

She suspected, when she saw the street on which the Montgomerys lived, that he meant "elevated" in social status as well as the island's topography. The houses here were large and grand. She found herself thinking, *Nouveau riche,* and then contritely reminded herself that the city was only about twenty years old. Charleston, by contrast, was nearly two hundred. All those years made a difference; time, certainly, to master bad habits.

Alice Montgomery was an airy dumpling of a woman with pale eyes that seemed perpetually misted with about-to-be-shed tears, and a small mouth permanently fixed in a hesitant smile.

Her husband, Clifford, appeared altogether too large and brutish to have wed her. The way he looked Joanna over reminded her of Vincent Mallory; indeed, it was Mr. Mallory who had arranged for them to stay with his acquaintances here.

"We're so happy to have you with us," Mrs. Montgomery said, showing Joanna and the children to their rooms; she had been chattering nonstop since they had arrived, an effort, Joanna suspected, to mask her shyness. Lewis and Clifford Montgomery had retired to the latter's study to discuss "business"—liquor business, Joanna supposed. Lieutenant Price had delivered them here and gone his own way.

"We get so few visitors of the right sort," her hostess was saying.

"What sort is that?" Joanna asked, and was at once sorry for the gibe; Alice Montgomery seemed to consider the question seriously.

"Why, you see, this is a seaport," she explained in earnest. "All kinds of ships put in, people you couldn't possibly invite into your home, if you follow my meaning. Ladies aren't even permitted in the wharf area unescorted—for their own safety. But of course, there's no problem up here—that class doesn't come this far."

"Except during the floods, I imagine," Joanna said.

"Oh, no, not even then; it wouldn't be right. Here, this is your room. I gave you one overlooking the garden, and it gets the breeze from the Gulf; the weather's been mighty warmish. Your daughter will be right here, right next door to you, and your sons across the hall, or we can switch them about if you'd rather. Such lovely children—they must give you a great deal of pleasure. Your nigras will be just fine now, in the sheds. Except for your own maids, of course, and the children's mammy; we'll put down pallets in the attic for them. I know you'll want them close at hand when you need them—it's so hard getting strange darkies to do things the way you're used to having them done. But I do just want to say one thing: I want you to treat ours as your own while you're here. If there's anything you want, you just let them know, and if they don't hop to it, don't you be shy of telling me. Mr. Montgomery likes a smooth-running house. Course, I expect you're used to that, coming from Eaton Hall. Mr. Mallory's told me how lovely it is."

She took a deep breath, smiling, and waited for her guest to respond to all this.

"It was," Joanna said, but the past tense seemed to slip by the other woman unnoticed. "I do hope we won't be too much trouble while we're here."

"I can't dream how."

"Well, it is difficult, with a houseful of people—just finding time to be alone, a chance to relax..."

"Oh, I don't care if I ever have a moment alone—I hate being all by myself. And I never relax—it makes me too nervous. I can't tell you, Miz Harte, how I'm looking forward to hearing all about Charleston. It's been ten years...." Alice Montgomery made an uncharacteristic pause and sighed. "I expect you'll find us hopelessly out of fashion here in Galveston."

"And San Antonio?" Joanna asked on an impulse. "Have you journeyed there?"

The teary eyes blinked with astonishment. "San Antonio? Oh, my, no, no one does—oh, I am sorry, I didn't mean—"

"It's all right," Joanna assured her. "I expect you're entirely correct."

In fact, as it turned out, quite a few people were apparently planning to make the trip with them.

"Word gets around when there's a party going," Lieutenant Price explained. "People who have some reason to make the trip arrange to make it together. Safety in numbers. And the company helps the time pass more pleasantly."

It would be several weeks before they were ready to go. Not only must a wagon be built and a team purchased, but supplies had to be laid in, some of them especially ordered and brought to Galveston on one of the many ships that sailed into the harbor.

Provisioning a wagon for a trip such as the one they were making was not, as Joanna came to learn, as easy as it might seem. Space was limited, the means of keeping food fresh in the Texas heat virtually nonexistent.

Beef had to be dried into jerky. Fruits—apples, apricots, peaches—were dried, too, into leathery strips not unlike the beef.

Water was precious; there would be weeks, the lieutenant informed them, when there was none available except what they'd brought with them in specially constructed barrels. Melissa, seeing one of the barrels, wailed, "But I'll need that much for bathing." She was unreservedly homesick for South Carolina, and not at all shy about letting everyone know.

Fortunately, the adventure had not yet begun to pale for the boys. Lieutenant Price took them with him one day on his way to the docks. They came home, to Joanna's surprise, wearing trousers of a peculiar cut and fabric in place of the woolen ones they'd left in.

"They're called 'dungarees,'" Jay Jay informed her proudly. "Lieutenant Price says all the cowboys are wearing them these days."

"Dugris," Gregory corrected his brother. "They come from the Bahamas. And they're ever so much more comfortable than the woolies."

"They wear like iron, ma'am," Lieutenant Price added, "and they are comfortable, especially on the trail. I guarantee your boys will find them much better for the trip."

"And we saw an Indian, too, a real one," Jay Jay went on.

"An Indian?" Joanna shot the lieutenant a worried glance, but his smile was reassuring.

"Nothing to worry about," he said. "This one's perfectly tame. His name's William Horse and he's going to join us on the train. He's quite civilized—I've talked with him at length myself. Been to boarding school back east, but his home's around San Antone. I thought he might be handy to have along."

"He's Nasoni," Gregory smiled. "The word *Texas* comes from a Nasoni word. It means friends, or allies."

Joanna laughed and shook her head. "Honestly, Gregory, I don't know where you learn all these things."

"From Lieutenant Price," Gregory said matter-of-factly.

It sometimes seemed to Joanna that if it weren't for the young army lieutenant, they would never have managed the trip to San Antonio—or, as he called it, San Antone. With their first setback, Lewis had lost that industry and determination with which he had first approached the venture. He still spoke glowingly of what lay before them—apparently, in his inner vision, some sort of Garden of Eden awaiting only his presence to make it bloom—but as the days passed, he grew less and less capable of coping with the myriad details essential to their departure. More and more, Joanna and the lieutenant between them assumed the responsibility for their preparations.

Lewis and Clifford Montgomery had apparently hit it off well. They were frequently out together, for increasingly long periods of time, sometimes all day and most of the night. Alice seemed

quite willing to accept her husband's often flimsy explanations for
their absence, though Joanna thought she herself had a better idea
what they were about.

When they were in the house, the two men were, more often
than not, closeted together in the host's study. Lewis's progressively
boisterous laugh, and the clink of glasses, could be heard often—
as could, later at night, the falls Lewis took on the stairs on his way
to their bed.

Clifford Montgomery had, it seemed, a thirst to equal Lewis's,
though he held his liquor a little better.

Alice Montgomery was a pleasant enough woman, but her endless chatter soon wore on Joanna's nerves. Joanna was used to her
solitude and found herself missing it sorely. Even with guests at
Eaton Hall, she'd had plenty of places to hide out by herself when
the need came on her.

She discovered the house by night.

The household retired early, except for the two men drinking
downstairs. Eventually they, too, came up and the slaves retired to
the attic and the outbuildings. There were whole rooms with no
one in them, not even a light burning to people them with furniture
and shadows. She discovered them by accident. She woke late one
night to find that Lewis had not come to bed. Once before, he had
passed out on the steps and spent the whole night sleeping there,
till the slaves had found him in the morning. Thinking that might
have happened again, Joanna donned her peignoir and went looking for him.

She did not find Lewis—she supposed he was with the Negroes.
She found the empty, blessedly silent house instead.

Even better, she found the gazebo, off by itself in the farthest
corner of the garden, scented with blossoms, teased by the welcome
breeze that blew in from the Gulf.

She took to going there late at night; while Lewis snored un-
evenly, only the sleepy whisperings of the palm fronds disturbed
the silence in the garden.

Not that she was alone. San Antonio sat there with her, the whole
of Texas came to visit, and mock her, and mutter dire imprecations
of what lay before her. And the sober spirit that fled Lewis's body
when he drank, sometimes that was there as well.

FIVE

They had been there six weeks
when Lieutenant Price came to
tell them their wagons were nearly ready.

"The whole train'll be ready soon," he said. "I thought maybe
you'd like to take a ride and come see them. And Mrs. Montgomery,
too, of course."

He did not even mention Lewis, who was not in the house at
the time anyway. By now it was understood that any decisions that
had to made would of necessity be made by Joanna. It was she who
had decided they must have two wagons—one for the family and
one for the slaves. She had been adamant in the face of one of
Lewis's increasingly rare objections.

"They're not animals," she had insisted. "I won't have them
walking behind the wagons like dogs."

In the end, the quarrel had simply died away; Lewis had had
another drink and forgotten it apparently, and Joanna had asked
the lieutenant to see to the extra wagon for her.

Watching her husband sink lower and lower into his drunken

abyss, and unable to do anything to reverse his course, Joanna had found herself dreaming of her husband as she had first known him, before they were married. Dashing, reckless, riding pell-mell across the fields at Eaton Hall; waltzing with her at a cotillion, his hand firm on the small of her back, his eyes gazing lovingly down into hers; or, eyes closed, listening to her read the verses she'd written (but perhaps he'd fallen asleep and she simply hadn't known).

He'd seemed to promise so much. Or had *she* written the promises onto the blank pages of his character? That was the tragedy of being young and idealistic: You saw things as ideal, things that never could be.

She'd forced herself to set those thoughts aside. Like a carriage that you'd driven till the wheels were worn and the seats sprung, Lewis would never be new to her again, or wonderful and shiny. The best you could do was keep it going and hope the wheels stayed on over the rougher stretches.

The ride with the lieutenant turned into a regular outing. All three of the children were delighted to go. Alice Montgomery sat beside Joanna, her voice rising and falling to the bobbing and swaying of the brougham.

Joanna had had few opportunities to venture out of the house since they'd arrived, and she savored the salt tang of the air, the noisy commotion of traffic, the potpourri of voices and accents common to a busy port town.

The wagons they'd come to inspect looked huge from the outside, and cramped when she peered within and saw all that they had been fashioned to accommodate. Most of the cooking and storage facilities had been crowded into the slaves' wagon. Even so, the one intended for the family had little room to spare, and no promise, it was clear, of privacy or solitude.

Well, Joanna consoled herself, she'd have solitude aplenty when they reached San Antonio, from all she'd heard.

They had just returned to the brougham, were about to step into it, when Jay Jay cried, "There's Mr. Horse!"

"The Nasoni," Gregory said in the way of explanation, and followed Jay Jay's erratic path around the assemblage of finished and half-finished wagons. They slowed their pace as they neared a young man standing some distance away.

Joanna did not know, really, what she had expected—someone in feathers, perhaps, with bright paint on his face, and little of anything on his body. What she saw was an austerely handsome young man, dressed as most of the men around him were dressed — Lieutenant Price was right, the new dungarees were certainly popular. His skin, to her genuine surprise, was anything but red. Umber, perhaps; actually no darker than many of the "white men" working on the wagons. That and the glossy blackness, like obsidian, of his hair were all that indicated his heritage, so far as she could see.

"Really, Miz Harte," Alice Montgomery intruded upon her thoughts, "you oughtn't to let your boys mix with savages."

"There's only one," Joanna said, annoyed, "and I can't say he looks particularly savage. At any rate, I've always taught my children to treat everyone with courtesy and respect."

"Well, of course, with people. But, my stars, an Indian's no more human than a nigra is. Why, there's no telling what your children might get just standing talking to him that way."

"Then I suppose it's better if we all get it; I'd hate to lose just half my family," Joanna said coolly. "Come along, Melissa, you wouldn't want to be an orphan anyway."

Melissa, who'd been envying the boys, jumped down from the brougham and followed in her mother's wake, actually rather enjoying Mrs. Montgomery's horrified expression.

"You're Mr. Horse, my sons tell me," Joanna greeted the young man as she approached. "I'm Joanna Harte. I understand we'll be traveling together."

William Horse stared stunned at the hand she had extended toward him. When it became inescapable that she meant him to shake it, he reached out tentatively and touched the tips of his fingers to hers before snatching them away again.

"And this is my daughter, Melissa. You've already met my sons. I'm sorry my husband isn't with us. I know he'd be delighted to meet you as well."

He recovered his poise than, and bowed formally from the waist. "It is an honor," he said.

"I understand that you are from the Na—Na—"

"Nasoni," Gregory supplied.

"Nasoni tribe? And Lieutenant Price tells me you've been back east, to school."

"In Boston, yes." He kept his eyes on the ground when he spoke to her.

"His mother was a princess," Jay Jay said happily. It was plain he did not share Mrs. Montgomery's fear of contamination.

As if to apologize for Jay Jay's pronouncement, William Horse said, "My father was a white man. I am what your people call a 'half-breed.'"

"Well, half royalty is certainly better than none at all, I should think," Joanna said. "Is San Antonio your home?"

His answer was a hesitant "Yes." After a pause, he added, "My father was there. At the Alamo."

"Oh. The battle. Was he..."

"He died. It was your General Houston who arranged for me to go to school in Boston. But now I wish to see my mother. I am grateful to be permitted to travel with your company."

"And we're very proud to travel with the son of an Indian princess and an American hero," Joanna said.

He looked up then, surprised, and wary, as if he suspected her of mocking him. Though he looked fierce and his manners were rigidly formal, Joanna was surprised to find his gaze timid and gentle. A child's glance, she thought, but a child who has suffered.

His eyes moved past her, their expression growing wary again. Joanna looked over her shoulder and saw the lieutenant approaching. He was scowling as though angry, and he barely nodded at the young Indian man.

"It's time we were going," he said.

"It was nice meeting you, Mr. Horse," Joanna said. "I'm looking forward to getting better acquainted on the trail."

He nodded, and bowed again, but made no reply.

When they were on their way back to the brougham, Lieutenant Price said, "That wasn't very wise."

Joanna turned her head to look at him, surprised. "What do you mean?" she asked.

"Talking to the Indian that way. Didn't you see people staring?"

Glancing about, Joanna saw that several people were indeed looking in their direction, and not with pleasure. "Actually, I hadn't noticed," she said. "But I can't see what difference it makes. Surely I have a right to speak to whomever I wish, even in Texas."

"In Texas"—he emphasized the word strongly—"there are a great many people who don't take socially to red men."

"Not even your better breed of Texans?" she asked, and saw his lips tighten and his face grow dark with anger. "I didn't come all this way, lieutenant, to suffer the same stupid conventions I left behind."

That, at least, she'd made her mind up to; she'd decided that in those weeks on their cramped ship; and lying in bed nights at the Montgomerys, wondering if this was the night her husband wouldn't make it home, her resolution on that point had grown stronger. That was the price it was going to cost the world for bringing her here, for asking this of her: If she was going to start a new life, it wasn't going to be on the old terms. She didn't know yet what the new terms would be, but they would be better than the old ones, about that she was determined.

"And," she added spitefully, "his skin is no redder than your own at this moment."

The lieutenant handed them wordlessly into the brougham beside a frostily silent Alice Montgomery; he got in after Joanna and slammed the carved door violently, making the little gilt cherubs tremble. In the distant sky, the thunder grumbled its disapproval.

William Horse remained where they had left him, staring after the carriage even when it had long since disappeared into the distance.

He was thinking of hair, red and gold—the color of a sunset sky over the great wide plains of Texas.

It had begun to rain by the time they reached the house, and the wind that managed to find its way into the brougham was wet and cool.

Joanna would have followed the others into the house without speaking—she and the lieutenant had not exchanged a word on the ride home—but he stopped her on the front walk.

"Mrs. Harte..."

"Yes?"

"If the weather should get nasty, it would be best to keep your family inside."

Joanna glanced skyward. It seemed surprisingly dark for mid-afternoon. "Will this be one of those bad storms?" she asked. They'd had hurricanes in South Carolina, but Eaton Hall was too far inland to have suffered any real damage beyond some occasional flooding from the river and a few shutters or shingles blown loose in the wind.

"I doubt it. The really bad ones don't come at all that often. But you can never be certain. Mrs. Montgomery will know what to do, of course. I'd promise to look in on you, but if things get really bad, I'll have plenty on my hands. And if there's flooding, just getting across town can be difficult. I don't mean to frighten you—just a word to the wise."

"Thank you, lieutenant." She smiled then and extended a gloved hand—the same hand she had extended to William Horse earlier, but if the lieutenant was afraid of "catching" anything, he gave no sign of it. He took her hand gladly and gave her one of his rare, slow smiles. "And forgive me," she added, "for being so churlish earlier. I realize you were only thinking of my well-being."

"I'm the one who should apologize. It's not my place to tell you how to behave," he said. He held her hand a fraction longer than was proper. "Well. Good day. And remember to be careful if it gets to storming."

"Lieutenant." He paused halfway down the walk and looked back. "You will be careful, too, won't you? Please?"

"You needn't worry," he said, looking altogether happy. "I'm not a careless man."

By five o'clock the sky had turned black, punctuated by an occasional flash of lightning.

Inside the house, the lamps had been lit and the shutters closed, giving Joanna the uncomfortable feeling she always got being cooped up. The air was stifling, while outside the howling of the wind rose to a fever pitch and the rain sounded like pebbles flung against the windows.

The tension among the house's occupants seemed to rise with the storm. They sat down to dinner as usual, but Alice Montgomery trembled visibly with every flash of lightning, and a loud thunderclap caused one of the slaves to squeal and drop a bowl of mashed potatoes on the floor, earning her a string of curses from Clifford.

Lewis had been drinking steadily from the time they had come in. He looked, Joanna thought, like an overwound clock about to explode.

When the slave girl had been sent from the room in tears, Lewis suddenly jumped up from the table. "Ah," he said disdainfully, "all these nervous women! This is worse than the storm itself. I'm going out."

"Do you think you should?" Alice ventured to ask, her own eyes fearful.

"Balls of fire, woman," her husband said with a growl of a laugh, "you think a little thunder and lightning will scare the man? Go right ahead, Harte—take the carriage if you've a mind. This'll all blow over in a couple of hours if I know anything about it. I'd go with you but I already got wet once seeing the house was closed up proper. Don't fancy another bath."

So far as Joanna had seen, his only contribution to the shutting up of the house had been swearing at the slaves, but she kept that observation to herself.

She followed Lewis into the hall, where he was tying a scarf about his throat. Here, the sound of the wind was ominously loud.

"Do you really think you should go?" Joanna said. "Lieutenant Price said—"

"Far too much, as usual," Lewis interrupted her. "He's not wet-nursing me, Joanna, though I fear he might be you. I'm beginning to think that young man pays you altogether too much attention."

"You might better be grateful for all he's done," Joanna said sharply.

Lewis took a step closer, looking down at her with red-rimmed eyes as if he'd been crying. "Maybe you'd better tell me, what all has he done? Things I don't know about?"

"Don't be disgusting," she said, turning away from his liquor-heavy breath.

He laughed. "Yes, I am disgusting—you've always thought that, haven't you?"

Joanna lifted her eyes then. "Not always," she said. "Lewis, I'm sorry, let's not quarrel. It's just—the storm does sound like it's getting dangerous. Wouldn't you be more comfortable—"

"I'll decide for myself where I'm comfortable. It's been a great many years, I might point out, since you've made any effort to make your company pleasant for me. It's a little late to be concerning yourself with my comfort now, my dear. Or my safety. Truth be known, wouldn't you just as leave a lightning bolt got me? You can't say you wouldn't be grateful, now, could you?"

"Is that what you want, Lewis? A lightning bolt to solve everything for you?"

He leaned down, his voice little more than an angry whisper. "If I thought they came in pairs, by God, I'd take you with me tonight, Joanna," he said.

She was too startled by his vehemence to think of a reply, and before she could make one, he had gone out, letting the front door slam violently back against the wall.

Joanna ran to the door, but he had already disappeared into the darkness. In the few seconds she stood peering out, she was soaked from the driving rain.

She stepped back inside and struggled to close the door. The wind made it almost impossible. Then, startling her, Clifford Montgomery was there at her side, reaching over her shoulder to help push at the door. Between them, they forced it shut.

Joanna leaned against it for a moment, water dripping from her hair and clothes, trying to catch her breath. Montgomery's hand was still over her shoulder, on the door. She became aware of the touch of his arm, resting lightly against her shoulder, and looked up, to find his eyes on her.

"If you'll excuse us," she said, brushing past him, "I think the children and I will go upstairs."

SIX

The wind rose to a deafening pitch, the house creaking and groaning as if in pain.

Alone in her room, the children finally asleep, Joanna tried to read, and found her nerves too taut. At length she decided simply to go to bed. Lewis would not be back before morning; at least she hoped he had sense enough to stay where he was.

For a long time she lay awake in the close darkness, listening, trying to reassure herself that there was no danger, and remaining anxious anyway.

She woke with a start, surprised to discover she had fallen asleep after all. But—what had awakened her? She listened; it was a moment before she heard the silence, and grasped its meaning.

The storm was over. No, no, it was too soon. This was the eye, more likely. Half over, then; the rest would be easier to endure, wouldn't it?

She got out of bed and went to a window, opening one shutter slightly to breathe deeply of the night air.

It was like breathing water, heated water; surely you could drown in air like this. Beads of perspiration stood out on her forehead and, in a twinkling, soaked her gown.

She fastened the shutters again and started toward the bed. Something creaked—outside her door? A floorboard? Or just the house, trying to settle itself after the battering it had taken?

It occurred to her that one of the children might have wakened, and she started toward the door, but before she could reach it, it swung unexpectedly open, startling her into immobility.

Someone stood framed in the open doorway. It was too dark to make him out, yet she knew at once that it was Clifford Montgomery.

"What are you doing here?" she demanded of him.

For an answer, he stepped into the room and closed the door after himself. The darkness swallowed him up. He might almost have disappeared into thin air.

Then she heard the sound of his breathing, quick, ragged.

"Get out," she said with all the authority she could muster. "Lewis..."

"Lewis is out—he took my carriage, remember?"

He bumped into something. She stood frozen, listening; his breathing was louder, nearer. She backed away, trying to remember the locations of the room's furnishings, but her mind was blank. There was a door, a connecting door...no, that wouldn't do; Melissa was in there, sleeping—no telling what this brute might do.....She half turned, and hit a chair; it scraped noisily on the wooden floor.

The sound led him to her. He was suddenly there, seizing her roughly, yanking her against him. She was afraid to scream, afraid of bringing the children to investigate; the two of them struggled in an eerie silence.

He tried to hold her head, to turn her face so that he could kiss her. She bit his hand and he swore under his breath. "Bitch," he said, and slapped her, once, twice, three times. She staggered backward, toppling onto the bed, her head striking the headboard.

Too dazed to do more than mutter a protest, she felt her night-clothes being torn from her, felt his weight on her, his knees forcing hers apart.

Then the brutal pain ripped through her.

Outside, the storm had begun to rage again.

She was barely aware of his leaving. She lay stunned, racked with pain, and began to cry noiselessly, tears not only of pain but of anger and frustration and, most of all, of humiliation.

She must have cried herself to sleep. She was aware gradually of a dim light shining through her lids. She opened her eyes and found herself looking up at her husband.

He was holding a lamp aloft, and by its flickering light she could see that he was drenched; his hair hung wetly over his brow and as he leaned down, the water dripped onto the bedclothes.

"Lewis? How...the storm..."

"I started back during the calm. I thought I'd made it just in time," he said. "Now it seems I was a bit late, wasn't I?"

In her surprise at seeing him, she'd actually forgotten Clifford's brutal attack, the pain, and fear. Her nightclothes were in shreds; there was blood on one breast where his nails had clawed at the delicate flesh....

"Montgomery?" he asked.

"Yes." She could think of nothing else to say. Everything was obvious anyway, wasn't it? Even his complicity, if you wanted to think of that. Though she would never have said it aloud, she could see that he had thought of that, too; Clifford Montgomery wasn't the only cause of the anger and the pain she saw building in her husband's eyes.

He set the lamp down on the table and started for the door.

"Lewis, wait," she called. "Don't. It's over and done with. There's nothing you can do now."

"It's not over," he said. "It's not done with."

He went out without a pause, looking straight ahead, walking stiffly, like a sleepwalker.

She sat for a moment propped up in the bed, stupidly clutching at a nightgown that could no longer begin to cover her nakedness. She was so unused to Lewis taking action. She didn't at first grasp what he intended to do.

It came to her all at once, like one of those flashes of lightning outside. That code of honor. God in heaven, of course, what else could a "southern gentleman" do? Even a drunk one? Even one who cared not at all for his wife?

"Lewis." She called his name again and jumped out of the bed. It took her a minute or more to find another robe. She rushed into the hall, to the top of the stairs. Alice Montgomery was in the hall below, in her own nightclothes—great flannel sprays of violets cascading over her rounded figure; she twisted her hands together like a Lady Macbeth reduced to the sniffles, and looked up wide-eyed as Joanna appeared.

"They've gone outside, to the garden," she said. As if to confirm her statement, a gust of wet wind swept along the hall, making the sprays of violets shudder on her bosom. "They took the pistols."

Joanna ran down the stairs. She was drenched before she even reached the open door to the garden; the wind was blowing the rain inside in sheets, like curtains at a window. Outside, her gown clung to her, her feet slipped on paths turned to mud. She waded through watery air.

The noise and the darkness conspired to hide them from her. She stumbled, colliding with an oleander bush that brought her to her knees, and staggered to her feet again. She thought she heard Alice shouting, but the words, if they were words and not just a trick of the storm, were indistinguishable.

At last a flash of lightning revealed the two men, in a far corner of the garden. They were standing back to back, pistols raised skyward.

"Stay out of this," Clifford yelled at her. Lewis ignored her completely; he might not have known she was there for all the notice he took of her.

The fool, Joanna thought, and didn't know if she was more angry or frightened. Lewis was no shot; even without knowing anything about guns, you could see that he was holding his all wrong somehow, it just looked inept. It had been a great many generations since the Hartes had had to hunt for their food, and not even for pleasure was Lewis likely to exert himself unduly.

They began to count together, stepping in time away from one another. "One," like a chorus, they sang. "Two..." Clifford's voice faded on the wind, but you could still see his lips moving.

She might have known, she told herself much later. Wouldn't Lewis *just* try to cheat, even in a matter of honor. They had reached the count of eight when he swung around, lifting his pistol toward Clifford's back. His foot slipped on the wet ground and he fell, the shot going wild, the gun flying from his hand.

"Oh, Lewis!" Joanna cried, relief and exasperation flooding together through her. She ran to him, kneeling beside him in the mud. At first she thought he had fainted, but then she saw that he was crying, sobbing soundlessly into the crook of his arm.

"Move aside," Clifford said.

She looked up. He was standing above them, the pistol aimed downward at Lewis.

"Don't," she said. "You can't. He's unarmed." She could see Lewis's gun on the ground beside her, gleaming wetly, where he had dropped it when he slipped.

"He asked for it," Clifford said. "It's his honor this is all about, not mine. He can die with it, if that's what he wants."

He pulled the trigger. Instead of the blast she expected, there was a sharp click as the hammer came down on an empty chamber, or it might have been a bullet soaked from the rain—she had no idea what.

Without thinking, Joanna snatched up Lewis's pistol and fired before Clifford could pull his trigger again. There was an explosion; the pistol leaped in her hand like a living thing, wrenching her shoulder. She'd never suspected—it looked so effortless.

It was impossible to miss, she was so close; the barrel was nearly grazing his belly when she fired. She was looking into his face. He looked surprised, amused almost, as if she had done something clever, something "precious." It was the movement of his hands, lifting toward his stomach, that brought her eyes down.

She stared at where his midsection had been, where a fragment of his watch fob still glinted. The blood was spilling from a great, gaping wound—blood, and something else, gray and coiled...

He clutched at his entrails, took a step backward, then toppled into some bushes, mercifully out of her sight.

She looked down. Already the rain was washing the blood from her hands in little rivulets. "My God," she heard Lewis say. "My God, you've blown his guts out. You've killed him, Joannie."

Why, he hasn't called me that in years, she thought.

Someone was screaming—Alice Montgomery, perhaps—but the scream faded on a roaring that rose up inside her, drowning out everything else.

She fell across Lewis, knocking him once again to the ground.

SEVEN

The hearings were mercifully brief. Alice Montgomery, sobbing and threatening every few breaths to swoon, told essentially the same story Joanna and a subdued—even a surprisingly sober—Lewis told. It took the judge only a matter of minutes to hand down a verdict of self-defense.

Lieutenant Price, who somehow blamed himself, had taken care of everything, or so it seemed—attorneys hired, doctors brought (Lewis was entirely unscathed, not so much as a bruise to show for the incident), the whole family moved to a boardinghouse the lieutenant found.

"You musn't blame yourself," Joanna said, not once but it seemed a score of times. "It wasn't your fault."

The wagons that had been assembled for the journey northward were in shambles from the storm. One of the Hartes' could be fixed up; the other was completely destroyed—it would have to be built anew.

SAN ANTONE

Lewis surveyed the wreckage grimly. "We'd better hope that train gets through with our household goods," he said, and wandered away, leaving Joanna to worry what exactly their financial position was.

She'd never concerned herself with money before; she'd never had to. But it took no great insight to see that this adventure had already proved expensive. A delay of several more weeks—a new wagon, the expense of boarding the entire family while they waited ...She would have liked to ask Lewis about the money—would have liked, in fact, to take over the responsibility for it—but he looked so beaten down with despair, so humbled. His shoulders drooped when he walked, and when he spoke to her now, it was in a much chastened voice, with none of the curtness, the insolence, that had marked his attitude toward her in the past. She couldn't bring herself to embarrass him further, to do any more damage to his pride.

The court hearings had not been easy on him. It had been necessary to tell of Clifford's assault on her. And how could she explain shooting the man without telling of Lewis's falling down, his defenselessness? He had held his head down while she spoke, refusing to look at her, at anyone in the courtroom.

So, she did not ask him about the money, but she began to think of ways they could save a little—not big things, not things that would be conspicuous, and force Lewis to be extravagant just to show they weren't in straits. Little things, here and there. At the boardinghouse Lieutenant Price found for them, she put all three of the children in one room—to general dismay.

"But, you and papa have your own rooms," Melissa protested. "And I'm sixteen."

"Which is quite old enough to be looking after your brothers for me," Joanna replied.

Gregory looked pained, and Jay Jay said flatly, "I don't need looking after."

Alone with her brothers, Melissa was quick to inform them. "I heard the whole business that night. Everything!"

The boys, whose comprehension of what "everything" entailed was only slightly scantier than hers, remained unimpressed.

"We'll all be sleeping in the same wagon on the trail," Gregory said, following some train of thought incomprehensible to the other two.

"I might not be," Melissa said. "I've already met Doña Sebastiano

46

and her daughter—they'll be traveling in the train, but they'll have an actual driver to handle the team for them, so they won't have to work. And they've already hinted that I might prefer to ride with them."

"Everyone has to work on a wagon train," Gregory said, and was ignored.

"Meskins?" Jay Jay asked; he had already picked up the local pronunciation.

"They're Spanish, which is a different matter altogether. Actually, she's full-blooded American, she came from Baltimore, but her husband is a Spanish grandee—that's like a nobleman. And they're going to be our neighbors, practically. Nancy, that's the daughter, plays the piano. She's going to teach me when we get to San Antonio."

"I'm going to ride with William Horse," Jay Jay announced.

"They're going to be our neighbors?" Gregory asked. "In San Antone?"

"She says it's no distance at all, by Texas standards. Whatever that means."

"Did she say what it was like there? What it looked like?"

"Not really." Melissa frowned thoughtfully. "I don't think she cares much for it, actually. I think they'd both rather stay in Galveston than go back there."

"Why don't they, then?" Jay Jay asked.

"Because her husband's there, silly."

"So what?"

"It's something you're too young to understand," Melissa said primly. "And you can't ride with William Horse. He's an Indian—he's liable to scalp you when no one's looking."

"Mama would be looking," Jay Jay said. "Did you ever notice? She's always looking. Only, sort of sideways, so you won't catch her."

"It's good to be observant," Gregory said.

"I think she's afraid," Melissa said. "I don't think she wanted to come any more than I did, only she doesn't want us to know."

"I don't see why she'd be afraid," Jay Jay said. "I'll protect her."

"Lieutenant Price wouldn't let anything happen," Gregory said. "That's what he's here for, to protect everyone."

None of them even bothered to mention their father's protecting them. He was automatically included in the "everyone" looked after by Lieutenant Price.

"Don't you think," Melissa said, "if she'd just let herself go a little—bend, sometimes... She always looks like she's afraid something's going to slip out of her fingers."

"She's carrying a lot on her shoulders these days," Gregory said sagely.

"Mama?" Jay Jay looked puzzled from one to the other. "I never see her carrying anything."

Joanna was surprised when Lewis came to her room the night of her acquittal. He had gone back to the bottle. Lewis's drinking seemed to come in waves, like the ocean's surf, sometimes receding, only to return, bigger, more advanced.

She was in bed. He came in the dark, wordless. She heard him undressing: the twin thump of his shoes on the floor, the scratch of wool over hairy legs. Hands clenched into fists, she lay on her back and waited.

A listening pause; why did he linger, what did he expect?

He belched, the sound sending the stillness fluttering like startled birds. Joanna turned her head away.

His hands felt foreign, and impatient; she could feel their tension, her skin soaked it up, and gave it back, magnified.

"Did you want him to?"

The question, the sound of his voice, startled her. They had been performing a mime; his question made it real.

"Want... who? What?"

"Montgomery. Was that the only time?"

She felt a growing stiffness against her thigh. The question's significance angered her more than its impertinence.

She slapped him, not very hard; the position made it difficult. "Get off me," she said, pushing.

"I'm your husband," he said, struggling to achieve his goal.

"Was that what you wanted? Was that why you were never here?" she demanded, still struggling against him. "You thought he'd tame your wife for you? You thought that was what I needed?"

"What do you need, Joannie?" he asked. "What is it that I can't give you?"

She stopped struggling all at once. "A man," she said. "You were half right anyway, Lewis. I do need a man. Not the way you thought, unfortunately."

His efforts continued a moment longer, but it was obvious they were doomed. Finally, he let out a long sigh and rolled off her.

The silence came back, descending heavily upon them. She felt ashamed of her cruelty, and angry with him for making her ashamed.

"I'm sorry," she said.

The bed moved. She heard him retrieving his clothes. "So am I," he said. "I knew it wouldn't work. I knew that before I came in."

"Then why..."

"I felt I owed you."

Owed me? She had to stifle the retort that rose to her lips.

"You saved my life." He hesitated; when he went on, his voice was bitter. "I came out a laughingstock, you know. A man, couldn't protect his wife's honor. Falling down, you had to rescue me. I could see people's faces there in the courtroom, see it in their eyes. Snickering. Embarrassed for me, some of them. I don't know which was worse. I don't know how I'll ever forgive you for that, Joannie."

"Would you rather I'd let him kill you?"

"Maybe. Then you'd never have forgiven yourself for that, either, would you?"

"Probably not."

"'Cause you've wanted me dead so bad yourself, sometimes?"

She felt suddenly tired; not just tired, but wearied. "Yes, sometimes. God forgive me, but that's the truth."

She was afraid she'd angered him again; he was a long time in replying.

"I can understand that," he said at last. "Sometimes I've felt the same way. About you. About myself. Maybe I did know, maybe I saw, when he looked at you, and wanted to give him an excuse to kill me. I am a coward."

She sat up; she could barely see him in the gloom. "Not completely," she said. "It took courage to bring us here, after all, to leave everything behind...."

He chuckled softly. "I didn't come *to* here, I came *from* there. I should have left you behind, Joannie. You're what I was running from, now I think of it."

"Me? Or yourself?"

He didn't answer. She was surprised when the hall door opened a moment later; she hadn't heard him cross the room.

"I won't bother you like this again," he said from the doorway. "It's no fun for either of us."

He went out, closing the door softly.

She lay for a long time, thinking of what had just happened, and of the things he had said.

Was it me? she asked some lingering essence of her husband, the ghost-husband that was never really gone from her side, that owned her, in a way her real husband could not. Did I do this to you? Did I make you what you have become?

She thought of Lewis lying in the mud and the rain, sobbing, waiting for a man to kill him, and she felt a pang inside her breast, a wrenching as if she was giving birth to a new—what? Not love for her husband, surely. Empathy, perhaps. How odd it was. For a time, not long after their marriage, she had come to hate the man she had wedded. Yet it seemed the lower he sank into his dissolution, the harder it became to hate him.

Or was that only the power of the weak over the strong?

EIGHT

J ay Jay could not help thinking his father was a fool. He would never have said so, of course, to anyone else. Like his brother and sister—it was one of the few things they had in common—he was intensely loyal to his family where other people were concerned. But in private he saw no reason for kidding himself.

He watched his father rushing up and down between the wagons, pointing out this crate and this barrel, bawling orders directing where this was to go, and that, and then shouting entirely contradictory commands the next moment.

Gregory stood in patient silence, his gaze following the pointing fingers, the waving hands, nodding from time to time to show that, yes, he did understand, yes, he had it exactly right; the contradictions seemed not to perturb him at all. When his father had gone on, Gregory went right back, Jay Jay observed, to following the same self-absorbed system he had been following before—just as incomprehensible to Jay Jay as their father's scheme had been, though apparently clear enough to his brother.

He supposed that Gregory was a fool, too, in his own way. To
some extent Jay Jay found his brother more maddening than their
father was. At least their father was drunk, and the same drunkenness that muddled his thinking or sent him sometimes into rages,
or clumsily falling all over himself, could just as easily turn into
hilarity, or even—though this was infrequent now to the point of
rarity—a maudlin sort of affection.

Foolish or not, it was possible to love his father in a way that he
could not love his brother or his mother. Their very competence
set them apart—you felt as if you had to reach up to them. Somehow Jay Jay never felt tall enough when he was with them.

Gregory was plodding. To see father and son together, you would
have thought he was the old man and Lewis his barely adolescent
child.

Most boys as they neared young manhood entered a period of
rebellion against their fathers. Jay Jay felt a secret kinship with the
man who had sired him, but he sometimes couldn't stop himself
from waging war on his brother. There was the time, for instance,
when their father had given them rifles for Christmas. It was Jay
Jay who had managed that, who had badgered and hinted and
finally, with no pretense of subtlety, begged. He'd come very close
to admitting that he could already shoot, had for the better part
of a year been surreptitiously taking the guns from the cabinet in
his father's den and practicing in the distant fields at Eaton. Luckily
his father gave in and bought guns for the boys before Jay Jay had
to confess.

Of course, he'd known he would have to suffer instruction from
his father, who could not even hold a gun properly, let alone hit
anything. He had even practiced shooting astray to conceal his
expertise. What he hadn't counted on was that Gregory would be
given a gun as well. The mere thought of his older brother, who
couldn't hit a tree throwing a rock, getting a rifle presented to him
gratis, after Jay Jay had spent weeks and weeks coaxing for one,
had very nearly spoiled the occasion for him.

In compensation, he had stolen into the den the night before
their first promised shooting lesson and, with a hammer wrapped
in one of his brother's socks—Gregory never did understand how
that sock had gotten a hole in it—he had managed to knock the
gunsight well off kilter.

Gregory's shot the following morning went right through the
window of one of the slave cabins, ricocheted off Big Pearl's cast-

iron pot that she kept simmering on the hearth, and embedded itself in her wall.

"Liked to kill me with it," she complained loudly and incessantly for several days, though as far as Jay Jay could see, to have been in any real danger, she would have needed to be hanging from the rafters.

Gregory's gun was put away "till he was older," and not brought out again. Jay Jay, who'd hit the target dead on his third shot (he could as easily have hit it the first time, but didn't want to tip his hand), was allowed to keep his.

One time he took the tip of his penknife to the seat of Gregory's best britches—this was the occasion of an enormous lawn party at Chester Glen. Chester Glen was not only the grandest of the plantations in the neighborhood of Eaton Hall, but the home as well of the Quincy girl, Diana, whom Gregory had recently been at some pains to impress. Jay Jay, with a neatness he did not often display, had carefully cut from inside every other stitch in the seam running down the seat of the trousers. The threads remaining were just sufficient to hold the pants together when his brother put them on. Gregory had alighted from the family carriage and mounted the great steps of the Quincy house in front of an army of people, Diana Quincy included, before anyone noticed his moon-white derrière protruding from a gaping wound in his velvet britches.

Then another time he had . . . but what was the use? The pleasure, for Jay Jay, was always short-lived. No matter what he invented to bedevil his brother, Gregory always seemed to come out a victim rather than a dunce, as intended. Even the time with the trousers, their mammy had taken the blame.

You couldn't make him cry, either, which particularly infuriated Jay Jay, who, for all his reckless derring-do, was maddeningly tearful; sometimes they welled up in his eyes for no reason at all that he could think of, even when he was not hurt or scared—he *never* cried then.

"My little man," their mother used to call Gregory, and "the man of the house."

Jay Jay's youngest memories of his brother were of an old man masquerading as a boy—just the opposite of him and Melissa, dressing up in their parents' clothes. Gregory had never done that. He'd never needed to.

Melissa, of course, was the oldest, but being a girl, she didn't count. To make matters worse, she was stubborn. And stuck-up.

And afraid of everything, from mice and ghosts to her hair coming undone at the wrong moment. (Jay Jay used to try to snatch a strand loose whenever the time seemed particularly ripe, but his sister got wise to that little trick, and these days, like as not, was ready with a sharp elbow for his ribs when he tried it; he was still trying to think of a good alternative.)

In fact, Melissa was the embodiment of everything you could think of to be wrong in a person, and it infuriated him to have to defend her to others, for no better reason than that she was his sister.

Not that he often had to. Over the years, the family had traveled less and less often to other plantations for rounds of visiting, and the visits to Eaton Hall had grown briefer and less frequent. "It's a good idea," their mother had informed them, "to get used to doing without others."

Of course, she wasn't stuck with just a sister and a stodgy brother for companions, or she might see things differently.

But the point was, people did disapprove of Melissa, which never failed to embarrass him. You could see it in other women when they looked after her, particularly when they didn't know anyone from the family was watching. And not just the women, either; the men watched her, too, though naturally they were better at concealing their true feelings than their wives were.

Jay Jay blamed his mother for everything, if only because his father was only too obviously inept to be held accountable. If you were going to be the strong one, it seemed to him, you had to expect things to be left up to you, didn't you? Where would Gregory be, after all, or Melissa, without his leadership?

"Papa says we own half of Texas." Their father, in fact, had said nothing of the sort, but Jay Jay had hit upon the remark as a means of getting an accurate perspective from Gregory, who was sure to know, without the necessity of stooping to ask him directly, which Jay Jay avoided at all costs.

"Not even a fraction," Gregory said. "Texas is enormous, the largest state in the Union. Better than eight hundred miles north to south, and almost that much east to west."

"I think it's awful," Melissa said, screwing her face up into a pout. Their mother had often warned her that someday her face would freeze into such an expression. At one time Jay Jay had watched daily in happy anticipation of the event, but it had unfortunately proved one of those times when their mother had turned out not to be right—and wouldn't it just have to be something he'd really wanted to see. "In South Carolina we were wealthy, we were somebody, and now here we are, living in a boardinghouse like Gypsies."

"Gypsies live in caravans, not boardinghouses."

"Well, and where do you think we're going to be living when we leave here? It'll be just horrible, I know it will."

"I wish we were ready to leave," Gregory said. "I think the journey will be interesting."

"I'm going to ride with William Horse."

If Jay Jay could not exactly love his mother, he could often feel sympathy for her: Staying on top of everything was a heavy responsibility, he'd discovered that already for himself.

He felt a real pang the day she went to pay a call on Mrs. Montgomery. She had her chin thrust out and up, the way she did when it was something she really didn't want to do, and she walked as if her black velvet dress were made of chain mail. Watching her from an upstairs window as she walked, ramrod-stiff, down the steps to the carriage, Jay Jay could easily imagine her going off to face fire-breathing dragons—which, funny enough, you could never picture their father doing.

Jay Jay admired pride greatly, it was something he just seemed to understand by instinct. Yet when his father, waking late, asked where she had gone, Jay Jay, who certainly knew, pretended ignorance. "She just went out," he lied. "She didn't say where."

He felt ashamed of himself later; he hated lying, and worse yet, he couldn't imagine why he had gone and told such a pointless lie.

He felt so bad, he would have to think of some really terrible way of tormenting his brother to work himself out of it.

Joanna felt, too, as if she were going into battle. Since that fateful night of the hurricane, she had seen Alice Montgomery briefly on two occasions—at the funeral services for Clifford, and in court, when Alice had told her version of what had happened that night. Joanna had not approached her or spoken to her either time. The ugly memory of Clifford's assault and the horror of what had happened subsequently were still too fresh in her mind. And she could hardly suppose the woman wanted reminding of her loss, in the form of the one who had killed her husband.

Still, decency did dictate a call before they left Galveston.

If they ever left Galveston. She had begun to wonder if they'd ever be ready. So much to be done, and redone; so many details, so many delays.

The weather grew hot, and hotter still. "Unusual for Galveston," Lieutenant Price would say, mopping his brow with his kerchief.

The gulf breeze withered in the heat and died, leaving a flotilla of ships frozen into immobility in the harbor. Work on the wagons slowed very nearly to a standstill, and supplies for which they waited did not come.

So, on a day when even the passing hours seemed to hang suspended, too wilted to move along their way, Joanna dressed in her "severest" dress and went to see Alice Montgomery. She would not have been surprised if Alice refused to see her altogether. But the little colored girl who answered the door—unfamiliar to Joanna—said, "I'll see," and disappeared into the shaded confines of the house.

Joanna waited on the veranda, behind a curtain of bougainvillaea, and in a short while Alice herself came through the screen doors.

"Joanna," she said, "this is such a surprise."

She looked—well, different, Joanna thought, though she wasn't quite sure just in what way. Her first thought was that Alice was already going to pieces; you heard of women doing that when they lost their husbands. A wisp of hair had escaped from the tightly coiled bun atop her head; in the past, a fidgeting hand would have been continually trying to put it in its place, but Alice appeared oddly unaware of the miscreant. Her face was bare of the customary rouge and powder. She looked, in fact, frowzy.

At the same time, though, she seemed completely unharried. Her smile, while it was still hesitant and shy, was less strained than it had appeared before, and her eyes, for the first time since Joanna had known her, seemed to look out of her face at you and not around some invisible corner. Indeed, were it not for her black outfit and the widow's weeds pinned to her bodice, Joanna would never have suspected the woman was so recently bereft, and she found herself wondering if perhaps the widow had been consoling herself with some sherry.

"I felt," Joanna said, "that I had to come see you before we left Galveston. We owe you so much, and, of course, there's what happened...."

For a moment, Alice looked at her as if she didn't remember exactly what *had* happened. "Oh," she said, looking far less em-

barrassed than Joanna felt. Unexpectedly, she said, "I was just
sitting in the garden—it's so much cooler. Would you like to...No,
no, of course, you wouldn't.....Let's just sit out here on the veranda, why don't we? It gets just as much breeze as the garden
anyway. If we had any breeze—though I swear, you can't get the
air to move even fanning it. Eliza, bring us some nice cool lemonade,
won't you? You will drink some lemonade, Joanna?"

"Yes, that would be nice." To cover her confusion, Joanna asked,
"Is that a new girl?"

"Yes, the other one ran off—a whole passel of them did, right
after Mr. Montgomery's accident. I expect they thought there'd be
no one to come after them. Lord knows, I don't mean to, not in
this weather."

"Ran off?" Joanna was surprised. In South Carolina, a runaway
slave was enough to rouse every man in the county to pursuit. Most
of those who tried were caught, and the punishment was brutal,
but that had never stopped an occasional effort.

"Oh, they're going in droves, people tell me. It's that Mr. Lincoln
and his talk of freeing them; it puts ideas in their heads. Leaving
good homes where they're treated like royalty, and like as not they
end up eaten by the Apaches. I don't know where they think they'd
go—Texas is Texas, from one end to the next, is what I always say.
Oh, here is our lemonade. Doesn't that look cool and delicious?
Eliza, dear, give Mrs. Harte the glass with all that ice you were so
extravagant with."

Joanna took the proffered glass with a polite "Thank you," and
sipped on the cool liquid. The ice, large chunks of it, tinkled and
glittered in the dappled sunlight. It was strange—with everything
else, she had all but forgotten President Lincoln, and the threats
of war between the states. In that regard, at least, Lewis had been
right: All that seemed so far away.

Or it had, until she'd been reminded. But the peculiar thing
was, so far as she knew, they had lost no slaves.

"Now, Joanna, I want you to know, I harbor no bitterness. You
did what you had to do, protecting your husband and all; any
woman would have done the same thing, I've told I don't know
how many people already. And after what happened, too. I don't
wonder you were half out of your mind. Why, I think that I myself
would have...Well, what's done is done, I always say."

Joanna was astonished; she had never suspected the woman
sitting opposite her of any grace in concealing her feelings.

"That's very kind of you," she said. "It has been preying on my mind, the thought that you're alone now because of what I ... Will you be all right, Alice? Have you family?"

"Oh, back in Georgia, what's left of them. I think I told you, I come from Savannah, but it's been so many years..." She paused, looking beyond Joanna, beyond the bougainvillaea, her eyes suddenly dreamy and young-girlish, as if for a moment she had shed a great many of her years. "I was fourteen when I married."

"That's very young."

"My papa was a gambler. He gambled away everything he had— his money and his horses, and the stock, and even his home. Finally he had nothing left to gamble away but his daughters." She sighed and gave her head a shake. "Fourteen. I swear, I don't even remember what it was like being that young, it might have all happened to some other girl."

It came to Joanna out of the blue that this woman wasn't concealing her feelings at all, that she really did harbor no regrets at what had happen. If anything, she was close to feeling grateful, though not even to herself could she admit that. Clifford Montgomery had been a brute of a man; life with him could hardly have been pleasant, especially for one little more than a child when she married.

Joanna felt a pang at some of the unkind thoughts she had had of this woman. No wonder she'd been so glad for some company. And what loneliness of the spirit, what unhappiness, had that tiresome volubility masked?

At the same time, she found herself wondering: Suppose.... Suppose things had ended differently, that it was Lewis who had been killed, not Alice's husband. That came very close to happening. Would she be feeling relieved, grateful, set free? Had she unconsciously wanted her husband killed that night? It was a cruel charge to bring against oneself, and in its wake left obligations, debts, duties that inevitably bound you all the more tightly to that other person. There were things you must make up for, things you wouldn't want left weighed against you in the balance.

But then, what did one owe oneself? Something, surely.

Alice was speaking, her voice easy and light. She was not a woman given to introspection, Joanna knew; quite likely Alice had not paused to reflect upon her feelings. Joanna found herself hoping that never happened.

"If there's anything you need..." she said aloud. Alice had made some mention of money; the exact statement had slipped by her. "Anything we can do..."

"Oh, I don't think so. Mr. Montgomery was a careful man when it came to money. And his business partner—his former business partner, that is to say; I still have trouble remembering—has made me a generous offer."

She smiled and for the first time Joanna realized she must have been exceptionally lovely, that fourteen-year-old girl, virtually sold into slavery by her gambler father.

"You know," Alice said, looking suddenly as pleased as if she'd managed it all herself, "I really never expected to be an independent woman."

There was a problem with the second wagon. Intending to travel from Galveston to San Antonio in the comfort of a carriage, Lewis had arranged for only one driver, William, who had driven their carriage in South Carolina. The other slaves in Texas with them were maids and household servants. Stable and field hands had been sent on the overland trek.

William, gifted with a coach and four, balked at handling the cumbersome prairie wagon. "I don't know nothing about no oxen," he asserted. "It's completely different."

"I don't see how you could know that without even trying," Joanna argued, without real conviction since she herself didn't know either.

"I just know," he said with stubborn dignity, and would not be budged.

Lewis, of course, blamed her, and seemed to relish the difficulty—it was she, after all, who had insisted on a second wagon for the slaves.

"I say, let 'em walk, the way I planned to begin with" was his solution.

Joanna brought the slaves together to ask if there were any among them with experience handling a team. There weren't, and none either, it appeared, eager to learn. She coaxed and questioned, pleaded, and finally threatened to leave them all behind to fend for themselves in the unfamiliar city, a threat that produced tears and consternation, but no positive results.

Joanna was about to concede that Lewis might have been right after all—but she couldn't let her people walk to San Antonio like cattle, she just couldn't—when their cook, Lucretia, asked to talk to her. She wanted to know if Joanna had found a driver yet for the slaves' wagon.

"No," Joanna admitted. "William could, I'm sure—it can't be that much different—but convincing him..."

"I can get around that William," Lucretia said confidently. "That man does anything I asks." She paused, glancing sideways, and then back again directly at Joanna. "Far as that goes, I expect I could learn to drive a wagon easy enough. Don't look to me like there's anything to it."

Joanna stared at her in surprise. Her efforts to locate a driver had been directed primarily at the men among the slaves. It hadn't really occurred to her to approach the women. The caste system among the slaves was as rigid as anything known in the East. House slaves simply did not put their hands to outside work—they would have considered it demeaning—and as head cook at Eaton Hall, Lucretia had reigned pretty much as the queen bee among the household slaves. Lucretia was the last person she would have thought to turn to for a solution to her problem.

"I have a feeling," she said, "that you're preparing to negotiate a deal."

"I don't know about no negotiating." Lucretia's sly glance belied her innocence.

"But there is something you want?"

"Mr. Harte, he says a slave is entitled to what he gets, and that's all."

"Which I suppose, is why you came to me and not Mr. Harte."

Lucretia took a while answering, and when she did, it was to make a seemingly unrelated remark. "Folks say...the slaves, they been saying, this here Mr. Lincoln, he's going to be freeing everyone one of these days soon."

"He says that he means to, yes," Joanna agreed, more puzzled than ever.

"What do you suppose is going to happen, to us, I mean, to the colored folk, when they is all freed? Who's going to take care of us if we don't belong to nobody?"

"Why, I don't know. I suppose..." But she had no ready answer; it was a question she simply had never considered. People talked about what would happen to the South, to the great plantations, to the whites—and she had been as selfish as anyone in that respect, hadn't she? Even when secretly, silently, she'd agreed with Mr. Lincoln that men ought to be free, she hadn't really thought about how the freed slaves were to fend for themselves in a society that could no longer afford them.

"Reason I ask," Lucretia said, indicating that she, at least, had been giving thought to the question, "is, Papa John, he been saying when he gets to this San Antone..."—she put the accent on the first syllable, giving the city an exotic, foreign sound—"...he says, from talk he hears, we'll be owning half of this here Texas."

"I don't think it's quite that much," Joanna said, smiling. "But it is a large piece of land, certainly, more than I can even imagine, to tell you the truth. But I still don't—"

"I been thinking," Lucretia went on with what sounded now like a well-rehearsed speech. "If we had just a small piece, William and me, just a little land of our own—I don't mean a garden plot like we had at Eaton Hall, I mean our own *place*—why, we wouldn't have to worry about what was going to happen to us, do you see? I mean, if this Mr. Lincoln, say, he was to free us, why, William and me, we could just get married like we been wanting to do, and the two of us, we could just look after ourselves. And our children, too. And besides, we'd be right there, wouldn't we? There's nothing to say we couldn't go right on taking care of you folks, too, at the same time. It seems to me, anyway."

She stopped and took a long breath, watching her mistress with a look both hopeful and wary, lest she'd gone too far. It was difficult to know, even with Mrs. Harte, who was different from the rest, who'd gone so far as to allow education for some of her slaves. Even with her, Lucretia made a point of pretending that the education hadn't "taken," talked a pidgin English intended to reassure that her intelligence was no threat.

Joanna, too, was thinking, indirectly, of Lucretia—of her intelligence, of her education. She had known the woman all her life; they were somewhere near the same age, though she didn't know Lucretia's exactly. And why don't I? she wondered.

Lucretia had worked in the kitchen of Eaton Hall when Joanna married. Joanna wasn't even sure now whose idea it had been to include Lucretia in her own rudimentary lessons, but she had taken pride in the fact that Lucretia could read and write, accomplishments unmastered by most southern white women.

Yet, she realized she didn't know her cook at all, not as a human being. She'd had no idea of Lucretia's dreams, her longings, her aspirations; hadn't even known of her involvement with William.

Why, I'm as bad as the rest of them, she thought. These people are invisible to me, as if they were nothing more than household furnishings. A chair you might know was handsome, or valuable, you might even notice that it needed dusting, but otherwise it was something you took for granted, used for your convenience and comfort, kicked when you were angry—threw away, perhaps, when it no longer suited.

Like Lucretia, standing here, holding herself empty. She realized how often they did that—you looked at their eyes, not into them, as if there were nothing behind the surfaces; your voice echoed through them, the way it did when you spoke in a cave. Only there was someone in there, someone listening, holding her breath, waiting for the bear to move on, or at least settle down to sleep.

For a moment, on the heels of this self-discovery, depression threatened her. I'm not nearly so mature as I thought, nor so bright, she berated herself.

But self-abasement was simply another excuse, wasn't it? It's all right to do this, so long as I whip myself for it periodically. I shall punish myself for them, and feel justified in my sins.

No, I shall have to do better, she told herself, and smiled at the apprehensive woman before her. "Yes, I do see," she said. "I can't promise you, you know, what we'll find when we get to this San Antonio, but certainly there will be land, and plenty of that. And I can promise you, some of it will be yours, yours and William's, to do with as you wish."

Lucretia stared, her eyes searching; she gave the impression of someone looking out for a trick, some catchphrase that would take all the good from what she had just heard.

Then a great, wide smile burst upon her face, and in her eyes, too, like sunlight splashing on the surface of a pool.

"That would be mighty nice," she said, and Joanna had just the faintest inkling that something had changed in Lucretia's speech, a discovery that came and went too quickly for her to seize upon it. "I'd best get William started with that team," Lucretia said, "if I'm going to learn to handle it by the time we start out."

"Whenever that may be," Joanna said ruefully; but at least one problem was solved, in a way that she could feel good about.

Then, as if it were overnight, their time in Galveston had vanished, the frozen days melting into a pool of yesterdays. They would be going soon—any day now—tomorrow....

And now, Joanna found herself longing for some of that time

that had so recently hung on her hands. Every moment seemed short of its appointed duration; the hours sped by. She heard conversations in broken fragments that barely penetrated her conciousness; her days were kaleidoscopes of fleeting impressions:

"...Not a damned darky fit to...Have your things moved tomorrow for loading, this is...Doña Sebastiano, how nice to know ...I've been invited to ride with...William Horse, Lieutenant Price says we...were part of the Haisini Confederacy, and besides that ...Dammit, I know they were fourteen trunks, Joanna, are you trying to say...Mr. Hansen owns a general store in San Antone... has an average rainfall of...plenty of room, and I don't want to travel from...sunup, or before, we can get several miles ahead of the...sunbonnet? But it's so ugly, I can't...Ride one of these, the saddle is so much bigger than...better than...harder...faster... almost...tonight...tomorrow...today...

"...Now," the lieutenant was saying, while Joanna took a last, sweeping look around—Gregory, sitting rigid beside his father in the driver's seat of the family wagon; Jay Jay, forbidden to ride with the Indian, William Horse, glowering petulantly from the seat beside William in the slave wagon. Melissa was with the Sebastianos in their wagon, though for herself Joanna could not see much to choose from between the Sebastianos' wagon and their own.

"Where's Jay?" Lewis asked.

"He's protesting the world's refusal to see things his way," Joanna said. "Never mind, he's with William and Lucretia, he'll be all right."

"Riding with the niggers?" Lewis asked, but Joanna ignored him.

"All set?" Lieutenant Price asked.

"Have been, dammit, for half an hour," Lewis said, and got only a polite glance for his trouble.

"Yes," Joanna said, letting out a breath she hadn't realized she'd been holding. "Yes, I believe so."

"Well, then..." The lieutenant nodded, and gave a signal to one of the horsemen at the front of the long column.

A moment later the call came back, from wagon to wagon, like an echo bounding off their canvas roofs—"Let's move out!"

Joanna climbed up beside her oldest son, taking a tight hold of the seat as Lewis got them off to a jerky start.

"We're on our way," he said. His laugh was high and giddy, like a child keyed up on nervous energy.

He was not the only one. In all the wagons, people were laughing or talking loudly. Voices shouted back and forth, and toward the rear of the train, someone was singing "Did you ever hear of Sweet Betsy from Pike?" in a bawling, off-key baritone. "Crossed the wide prairie with her husband, Ike...."

Like syrup dripping from a spoon, the tight ball of wagons and horses and oxen spun itself out slowly into a long, thinning strand across the flat Texas earth, stretching, stretching, until you expected actually to hear the snap of the thread that held them.

At the head of the train, one of the cowboys suddenly gave a nasal yell—"Ahhh-haaa, San Antone!"—and larruped up his horse. Behind him others took up the shout. Horses galloped, and the wagon drivers whipped their animals to a brief burst of speed as well—pointless, foolish even, but spontaneous and exhilarating.

The dust rose up from the ground in raucous clouds, and the cries came and went:

"San Antone! Ahhh-haaa, San Antone!"

NINE

By the time the sun had climbed halfway up the morning sky, Lewis had begun to feel his thirst.

He drove on, trying to ignore the sweat dripping from beneath his hatband into his eyes, and the increasing soreness of hands unaccustomed to handling a team. He'd promised himself he would drive the first day. People were looking up to him, after all—Lewis Harte, of Eaton Hall, South Carolina. The head of the train. He'd heard it referred to in Galveston as the Harte Train. So, even here in Texas, his name had begun to acquire significance, hadn't it? Which was only right.

"Just wait till we get to San Antonio," he told himself.

It almost seemed as if everything had been hanging in suspension since they had left South Carolina. Even the things that had happened he saw through a haze like that blurring the far-off Texas horizon. His senses, his entire being, everything was focused on their destination.

San Antonio. A half-million acres, to make a new Eaton Hall, the biggest, grandest plantation anyone had ever seen, and he its master. Rice growing as far as the eye could see, farther, even. And cotton, too; he'd brought cottonseed, enough to grow what they needed, anyway. And fruits and vegetables; they'd need to look out for themselves, obviously, with San Antonio far more isolated than they had expected. Lucky for them all, he'd had the foresight he did.

Joanna and all her lessons, he thought scornfully; a lot of good her geography books had done them. He had made up his mind, there were things he meant to put his foot down on. All this learning business. And the way she'd changed since they'd left home; half the time she acted like she'd forgotten she had a husband.

Of course, he had to give her her due, she'd done a good job of managing things. Not that a woman wasn't supposed to help; that was her job, wasn't it? A helpmate. Obviously she hadn't found that in any of her books, or taken the time to study its meaning. Too clever by half for her own good, Joanna was.

Well, yes, he could feel admiration for her. And disappointment at the same time. He didn't know why he always felt cheated when she handled everything in that level-headed way of hers, like she'd taken something from him to do it.

His throat was dust-dry. He reached for the flask in his vest pocket and caught a movement out of the corner of his eye: Joanna, watching him.

Dammit to hell, always waiting for him to fall on his face—you'd think she was expecting him to. It put a curse on a man, made him trip despite himself.

"Watch out," she said.

"I see it." He snatched the rein in both hands and wheeled violently around a boulder, making the wagon rock violently. "You could wreck us, shouting in my ear that way. I'm not blind, you know."

Admiration and disappointment. Now, what kind of a man could make a marriage out of that?

Take their wedding night, for instance. Wouldn't you think a woman would be glad for a man who knew what he was about? Wouldn't you think experience would be a good thing at a time like that?

But, no, there was Joannie, just looking at him in that way of hers, cold, unforgiving. He could still see that look in her eyes—

maybe he had ought to have put out the lamp, but, dammit all, a man did like to watch.

Disappointed, yes, even on their wedding night. He had known that before he was even done, had seen in her eyes that he had done it wrong, and how the hell would she know? . . . No, wait, that wasn't right. It was *him* that was disappointed, had been all along. . . .

There was a sudden crash and the wagon gave a lurch. The oxen bellowed.

"What the hell . . ." Lewis leaned out to see, and almost fell from the seat—the heat made a man dizzy, God Almighty.

They had broken a wheel. Despite Lewis's insistence that the others push on, the whole train ground to a halt.

"It was that fella in front of me," Lewis said, angry because everyone seemed to be blaming him for the delay. "Kicking up a dust storm, you couldn't see hand in front of face."

"You've been driving all morning," Joanna said in a sympathetic voice. "Why don't you rest awhile out of the sun and let me drive?"

"Makes a man thirsty," Lewis said, taking out his flask and drinking; he cast a defiant glance around, but no one seemed to have paid any attention.

He demurred at first, but Joanna pointed out that women were driving in some of the other wagons, and would be throughout the trip. "And I've got Gregory up here if I get tired," she added.

Lewis found a patch of shade on the far side of the wagon and sat sipping from his flask while the lieutenant's men saw to changing the wheel. By the time they were ready to start up again, Joanna had convinced him to climb inside out of the now scorching Texas sun.

In no time, he had fallen asleep.

Joanna quickly learned that handling a team of oxen over the rough ground was a far cry from driving a buggy or even a farm wagon in South Carolina. Her arms ached, and she began to sympathize with the thirst that had plagued Lewis. The sun beat mercilessly on her, despite the protection of the sunbonnet she wore, and she was covered from head to foot with the dust of the trail. Gregory crawled into the back of the wagon and fetched her a dipper of water, but Joanna was too aware of the importance of stretching their water supply to have more than a few sips.

"I'll drive if you want," Gregory offered.

As welcome as a period of respite sounded, however, she declined. For all his willingness, Gregory was little more than a boy; it would not take long for him to be exhausted as well. It was not yet even midday, and so far none of the other wagons had changed drivers.

"I'll drive till we stop at noon," she said, and was soon wondering if she could stick to that promise.

Just when she was beginning to fear she could go no farther, there was the clatter of hoofbeats alongside, and the Indian, William Horse, rode up to the wagon. It was the first she'd seen him since they had set out, or in any case, she hadn't noticed him. He was dressed indistinguishably from the cowboys—the same dugris, which seemed to be standard for everyone but the soldiers, with a kerchief at his throat, and atop his head one of the wide-brimmed Stetson hats, the practicality of which she could now more fully appreciate.

He tipped his hat toward her and then, as gracefully as a dancer, leaned sideways from his horse, slid from the saddle, and, while her breath caught in her throat, leaped to the wagon and was sitting beside her.

"I will drive the wagon for you," he said matter-of-factly.

"Oh, but that's not necessary ... your horse ..."

"He will follow, he is an Indian pony," he said, and without further ado, took the reins from her.

She smiled, too weary to pretend she wasn't glad to have them go. "I am grateful," she said.

His face remained expressionless, but he nodded, and concentrated his attention on the team. It was immediately evident that he knew what he was about; you almost fancied you could see the oxen falling into step, shedding the lackadaisical manner with which they'd followed her plaintive suggestions.

Gregory was more than grateful; he was soon leaning back and forth, one time in front of his mother and the next behind her, fairly threatening to topple her from the seat while he plied their working guest with an endless stream of questions: "What kind of trees are those? Is it always this hot and dry? How long can the horses travel without water? Is that really an Indian pony? Did you catch him wild?"

Joanna was certain she'd never heard her son so voluble. After a while, his voice faded into a sort of droning noise, and the heat seemed to lessen; she could actually feel herself growing cooler. . . .

The gentle touch of a hand on her shoulder brought her back—

she realized with a start she'd been about to pass out.

It was Gregory's hand on her shoulder, and William Horse, with one eye on the team and the other on her, was giving Gregory directions.

"She must lie down, inside, out of the sun," he said. "Water, but only a little. Wet her wrists and her face, and a small amount to drink, but no more."

"No, really, I'm all right," Joanna tried to insist, but truth to tell, she did still feel light-headed, and found herself hanging on tightly to the edge of the drive board.

"Do as he says, please, mother," Gregory said. "We can handle this."

"Oh, well," she murmured, but she let him help her into the shaded interior of the wagon.

It did feel heavenly to lie down and rest her eyes. Gregory was back in a moment, helping her to sit up while she took a few sips of water, and draping a wet cloth over her brow afterward.

Lewis was snoring faintly nearby, and, lying inside like this, the constant motion of the wagon was far less wearying than it had been in the driver's seat. She rose and fell with it, rocking gently to and fro, letting it lull her into a dreamy state of suspension between sleep and waking. It was the most peaceful moment she could remember since they'd left Eaton Hall. She drifted contentedly into sleep....

And woke to an uproar.

At first, her brain refused to tell her where she was or how she'd gotten there, keeping secrets from her, teasing her, the way her mother did when she was little.

"God damn thieving Indians!" Lewis's voice, an angry bellow.

Lewis. Indian. William Horse! She sat up abruptly, banging her head on something hanging from the crosspiece ("Space is precious inside a wagon; you must learn to move around things"), and pushed aside the flap over the opening.

Lewis was there, just alongside the wagon, his riding crop raised in a violent pose. They were stopped—that was the first thing she grasped; the rest came more slowly, seeping upward into her consciousness, like something she'd known long before, and forgotten, that was just coming back to her.

William Horse, standing in front of Lewis, neither cowering nor defending himself. Gregory, to the side of the two men, not cowering either, but holding himself back: You could actually see the man, not quite ready yet for action; the boy, relinquishing submission, while her son teetered between boyhood and manhood.

Time, holding her breath, blinked and went on, content to let her handle this. The fist with the riding crop in it (Where on earth had he found that? It gave this whole scene a touch of the ridiculous) lifted to come down.

"The minute a man's back is turned," Lewis was ranting.

"Lewis! For heaven's sake!" She nearly fell from the wagon, reaching out to snatch the whip from his hand.

Unexpecting, he let it slide easily from his fingers. His head snapped around, mouth open, eyes red and graveled. It was the first time she had ever taken physical action to defy her husband, and it would be hard to say which of them was the more surprised.

"Have you gone daft, woman?"

She crawled out, clambering to the ground, heedless of skirts and bared legs and people watching, though it did just register that the Indian moved involuntarily toward her.

"He was helping us," she said, sorry that she hadn't stayed in the wagon where she could look down on her husband; he was too tall to scold this way. "The driving was too much for me. He came up to help."

"Help?" You could see comprehension struggling its way through sleep and liquor. Heaven alone knew what he thought he'd seen, waking up.

He looked around, uncertain, suddenly self-aware. People were staring. By now, Joanna realized, the whole train was stopped. It was midday.

She stepped to her husband, put a gentle hand on his arm, was surprised to discover that he was trembling. "It's all right," she said in a lower voice. "I told them you were ill. I said you had a fever."

And now I am lying, she thought; it was inescapable: Whatever spoiled, spoiled whatever it touched. Unless you cut off the rot. But the rot was in Lewis; how could she cut him off without sacrificing him?

"A fever..."

"Rest here awhile, in the shade of the wagon. I'll see if Lucretia hasn't some lunch ready. And this afternoon you can rest inside the wagon. There's three of us now to handle the driving, no need for you to wear yourself out. You'll need to be fresh and rested when we get to San Antonio."

"San Antonio, yes." He let her lead him to the side of the wagon and sank gratefully to the ground in the small patch of shade. "Yes, I'll have everything to do once we get there."

He was already reaching for his flask when she turned away from him.

William Horse was still standing where he had been, one hand on the shoulder of an ox. She tried to read his dark eyes as she came up to him, but without success.

"I am sorry," she said. "Are you all right?"

"Yes." He made no elaboration. His eyes bored into hers for a moment; she had no idea what he was thinking or feeling. Then, abruptly, he turned away from her and walked toward his horse, eating grass nearby.

Gregory, looking embarrassed now by the step he had nearly taken, said, "I'll water the stock," and the incident apparently was ended.

But not entirely. A wagon train, Joanna quickly learned, became a small community of its own, even more circumscribed than the society they had known in South Carolina.

The first effect of all this was the return of Melissa, flouncing over the hard-packed earth as if her feet could not deign to touch it, to announce that Doña Sebastiano had suggested perhaps after all she would be more comfortable traveling with her own family.

"That's rather a change of heart, isn't it?" Joanna asked. Up to now, Doña Sebastiano had been fervently in pursuit of closer ties.

"And what do you suppose brought it on?" Melissa demanded angrily, lavishly sprinkling her throat and wrists with water from their dipper.

"Oh, dear," Joanna said. William Horse, obviously; she had been warned how Texans felt. "Well, it can't hurt to follow her suggestion for a while, and I promise, I'll see if I can't patch things up with Doña Sebastiano this evening. Please, darling, no more quarrels just now, all right?"

She had no sooner mollified her daughter, however, than Lieutenant Price was there, strolling up for all the world as if he had nothing on his mind but the time of day.

"Your husband all right?" he asked in an overly casual voice.

"Yes. I've suggested he rest for a while."

"This Texas heat gets to a man when he's not used to it."

"It gets to a woman, too, it may surprise you to know."

"Liquor can make it worse."

"There aren't any things liquor makes better that I've noticed,"

Joanna said, too sharply. She was not, just at the moment, in a frame of mind to discuss her husband's drinking.

Webb Price's lips tightened, but he stood his ground. "About that Indian," he said. "There's people grumbling about his riding with a white woman—"

"If it's anyone's business," Joanna said, giving vent to pent-up anger, "you may tell them I have hired Mr. Horse as our driver. I'm sure even Texans can't object to an Indian working for them, if the wages are low enough."

He turned away and would have left her, but she was immediately sorry for her rudeness. "Lieutenant, I am sorry," she said contritely. "Please, you must see, we do need someone, and there's no one else. You've got a train to lead and no men to spare, and the other families have their hands full with their own wagons. If I must handle our wagon by myself, it's only going to end up slowing everyone down."

He paused, giving her an appraising look. "You're a tough woman," he said, without making it clear whether or not it was meant as a compliment.

"Texas women aren't soft, are they?" she said, smiling. "Not in country like this, surely."

After a moment, he returned her smile. "No, ma'am, I guess they aren't, not the ones who survive here."

"As I intend to do."

"And I reckon you will. I'll straighten folks out if there's any trouble." He tipped his hat to her and left.

TEN

Lewis gave up altogether the effort of handling the wagon, and retired inside. He drank and slept, and rode for a while on the rear gate, his legs dangling, like an overgrown boy.

It seemed to Joanna as if the more responsibility she herself assumed, the more Lewis surrendered. She wondered briefly what he would do if she simply stopped coping. Would Lewis's manhood reassert itself? Would he take charge and relieve her of the burdens? Or would this entire enterprise simply flounder with no one to manage?

Looking around at the increasingly barren plain they were entering, she felt disinclined to take the chance of depending on her husband. At least she was not on her own. Lieutenant Price had proved his willingness to be of assistance, and now William Horse, too, had taken on some of the responsibility for her and her brood. It appeared that he meant to act as their driver for the entire trip.

There was only one awkward moment between them. While they

were stopped, mindful of what she had told the lieutenant, she had approached the Nasoni about actually hiring him.

"Of course, I won't be able to pay you much," she had said, faltering—this sort of business arrangement was unfamiliar to her. "But I thought something in the neighborhood of—"

An angry look crossed his face, his wide nostrils flared wider, and to her amazement he simply stalked off, leaving her in mid-sentence.

"Now, what on earth?" she murmured, staring after him.

Lucretia, who was nearby dishing out the midday meal, looked after him, too. "Pride comes in many colors," she said, and went back to her work.

"But that's ridiculous," Joanna said. "He can't work for nothing, like a—"

She caught the quick, almost imperceptible look that her cook gave her, and hesitated. "Well, of course, there are slaves, and then there are..." She hesitated again, and finished lamely, "Others."

"I expect you're right," Lucretia said, and turned her back, leaving Joanna to wonder why it seemed as if she were just now on the verge of getting to know this woman with whom she'd shared most of her life.

In the end, Joanna had followed the Indian to the wateringhole near where they had stopped, and apologized for any unintended offense.

"I am most grateful for your help," she concluded, and for the very first time since she had met him, was rewarded by a smile from him—a smile so tentative, so fleeting, that it was gone before she even recognized it for what it was.

But the memory of it warmed her as she walked back to the train.

So William Horse became their driver, and with her entire family for the moment ensconced in one wagon—Jay Jay had immediately taken his place alongside their new driver—Joanna allowed herself the luxury of a sense of well-being. If she could just get them to San Antone—now, there, she was beginning to call it that; she must ask Lieutenant Price why the natives did not say San Antonio, the way it was written—if she could hold things together just that long ...the rest of the help would arrive soon enough, or might even be there waiting. Campbell, their overseer, had been with them for years: he was used to running things with little or no supervision from Lewis.

Yes, just get them to San Antone. After that, everything would be easier.

Getting them there, however, was not likely to be easy. Things kept popping up, demanding attention, provoking worry.

While she was preparing their supper, Lucretia informed her with the utmost casualness that some of the slaves were gone.

"Gone?" Joanna had trouble grasping what she meant. "Gone where?"

Lucretia shrugged and shook her head.

"You mean, ran away?"

"Seems that way."

"But, ran away where, in this wilderness?"

"I expect they slipped away before we left Galveston. All that dust folks was kicking up, you couldn't have seen."

Joanna was silent for a moment. Lucretia and her assistants had been preparing food for days before they left, and now she was spreading out enormous hampers of fried chicken, rolls, vegetable salads. Later there would be the chore of trail cooking, but for now they might almost have been on an elaborate picnic. It lent an air of unreality.

"How many went?"

"Five. Six maybe. Ulysses has a way of disappearing. Hard to say yet if he's around somewhere or not." She paused to look directly at her mistress. "What you going to do?"

"I don't know. I can't see what we *could* do," Joanna said.

"You going to tell the master?"

"No." That much she was certain of. Lewis, with his volatile temper and his ever-increasing foolishness, was not above turning the whole train around and going back to look—or, worse yet, leaving the train to go on without them while they went back alone.

"No, we won't say anything to anyone," she decided aloud.

"I think that's best," Lucretia said with an unmistakable air of complicity, so that Joanna felt no problem in appealing to her.

"Lucretia, what can I do about it?" she asked. "Would it help if I talked to the others? Would it do any good to threaten them?"

She could tell by the involuntary stiffening of Lucretia's shoulders that the idea did not sit well.

"I sho nuff couldn't say." The patois was back, and the shuffling movements as she turned to spoon out a salad of rice and curried fruit.

Joanna felt she had been dismissed. Irritated, she glanced around and, seeing Melissa, remembered her difficulties with Doña Sebastiano.

That, at least, was a problem she could do something about. She took one of Lucretia's pound cakes with her as a peace offering and went to call on the señora.

She found her seated under an elaborate canopy extended out from the side of her wagon, fanning herself while a trio of Mexican women chatted and cooked at an open fire. With their floridly colored clothes, their high, melodious voices, they might have been a trio of tropical birds. Two men—presumably the hired hands who were to drive and manage the animals—were busy nearby. Doña Sebastiano's daughter was seated beside her; the two gave the impression of holding a royal audience.

Despite her name, there was nothing Spanish about the doña or her appearance. She came from Baltimore, according to Melissa. Her Spanish husband had met her there while traveling, and married her after what Melissa described as a "whirlwind courtship."

Admittedly, the señora's attitude might have prejudiced Joanna against her, but she had difficulty now imagining what that Spanish nobleman had seen that had so smitten him. Doña Sebastiano's hair must once have been a fiery red, but it was faded now to the color of dying rose petals, and her skin, despite the insistent Texas sun, was pale and parchment-brittle. Seated stiffly, unsmiling, she watched as Joanna approached. There was nothing welcoming in her manner.

The daughter, at least, was a beauty, Joanna had to concede that. Younger than Melissa, she appeared years older; far too mature and sophisticated for her age, in Joanna's opinion, but there was no denying that she was ravishing. Her hair was a burnished chestnut color, her eyes very nearly the same, wide and luminous, and almost never at rest. Only her mouth was out of proportion; too tiny, it gave her a speculative look, as if she were weighing everything she saw. One could only assume that she found much of it wanting.

"I've brought you a gift," Joanna said, "as a way of saying thank you for being so hospitable to my daughter. She's finding this entire business an ordeal; making new friends has helped take her mind off the inconvenience."

Doña Sebastiano eyed the gift with some reluctance, but her daughter's diminutive hand darted out and snatched it greedily.

"Our cook's quite proud of her cakes. Justly so, I like to think," Joanna said.

"Thank you." Doña Sebastiano's smile required obvious effort.

Joanna, who had not yet been introduced to the señora's daughter, extended a hand. "I'm Mrs. Harte. I don't believe we've met, but Melissa has spoken of you most favorably."

"My daughter, Nancy," Doña Sebastiano said, and Nancy murmured a quick "How do you do?"

"Your only child?"

It seemed to Joanna that the señora's prim look grew a shade sterner as she said, "No. I have another daughter, Carolyn. She is with her father, in San Antonio."

"Oh, yes, San Antonio," Joanna said. "Perhaps while we're traveling you'll be able to tell me a little about the place, seeing it's to be my new home. Is it much like Galveston?"

"Not in the least," Doña Sebastiano said, and Nancy added, "Galveston is civilized."

Joanna was somewhat taken aback by the obvious distaste the two women showed for their destination. "Is San Antonio as unpleasant as all that?" she asked.

"If it were up to me," Doña Sebastiano said, "I would remain in Galveston. But my husband heard of your train; it meant we could travel with an escort. So..." She shrugged. It was evident that she was returning to San Antonio at her husband's request and not of her own volition. And she seemed to hold Joanna personally responsible for this turn of events.

Joanna found herself disliking this arrogant, unfriendly woman; after all, if her husband was there, and her other daughter...what kind of woman...

But she caught herself—she had come to make peace, not judgments. She cast a quick glance about. "I must say, you've shown admirable foresight," she said.

Doña Sebastiano was a woman who enjoyed compliments and was ever ready to agree with them. "Yes?"

"In hiring your hands before we left Galveston." Joanna indicated the two workmen. "If I'd anticipated my husband's health... As it is, I've had to make do with what was available. I do hope the young man I've hired proves reliable. I should hate to hold up the entire company."

"You hired that Indian, did you?"

Joanna allowed herself to look surprised by the question. "Why, yes, I thought everyone knew." She hesitated and then, with the air of one badly in need of guidance, added, "Have you had any experience working Indians? I'd appreciate any advice...."

Doña Sebastiano appeared gratified by the request. "My advice," she said, and her ladylike airs faded temporarily, "is to watch him like a hawk. An Indian's no better than a Mexican—a pack of low-down, lying skunks. Of course, when that's all you can git...just mark my words, you sleep with a gun by your pillow, you never know...." And she shook her head, clucking her tongue in her cheek.

Joanna restrained a sudden urge to lean forward and slap the other woman. "I shall. And I'm grateful for your advice."

"Just mark my words."

Doña Sebastiano's words had the air of finality about them, and Joanna seized upon the opportunity to take her leave.

"Well, I hope we'll have more opportunities to chat like this," she said. "The advice of one of your station is bound to serve me well."

"Anytime," Doña Sebastiano said with a queenly nod. Her daughter, Nancy, pursed her mouth consideringly. It was difficult to tell, Joanna was thinking, whether the daughter was less a fool than the mother, or simply less flagrant about it.

In any case, Joanna concluded, making her way back toward her own party, she could not say she cared much for either of them. Which was unfortunate, considering they were, if she understood rightly, their nearest neighbors in San Antonio.

She saw as she approached the wagon that they had company: Melissa and the boys stood chatting with a tall, blond gentleman. Joanna had seen him driving one of the other wagons, and rather thought she had been introduced to him, though she could not at the moment put a name on him.

Melissa took care of that by introducing him as "Mr. Hansen."

"I came to bring your daughter some cream," Mr. Hansen said. Like Doña Sebastiano's, his manners were old-world stiff, but despite his formal manner, he seemed friendly. He was, she saw at closer range, older than she had originally assumed. His hair and his ruddy complexion gave him a boyish look, but there were creases about his eyes and the corners of his mouth, and his hands showed years of exposure to hard work and the elements.

"Cream?"

"For the skin. Of course, it is meant for both of you." His embarrassment only served to underscore the fact that Joanna had been an afterthought.

"Mr. Hansen has a general store in San Antonio," Melissa said, and Jay Jay added, "He's German."

Joanna was mildly surprised. She had detected no accent in his voice, other than what she had come to think of as a Texan accent, though she was not quite sure how to describe what that was.

"I came here as a child," he said. "To New York my family came, and much later, to Texas."

"To San Antonio?"

"No, first we came to New Braunfel. Do you know it?"

"I'm afraid not."

"It is east of San Antonio, not far. We farm there. But there are many brothers and not enough farm. So when I marry, I take my wife to San Antonio and we start a store there."

"Is your wife with you on this trip?" Joanna asked. She did not recall seeing him with anyone.

His eyes fell away from hers. "My wife is dead," he said.

"Oh, I am sorry."

"It is many years," he said. There was a moment of awkward silence; then he looked up again, at Melissa first, and then Joanna. "Please—you do not take offense at my gift? This sun, it is very hard for the ladies. This lotion is one my wife favored. It is one of the items I traveled to Galveston to procure."

"We're most grateful for it, I'd begun to fear we'd be indistinguishable from the saddle horses by the time we reached our destination."

"But—such beautiful ladies, you could not be mistaken—oh, I see, you jest."

Humor, Joanna had begun to suspect, was going to be in short supply on this journey. To alleviate the awkwardness, she said, "You must let us pay you for this, however."

"Please, no, it is my honor."

"Well, then, you must eat with us one evening, perhaps tomorrow night?"

"I shall be most grateful; but when we arrive in San Antonio, you will come to my house for dinner, yes?"

On that note, he took leave of them, walking stiffly erect.

"Our first invitation," Melissa said when he was gone.

"And your first conquest, it seems to me," Joanna could not help mentioning.

"Mr. Hansen? Don't be ridiculous," Melissa protested, reddening. "Why, he's years older than I am—anyone can see that. He's probably your age."

"Imagine that," Joanna said, "and still able to get around under his own power."

She noticed, however, that her daughter stole another glance in the direction of Mr. Hansen's departing back before she turned once again to the wagon.

ELEVEN

B y day, nearly thirty slaves were
grateful to ride packed into the
Hartes' second wagon. At night, Lucretia and William slept alone
inside while the others found room on the ground about and beneath.

Lucretia loved William because he was an essentially good man.
He was, as well, an uncomplicated one, that rarest of all the plantation master's possessions, a slave without resentment of his slavery.
His acceptance of his status mirrored that of the white masters he
had served all his life: It was the natural order of things. Born and
reared at Eaton Hall, he had known only one way of life, and that,
for a slave, had been singularly lucky. His father had been major
domo under the old massa; his mother, cook before Lucretia. As
a boy, William had been beaten only twice, and both times he had
regarded the punishment as fitting. As a man, he looked down
with kindly conceit on most of the other slaves he knew; and had
prejudice been less ingrained, he would have seen himself as the
better of many whites, too.

Lucretia both admired and despised him for his tolerance. She was not so lucky. There were days in the old house, in South Carolina, when she had not dared pause before a mirror, nor glance in the direction of her own reflection, lest her hands rise of their own accord and try to strip the blackness from her face.

Lucretia's first beating had been a matter of color. She had been five, perhaps six—she was no more certain of her exact age than her mistress was—when she had stolen into the bedroom of Joanna's mother, in itself enough to bring punishment down upon her head. She was found there seated at the vanity table, her face hidden under a thick mask of lotions and creams, and over them a caked layer of white powder that crazed and cracked when she howled at her punishment, falling in chunks to the floor, ground back into powder by her flailing feet. All for nothing. What she had seen of her handiwork in the vanity mirror had been punishment enough.

She loved Joanna, and hated her, too; hated herself for loving her, hated herself for hating her. She thought sometimes she would be happier under a harsher mistress. Joanna was kind and gentle, good to her slaves, good to Lucretia in particular. And how could you not resent the necessity of feeling grateful for that? What soul could not fester, bearing such a wound?

How lucky she had felt when Joanna first helped her learn to read. But why, then, had it come to feel a gift she gave the writer, too, something essential to the very urge that had driven him in the first place? Why did only she bear the burden of obligation for something the inherent rightness of which seemed to blossom and spread like a field of dandelions within her?

Oh, the hunger that had spawned, insatiable, gnawing, making the hunger she fed in others seem puny indeed.

Words, clogging her innards, threatening to break through the fragile shell of her skull and print themselves across her brow, for all to realize her guilt.

Like a secret drunk she was, stealing at night into forbidden rooms, dens and studies and parlors; pawing with trembling hands through trunks and valises and letters bound in molding ribbons, thirsting for words, words, more words.

Books, smuggled under her apron. Letters, the possession of which meant the hide off her back. Labels on patent-medicine bottles, and the ragged scraps of newspapers, discarded by those who could read without danger.

For she knew the danger; it had come up like gorge within her. She had awakened one night in a cold sweat of terror and known in an instant why the others did not let their slaves read, and why she dared not let even Joanna know of the books and letters, of the pages and the thousands and thousands of tumbling words that beat against the backs of her eyelids.

It wasn't the words. They were only seeds. It was their harvest of ideas, that was the danger; she'd known that when the first one rotted in her mouth and made her world taste sour.

That was the bitterest lesson of all, and she could thank Joanna for it as well. She could look back now and see, its seed had been planted in the very first lesson ("*A* is for apple..."): There was *no* unthinking an idea.

So, she lay in the dark, with her William snoring beside her, and listened to the sounds of slaves creeping away in the darkness, and did not move to stop them or warn her mistress. She wished them well, and ached for what lay before them; envied their courage, and mocked their foolhardiness. She knew what they felt, what drove them to the risks they took. And her burden was worse than theirs: She had the words for it. And the idea of it.

And now, like a fragile bud she had cupped in her hands, lest her very wishing crush it, she had the dream of it, too.

Their own land. The freedom of it, for her and William, and the children whose sprouting waited in her belly, and the children to come from them.

She would get it; she would use her mistress's own goodness against her to get it, and without shame.

Because that was the shape the words had taken for her, the idea that had come to live in her, and become her: Freedom was a right. You owed no thanks for it. And the very loving goodness that would make a gift of it was in itself a chain that must be broken if you were to be free.

Joanna did not learn until the midday stop the following day that three more slaves had run away during the night.

She stood, worrying at the far horizon. Why was this happening now, here, of all places? She might have understood it in South Carolina, where they at least knew the lay of the land, but here, in this trackless wilderness—or was that the point? All that space, it made you dizzy almost; you felt barely anchored to the earth. And it would be easy enough, surely, to lose yourself; given enough time to put distance behind you, it was hard to imagine anyone ever finding you.

"But they'll die out there," she said aloud.

"Pro'ly," Lucretia agreed.

"All for the sake of freedom?" She could see an effort to live free; but simply to die free—could it be worth it?

Lieutenant Price came up then, with the suggestion that perhaps she would like to ride ahead for a while. "I have to scout the next water hole," he said. "And now that you've got a driver..." He cocked an eye in the direction of William Horse, who looked not at all happy with the suggestion.

Joanna, however, jumped at the chance to put the wagon train and its problems, temporarily at least, behind her. "My sidesaddle's in the wagon," she said.

"I'll get it," Gregory offered, and headed for the rear of the wagon.

"I'll have one of the men fetch a horse," the lieutenant said, but the Nasoni said, "That is not necessary. My horse is here."

The lieutenant gave the pinto a dubious look. "I don't know. That horse looks half wild to me."

"He is an Indian pony," William Horse said, as if that explained everything. "Here, I will show you."

He gestured for Joanna to approach the pony with him. She had to admit, though she was a good rider, the pinto looked plenty skittish.

"Do not be afraid," William Horse said. "Animals smell fear. Here, breathe into his nostrils, like so." He snorted hard and loud up the horse's nostrils. To Joanna's surprise, the horse responded in kind, his nostrils flaring as he breathed a powerful stream of air into the Indian's face.

"It is the horse's way of greeting a friend," the Indian said. "Now, you do it."

Joanna approached the mount shyly, feeling a trifle foolish. The pinto whinnied nervously, but his large, limpid eyes regarded her with a steady appraisal.

Well, she told herself, it was already obvious that she wasn't going to conquer Texas without a horse, and who better to teach her about horses than an Indian?

She leaned forward till her nose was almost touching the pinto's, surprised that the horse waited patiently and motionless. She breathed out hard, trying to direct her breath up his nostrils, and was rewarded with a blast of hot breath that all but choked her.

"Again," William Horse said. She repeated the strange ritual. "Now," he said, sounding satisfied, "he is your friend, you can ride him anywhere."

The horse gave a friendly-sounding snort and, when she reached up to pet his muzzle, rubbed gently against her hand.

"Well, I'll be," Lieutenant Price said, clearly impressed. William Horse, looking pleased with himself, went to take the saddle from Gregory.

A short while later, William Horse—and a great many others in the camp—watched Joanna ride off ahead of the train with the handsome army lieutenant.

Gregory, on the other hand, was not watching his mother, but William Horse. Jay Jay was enthralled with their new driver, Gregory uncomfortable, and not entirely sure why. He bristled like a jealous suitor whenever William Horse looked at their mother, and because he was constantly watching for such things, he knew the Indian looked at her often.

His reactions were peculiar when you considered that he was not at all perturbed by Lieutenant Price's attentions to their mother, and they were far more obvious. But in a sense, Lieutenant Price's presence was official; he would have been there, looking after them, even if he didn't like them. Good feelings just made it all the better.

It wasn't that William Horse was an Indian, either; to some degree, that was in his favor—Gregory could not help being interested in the first Indian he'd ever met.

The Indian had, however, thrust himself upon them, unlike the lieutenant. Grateful as Gregory was for his help—and he *was* grateful; there were many things he just couldn't do yet for his mother—he was wary, as well, of any deliberate intrusion.

Besides, the lieutenant didn't exactly belong just to them; he had the whole wagon train to look after—and more than that, you could see that he belonged to the army first and foremost. William Horse was suddenly and simply there, with them, riding in the wagon, driving it most of the time, or right alongside it, with nothing to occupy his attention but them—with nothing most of the time, it seemed, to occupy his attention but their mother.

Being occupied so much with her himself, Gregory couldn't help noticing, or minding. Gregory thought of himself as his mother's partner in things. An apprentice, to be sure, with much still to learn, but it was understood between them that he would take over more responsibilities as time passed. It had always been that way; it was what he had sacrificed his childhood for.

He'd never actually played, for instance, with other children. Not that they wouldn't have let him, or even that he wouldn't sometimes have liked to. Take Jay Jay, for example. His brother was an evil, *evil* child; there was nothing so dangerous or so monstrous that he couldn't delight in it, thrive on it. Gregory would have worshiped him if it hadn't seemed like going over to the enemy somehow.

Or his father. Gregory loved to cope, he loved to make something his duty merely for the sake of doing it. And he could well have been father to the man whose son he was.

But when the time had come for choosing sides, his father had been on the wrong one. Because no matter what he had done for his father, it seemed as if he had always known it was his mother who managed. His father had problems. His mother solved them. It hadn't been difficult to choose between those two directions. Not for him, anyway.

Jay Jay and Melissa never really had chosen, but that was a choice, too, wasn't it? For himself, he had to belong, and if he could only belong to one of them, then that belonging must be total.

Which made him wary of people like the Indian seated next to him, who otherwise by now might have become his friend, if more than one were permissible.

And wary, too, of the fact that his mother was changing, he could see that, and it worried him, because he didn't yet know how he was supposed to change with her.

There was a moment, when they first started to ride from the camp, when the lieutenant glanced at her, frowned, and reined in his horse abruptly.

"Oh, no," he said, "you're not taking that with you."

"Taking..."—she looked around, puzzled—"...what?"

"Whatever it is that's making you frown like that," he said. "Don't worry, if it's that serious, it'll wait here till you get back."

She laughed self-consciously. "You're right," she said. "Very well, I promise."

"Good." He rode ahead and she followed, the pinto moving easily and gracefully in the wake of his huge stallion.

86

It felt wonderful to ride, to feel the problems fading into the distance behind her, as the wagon train faded. She had liked to ride in South Carolina, too, but that had been different. She'd almost always been on Eaton Hall land, and even when she was out of sight of house and buildings, even out of sight of all the people on the plantation, she had still felt hemmed in.

But you couldn't feel that here; by the time they'd crested a ridge and ridden down into a shallow in the earth, it seemed as if they were alone and a thousand miles distant from everyone and everything else.

For a while they rode without talking. They mounted another ridge, the lieutenant pulling ahead and then slowing to wait for her to come alongside him. She saw water in the distance and pointed. "Our wateringhole?" she asked.

So he explained to her about mirages, those illusionary pools of water that vanished as you neared them; vanished as this one was vanishing while they rode closer.

"Men have died following them across the desert," he said, "going straight away from the real water they needed."

After a moment, she asked, "Is that what my husband is doing, here in Texas? Following a mirage?"

"Hard to say." He pointed down; at their feet, a brief stretch of wagon tracks could just be made out in the tall brown grass. "At least he's not the first."

"It's hard to imagine anyone else has ever been here," she said, marveling.

"The land heals itself. That's part of what I like about Texas. People keep coming, more and more of them, and there's so much Texas, it just soaks them up, the way the desert soaks up the spring rains, till there's scarcely a trace of them, and the land is still just as big and open and wild as it ever was."

"Will it always be, I wonder?"

"There's something in me likes to think a part of it always will be. If God had anything in mind when he made Texas, it must have been to let a man know what freedom feels like."

Freedom. Yes, she'd been thinking something like that earlier; that was what she'd sensed here, since they'd left Galveston. Those pushed-back horizons, faded far off into the distance; why, even the boundaries of her marriage seemed to have moved back from her, to give her room she'd never had before.

She tried to look at this moment in time over her shoulder as it were, as it would look when she had gone on into the future.

Wouldn't it be funny if this, here, turned out to be happiness, the happiness she'd been waiting for all her life, that had seemed always to elude her. This immense dome of sky, faded to a washed-out blue-gray. The endless, wrinkled prairie unfolding itself before them, and the tall grass burning brown in the hot sun. The sky-searching of a hawk, her hair loose from its pins, whipping in her face, and the steady thrumedy-thrumedy-thrum of horses' hooves on the iron-hard ground.

She laughed aloud. Webb Price gave her a surprised look, and then he laughed with her. Suddenly, he spurred up his horse and with a loud yell, Yippee-i-o, he raced forward. She kicked the pony's flanks and ran after him, the two of them thundering over the plains. The rest of her pins came loose and her hair made a golden red cloud trailing after her, a web to catch the shining rays of the midday sun.

"There," he said, pointing to where a greener patch of grass and a low outcropping of brush marked the location of the water hole they were seeking.

They slowed to a more sedate pace. "It got to you, didn't it?" he asked, grinning. "Texas? It does that, it gets to you all of a sudden. I may as well warn you, once it's in your blood like that, you like to never get it out."

She laughed, and shook her hair about her face. "I like it," she said. "I like it here." And she did, as simply as that; she felt suddenly as if she'd come home, home to some place where her heart had been all along, without her even knowing it.

"It can be a rough country, too. Hard to tame," he warned.

"I don't know that I'd want to tame it, exactly," she said, looking around with a newfound sense of recognition.

"Like a horse, you mean, just tame enough to stay on, and still wild in the heart." The way a man wants a woman, he was thinking, but didn't dare say. The way I want you.

"Like this pony," she said, and he was immediately sorry for his analogy.

They had reached the water hole. He dismounted and came to help her down.

Their touch, when he took her hand, was like a flash of lightning crackling about them. The tension that had long been mounting between them broke. Whether by accident or by design, she half fell into his arms, against his chest, and somehow, never knowing quite how it had come about, he was kissing her—her lips, her throat, her hair, even the closed lids of her eyes. She crowded into his senses, merged with the scent of hot prairie and tall grass and mirrored surface of the pool. Something pierced his chest like a knife, but sweetly for all its pain.

"Joanna," he murmured, and in her name alone was his declaration of love.

Suddenly she was struggling against him. For a few seconds he held her tight, body crushed against body, softness yielding to rock-like hardness.

"Don't, please," she cried.

He let her go then. She took a step backward, half staggering drunkenly. He could still feel the heat of her breasts where they had been crushed against him.

"I'm married," she said, breathing heavily.

"Your husband..."

"...Is my husband, for better or for worse," she finished for him.

"Most would say for the worst."

"And so you would make of me a poor wife? A cheap woman?"

"You could never be that."

"I would be to a husband I betrayed. And what man would ever be sure afterward that he could trust me either? Is that what you want, Lieutenant Price? Because I can tell you truthfully, you are very dangerously close to having it. To something we can't do without feeling ashamed afterward."

For a long moment they regarded one another steadily. Then, with an angry set to his mouth, he turned away from her. "No" was all he said.

Their horses, mindless of the passion hovering in air, had gone to drink at the muddy pool. They waited silently for the animals to finish, then mounted again and turned back toward the wagon train. He let her ride ahead of him, but when they had ridden a short distance, he spoke her name, in a formal, businesslike voice.

"Mrs. Harte?"

She looked back at him, trying not to show the pain that distant tone caused her. "Yes?"

"I think you'll be happier here if you learn to manage a western saddle."

TWELVE

Lucretia was making coffee. She brought the water to a boil in the big enameled pot. A whole egg was wrapped in cheesecloth with the coffee and a bit of salt. When the water was boiling hard, she crushed the egg inside the cloth, dropped the whole package into the pot, and set it off the fire to steep briefly.

Already others in the train were talking enviously of the Hartes' coffee.

Joanna was watching Lucretia, but her thoughts were not of coffee. She was wondering if she dared to follow through on the idea that had come to her the day before, riding back from that wateringhole with Webb Price.

It was that talk about freedom, about the way Texas affected you, that had put the idea in her head. At first she'd rejected the idea as impossible. There were too many risks, too many problems. If nothing else, there was Lewis to worry about, and she didn't have to ask to know what his reaction would be.

On the other hand, something had to be done, and done soon.

Their slaves were running away in droves. More had gone last night; she supposed they were eager to be on their way before the train had advanced too far into the open Texas prairie.

They'd started out with better than thirty slaves. They now had fewer than twenty—seventeen, if she counted rightly, and five of them were youngsters, not much good for anything but the simplest chores.

And the idea that had been circling around inside her head all night long had begun to seem less preposterous.

She watched Lewis clamber out of the wagon, yawn and stretch. He'd seemed sullen when she rode back yesterday, and had scarcely spoken to her since; meaning, of course, that he'd spent most of another day drinking, and sleeping off the liquor, simply to start drinking all over again. He looked puffy now, and bleary-eyed, and it came to her quite clearly that *he* was no argument for not doing what she was contemplating.

"Jay Jay," she said when her husband was out of hearing range. "Yes'm?"

"I want you to spend this evening with your father."

"Ma'am?"

"Take a walk with him, about sundown. Get him to go riding with you, if he will. Keep him occupied." She hesitated, then added, "Get him drunk if you have to. And, Lucretia, I want you to get all the slaves together for a meeting. Just after sundown, on the far side of their wagon, where we won't attract notice."

"What you fixin' to do?" Lucretia asked the question on the faces of Jay Jay and Gregory.

"I'm going to promise them their freedom, when we get to San Antone," Joanna said.

The others stared wide-eyed. Melissa, who'd come up in time to catch the tail end of the conversation, gasped and flung her hands to her cheeks.

"You can't!" Jay Jay exclaimed.

"Who'll curl my hair?" Melissa demanded, but no one paid her any attention.

"He's right," Gregory said. "Papa would have to sign the papers of manumission." He looked less bewildered than the others, his tongue thrusting out one cheek thoughtfully. Joanna took that for encouragement.

"Well, we won't need those till we get there," she said. "And I don't want anyone saying anything to him till I think how to do it, you hear?" She fixed each of them in turn with a steely gaze. "You all just do as I say, and leave me to handle him."

She reached for one of the cups lined up by the fire. Lucretia, barely able to contain the sense of excitement and triumph within her, moved swiftly to snatch up the coffeepot and pour the cup full of steaming black coffee.

"I think mama has lost her mind."

Gregory ignored his sister's comment and asked instead, "Aren't you coming to hear what she has to say?"

"I don't care to take part in giving away everything we own, thank you, behind my father's back."

Gregory narrowed his eyes at her. "You're not going to tell, are you?" he asked.

"I don't see how I could even if I wanted to, 'less I wanted to chase papa clear across Texas. Lord only knows where Jay Jay has taken him; they could be in San Antonio already for all we know."

Jay Jay had obediently spirited his father away immediately after supper; no one knew just where or what excuse he had used. It was exactly the sort of deviousness for which, in Melissa's opinion, he was ideally suited.

"Anyway," Gregory said, "the slaves are not everything we own, and she isn't trying to give them away, she's trying to hold on to them."

"Well, she's got a most peculiar way of doing that, is my opinion. What I say is, if something is yours, you hold on to it tight, and try to get more while you're at it. That's the way progress is made."

"There's mother," Gregory said, catching sight of her across the camp. "I'm going." He waited a few seconds, but when there was no response from Melissa, he left her alone by the wagon and went after his mother.

Melissa waited until she was certain he was gone and not coming back. Then she leaned into the opening of the wagon and reached unerringly into her bag to extract her hand mirror. Propping it into a fold of the canvas, she squinted slightly to gaze at her reflection in it. It was nearly dark and the image she saw was a shadowy one, but that did not deter her interest in it. Not even the ridicule of her brothers could do that, though she had learned to avoid their mockery when she could.

She could hardly be expected to think kindly of giving things away, useful things that you were accustomed to and couldn't be expected to manage without. It was all right for the others—they all managed to take care of one another, in some fashion. But if no one understood her—and it was certainly obvious they did not—how could they be expected to look after her properly?

Slaves were different, of course; that was what they were there for, whether they understood or not. You couldn't very well throw something at, say, your mother, and not even know yourself why you wanted to. The problem with real people was that they expected so much of you, as if they thought you owed it to them. It made everything so much more difficult.

The light was almost gone now; she had to squint hard and lean with her nose practically against the glass, and then she was alarmed by how dreadful she looked, with her face all scrunched up like that. Piqued, she stuck out her tongue at herself.

One of the shadows beyond her reflection moved, and a masculine voice said, "Now, that is a shame, to spoil such a pretty picture in that manner."

She squealed and whirled about. "Oh, Mr. Hansen, it's you. You scared me half out of my wits."

"I am sorry," he said, looking abashed. He glanced around. "No one is here? Perhaps I should return another time...?"

"Oh, no." She reached quickly to lay a delicate white hand on his arm. "No, don't go, please. It's getting dark, and I'm so frightened of wild beasts, with no one around to protect me."

"I do not think animals would come into the camp, with so many people—so many fires...." His eyes fell to the hand on his arm. He looked both pleased and embarrassed.

"Even so..." she said, and let the sentence dwindle. "Won't you have some coffee? I do believe there's some left, though it seems I'll have to pour it for you myself, if you don't mind my clumsy efforts."

"Mind?" he repeated, and was struck dumb by the contemplation of that possibility.

"Do you know," she went on, leading him toward the low-burning fire and seeming oblivious to his uncertainty, "I have been just dying to hear all about that store of yours, in San Antonio? Tell me, is it a large store, would you say, or just a little bitty one? Approximately how many people would you say you have working for you, exactly?"

And Mr. Hansen, who had stood for nearly twenty minutes trying to screw up the courage merely to greet this lovely young creature, found himself in no time chatting at great length about his store, its merchandise, the home in which he lived ("Fifteen rooms! And you a widower, too. Why, it must be ever so lonesome for you") and even astonishingly detailed descriptions of each room's furnishings.

He told her things he wasn't even aware he had known, and was delighted at the obvious interest she displayed in everything she heard. In his experience, it was unusual to find a female, especially one so young and beautiful, with any interest in business or financial matters. Truly, this daughter of the elegant Mrs. Harte was some sort of a paragon.

"How are you going to explain this to papa?" Gregory wanted to know. He had caught up with his mother and together the two of them were approaching the waiting group of blacks.

"I don't know," Joanna admitted frankly.

"Legally, he'll have to sign."

"It's ridiculous, isn't it? Legally I'm not much better off than the slaves. What's his is his, and what's mine is his. I'm making all the decisions, but legally I have no right. He can lie drunk in the back of the wagon, but the law says he's the only one smart enough to know what to do."

"When your sons are old enough..."

"I'll become their chattel, instead of his. Oh, I didn't mean to be offensive—God knows, you're bound to do a better job of things than he does. But why shouldn't a woman have the authority if she's capable of it? For that matter, why shouldn't a woman help elect a president? We have to pay for their mistakes as much as anybody, maybe more in some ways."

"That'll never happen," Gregory said.

"There's women who talk about it," Joanna said.

"Up north, maybe. Not in the South."

"This isn't the South. Not really."

"It's a slave state," he pointed out.

"This," she said, raising her hand in a sweeping gesture that took in the whole darkening plain, "is Texas. And I'm beginning to think that Texas is just not like anyplace else." She paused, and then added, with a slightly timorous smile, "After all, where else would I be about to do this?"

Her son's look was not encouraging, however, and Joanna turned from it to the waiting, watching faces.

What she saw was anxiety, apprehension, fear. It had never really occurred to her before that her whole bond with these people—these people with whom she in fact shared her life—was fear. It was fear, not loyalty, that kept them with her. Fear, not love, that made them concerned for her well-being. Fear, not pride, that governed the quality of their work.

"Well, here's my chance to change all that," she told herself, and squaring her shoulders, she gave the slaves a look intended to put them at their ease.

The effort was only partly successful. Meetings like this, though usually called by the master rather than his wife, almost invariably meant trouble, and when Joanna started by mentioning the runaways, there was a great shuffling of feet, and nervous glances tossed about.

"I've no doubt there are others of you who have been tempted to do the same," Joanna said. "And, frankly, I've begun to understand how you feel. I myself never really knew what freedom felt like until just these last few days. I feel as if I, too, have been in chains. But all that is changing. This is a new land; we're going to a new home, a new life—and I want you all to share in that new life with me. Not by running away in the night. To begin with, with each day we're advancing farther and farther into the wilderness, and the chances of survival grow slimmer and slimmer for those who run. And even if some of them do make it back to Galveston, more than likely what they face there is recapture, and a new master. Maybe a worse one."

"They say, up north—" someone in the rear, she couldn't tell who, started to say, but another voice quickly and softly shushed him.

"Yes, up north," Joanna agreed. "Things are different there, so I understand. But I don't know if any of you realize just how far 'up north' is from here—much farther than it is from South Carolina. And anyway, we don't have to go up north to have things different, that's what I've come to tell you. We can *make* them different right here, in Texas."

"What you mean?" one of the men asked.

"I mean, I'm setting you free. All of you." She took a deep breath and paused, waiting.

Her announcement was greeted by a stunned silence. Even Lucretia, who had already known, waited as if for the other shoe to fall.

"You mean right here?" someone asked, and someone else said, "You just going to leave us here?"

"No, no, I don't mean that at all," Joanna said quickly. "And I can't just send you back to Galveston either—you wouldn't be any better off there. What I mean is, if the rest of you will stay with us, continue with us and go on doing your work, you'll arrive in San Antonio as free men and women."

"What d'we do there?"

"The same jobs you've always done, only instead of doing it just for me and my family, you'll be doing it for yourselves as well. For wages, modest ones anyway. And what's more, hopefully, for your own land as well. The land we're going to is enormous, I can't even picture myself how big it is, but I'm going to ask my husband to give each of you a parcel of your own, a few acres anyway. Enough to make a home on."

The expressions on the faces before her were uncomprehending still, and even suspicious.

"The massa, he don't know nothing 'bout this?"

"Well, no, not just yet," Joanna admitted reluctantly, and saw the fear come back like a prairie wind sweeping over the group. There was more shuffling about in the loose dust.

Sulie, one of Lucretia's assistants, a pretty young girl of sixteen or seventeen, got up from where she'd been sitting on the ground. "If the massa don't say we're free..." she said, and shrugged, avoiding Joanna's eyes.

"I'll talk to the master. Mr. Harte," she corrected herself. "When the time is right. Before we reach San Antonio, I promise. I give you my word."

The slaves, however, had begun to drift away without even waiting to be dismissed. Watching them vanish into the darkness, Joanna felt her determination fading with them.

She hadn't even managed to convince the slaves she was freeing them. How on earth was she going to convince her husband?

THIRTEEN

B y morning, however, Joanna had regained some of her courage.

For one thing, Lucretia had no more runaways to report. If they didn't yet quite believe what she had told them, at least the blacks seemed to be adopting a wait-and-see attitude.

"You've got to help convince them I'm sincere," she told Lucretia.

"Yes'm," Lucretia agreed, and almost as an afterthought said, "Maybe if you told them you needed their help..."

"That's ridiculous, of course I need their help, just as they need mine," Joanna replied.

"Yes'm." Lucretia went back to stirring the big pot of oatmeal over the fire.

"They can see that for themselves, surely."

"If'n you say so, Miz Harte."

So of course she spent the day talking individually, whenever the opportunities arose, with the blacks, trying to make each of them understand that the plan she had proposed might be not only the best future for all of them but perhaps the only future for them.

"Running away isn't the answer," she said time and time again. "Your chances of surviving out there are slim, practically non-existent. And my chances of surviving without your help are no better. But working together, free, we have a chance to make for all of us something different, something far better than what we've left behind."

As she talked, she began to see that depriving slaves of education had worked to her detriment as well as theirs. It was those few whose minds had been developed, even minimally, who first began to nod their heads in agreement, to look less bewildered and frightened by her idea.

But it wasn't only the slaves that she began to convince. The more she talked, the more she persuaded and sold her plan, the more she convinced herself, the more she put to rest her own fears and doubts.

It wasn't Lewis who was her enemy, it was fear, she saw that. Fear that made you hesitate, and made you feel sorry for what you had not. True, she lacked the privileges of manhood; but there were men who tried and failed, notwithstanding those privileges.

She made up her mind that if she failed, it would not be because she was a woman. It was going to take all her courage and will to succeed; it would be all to easy to blame the lack of them on her femininity, and she promised herself that she would not again fall into that trap. Certainly that would recompense her little if she lay dying in some burning desert, wouldn't it?

It wasn't fear that would make a success of this venture, that she needed to drive her. It was determination; she wanted what she had begun to discern, as yet dimly before her, awaiting her where they were going. She had a sense that this was her destiny, that this was what had haunted and teased her all those years at Eaton Hall, whispering to her in the darkness, vanishing out of sight as she sought to follow. Always there, beckoning just beyond her vision.

She'd wanted something different from life, had been unhappily convinced that something better was meant for her. Now, she'd been given Texas. But she must earn it, must mold it to herself, or herself to it, more likely. Yes, that was it: Texas was the form, and its shape was freedom; new and vast horizons, bigger than men had dreamed before; huge and rich and burning with life as it had never been lived before, as perhaps it could never be lived elsewhere.

That was what she'd discovered here in Texas, because she had discovered it as well inside herself. That was how she knew she was right.

And that would be the source of her strength. She would make the slaves believe, because she believed. She would convince Lewis of her vision, because she now saw it so clearly.

"You're changing, Joannie," he said, looking at her oddly.

"Yes, Lewis," she said, and surprised herself by laughing aloud, "I have changed."

And she had, too.

Her new commitment was like a religious fervor and she cloaked herself in it. But it was not long before her new faith was tested and her hopes of trying to find an easy way of approaching Lewis with these matters were dashed.

Wrapped up in the rote of what they were doing, lulled into lethargy by drink and the Texas heat, Lewis had been almost a ghostly presence among them, visibly there, yet insubstantial.

It was the following night, however, when he made a fateful decision to bed with one of the slave wenches. Worse luck, he chose Sulie, whose inherent intelligence and high spirits had more than once threatened to get her into trouble in South Carolina. She was pretty, and rebellious, and the combination made her particularly desirable to a man like Lewis.

Joanna, who did not share Lewis's long stretches of inactivity, was inside their wagon when the uproar began. She lay, awake enough to be conscious of voices, arguing, shouting; asleep enough to pay them little mind.

Until Lewis threw back the canvas flap and half crawled into the wagon, muttering and shoving things about.

"God damn niggers, I'll kill every one of them," he swore under his breath. "Where is it, damnation, where's my whip?"

Joanna sat up quickly. "Lewis, now what are you..."

"Stay out of this," he said, snatching his black snake whip from beneath a barrel. "I got plantation business to tend to. Man's business." With that he was gone, the flap snuffing out the moonlight that had illuminated the interior.

Man's business? But wasn't she taking care of that? Joanna fumbled sleepily for her clothes; in the distance, the babble of voices grew louder, Lewis's soaring above the rest. She threw a blanket over her nightdress and half climbed, half fell out of the wagon.

"Mother..." Gregory said.

"Stay here. All of you," she added, well aware that the inquisitive Jay Jay would likely be hot on her heels.

She found the slaves assembled alongside their wagon. Men and women alike were stripped to the waist, the light of a dwindling campfire gleaming darkly off sweaty skin. Beyond, neighbors from the other wagons, drawn by the ruckus, had begun to gather in a semicircle, watching.

Sulie was kneeling on the ground, her pose, despite the situation, as graceful and poignant as a ballerina's. Lewis towered over her, the firelight casting him a giant's shadow and making him for once look imposing. He had the whip raised, and as she ran up, Joanna caught sight of a long red welt across Sulie's back, already beginning to ooze blood.

She ran directly between them, almost getting the whip across her face. "Lewis, don't!" she cried.

He blinked, his arm momentarily frozen in midswing. "Get out of my way, Joanna," he said. "This has got to be done. They're talking about freedom. A man can't tolerate that kind of sass from 'em—it makes 'em dangerous...."

"Lewis, I've got to talk to you," she said breathlessly.

"Not now, Joanna...."

"Now."

He lowered his arm, his look menacing, angrier than she'd ever seen it, but not just angry, either. She saw his half-glance in the direction of the people watching in the distance, and knew she was making a fool of him, in front of an audience; but that couldn't be helped now.

"Joanna, I am ordering you—"

"No," she said, lowering her voice. "You're not going to whip the blacks, and I am no longer taking orders from you. We're not your property anymore, Lewis, that's what I'm trying to tell you. None of us is."

He stared at her for a long moment, plainly unable to believe what he'd heard. "You must be crazy," he said, dropping his voice as she had done; but not hearing couldn't hide from their audience what was going on.

"Lewis, I told you, I've got to talk to you. I should have before now, but I was afraid. That was my mistake. But I won't let you compound it. Please, come back to the wagon with me where we can talk."

"I am running things here, in this train," he said, "and I'm telling you—"

"But you're not, Lewis," she said, speaking as slowly and as carefully as she had to the children when they were small and some lesson of major importance had to be imparted to them. "Even you must see that. You aren't running things anymore. Not since we got here. You made me take over all the responsibility, Lewis, and I've done the best I could with it. Now you're going to have to abide by what I've done."

For a few seconds, she thought he was going to strike her after all with the whip. She doubted if any of those watching would try to stop him, either; legally, he would be entirely within his rights to whip not only the slaves but her as well, if he chose.

Then, slowly, he brought his arm down—it must have begun to ache, surely, holding that heavy whip aloft all this time.

"Please," she said gently, "come with me where we can talk, and I'll try to explain everything."

She put a hand toward him, but he leaned away from it, looking at it as if it might have been a snake. He looked, too, like a child, a scolded child, hurt and bewildered, but beginning to comprehend.

He shook his head. "I didn't make you, Joanna. I never made you do any of it," he said.

She looked at the ground, away from him, away from the pain in his eyes and the droop of his broad shoulders. "Maybe..." she hesitated, confused. "Something did, something made me."

"That was in you. In you, all along," he said.

He turned away from her, not even glancing at the others, and began to walk back toward their wagon. He stumbled slightly over something on the ground. The ground's surface here was rough, it was hard for anyone to walk without stumbling here and there, but just now it made him look particularly clumsy and foolish.

Sulie was still on her knees; the other slaves were motionless, wide-eyed.

Well, at least, she thought, *I've got them convinced now.*

"Sulie, get up," she said, sounding angry. "And the rest of you, cover yourselves and go back to bed. I'll handle this."

Sulie's legs had gotten stiff, so that she staggered when she tried to rise. Joanna saw, and made no move to help. It was Lucretia who stepped forward to give her a steadying hand. "I'll clean up her back for her," Lucretia said; and as Joanna started away, she added, "Miz Harte? That was very brave, what you did."

Joanna glanced at her, then looked into the darkness that had swallowed up Lewis.

"No it wasn't," she said. "It was very cruel."

Lewis was again rummaging in the wagon when she came up, this time for his bottle. He found it and took a long swig from it, eyed her over the bottle's rim while he drank. Joanna waited, for once not begrudging him his whiskey.

"You freed 'em?" he asked finally, wiping the back of his hand across his mouth. "You turned my slaves free?"

"I promised them they would be free," she said, as mindful as he was of the fact that she could not legally set them free. Just as they were both aware—it was evident in the way he'd worded his question—that they were discussing something that was already a fact.

"It had to be done," she went on. "They were leaving us, running away in droves. We'd have arrived in San Antone with none left."

"No one told me," he said.

"Would you have liked hearing it?" She didn't say that if he'd been running things as he'd said earlier, he wouldn't have needed telling.

"A wife can't give away a husband's slaves, nor free them, either. Unless he's dead. Or were you planning on killing me before we got there, Joanna, along with all your other ideas?"

"Oh, Lewis, you know I'd never deliberately, consciously set out to hurt you. I might not be much of a wife to you, but I'm better than that, and so are you. Not *everything* is wrong with our marriage. No, please, don't drink any more just yet. Wait till we've talked first."

He drank anyway, but, she noticed, only a sip this time. And he waited for her to go on.

"I didn't ask to come here, Lewis, you know that," she said. "You brought us here over my objections. Don't look all angry at me now. What I'm trying to say is that you were right all along about coming to Texas, and I was wrong. Whether it was luck or the lot of the devil, I don't know, but we're here and, Lewis, I know it's the right thing for us. Do you hear me? I can feel it in my soul, I can look around, I can look up—oh, look, Lewis, look up there, did you ever see..." She gestured upward, at the heavens. She'd never seen so many stars; when she tilted her head back, like this, she felt she could almost fall upward into them, among them. What couldn't you do ... ? The words she'd been trying to find to convince Lewis, the words she chased like a will-o'-the-wisp, came tumbling out of her, so that even in his anger, her husband stared mesmerized, could almost feel the heat of her ardor—an ardor he'd never felt from her before. It was the first time he was seeing his wife in a passion, but it wasn't him she was making love to, it was something else, something he couldn't see or put a name to, but couldn't doubt was real.

It scared him, but it thrilled him, too; and, perversely, aroused him, as she had never aroused him in their marriage. Though anything would be doomed to fail in the wake of what was gleaming now in her face.

"It's so free here," she said, "so open—it's like God gave us back a piece of the world, without all the mistakes and the fools and the fripperies that hemmed us in before, where we were. Like being born again. I never understood what that meant till I came to Texas. We can make something here, Lewis, I know we can. A new Eaton Hall—no, no, even the name has to be different. It'll be nothing like what we left behind, but it'll be good, I know it will, I can feel it buzzing around inside me, about to burst. And we'll do it. *I'll* do it. I'll do it for us, I know I can, if you'll only let me. You won't have to trouble yourself again, do you hear what I'm saying? Never to bother yourself again, never to worry or fret over things ... Just leave it to me. Let me do it. Let me do it my way and I'll make it right, I'll make something to be proud of, I swear it. I know it. And I'll never ask for your help, Lewis, I'll do it all. Only, all I do ask of you, all I'm saying is, don't stand in my way, don't make it harder for me. It's the first time I've ever asked anything of you, and it's all I ever will ask, Lewis. Give me Texas. I'll do the rest."

The silence that followed her rush of words was thunderous. There were sounds, distant sounds from the other wagons, voices and cooking pots being put away for the night, and even an animal baying somewhere far in the distant darkness; and, closer, Joanna's excited breathing, panting almost, as she watched him with eyes that looked glazed over, near-demented. But the sounds only made the silence more intense.

Lewis felt like a field after a brush fire had swept over it, seared, exhausted, with an aching emptiness for the new growth that would follow—but, oh, what a hollow it left in you, waiting for the seed.

"All right," he said, because it was all he could say; because it would take more than what he knew was in him to stand up to what was in her; and because, resentfully, and hopefully, too, he knew she was right—you couldn't stand in the face of her obvious conviction and not be convinced. "All right, Joanna, take your Texas, take your slaves and your Eaton Hall, whatever the hell you call it, and be damned if it fails."

He started away from her, but then he stopped and turned back to her. "Did you ever ask yourself why you married me, Joanna?" he asked, his voice angry and accusing, but laden with pain, too. "Why you didn't marry someone different, some strong-willed ram-rod like your fancy lieutenant? A baby every year and a plantation managing itself without a twitch of your finger, and he'd run every-thing for you, and every night pound that day's notions out of you. There's men, you know, could've given you everything you wanted, except what I had to give and didn't realize it, what you got off of me."

"And what was that, Lewis?"

"Don't you know yet? You got so much in that head of yours, Joannie, I'd have thought you had that figured out by now. All that freedom, all those things you were raving about just now, you couldn't have them—a woman couldn't think that way, let alone talk it, except she married a man weaker than she was. That's why you married me, Joanna. You married what you needed, and then hated me for it. I've been seeing that in your eyes night after night, day after day, since the day we were wed. And you never once thought what that was costing me."

She made no answer, unable to think of what to say that wouldn't set badly with one or the other of them; and she was still drained by the emotion she had just expressed so fervently.

Lewis did go then, disappearing into the night, taking his whiskey bottle with him. She watched long after he had gone.

FOURTEEN

Texas. It seemed to go on forever, its terrain varying little from day to grueling day of their laborious journey.

As they will on long journeys, the passing days began to blur together. Unable for long to contemplate that endless enormity of earth and sky, scarcely able to discern a horizon so far distant, people weary and bored turned their attention closer to home— to those details, some large, most little, that alone served to mark the time's passage.

Though they had been strangers a short time before, and under other circumstances might have inclined toward no more than mere acquaintance, those in the wagon train became, for the duration, their own community; excepting a store or two, and a permanent site, they were a small town, inching its way slowly over the plains.

What they did not lack, certainly, was the stuff on which such towns seemed to thrive: gossip. And just as inevitably, the Hartes were the stuff of which they gossiped.

Lewis's fondness for the bottle had already begun to pale as a

source of interest by the time they had started out, and aside from
the abortive attempt to whip his slaves, his significance soon dwindled to next to nothing. When, in later years, these travelers would
look back upon themselves as "the Harte Train," it was Mrs. Harte,
and not her husband or her family, whom the name conjured up.

Now *there* was someone you could get your claws into!

For all the clucking and the nodding of heads, no one could
really pretend any surprise at her ascendancy in her household.
But when she took—literally—to wearing the pants in the family . . .

Webb Price's suggestion that she take to the western saddle was
what brought this about. It was clear that he was right—her elegant
sidesaddle and the voluminous skirts in which she was accustomed
to sitting it were plainly not the gear of the Texas plains. Having
spent several days observing the western saddle and its use, Joanna
started by taking up the hem of one of her skirts. Though this left
her ankles and even a little of her calf shockingly exposed, it gave
her the freedom she needed for the stirrups—and gave those in
the party a new antidote to the journey's tedium.

Of course she could hardly have several layers of ruffled petticoats dangling beneath the shortened skirt. Anyway, she had stolen
out one night with Gregory's connivance to experiment, and had
discovered that when she attempted to sit astride a saddle while
wearing them, in itself an almost impossible feat, the stiffly starched
ruffles became a considerable barrier between herself and the horse.

A second try without the petticoats proved more manageable,
but with the skirt hitched up sufficiently to allow her to sit astride,
she found that considerably more than ankle and calf were left
exposed. She flirted briefly with the idea of borrowing Gregory's
dungarees, and went so far as to try them on, but even her newfound sense of independence withered before the prospect of appearing publicly with her body revealed so blatantly.

What was needed was something that would provide at least a
measure of a skirt's modesty with the freedom of movement men
enjoyed in their trousers.

Finally, she hit upon the solution of slitting her skirt up front
and back and resewing the two sides together so that they formed
trouser legs of a sort, separate from one another, but far fuller
than a man's pants. Except when she was riding, or walking with
long strides, the fullness of fabric made it difficult to tell she was
wearing anything but a peculiarly short skirt.

But when she screwed up her courage sufficiently to put her new design to the test of riding, a veritable chorus of gasps went up from the other wagons in the train. Doña Sebastiano paled so visibly that she had to be helped inside her wagon, ostensibly to lie down, though she could not be restrained from poking her head out every few seconds to stare.

Of the men, only William Horse seemed unperturbed. "Now you ride like an Indian" was all he said, leaving her to presume that was a compliment.

Webb Price, who had accepted with enthusiasm Joanna's suggestion that she would like to go for a ride, looked considerably less enthusiastic when she was mounted and ready to go.

"You've no one but yourself to blame," Joanna teased him. "You were the one who gave me the idea."

"In the future I'd guess I'd better be more careful with my suggestions," he said wryly.

"Of course, if you're embarrassed to be seen with me, I'm sure Mr. Horse would keep me company."

"That won't be necessary," Webb said. His look was grim, but he rode beside her out of camp, stonily ignoring the stares and even some guffaws from his own men.

Despite the consternation she caused, however, Joanna was quick to pronounce her experiment a success. That same evening, she went to work with scissors and needle on several more of her dresses, and in time the others in the group became accustomed to her unorthodox costume, though none of the other women attempted to emulate it. Melissa, declaring herself "mortified beyond description," burst into tears at her mother's offer to modify her dresses.

"The Brazos," Webb said, indicating the swift-flowing muddy brown water before them. He had called this a stream, but to those in the train, contemplating the task of getting their cumbersome wagons across to the other side, what they were looking at was a river, plain and simple.

"We'll camp this side for two days," Webb declared. "It's best to make the crossing with everyone rested."

As they had left behind them the marshy lowlands of Galveston and made their way onto the prairie, Webb had taken the precaution nightly of having the wagons pulled into a circle about their camp, and sentries posted.

For they knew, even without a formal announcement from Price, that they had entered a land unsoftened even by the token amenities of Galveston. They were entering a land still owned by resentful Apaches, who would fight and kill to preserve their natural domain. They were entering the unyielding land of Texas.

FIFTEEN

They crossed the Brazos, then the Colorado, and a half-dozen smaller streams, with no more loss than a couple of crates that came loose from one of the wagons.

Twice, small bands of Indians followed and watched from a distance, but did not attack, and once Apaches came close enough to attempt to steal horses from the remuda, but they were spotted and driven away with nothing but one mare for their trouble.

It began to seem to the travelers as if the Texas plains were the whole of their existence, the routine of their journey the pattern of their lives. They had begun to forget what it felt like to sleep in real beds, in houses with solid walls about them, to eat at real tables.

Then, to their surprise, the lieutenant called an assembly one evening soon after they had made camp, to make an announcement.

"We'll reach San Antonio day after tomorrow," he informed them, "barring any accidents."

Excitement ran high; people sat up late that night, in a party mood, some of them talking brightly about their plans for a future that was suddenly far nearer than it had been; some just sitting staring quietly into the night. The following day, even the most staid among them had trouble restraining themselves from whipping up their animals to make faster time.

"San Antone'll still be there when we get there," Webb said more than once to an impatient driver.

And he was right. The day after that, it appeared as a collection of fly specks on the horizon, specks that gradually grew to take the shape of houses and commercial buildings, and by late afternoon they were riding into a village of dusky beige houses and wide, dust-clouded streets.

Virtually all of the children and a great many of the adults had jumped down from the wagons to enter the town on foot; Lewis was among them, laughing and gamboling for all the world as if he, too, were a child.

Joanna, with a thought to the impression they would make arriving, had arranged it so that she was driving the team of oxen, and William Horse riding alongside.

She looked around with interest, noting that most of the buildings where they were passing were of adobe, pink-tinged and cool-looking. There were larger houses, too, several-storied wood structures with porches, gables, steep pitched roofs. The sounds of music drifted out from an occasional cantina, as the local taverns were called, and the cooking smells, it being near the supper hour, were foreign and spicy, but with that tang that Joanna had come to associate with Texas. A Mexican youth, as slim as a rapier, sat atop a hitching rail, idly tuning a guitar, disassociated notes cascading to the dusty gound; and as they passed, women came to the front doors and porches to observe their progress.

The people were as varied as the sights and sounds and smells of the village—many of them dark-haired and dark-eyed, plainly of Mexican or Spanish descent, but others as blond and Germanic-looking as Peter Hansen, and every coloration in between. To Joanna's surprise, a pigtailed Chinese darted across the street just in front of her wagon, incongruous and exotic in this western setting.

Lewis ran up alongside. "We're here, Joannie," he called, "we're here," and ran ahead again.

Peter Hansen had graciously invited them to stay as his house-guests until they were ready to start building their new home, and

Joanna had gratefully accepted. She supposed his hospitality depended a great deal on his bewitchment by Melissa, who had been
openly and often mercilessly flirting with him for much of the trip.
Joanna had not been unaware of the time the two spent together,
but with a whole wagon train of chaperons keeping an eye on them,
she had not worried herself unduly over the situation.

His home surprised her with its size, considering that he lived
alone with, as she understood, a handful of servants. Three stories
tall, it was darkly imposing, even intimidating, in what she thought
of as a Gothic style, complete with turret and spire, and atop the
latter a rooster weathervane that turned spiritedly in the Texas
breeze. But Joanna had seen enough now to know that in local
terms, this was a mansion in the grand style, and in any event the
comfort it promised after weeks on the trail could not have been
more appealing if she had been invited to stay over in the Taj
Mahal itself.

She luxuriated in a hot bath, after finally persuading Melissa to
end her bath, and that night slept in an enormous four-poster bed
on a veritable sea of down.

The following day, Lieutenant Price had offered to show them
about the town. Everyone went but Melissa, who declared she wanted
only to sit and rest her weary limbs—and, as soon as the others
had gone, asked Mr. Hansen if he couldn't somehow be persuaded
to show her his Emporium, which she was utterly dying to see. Mr.
Hansen allowed himself to be persuaded with a minimum of effort
on her part.

Lewis and the boys were constantly off on their own, chasing
after first this, then that subject of interest to them. Joanna could
not help noting the change that had come over her husband in the
past few weeks, dating from their confrontation over the freeing
of the slaves. He seemed at times more childlike than ever; she
sometimes had to remind herself that he really was not just another
of her "boys." He remained distant from Lieutenant Price, and he
was still sometimes churlish and resentful toward her, but again, it
was more the petulant rebellion of a difficult child than the re-
monstrances of a husband.

More and more, however, as the journey had progressed, she
had detected something else in his attitude. Finally, she had realized
that it was a sense of relief. Though he might resent it, and even
pretend otherwise, Joanna was convinced that Lewis was grateful
to have the responsibilities taken from his shoulders. He had never

been a man who coped well. Now, even his drinking had abated; he drank less, and suffered less from what he did drink. So far as she could tell, observing him, he looked happier than he had since she'd known him. And if it was a childish happiness, why should she begrudge him that?

She was enchanted by San Antonio's *mercado*—a sprawling marketplace of shops, lean-tos, and open stalls where vendors, mostly Mexicans, sold a variety of goods and services that would have done a city like Charleston proud. Joanna saw workers in leather and tin and silver, stalls displaying brilliantly colored pottery. There were flowers and toys and jewelry. And food, luscious displays in infinite variety, mouth-watering fruits and vegetables, rich baked goods, sweets, and great slabs of meat dripping hot juices on their fires.

"I'm surprised to see so many Mexicans," Joanna commented. "Wasn't there a war between the Texans and the Mexicans?"

"And there's still a lot of prejudice, both ways," Webb admitted. "But most of these people consider themselves Texans, too. A lot of them took no part in the fighting, and a few even fought on our side."

"And I suppose I'm not to mingle with them, either?" she asked, glancing sideways at him with a teasing smile.

"Mrs. Harte, I've given up trying to tell you what to do," he said. "In my experience, it only makes you more insistent."

She followed her nose to a stall where an enormous caldron sat over a low burning bed of coals. In it was simmering what appeared to be a cross between a thick soup and a thin stew.

"This smells wonderful," she said. "What is it?"

"It's a San Antone original," Webb said. "Invented right here. We call it 'chili.' I guess you could say it's the local dish. But I think for once you'd better do what I tell you."

"There you go again," Joanna chided him. "It's no use treating me like a child. I simply must try this."

She managed to negotiate the purchase of a bowl of the stew from a grinning Mexican girl, who took the proffered coins and ladled a steaming bowlful for her. Those at the nearby stalls seemed pleased to observe the purchase, and comments were called back and forth in Spanish, which Joanna did not yet understand. To her surprise, several of the locals came running up to stand and watch, smiling.

"I seem to have created a sensation," she said, dipping the offered spoon into the chili. "I suppose most newcomers don't take so readily to the local fare, do they?"

"It does take most folks a while to get used to it," Webb admitted, watching with interest as she took her first bite.

"I can't imagine why," she said. "It's absolutely delicious. And it's so—so..."

It suddenly felt as if she had swallowed one of the embers from the fire. Tears sprang to her eyes and she found herself literally gasping for air.

"So hot?" Webb suggested, and laughed aloud with the watching Mexicans as she hopped frantically from one foot to the other. "I tried to warn you, you know. No, wait, not water," he warned as she reached for the dipper in the nearby pail. "That'll only make it a river of fire all the way down. Eat a piece of this bread—that'll soak some of it up. And then a little *cerveza*—beer. I think you'll find that suits it best."

She ate the bread that someone had immediately produced, and found that, as he had said, it did help to soak up some of the fire in her mouth. Afterward, she took a sip from the cooling beer he offered, and though the burning sensation lingered, it was much less than before.

"Well," she said finally, with a rueful smile around, "maybe the next time I will at least listen to your advice. Is it always like that?"

"Or worse," he said. "Texans like their food hot. It's the chilis, the peppers—that's what it's named for. And they've got a fairly simple test to see if they've got it hot enough. They give a little to a Yankee, and if it makes him holler and hop around, they figure it's about right."

"Then I think they can safely assume this is satisfactory."

He translated her comment for the still-watching Mexicans, and they laughed good-naturedly before returning to their work.

"It is delicious, though," Joanna said again. "I suppose in time one grows accustomed to the heat."

"In a few months, you'll think that's too tame," he said.

Joanna, still tasting the chili all the way down to her stomach, wasn't entirely sure. Becoming a Texan was going to require more, apparently, than just learning to ride a western saddle.

They arrived back at Mr. Hansen's house in the late afternoon, to find a tearful Melissa waiting in the parlor for them. Mr. Hansen, looking embarrassed, stood directly behind her, as if he had been trying to console her, and seated in front of them was Sergeant Burke from the wagon train.

"Oh, mama, it's dreadful," Melissa burst out when they came in. "We've lost everything."

"Everything?" Joanna looked from one to the other, startled by the announcement.

"I'm afraid I've got some bad news," the sergeant said, standing.

"What is it, sergeant," Webb demanded when Burke hesitated nervously.

"The Hartes' wagon train," the sergeant said, twisting his hat in his hands. "The other train, the party they sent overland with their household goods. It was attacked by Comanches, just across the Texas border. Two of the men escaped and made it here to tell what happened. The rest of the train was wiped out entirely. People, wagons, everything. It's all gone."

Peter Hansen was nearly asleep when the sound of his bedroom door softly opening and closing brought him to a sitting position.

"Who's there?" he demanded in a whisper. He was about to repeat his demand when a voice, so close it made him jump, said, "It's me."

"Melissa?" He was beset at once by a tornado of emotions. "Wait, I'll put some clothes on and get a light—"

"No, don't, someone will see," she said.

"But—you can't," he tried to argue, and lost track of what he meant to say when the bed tilted, and suddenly she had flung herself against him. He felt something wet on his shoulder through the flannel of his nightshirt.

"Oh, Peter, I'm so unhappy," she sobbed, "and so frightened. It's all so strange to me. And now we've lost everything. My life's practically over."

A part of him was perfectly well aware of the impropriety of permitting her to stay where she was—in his bed, in the dark, the two of them barely clothed, for he needed no lights to discover that she, too, was in her nightclothes.

It would have taken sterner stuff than he was made of, however, to send her away uncomforted when she was clearly so miserable.

The minutes passed, and with them the opportunity of doing "the right thing."

"You're so kind," Melissa said after a while. "And so strong. What a lucky woman your wife must have been, having you to take care her. I can't imagine anything more wonderful."

Peter, whose first wife had, to all appearances, been unaware of her good fortune, was moved deeply by the compliment. "Oh, it would be an honor for any man to take care of such an angel as you," he said. "If I were not so old—"

"Old?" Her voice went up incredulously. "Why, you're not old. When a girl dreams of the perfect man, she never thinks of those silly young men; she wants a man with some maturity, a man she can look up to—someone like you. There, yes, I've said it at last, and little I care if you think me a fool for baring my heart this way. I can't tolerate artifice between us when you've been so very good to me."

"My precious one," he breathed, scarcely able to believe what his ears had heard. He leaned toward her, meaning to give her cheek a chaste kiss (now, truly, if this was the way things were, he must send her away), but his lips defied his intentions, and met her lips instead. They kissed. And kissed some more. And somehow went from sitting to lying.

He was never clear afterward what had come over him, how he could possibly have assaulted her as he did. Yet it happened. Night-clothes, hers and his alike, were somehow put aside; flesh rigid and yielding met and was joined; seducer and seduced became one.

Lying beneath him, feeling the restrained ardor of his thrusts, Melissa stared over his shoulder at the distant ceiling, barely discernible in the moonlight, and mentally toured the house that she had decided some time earlier would be hers. It was not Eaton Hall, of course, but Eaton Hall was now far behind her, and would never be again. This was Texas, and this house as fine a one, she had noted, as the state had to offer. Certainly she had no intention of groveling in the dirt like common farmers, as her mother apparently planned to do. No doubt her mother would have had her working alongside the slaves—free darkies they were now; she couldn't even rightly order them about. Why, it had come to her the moment Sergeant Burke delivered his news (it was the exact reason she had burst into tears) that the Hartes were actually poor now.

Peter Hansen, on the other hand, was not poor; if anything, she had come to the opinion that he was better off than his conservative life-style indicated. This house, for instance: It could be made livable, with her taste and a little money.

She discovered a trifle belatedly that her paramour had finished what he'd been about. She sighed in a reasonable facsimile of contentment. "Oh, my beloved," she murmured, "you've made me so happy. Even if it means my ruin—"

"Your ruin? But, no." He sat up again, shocked, as much by his own dastardly behavior as by what she'd suggested. "I will speak to your father at once, in the morning."

"And my mother." Melissa was not without her practical side.

"And your mother. I will make them see—they must permit—"

"Oh, they will, my dearest, when they see how much you care. You do care for me, don't you, Peter, at least a tiny bit?"

"My darling, my true heart," he gasped, and again smothered her with kisses, with much the same result as before.

Eventually he lay exhausted beside her, once again very near to sleep, hardly listening to the words she was saying, only the heavenly music of her voice.

"We'll be so happy together, you and I," she was saying, tenderly running her fingertips through the damp tangle of his hair. "And I want to be more than just a mere wife to you, truly I do. I want to be a partner, in everything. In the store, too, though of course I'm only a woman, I don't pretend to any business sense. All that profit-and-loss nonsense, I'm not even sure what it means, honestly. Would you hate having to explain things to me? Like, profit—what does that mean, exactly?"

"Profit? That is the money the store actually makes for us," he said sleepily, amused at her efforts to share his concerns. What a lucky man he was, he congratulated himself. How many women would take such trouble?

"Does your store—"

"Our store."

"—Our store make a profit?"

"Yes, indeed," he said proudly.

"Really?" She sat up, gazing down at him with an interest that, even in the pale light, was unmistakable. "How much? I mean, approximately. I've got no head for figures, I'm afraid, but I do so want to learn."

"My daughter?" Lewis seemed not even to have considered the possibility. "But she's a mere child."

Joanna was less surprised, though she hadn't been aware that things had progressed anywhere near so far.

"I think," she said, considering their host in a new light—one not altogether flattering to him, though she kept that to herself— "a girl knows better than anyone else when she's ready to become a woman. I should point out, however, that your acquaintance has been brief. Scarcely time enough to get acquainted, I should think."

"I have bared my soul to your daughter," Mr. Hansen said soberly. "Such as I am, she knows me."

Joanna had in fact been thinking the other way around. She felt that even she had underestimated her daugther, whose head she had long assumed to be filled largely with air.

"And you have perhaps observed," Peter went on, "that Texans are brash. We stand less on ceremony here."

"And my mother has never been one to be bound by convention," Melissa said, a shade too sweetly. "Why, you saw yourself, on our journey here, she believes in a woman's independence."

Glancing in her daughter's direction, Joanna had the thought that perhaps after all it was time Melissa had her own home. Certainly she was less a child than Joanna had heretofore realized.

"I'm sure I speak for my husband, Mr. Hansen, when I say we will be honored to have you for a son-in-law," Joanna said aloud.

"Oh, mama," Melissa cried, and for a moment, rushing to hug first her mother and then her fther, she was once again a little girl.

Lewis looked briefly as if he meant to argue the matter further; but looking from mother to daughter, he changed his mind and extended his hand to his future son-in-law with only slight reluctance. "If it makes the women happy," he said, in the way of congratulations.

"Now," Melissa said brightly, and Joanna caught a glimpse of exactly how this state of affairs had come about, "if that's all settled, there's at least a million things I've got to think about. And there's really not much sense, is there, mother, in my going to look at the new land with you? I mean, seeing as I won't be living there anyway. And I do have so much to do."

"I understand," Joanna said.

Lieutenant Price had arranged to take them to see their land. The exact boundaries, of course, would need to be established by a surveyor. "And it would take several days to get all the way round it," Webb added.

But with the exception of Melissa, everyone was eager to see where they were going to be living. The losses they had suffered only emphasized the finality of their move, and made all the more imperative getting themselves established as quickly as possible.

The boys went, too; on that, Lewis had been adamant. "You may run things for now," he said, "but they're the ones who'll inherit it eventually. They may as well know right off what they've got to look forward to."

Since they would not be staying on this occasion, they went on horseback rather than in the wagon. Jay Jay rode like one to the saddle born anyway. "Could pass for a born Texan" was Webb's assessment. Gregory rode competently, but with no illusion that horse and rider were less than two separate entities.

It was an easy two hours of riding before they crested a ridge and Webb, reining in his horse, pointed into a shallow valley before them. "As best I can judge," he told them, "your land starts about here and goes on a long ways out of sight."

Joanna sat for a long while looking in every direction. Once again she had that eerie sensation of coming home to someplace where her heart had always been.

Not too far distant, a small stream meandered its way into the valley, and on its opposite bank was a thick grove of trees. The grasses were deep and lush, still greenish near the water, fading to brown farther away. For the most part, the land was flat, with here and there a low, gently curving hill to break the monotony.

"It's beautiful," she said finally, getting down from her horse to walk through whispering grasses.

Lewis had dismounted before her and walked toward the stream, where he stood studying its flow. She went to him.

"We'll never make it work, Joanna," he said grimly. "There's not enough water for rice."

"We'll make it work," she said determinedly. "There's water enough for cotton."

He looked at her speculatively. "We don't have all that much cottonseed," he said.

"We've got enough to start."

"Cotton takes hands."

"There's four of us. I'm not afraid to work. And we've got better than a dozen blacks."

He nodded, considering. Stooping, he ran a handful of dirt

through his fingers. "It's rich soil," he admitted, looking less discouraged.

"The weather's hot. We'll have a long growing season."

He stood up, facing her. Webb had strolled away, probably out of tact. The boys were wading in the stream while the horses watered. "You've set your mind to it, haven't you?" Lewis asked.

"I have," she said.

"Well, then..." He shrugged and left it at that, seeming glad to be done with the matter.

"We'll set the house there," she said, "in that grove of trees. They'll give us plenty of shade."

"That's pecan trees. We'll get more than shade out of them."

"And I want a gate, first thing, over there. Rock and iron. With a sign from post to post, letters big enough they can read the name while they're still miles from the ranch."

He cocked an eyebrow. "A ranch, is it?"

"They have ranches here instead of plantations."

He looked off into the distance, his expression momentarily unreadable. "Nothing's the same, is it?" he asked.

"No. It's all different now," she agreed.

He turned back toward her. "What name are they going to read, by the way, while they're miles away?"

On an impulse, she said, "You pick one."

"Anything I want?"

"As long as it's not Eaton Hall."

He thought for a moment. She had always considered her husband a humorless man, but of late he'd begun to develop a wry, self-deprecating brand of humor. Now he grinned slyly at her and said, "How about Harte's Folly?"

"Harte's Folly?" She said it to herself a few times. "Yes, that'll do just fine. It'll make a great joke, won't it, when it's the biggest and best ranch in all the state of Texas?"

"Biggest. Best. That's the way these Texans talk, Joanna."

"We are Texans now," she said, smiling.

Peter Hansen took them to a sign maker, a Mexican who spoke broken English and nodded often while Joanna explained what she wanted.

He had seemed to understand; but two weeks later, Lewis rushed into the house, angrily disconcerted. "Damned stupid Mexican," he was bellowing. "Joanna! Joanna!"

"I'm here," she said, coming from the kitchen.

"He's ruined it. The sign. Wait till you see."

"What on earth has he done?"

"You'll have to see for yourself, it's too blamed silly to be believed otherwise," he insisted.

It was only a few blocks. Despite the heat, Lewis was practically running, and Joanna was hard pressed to keep up with him.

Though the letters, in wrought iron, were two feet high—not big enough, perhaps, to be read for miles, but certainly legible at some distance—the sign was lying flat just now, so that Joanna had to go stand before it to see what had happened.

She discovered that the "biggest and best" ranch in Texas had been named not Harte's Folly, as intended, but Heart's Folly.

"It'll have to be done all over again," Lewis said petulantly.

To his surprise, however, Joanna began to laugh. "No," she said. "No, let's leave it as it is."

He looked at her incredulously. "Like that?"

"Yes."

He thrust his tongue at his cheek, in a mannerism he seemed to have acquired from Gregory. Then he, too, began to laugh. "Joanna" was all he said, shaking his head. "Joanna."

In a rare gesture of affection, she suddenly linked her arm with his. "Lucretia's been experimenting with those pecans. She's just made a pie, and if it tastes anywhere near as good as it smells, it'll be sheer delight. Let's go plague her for a sample, shall we?"

They walked back more slowly than they had come, arms still together, and occasionally laughing. Those who saw them were surprised, for they had seen little display of affection between these two rather peculiar newcomers.

So, the ranch got its name; and for years to come, those who read it while riding up to its stone-and-iron gates wondered how it had come to be called that.

But none of the Hartes ever offered to explain.

PART II

HEART'S FOLLY

SIXTEEN

The Indians had a legend: During a time of great drought, one young girl, fearing that her people might starve, decided she would burn her favorite doll as a sacrifice to the rain gods.

That very night a gentle rain began to fall, and in the morning, wherever the doll's ashes had fallen, the earth was covered with beautiful blue flowers.

In the spring, the hill behind the main house turned into a sea of wild bluebonnets, shaming the washed-out blue-gray of the Texas sky.

Joanna came out the front door, pausing on the long, covered porch. Only eight in the morning, only April, and already the air was scorching hot; the breeze blowing along the porch seemed to lift the moisture right out of you and leave you raisin-dried.

The others complained, except for Gregory, who seemed oblivious to weather. For herself, Joanna liked it. She felt like one of the seeds the hands were right now planting in the ground, as if she, the whole ranch, took sustenance from it, grew strong and powerful feeding on that energetic heat.

They would have a good crop this year, she was sure of it. They had even managed a small crop the year before, despite planting as late as they had. The summer had just seemed to go on and on forever. She'd taken that as an omen.

In the distance was the clatter and thrum of hammers and saws. The main part of the house had been put up right away: neither brick, which was too like the old Eaton Hall, nor adobe, from which most of the local houses were constructed. Good solid wood, three stories high, with porches on the front and two sides—in the opinions of the others, wasted, since everyone deemed it either too hot or too cold to sit on the porches, but Joanna took to them season in and out. She had a balcony, too, above the main porch, outside her bedroom.

"You might as well have camped outside, saved all this building," Lewis complained, but she could see he was proud of the house, the way it sat, not dominating that giant landscape—nothing could do that, and this house didn't try—but not intimidated by it either; proud, commanding, a house to be reckoned with.

Now, with the diminishing of the spring rains, Joanna had set the workmen to expanding it—"Just finishing it off" was her explanation. Only, "finishing it off" meant practically doubling its size. A whole wing for guests. She had suspected that here, the same as South Carolina, people came for visits and liked to stay. She meant to have them out of her way, where they could be comfortable without infringing on her comfort.

Another wing that, in her mind, though she didn't spell it out to the family, would eventually be for her sons and their families. Sooner or later they would marry; she did not want that to mean their moving away—she'd need them for the Heart's Folly she envisioned. So she meant to be prepared.

Lewis had wanted a ballroom, and though she had difficulty picturing the Texans she'd met at such a formal gathering, she'd put one in, above the guest wing. They had plenty of room, and it balanced off the other wing.

Inside, past an immense entry hall, the parlor had already taken on a look of its own. Jay Jay had brought down an antelope, and a longhorn steer that, at the time, he'd somehow mistaken for a buffalo; the heads of both were on the darkly varnished walls, and beneath them, startling visitors who came from the blinding sunshine into the thickly shadowed gloom, was the stuffed carcass of a puma Lewis had killed, more or less by accident, while they had been on a trip to survey the boundaries of the property. Joanna had had it stuffed and placed in the parlor as a Christmas surprise for him; Lewis had been thrilled to the point of tears and had subsequently invented an absolutely preposterous version of his stalking and killing it, which she tactfully never challenged.

Joanna's contribution to the animal population was a bobcat, which, likewise mounted, she kept in her bedroom, not, as some presumed, out of modesty but because there she could look at it as often and as proudly as she chose, savoring the feeling of accomplishment it gave her.

She had learned about guns from Webb Price, their use and their care. She was a better shot than either Lewis or Gregory, though she was careful to play down the fact. Jay Jay, on the other hand, was the undisputed sharpshooter of the ranch; he liked to boast he could shoot a gnat off a prairie dog's nose and not get a whisker, and no one was altogether certain he was boasting.

From William Horse, Joanna had learned to use a bowie knife. With that, she outstripped even her youngest son. She could throw a knife twenty feet or better and hit a target dead center. Lewis had scorned this as a useless and unwomanly occupation, until she had taken a rattlesnake's head off one day, just before it got its fangs into Gregory's leg. No one had scoffed since then.

Exactly how William Horse had become a fixture on the ranch, not even Joanna could explain. He had simply been there one morning, working alongside the blacks, only a short while after they had parted from him in town.

"What's he doing here?" Lewis had demanded.

"Planting seed, apparently" was the only reply Joanna had to offer.

And that was, it seemed, what he had done; he had merely taken root, unobtrusively grafting himself on to the place until he seemed as natural to it as the sunbaked earth. He worked tirelessly, too, mostly outside, like some physical extension of Gregory's ideas.

Gregory had proved particularly adept at the business of farming; at least, at its management. He kept the books, ordered seed, planned the planting—always with the manner of acting on Joanna's behalf, rather than usurping her authority in any way. Even in the office the two of them shared, just off Joanna's bedroom, his tiny desk was dominated by hers, shoved off by itself into an airless and badly lighted corner. He spent most of his time there, and it sometimes seemed as if, from there, he could hear each individual plant growing and assess its progress.

William Horse, who almost never set foot in the house, and then only with the utmost discomfort—he looked forever on the verge of bolting—functioned in some undelineated way as Gregory's field officer. "You'd think they were out of the same seed pod," grumbled Lewis, who never got over his dislike of the Indian, and Jay Jay from time to time displayed a quick flash of jealousy, though of which of the two Joanna wasn't sure.

What the others saw as a brotherly closeness, however, seemed something different to her. She got the impression the two distrusted one another, and that in working together as closely as they did, William Horse and her son were keeping tabs on one another for some reason.

Jay Jay, too, worked hard; at least he always seemed busy, though if she'd been asked to make a list of his actual accomplishments, she wasn't sure what she would have put down. He was splendid with the animals, ruinous to crops. He and William Horse had made a foray onto the range and come back with a trio of wild horses they had managed to tame—at least well enough that they could ride them, though no one else had yet gotten up courage enough to try.

Yes, it was in Joanna's mind, standing on the porch of the main house this hot, clear morning, that they had accomplished a great deal already. Lucretia and William, married now, had their own place; each of the blacks did, just as she had promised, and William Horse did, too. It wasn't until after his had been put up that she realized it looked right up at the balcony outside her bedroom, but so far apparently no one else but her had realized this.

In true Texas fashion, the ranch already sprawled, numerous buildings of all kinds and all sizes, taking up more space than many a farm back east had occupied altogether. Of course, they owed a lot of money: an enormous sum to the local bank, and even more to Peter Hansen. (She hadn't married him, had she? But if you were given a rich son-in-law on a silver platter, so to speak, there was surely no harm in benefiting from it.)

A billowing of dust in the distance foretold someone's approach. Joanna squinted—she had begun to collect a little network of lines at the corners of her eyes; you really had to work to see Texas distances. After a while she could make out a farm wagon, and eventually the man driving it. Smiling readily, Joanna came down the steps and walked out to meet the visitor, moving slowly out of respect for the Texas sun.

Don Sebastiano, their nearest neighbor, drove with a solemn dignity; not until he brought the horses to a stop and looked down at her did his somber expression melt into a warm greeting. His youngest daughter, Carrie, gave Joanna her own shy, sweet smile.

"You said you needed more cottonseed," Don Sebastiano said. "I had more than I needed, so I've brought you some."

"You know it'll be fall before I can pay," Joanna warned.

Don Sebastiano shrugged eloquently. "I cannot give it back to the plants from which I got it," he said.

"You're far too generous. I'll have someone unload it. William Horse," she called, unnecessarily, since almost before the name had escaped her lips, he was there, gesturing to a pair of workers to help with the seed bags.

Unnoticed by anyone but Carrie, Gregory had come to an upstairs window. He counted the bags as they were unloaded, his lips working silently, his brain adding up figures. Without losing count, he watched the girl, too, until he suddenly realized she was staring back at him. Blushing, he stepped aside, behind the window curtain.

"Come inside and have some coffee—Lucretia's just made a pot. Better yet, let's have it on the porch. I like to watch the day get going."

He was almost the only one who would share the porches with her. He said it was because he came from Spain and was used to the heat, but Joanna, mindful of the fact that he'd made that journey as a small boy, suspected it was Latin politeness more than anything else.

No matter. She was fond of his company, of him, in fact, though she never ceased to wonder that this gentlemanly Spaniard could be the husband and father of that pair who'd traveled from Galveston with them.

Carrie, now, was different—she was plainly Don Sebastiano's daughter. It was evident that she loved her father, and his ranch, in about equal measure. Martha, his wife, and Nancy, the older daughter, would have liked nothing better than to live in Galveston, if the ranch were rich enough to afford that, and they never tired of telling him so; but Carrie only left the ranch to accompany her father on some errand such as this.

"There's pecan rolls in the kitchen, fresh baked," Joanna told her. "Go fetch yourself a couple, and while you're there, tell Sulie to bring some coffee, all right?"

She watched the girl go, dark pigtails bouncing as she ran along the porch.

Don Sebastiano was watching the work of unloading the wagon. "That Indian reads your mind, or so it seems," he said.

"William Horse? He's a godsend, I can tell you that. He works endlessly. Never seems to get tired. Sometimes I wonder what is on his mind."

Don Sebastiano gave her a measuring look, but she ignored it if she even saw it, and smiled brightly at him. "I've long since stopped worrying about his scalping us, though."

Sulie came out the screen door, bearing a tray with two oversize, steaming mugs. "Beats me how you can drink this in the heat of day," Sulie said, juggling the tray to hand each a cup. "Morning, Mr. Sebastiano."

"It makes me feel cooler inside," Joanna said, which made no more sense to her than it did to anyone else, but it was just how she felt.

"Huh," Sulie said, and turned to watch the men working. "Is that more cottonseed? We ain't got hands enough to plant what we got now; who's going to grow this?"

"We are," Joanna said. "I've been thinking, Don Sebastiano— there's plenty of Mexicans without work, aren't there?"

"There's places won't hire them, not since the war. Afraid, probably, of what might happen if there's more trouble, though I truly doubt there will be. I think everyone would like to get on with the business of living."

"How you goin' to pay Mexicans, I'd like to know?" Sulie asked.

"I'll give them room and board," Joanna said. "And a dollar a month. When I get it."

"When'll that be, I'd like to know?"

"Sulie, it's really too early in the day to argue," Joanna said sharply.

Sulie made an exit full of wounded dignity. The screen door banged loudly enough to make William Horse pause and glance in that direction. Inevitably his glance went first unerringly to Joanna, and then swept the area surrounding her.

"Oh, dear," Joanna said. "Now I'll have to patch things up with her, or prepare myself for cornbread baked like adobe."

"Someone's coming." Don Sebastiano pointed down between the stone gateposts. Another cloud of dust was approaching, this one at a speed considerably faster than his wagon.

"Why," Joanna said after a moment, "that's Melissa's trap, I do believe. Lord, she looks like the devil himself is after her the way she's flying."

Melissa did indeed look, as she drove up the long drive and around the circle it made in front of the house, as if the devil were after her. Her face was flushed—never mind the lather she'd whipped the horses up to—and wisps of hair had come loose from beneath her hat—a stylish hat, Joanna couldn't help noting. Melissa seemed to have brought, almost single-handedly, the concept of "style" to Texas; it was as if all those women who were suddenly flocking to Hansen's Emporium had simply been waiting, prairie-like, to soak up the rain of her fashion.

Still, Joanna could not look at her without seeing the little girl playing at "dressing up." Did all mothers think that way? she wondered; of course, she would be the first to admit her motherhood was probably not typical.

Melissa's agitation on this occasion only accentuated, to Joanna's mind, the discrepancy between Melissa's "style" and Melissa herself.

"War!" the elegantly dressed young lady shouted, and practically leaped from the buggy before it had quite stopped. "We're at war!"

It took Joanna a moment to grasp the meaning of her words. She had been so involved in more immediate matters here in Texas, here at the ranch, she'd had little thought for the bickering and saber rattling they had left behind in South Carolina. She knew Webb was worried; but she had cotton to be planted, a ranch full of people to feed, stock to be tended—and her slaves were already freed, weren't they?

"We fired on Fort Sumter. Leveled it, some say," Melissa rushed on, while the others, from the sheds and barns, from inside the house, began to gather toward her, reeled in like so many fish by her pronouncements. "And Mr. Lincoln has asked to raise an army. They say he's told his Yankee minions every woman of the South is theirs to do with as they will!" Her eyes were so alight it would have been difficult to assess exactly her true response to that proviso.

"Webb." Joanna was scarcely aware she had spoken the name aloud. Her first thought was that he, even more than the rest of them, would be caught in the middle of events.

Melissa turned on her angrily. "If you mean Mr. Lieutenant Traitor, he's holed up inside his stockade with what's left of his blackguard soldiers."

Only a few weeks before, Texas had voted to join the Confederacy and secede from the Union; their famous governor, Sam Houston, had been voted out of office—ignobly, in Joanna's opinion—for refusing to sign the secession papers. Since then, Webb's position had been tenuous. An officer of the U.S. Army, he was sworn to obey his commander in chief, the president. At the same time, he was a Texan, and Texas was now a Confederate state. Helplessly, Webb had watched one after another of his own soldiers drift over to the Confederate Army, while the numbers within the garrison dwindled ominously and he awaited orders from Washington.

"You don't mean there's trouble in town?" Joanna asked.

"Well, that depends on what you'd call trouble, I suspect. There's folks collecting outside the stockade, I did see that, and one or two of them looked like they wouldn't be adverse to stringing up a Yankee-lover if they got the chance. Why, where are you going? You can't take my trap."

"I can, and I am," Joanna said, already in the driver's seat.

"But what am I to do?" Melissa wailed.

"You'll be entirely safe here from Mr. Lincoln's Yankee minions," Joanna said, and drove off, whipping the beleaguered horses once again to a run.

"Well, I never," Melissa declared, and looked around for some support; but as quickly as she had claimed it, she had lost center stage to the news she had delivered. Those on the porch and milling about on the lawn seemed to have lost any focus, they hardly looked at one another, and few words were spoken as each silently weighed what they'd heard and its personal significance to them.

Melissa's eyes landed on young Carrie and, angry with her mother and feeling herself all at once a castaway, she pounced. "Is that a pecan roll? Give that to me," she demanded, and snatching it from the child's hand, she stuffed a monstrous portion of the sweet into her mouth before dropping like one wounded into the chair her mother had recently vacated. "Well, I never," she said again.

She came to the ranch only infrequently, and stayed but briefly, just long enough to confirm in her own mind that she had, after all, done the right thing in marrying Peter Hansen. Not that she had ever entertained any serious doubts. It had seemed to her then, seemed to her now, a perfectly obvious choice. For one thing, it cost her so little. It was really only one of the many parts of her that had become his wife, one she felt sure she could spare. The rest of her remained untouched, even when, with tedious regularity, he claimed his conjugal rights.

The real Melissa, on the other hand, the clever and enchanting collage of delightful aspects (she'd just recently penned that description of herself in her diary), had gained so much. She had the Emporium. It was true she still had to work "around" her husband, but with each day the store was becoming more clearly hers.

For that, Peter could hardly fault her. In a few months, their volume of business had doubled, and their profits—which so recently had had to be explained to her—soared monthly.

At first, Peter had been amused, even charmed, by her interest in the business. And what harm could there be in indulging her suggestion that they begin to stock more of the sort of luxury items she insisted were dear to the hearts of all women? Personally, he thought he knew these hard-edged Texas women well enough by now; they weren't the sort to interest themselves in fine lingerie, the latest fashions, expensive perfumes and powders. It had come as a great surprise to him to discover how wrong he had been. Gaunt pioneer women came, and bought elegant silks and linens. Mexican women in cheap print dresses marched out of the store with the latest French chapeaus upon their heads. And, even more astonishing to his way of thinking, leather-skinned cowboys with embarrassed sideways glances bought tiny flasks of expensive perfume, wrapped as gifts.

"We've got too much in the way of yard goods," Melissa declared. "There's lots of women want their dresses ready-made."

"It's too difficult," he had argued. "You can't predict what style a woman is going to want. You'd need a hundred different dresses, in every possible size, to please everyone."

"Don't be a goose," Melissa replied. "They'll want the style I wear, once they've seen it on me."

And once again she had been entirely right.

After that, Mr. Hansen was less amused than he had been. When his wife talked of this change they would make, or this department they would add, he listened carefully, but there was something puzzled, and suspicious, too, in the way he looked at her.

Like wildfire, news of the Civil War had spread throughout San Antone, and as if battle were to be joined at once, its citizens had abandoned their homes and pursuits to pour into the streets.

It made driving difficult, and Joanna decided to return Melissa's buggy to her house and go the rest of the way on foot.

Peter Hansen came out the front door while she was tying the horse up. "Melissa's at the ranch," she explained before he could ask. "Someone will bring her in later."

"But, wait," he said when he saw she was planning to go on. "It's not safe. You must come inside."

Joanna had no time, however, to waste on argument. With a quick shake of her head for an answer, she set out on foot for the stockade.

It was still not easy to travel. By this time the "folks collecting" that Melissa had described had become a mob, growing thicker the closer she got to the garrison. Her impression was that not all of them were concerned with the Yankee soldiers inside the stockade; some of these people were simply "there," because it was where other people were, congregating as people will in a time of confusion. But, it was equally plain, some of them were there with a purpose, and it was not a friendly one.

Suddenly she emerged from the crowd to find that the dusty street just in front of the wooden stockade was empty. A no-man's-land between enemies at war. She started across the empty space, and was immediately aware of the silence that fell in her wake, as if her passing burst the varied bubbles of conversation floating about.

"They're not letting anyone inside," someone called to her, and when she ignored that information, a strange man ran out from the crowd to grab her arm forcefully. "You can't go there, missus," he said.

"I am Joanna Harte, of Heart's Folly, and I will go where I choose," she informed him coldly. "Kindly take your hands off me."

Surprised, the man did so, taking a quick step back as if afraid she might strike him. Joanna went on her way, unmolested by anyone further.

"Lieutenant?"

Webb looked up from the communiqué he had been reading. "Yes?"

"There's a woman at the gate," the soldier, a fresh-faced recruit newly arrived from New Hampshire, informed him. "Says she's coming in the gate or over the fence, one or the other."

To the soldier's astonishment, his harried lieutenant gave a shout of laughter. "Joanna," he said, and all but knocked the soldier aside in his rush to get through the door.

"Joanna, what on earth..." he demanded when he'd fairly dragged her through the gate, and ordered it barricaded again. "Didn't you see that mob out there?"

"And they've seen me," she said.

He laughed again, and said, "Well, that ought to keep us safe." But then he grew serious. "I can't let you stay."

"I didn't intend to. I just wanted—I don't know, to see for myself, I suppose. I thought, something has changed here, not just some temporary upset, but permanently. I think that's what I always dreaded about the prospect of this war—it's too deep, too serious to get over it." She shook her head as if to ward off some hovering insect. "I'm rambling. What about you? What will you do?"

"We just got our orders. We're to leave in the morning. And, in the meantime, not to make any trouble. We're to pull back to Kansas. We're too outnumbered here. If they ever get that Confederate Army mobilized in Texas, they'll wipe us off the map."

"But they're people you know. Texans, just like you. Like us."

"We're on different sides now," he said. A surprised look suddenly passed across his face. "Why, we're on different sides," he said. "You and me. You're consorting with the enemy, that's what they'd call it—we both are. They've made enemies of us, Joanna, that's what they've done to us."

They had made their way back to his office, oblivious to the curious and occasionally lecherous looks they had gotten from his men. Now they both stopped, turning as one toward each other.

"How can we be enemies," Joanna asked, "when we're both on the side of love?"

For what seemed an eternity, they stared into one another's eyes. Then, as one, they came together, bodies straining, arms clinging, lips sweetly savoring a kiss that went on and on, that might have lasted forever if a distant shot hadn't broken it off.

"Wait here," he said breathlessly, and was gone, leaving the weight and taste of his mouth still lingering on hers.

He was back in a moment. "Some blamed fool outside fired his gun accidentally. Everybody's laughing at him, but it might just as easily have set things off. I've got to get you out of here."

She smiled ruefully. "They'll never let you just ride out with me," she said.

"Leave that to me." He went to the door and bawled, "Sergeant Burke."

The sergeant appeared in the doorway, pausing to touch the brim of his hat and nod in Joanna's direction. "Mrs. Harte," he said. If he was surprised to see her, he gave no sign of it.

"I want a distraction at the front gate," Webb said. "Nothing that'll rile them up, just enough to get their attention. Give me time to saddle a horse, then march some soldiers up and down as if we were getting ready to do something, but no clue of what."

The sergeant nodded and was gone. Webb took Joanna's hand and wordlessly hurried her to the stables, saddling one of the army's horses for her. They walked to the back gate on either side of the animal.

"Just this once," Webb said, "I'm glad for those damned pants you wear. If anything happens, get on and ride, never mind about me."

Sergeant Burke's distraction at the front gate worked; even as Webb opened the rear gate a crack and peered out, the people who had been hanging about there heard of "something going on" and ran to the front of the stockade, leaving the way clear for Joanna and Webb. They crept out, making as little noise as possible, not talking at all, along an alleyway, through a momentarily deserted blacksmith's shop, down another alley. They reached the local stables, likewise deserted. They were beyond the fringes of the mob now. "You'll be all right from here," Webb said. "I'd best get back."

"You'll be leaving. Tomorrow," Joanna said, making it a statement rather than a question.

"Yes." He made no move to leave.

"There's no telling when you'll be back." She did not voice her fear that he might not return at all. Some men didn't from war.

"No. They'll send me someplace else, most likely. I'm a Texan. They won't send me back here."

There was a volley of shots, not too far away. "It's started," Webb said, but still he did not move; he was looking into Joanna's eyes. They heard the outside sounds like something far away, an echo down a distant canyon.

She took a step toward him. It was all the encouragement he needed. He gathered her again into an embrace. Their kiss this time was longer, more urgent; she felt numb and at the same time alive as she had never been alive before. She had wanted this so long, fought so hard against it, not for her husband's sake but for her own, and for Webb's as well.

His fingers fumbled with the ribbon holding her hair, until her hair fell in a shimmering cascade, and he kissed it too, kissed her throat, her earlobes, a shoulder that had magically become bare.

Joanna arched her spine to press more tightly against him, her lips parting to welcome the thrust of his tongue. His breath was hot, feverish; it seemed to ignite trails of fire over her skin. Despite her years and her marriage, even her motherhood, this sensation of passion, of desire, was something new to her. She found herself reveling in it, discovered a woman she hadn't known existed within her.

So this was what all those words, those songs and poems of love, meant! She shuddered with delight. What did right or wrong matter at such a moment as this? She felt she had been born to feel Webb's arms about her, to taste his kisses, to feel his hands caressing her body.

Chills raced through her as his fingers worked at the buttons of her blouse. His hand cupped one firm breast, its nipple hardening against his palm. Joanna gave a low moan.

"I love you," Webb breathed. "God help me, I love you more than I can bear."

After a moment, Joanna moved away from him. His glance was startled at first, until he saw that she had moved toward a pile of straw in one corner. The straw made a whispering sound as she lay back upon it.

His blood pounding, Webb lowered himself over her.

They dressed later in heavy silence.

"So, now you go back to your husband," Webb said, with the sound of bitterness in his voice.

Joanna laid a hand on his arm. "Don't," she said. "We've had this moment at least. It will be ours forever, no matter what happens. Let's not taint it."

"You're right," he said. Reluctantly he got to his feet and helped her up. The gunfire they had heard earlier had continued sporadically, and just then there was a fresh volley. "I've got to go," he said. He smiled sadly. "Already I'm a traitor, for your sweet sake."

They kissed again, more gently than before. There seemed to be no words they could say that would add or take away from what was between them.

He helped her into the saddle. She leaned far down for one last kiss.

"Goodbye," he said, and then he was gone, already running, back to his post and the war that claimed him.

Tears blurring her vision, Joanna turned her horse toward home.

SEVENTEEN

Lewis's predictions that the war, when it came, would not reach far-off Texas, proved in large measure accurate.

There were skirmishes, mostly between locals who had taken opposing sides. Men went off to fight, and women mourned them. Crops and livestock and other valuables were requisitioned in the name of the Confederacy. Joanna, having barely gotten her ranch started, watched much of what her first year had achieved being carted away by soldiers.

At that, however, she counted them lucky. The war, for most Texans, was like distant thunder just over the horizon, ominous, but not directly dangerous.

It was already said by some, however, that the Hartes had a penchant for attracting trouble, the way the tallest tree seems to call down the lightning upon itself. There was resentment of the position of the blacks on Heart's Folly: free, working not only for wages—better wages than some whites were paid, though Joanna would have argued both were paid what they were no doubt worth—but owners of their own little landholdings as well.

Women whose husbands and sons had gone off to fight for slavery; those who'd managed to talk their way out of the army and so were glad to help turn criticism in another direction, the ones who had wanted to serve and were too old, or otherwise unsuited for battle—all the malcontents who were always the most likely to be left behind in such a situation—turned their gazes upon Heart's Folly, and pronounced themselves angry at what they saw.

Joanna remained impervious to their grumbling, and Lewis largely unaware of it. Melissa made such a to-do over her own disapproval of her mother's policies that she won for the Emporium new customers from among the very ranks of those who complained most loudly. "True daughters of the South must hang together," became almost an unofficial motto of the store—to which Joanna on one occasion was heard to reply, sotto voce, that there were several of the ladies whom she would happily have accommodated in that respect.

Most of the blacks, who rarely ventured from the confines of the ranch, were removed from any danger of reprisal. Lucretia could have been, too. It began to seem as if she went out of her way to flaunt her freedom. She and William had married soon after their arrival in San Antone, and by the war's outbreak she had already informed Joanna, with touching pride, that she was expecting their first child. Joanna was delighted for her, and from the first had urged her to let someone else attend to the shopping. "That trip into town will get more tiresome as the months progress."

Lucretia would not hear of it. Saturday was the traditional market day; Farmers with produce to sell, housewives with a few extra eggs, children with berries or nuts they had gathered swelled the *mercado* to overflowing, spilling out into the surrounding streets.

Each Saturday William hitched the horses to the cart and helped his wife up as politely, as delicately, as he had once helped southern aristocrats into the Hartes' fine carriages. With a parasol to protect her from the sun, and William and one or the other of the young men from the ranch to carry packages, Lucretia did not so much stroll about the town as march, chin defiantly thrust up and out, badgering merchants mercilessly to get a good price on the best they had to offer.

And, inevitably, she rubbed a great many people the wrong way, although she affected not to notice.

Lucretia despised in the other blacks, in her husband in particular, what she called their "pickaninny act." People who were natural and at ease among themselves, in the safe confines of the ranch,
would, in the presence of whites, suddenly begin to act the fool.
Men and women alike tittered as if bereft of their senses; they
slouched, they grew blank-faced, they shuffled their feet as if on
the verge of dancing a jig. What infuriated her the most was the
need to check in herself the very same impulse to seek safety in
thus effacing herself.

"God didn't make me a fool," she argued scornfully with William
when he issued dire warnings of the trouble she was inviting on
herself, "and I won't let an ignorant bunch of redneck cowboys do
it for him."

So she sashayed and scorned, and resentment fed anger, like
the spring rain clouds feeding the creek that cut across Heart's
Folly.

The conflagration back east only served to intensify the heat of
the summer. June and July were scorchers, August hotter still.

In September, the trouble of which William had warned descended on them with a fury.

It came on a Saturday, one of those outing days of which Lucretia
was so determinedly fond. She was, by this time, well along in her
term, the swelling of her pregnancy accentuating, exaggerating
even, her stiff-spined manner of walking when she was in town.

They had finished the marketing; the purchases were in the
cart, under the eye of one of the younger boys from the ranch. "I
want to go to the Emporium," Lucretia said when the last of the
purchases had been stowed away.

William gave her a doubtful look. He knew, as she did, that
Melissa did not favor the blacks coming in to shop at "her" store,
though she had no qualms about taking their money from Joanna
as their proxy.

"What you want to go there for?" he asked, and got a withering
look for his trouble.

"Things," Lucretia said, which he took to mean that her purpose
was merely to make an appearance, and that if it followed her
custom, it would be dragged out to the maximum she could manage. With most, Lucretia, however belligerently, was precise in demanding no more than what she regarded as fair, and due her.
With Melissa, she seemed intent merely on aggravating for aggra-
vation's sake.

With trepidation, William followed her along the board sidewalk, at her side, yet always a slight bit behind, like some royal consort following in her wake.

They were almost to the Emporium's entrance when Doña Sebastiano and her daughter, Nancy, came out of the store, their arms laden with packages. All four stopped. The sidewalk here was too narrow to permit more than two people to pass one another without someone's having to step down into the street or fall back behind another. Heavy rains the previous spring had left a little wash just at this point of the street. The step down was a long one, awkward for any full-skirted lady, doubly so for one well along in her seventh month of pregnancy. William instinctively moved behind his wife, but this left the three women still at an impasse.

The awkward moment grew long, and more awkward. To make matters worse, Saturday was the town's busy day; the streets were inevitably crowded, with shoppers, farmers and cowboys in for the day, drifters and ne'er-do-wells, and a score of others. Another pair of customers came out of the Emporium, stopping behind the Sebastianos, and one of those women was heard to declare, loudly, "Well, when decent white folks can't even go about their business untroubled..."

Her remark drew attention; people began to stare, some to gather closer. Faces were angry, and few were sympathetic toward Lucretia and her husband.

"Lucretia," William said, and stepped into the street, taking his wife's arm as if to pull her down with him. Haughtily, Lucretia shook off his hand and stepped in the other direction, toward the storefront, as close as she could get to the building without actually cringing against it.

Perhaps emboldened by the addition of two others behind her, Doña Sebastiano gave a toss of her head and, taking her daughter's hand, stepped forward. "Pardon us," she said coolly, and attempted to make their way by. But they were wearing crinolines and hoops beneath their skirts, as the fashion of the day demanded. Moreover, both were at pains to ensure that they made no physical contact with the black woman.

The sidewalk was simply too narrow. Walking at its very edge, Doña Sebastiano lost her footing and would have fallen into the street had not William, standing just there, moved swiftly, unthinkingly, to catch her.

The result of his actions was pandemonium. "Don't touch me,

you animal!" the doña shouted, and her daughter screamed loudly.

"He tried to fling her into the street," the woman behind them shrieked, "to make way for his nigger wife!"

It was all that was needed. Strangely, Lucretia herself seemed almost forgotten in the melee that ensued; she was knocked about by the suddenly tumultuous throng and nearly pushed through the glass window that fronted Melissa's store.

But it was William toward whom the crowd's anger was directed. Like one of those flash floods that appear in the twinkling of an eye, scour the desert floor, and are gone as quickly as they came, the mob seized up the hapless Negro and swept on, their roar already diminishing in the distance by the time the frightened boy in the farm cart, thinking both cook and her husband taken, had leaped to the driver's seat and, with a ferocious crack of the whip, sent the horses galloping in a homeward direction.

It was nearing evening by the time Joanna arrived in town. Despite her objections, Lewis had insisted upon accompanying her. She had objected less to Jay Jay's coming along; though he was still only a boy, his prowess with a gun was not unknown in the town. And they had hardly driven by the gateposts before Lewis, looking over his shoulder, spat noisily and said, "Here comes that goddam Indian."

So their appearance was not inconspicuous—three of them in the wagon, and the Nasoni riding a discreet distance behind. People observed them from sidewalks and open doorways, and many slunk away from Joanna's gaze; she took that for a bad omen.

They had driven clear to the far edge of town before they found him, hanging from the branch of a big old magnolia tree. Driving near, Joanna heard a buzz, like the distant hum of saws. It puzzled her until they were close enough that she could see the flies already thick on his face and bare chest.

It was hot, and there was a putrid underodor to the perfume of the magnolias.

He looked smaller than she remembered him, as if death had diminished the man. She did not try to see his face, although the body kept turning slowly to and fro on the rope. That, and the constant movement of the flies crawling and buzzing about him gave an eerie impression that he was moving, flexing his muscles perhaps. Joanna stared and as she did so a trickle of sweat inched down between her breasts. The shame she felt was as irrevocable as his death was.

"Señora?"

Joanna, who had climbed down from the wagon, turned and found a Mexican woman standing some distance away; a little girl hid warily behind her and peered wide-eyed around her mother's skirts.

"His woman," the Mexican said. "Her time came. I brought her in here." She motioned toward a shack set off by itself with an air of rejection.

Joanna started to follow her, but just then saw the sheriff approaching, with a smattering of townsfolk trailing after him.

"This your slave?" he asked as he came up.

"He was my employee," Joanna said. "And my friend. Have you arrested the guilty parties?"

"Well, now..." He attempted to stare her down, and quickly gave up the attempt, looking first at his own dust-stained boots, then over his shoulder at the watching citizenry, and finally at some point over Joanna's head.

"That's not so easy to ascertain," he said. "There was like a mob, you see. It's hard to get a clear picture in a case like that. What we've got straight so far is that your nigra there attacked some white women, in broad daylight, no less. Well, say, you can imagine about how that went over. This is wartime. People are touchy."

He waited for her to respond. The silence grew awkward and he shifted his weight from one foot to another, hitching up his trousers.

"In other words," Joanna said coldly, "you're saying you intend to do nothing?"

"Why, I don't see that there's a whole lot I could do, do you? Looks like things have pretty much worked themselves out without any help from me. In a manner of speaking, you could even say justice has been done."

"Then, sheriff, let me make something clear to you. In the future, I will handle justice where Heart's Folly is concerned. You see that people are informed of that."

"Now, Mrs. Harte, I am the law here, don't you be forgetting—"

"The law *here*, perhaps. Henceforth, sheriff, I'm the law at Heart's Folly, and don't you be forgetting that, because I promise you, that badge you wear will protect you no more than it protected him."

She turned back to the Mexican woman, who had edged cautiously away at the sheriff's approach. Now she nodded, and led Joanna toward the shanty she'd indicated before.

"I don't know if you're aware, Mrs. Harte," the sheriff called after her, "what sort of place that is you're thinking of enterin'."

"I'm well aware," Joanna said without so much as slowing her steps. "It's a haven in an otherwise hostile community."

There was no door, only a ragged-looking curtain hanging in the opening. The woman held it aside for Joanna to enter.

Lewis, looking embarrassed by the attention they were receiving, ambled up and down before the shack with the air of a man killing time, but Jay Jay planted himself squarely in front of the doorway, feet wide, face set in so ferocious a scowl that, notwithstanding his youth and diminutive size, those who were tempted to laugh looked again and thought better of it.

Then there was the Indian, sitting quietly motionless on his pony, not so near as to seem "interfering," not so far that his presence could be ignored. There were plenty in the town who resented his presence, too, at Heart's Folly, and occasionally some sniggering comment was made on the exact nature of the relationship that existed between him and the mistress of that ranch; but they were not made within range of his hearing, and when he walked down the town's streets—he did not use the sidewalks, but walked in the dust of the street, with rarely a glance right or left—no one thought to challenge his passage.

Just as no one challenged Joanna when the Indian was around; that much of the relationship between the two was clear enough, at any rate.

The interior of the shack was shaded in gloom. It took Joanna a moment of blinking before she was able to make out the dark figure lying on a bare mattress in one corner.

She went to her, but Lucretia, after one bitter glance, turned her face toward the wall. The dim light glinted on the wetness of her cheeks.

"*Señora, su hijo,*" the Mexican woman said.

At first glance the bundle she offered seemed too small to be a child; but then a howl of protest put that question to rest.

"Oh, a son," Joanna said, taking the indignant baby into her hands.

That got Lucretia's attention. "His name is Abraham Lincoln," she said. "I want him baptized. I want him christened that."

"Abraham Lincoln *Harte*," Joanna said; like most slaves, neither Lucretia nor William had ever had a last name; but their son had been born free, and fatherless; she would not have him nameless as well.

"We'll build our own chapel," she said on an impulse. "On the Folly. Abraham Lincoln will be the first child christened in it. And our own school, too, for all the ranch children. We'll make our own world, right there on our ranch. And from here on, we'll run it as we see fit."

Joanna took the Mexican woman's smile as encouragement, though in fact she had understood almost nothing Joanna said; the English had been too rapid for her. Glancing around, she suddenly discovered her daughter was missing.

"Yolanda? *A donde?*"

Outside, Jay Jay happened to look around as well and saw the child peeking around the corner at him. He gave her one of his disarming smiles, so embarrassing the girl that, with squeals of laughter, she disappeared behind the house, shouting in Spanish to some distant playmate.

EIGHTEEN

Everyone but Sulie found it odd that she should become Lewis's mistress. After all, it was her refusal to bed the master that had provoked that confrontation during the journey from Galveston, and though the fact had never actually been announced, it had clearly been from that point that Joanna had taken command of things.

Sulie, however, marked that incident as the moment when she'd begun to feel sorry for her past master. He had looked so broken, so pathetic. And after that, he'd been a different man, any fool could see that. He'd lost something of his manhood, instinct rather than experience told her that; told her, too, that it was something only a woman could repair.

Joanna was perhaps the last to realize what was going on, and then only because of a remark made by Lucretia.

Sulie had received her plot of land, as had the others, when they first arrived in San Antonio. Being single, however, and disdaining to marry any of the available males in the group, she had declined the offer of her own house. As her landholding was adjacent to that of Lucretia and William, and as she already worked as Lucretia's "second-in-command," it had been convenient for all three of them to treat the two pieces of property as one, and for Sulie to occupy the unused second bedroom in the house belonging to Lucretia and William. The intention had been that when that couple began to produce a family, Sulie would move into her own quarters and the extra room become a nursery.

William's death, of course, changed all that; it was more convenient than ever for Sulie to remain where she was, where she could be a ready nurse and companion for Lucretia during the weeks when she recovered from the twin shocks of birth and death. And a child born two months early required even more attention than ordinarily necessary.

In time Lucretia did recover, though there was a hard-edged quality to her that had not been there before. Joanna's new chapel was built, as promised, in the grove of pecan trees, only a short distance from the main house, and Abraham Lincoln Harte was duly christened in it, by a priest whose initial reluctance was overcome by the generosity of Joanna's charity. Too, a visit to the ranch helped convince that really quite good man that the future patronage of the Hartes might well be worth cultivating.

Despite his inauspicious entry into the world, the boy proved healthy. Sulie's presence in Lucretia's house remained a convenience, but a less pressing one than before. In time, in fact, it became apparent that the convenience of Sulie's living elsewhere had begun to weigh more heavily with Lucretia than the convenience of having her remain. She several times remarked to Joanna that Sulie was of an age when she ought to be thinking of her own future; it was implied that this would be easier if she were in her own house.

"Why, yes," Joanna agreed finally, "I can see it might be better for her if she were."

"For others, too, maybe," Lucretia said, giving Joanna a veiled look she did not, at the moment, comprehend.

On this occasion the conversation was interrupted by the most unexpected of arrivals. Jay Jay, coming in from out of doors, remarked somewhat offhandedly that there was "company coming." Joanna, curious, came to the front door, watching a speck shimmering on the horizon grow ever so gradually into the figure of a woman, trudging with unmistakable weariness in the general direction of the ranch, with a detour to find the right crossing place for the stream, and a half-dozen stops to rest—seating herself, they could see when she came a bit closer, on the carpetbag she otherwise dragged with her. Thus interrupted, her progress, slow in any case, was at a snail's pace.

Joanna had actually been watching her for the best part of half an hour when something arrested her attention—a fanning gesture, no more than that. "Why, it surely can't be," Joanna exclaimed. She hooded her eyes with one hand and strained to see. "Jay Jay, quick, fetch me the trap. I'd swear that's Alice Montgomery."

And it was, too. Panting for breath as she trudged, her face of a redness that threatened a stroke on the spot, that hapless creature was barely able to smile a greeting when Joanna drove hastily up to her.

"Alice, in the name of heaven, I can hardly credit this!" Joanna exclaimed, leaping down to help her. "No, don't try to talk now, just get your breath, we'll talk at the house."

"You are—most kind," Alice gasped, and fairly swooned back against the horsehair seat, her gaping mouth of momentary interest to a passing fly.

At the house, Joanna and Lucretia between them helped her into the dim coolness of the parlor, where it was immediately necessary to assure her that the puma with which she suddenly found herself face-to-face represented no threat to her safety.

"Oh, you can't imagine," Alice said, still out of breath. "Do you know, I couldn't find a single soul in town willing to drive me here. They couldn't be more leery of this place if General Sherman himself were encamped— Great Gawd Almighty." She interrupted herself with a squeal, and threw her hands to her cheeks.

Joanna, looking, saw that William Horse had brought their visitor's carpetbag into the room, setting it on the floor.

"You remember William Horse, surely," Joanna said. "We met him in Galveston. He traveled here with us."

"The same one. Upon my soul. Don't tell me you've purchased him?"

"Thank you, William," Joanna said, nodding as he went out. "No, we own no slaves here. He's as free as the rest of us."

"No—but what of the nigras—I'd swear that was the same one you had with you—and those pickaninnies in the field, not a one of whom lifted a finger, I might mention, to help me in my most laborious sojourn, though they were interested enough to neglect their work so as to stare?"

"All free. And landholders, every one. We make our own rules here at the Folly. But tell me, what on earth brings you here, of all places?"

"Of all places, indeed. Who'd ever have thought...the very ends of the earth...oh, if my mother could see me this day, to what depths I've fallen—no offense meant, I do assure you, Joanna."

"And none taken, but that hardly answers my question: How have you managed to fall to such depths as these?"

"The war," Alice said. "What else but this horrible war? The Yankees have occupied Galveston, came right up Broadway, to my very house, set their headquarters up in my own front room, can you credit that? They said, of course, they'd do no mischief, but what good's a Yankee's word, I ask you, when everyone knows the flower of southern womanhood has been but fodder under their marching boots? Well, I could hardly stay in the house, my own house, mind you, but you know how people will talk, and anyway, I couldn't once close my eyes in restful sleep, never knowing when one of those grinning apes they call 'soldiers' might take it upon himself—well, absolute hordes of people were fleeing, all the decent folk, and the sensible ones, by boat, and by wagon, on foot, even. I could have gone to Charleston—Luisa Mary Honeycott was practically on her knees begging me—but I knew my dyspepsia would never survive a sea voyage, not the state my nerves were in at the moment, and anyway, I never could stomach that Luisa Mary; she's sneaking, that one—I've always said that about her. You remember her—lived three doors down, bragged all the time about her chutney, which I personally found sour. So, as luck would have it, the Andersons—Dr. Anderson and his wife, Millicent, you met them, I'm certain—were on their way here, with a large party, and they were gracious enough to say that I might ride with them, though I can't say their graciousness lasted more than a day or two on the trail. Got me here, they did, and fairly threw me out of their wagon into the very dirt of the streets, let me down, they did, and drove off, as well as if they didn't know me. If I hadn't known that I could—Lewis."

Joanna, struggling to keep hold of the thread of this story, was surprised by this change of direction, until she looked and saw her husband in the doorway.

"Oh, Lewis, come in," she said. "You remember Alice Montgomery. She's dropped by for a visit."

"From Galveston?" Lewis asked, surprised.

"We might as well be frank," Alice said, wagging her finger. "It's likely to be a long visit. I don't know when I'll be up to making that journey again. But I said to myself, Where can I go? and the answer came to me right off. Joanna, I said to myself, why, I can't count the times she pleaded to be of some service to me. And after all, I told myself, it's not as if she had no part in making me a widow."

Alice's eyes did not join in her little burst of laughter that followed this sally, but went from Joanna to Lewis, and back to Joanna.

Joanna, having already seen her way through to the blackmail at the core of Alice's story, was ready to yield to the sense of it, though she was silently congratulating herself on her foresight in having arranged large—and distant—guest quarters.

"We'd have taken offense if you'd gone anywhere else," she said aloud. "Jay Jay, tell Lucretia to have one of the girls make up a room for Mrs. Montgomery—the far bedroom, I think; she'll want her privacy, I'm sure. And ask Sulie if she won't bring us some sherry."

Alice prattled on. Joanna had learned previously that it was not necessary to really listen to Alice's words, all of them, in order to follow the flow—the flood, you might call it—of her conversation.

She couldn't, of course, turn Alice out; Alice's moral blackmail was very much to the point, though she could not help being surprised that Alice had actually come here, made that difficult journey. Well, you couldn't tell about people, could you, even those who seemed the easiest to categorize? Often, they fooled you the most.

Sulie came in, setting a tray with glasses, a decanter, little napkins on the table in front of Joanna. Absently, Joanna thanked her; she was mentally weighing what Alice's arrival would mean to them, what effects it would have, when Lewis surprised her with a remark.

"Don't you think, Joanna," he said in that way he'd developed of sidling around her possible disagreement, "Sulie ought to have a place of her own?"

Joanna looked up at him. "Why, what a remarkable coincidence," she started to say, and stopped.

Lewis was not looking at her, he was looking after Sulie, his eyes glazed in that way besotted men get over the objects of their affections. It spoke more plainly than words.

"Coincidence?" Lewis echoed her word, and turned his glance toward her.

"I was just thinking the same thing myself, earlier today," Joanna said, surprised at the evenness of her own reaction, at the completeness of her discovery. Like a single piece that makes a whole puzzle fall together with such obviousness you wonder it had mystified you a moment before, there flashed before her an entire sequence of moments, too minor to be called events—glances; almost indistinguishable changes in inflection; gestures. Why, the surprise wasn't Lewis at all; she'd wager money the suggestion hadn't even come from him in the first place, though by now he quite likely thought it had. The surprise was Sulie.

"Were you?" Lewis was too much a child for successful dissimulation. He emptied his glass of sherry and wiped his mouth with the back of his hand, smearing a grin across his face.

"Yes. I wonder if you wouldn't see to it for me? The men have time enough just now; they ought to have it taken care of well before harvest."

"Yes, yes, I'll see to it," he said, and jumped up as if she had said "This instant."

An errant sunbeam had finagled its way between the closed draperies. Joanna followed its dust-laden track with her eyes, straight, a pointing finger of light slicing the air between her and Alice Montgomery, splintering finally in the crystal of the decanter.

Her first real judgment of the situation was, It will make things easier. The immediate question, of course, was, for whom? But that answer, too, was easy to come by: for the Folly. Contented people, satisfied people, they were easier to manage, to count on.

But surely that was a fanaticism, wasn't it, putting a thing, something inanimate, above everything else, above what any sane person would call "decency"? A married woman—there were vows, after all, taken before God—arranging for her husband and his mistress.

But she had taken a vow, too, that things must be different here, and how else could they be except she made them so?

For that matter, how could you think of the Folly as a "thing," as inanimate, when surely it was alive, its life larger than her own in a sense?

She was suddenly aware that Alice had asked her something, or was waiting for a reply to something, her mouth open as if barely able to contain the words she had ready in response.

"I'm sorry," Joanna said. "My mind was wandering."

"I said your husband seems a different man altogether from what he was in Galveston. This place certainly seems to agree with him, at any rate, though it's the last thing I'd have expected."

It was exactly what Joanna needed to hear at the moment. She laughed unexpectedly, mostly at herself. It's a little late in the game, isn't it, she asked herself, for me to start dithering over convention?

"Whatever is so amusing?" Alice asked.

"I was thinking of something. I believe it was Machiavelli who said, 'When a woman ceases to be desirable, a procuress is born.'"

Alice's eyes went wide with shocked confusion. "I don't think I see…"

"Oh, it's nothing," Joanna said with another laugh. "I sometimes think my husband is right—I read too much for my own good. Come along, dear. Let's see what they've done in the way of a room for you, and later we'll have a nice juicy gossip. I'm certain you must have a great deal to tell me."

NINETEEN

T he Folly—both the house and the ranch itself—was already large enough and busy enough that it easily assimilated the presence of Alice Montgomery with little real effect upon the lives and schedules of the other inhabitants.

Her presence, however, was not entirely without its effects, and these were felt most keenly in the somewhat tenuous relationship that existed between the residents of the ranch, on one hand, and the residents of the town of San Antonio, on the other.

Alice Montgomery was determinedly social. It was not to be expected that she would long suffer the isolation of Heart's Folly, an isolation of spirit as well as distance. She had come to what she considered a "frontier outpost" under duress; now she began to perceive herself as "godsent," and her visit as "ordained." Why, the very gifts that she possessed in abundance, as she was all too willing to point out to Joanna, were those most conspicuously lacking in local circles. Surely she had come for the express purpose of—it was her duty—sharing with these socially starved creatures her city sophistication, her "niceness," as she so aptly put it.

Having thus provided herself with a mission, Alice set about it with a vengeance. Against her voluble onslaught, few could muster argument—few, in fact, could find the opening in which to insert more than an occasional word or two.

Alice visited. She dropped by. She attended—everything and anything. Not a wedding, not a funeral, not an afternoon get-together of neighbors around a pot of coffee escaped her notice or her attendance. She made full allowances for the difficulties in extending formal invitations under such primitive conditions, and graciously dispensed with the necessity of waiting upon them. No one was safe from her. Closed doors—and they were rare in the heat of a Texas summer—were to be tapped on, softly, certainly, but with a persistence that could reach any level. She could veritably fly down the streets of the town in pursuit of quarry. She was blithely, cheerily, impervious to rebuffs, even to direct insult—after all, that was the point, wasn't it? These poor people had had no opportunity heretofore to "learn."

In all this, Alice might simply have made herself ridiculous; indeed, some thought her so. Joanna herself might have subscribed to that opinion, had chauvinism not prevented her doing so. Alice was her guest; more to the point, for better or for worse, she was part now of the Folly; and as such, in Joanna's mind, clothed in a mantle of superiority.

But Alice's efforts bore fruit.

In part, this was because the soil was ripe for her planting. However foolish her version of logic, Alice had instinctively hit upon a truth: The women of San Antonio were indeed ready—waiting—for the social niceties that they had been lacking. Only a few years before, the town had been a frontier outpost of the most rugged sort. Little more than a cow town, it had been the site of the bloody battles climaxed at the Alamo. Life had been hard, and there had been little time or energy for more than survival.

That was in the past, though. In more recent years, San Antonio had reached that stage where its citizens found life, if not easy, more commodious than before. Women whose days had not held enough hours to attend to necessities now looked about for those gracious touches that make subsistence in the end worthwhile. What they had lacked was a social leader; in Alice Montgomery, they were handed one full-blown, whose blandishments were no more resistible than the winds of a tornado.

Alice had one other advantage as well, and that was Heart's Folly.

People might resent the ranch and its inhabitants, might feel anger toward them and occasionally vent that anger; but, as people will, they knew curiosity, too, and a spiteful kind of awe. Even by Texas standards, the ranch was huge, and there were few locals who hadn't found some opportunity to drive by closely enough to see that immense, still-growing house the Hartes had built.

Like it or not, it was undeniable that the Hartes had already made themselves preeminent. About such people, lesser individuals like to hear—preferably ugly things, but any gossip will do when little is to be had.

Alice Montgomery was privy to what were supposed to be the "secrets" of that place, and she showed no disinclination to share them. Nothing could ensure the success of Alice's visit more than finding others willing to listen—listen they must, of course, but the pleasure was doubled if it pleased them to do so—and, why, if Heart's Folly was what they most liked to hear about, it was what she was most supplied with, too.

Sulie had not moved into the little cottage being built for her before Alice had made much of Lewis's interest in that matter— though others had to draw their own conclusions from her inferences: "Far be it from me," she declared with unimpeachable sincerity, "to gossip about the very master of the place in which hard necessity has made me a guest." And, after a pause, "If he can be called the master," a remark upon which she was easily coaxed to amplify.

One may be foolish without being a fool. For all the jokes at her expense, for all the patience that she tried, Alice had soon enough established herself as a fixture, perhaps *the* fixture, in local society. It was certainly she who launched what many came to call, laughingly, "The Battle of the Ranch Queens," a battle that, by virtue of its immediacy, for a time occupied local attention more fully than did that bitter war raging at a distance.

In time it became necessary that Alice do something more to cement her newly acquired position beyond repeating what had now come to be common talk in the form of gossip about the Hartes. Morever, she had been entertained, willingly or not, time and again by virtually every household of any significance in the area; she was overdue in repaying hospitality, and certain less than kindly souls began to hint at that fact.

True, she had once or twice assumed the role of cohostess at little socials at Melissa's home, somewhat to Melissa's chagrin. But with the coming of another spring, it became evident to Alice that something more was needed, and that the time was ripe to show her hand, to show just what she could deliver when of a mind to.

In short, she decided to arrange a festivity at Heart's Folly itself.

With an instinct for generalship that might have done the Confederacy justice, she made it a point first to test the waters. The results were double-edged: Everyone to whom she hinted at her scheme was titillated by the prospect; but most were openly skeptical as well, so that if she failed to deliver the goods, so to speak, there was a real danger of losing the ground she had already gained. That she had no mind to do.

At first Joanna was astonished by the suggestion. "You can't have spent this much time here without seeing for yourself there's not much love lost between us and the townspeople," she pointed out.

"But that's exactly the point," was Alice's rejoinder. "Here you are, and here they are, and neither likely just to vanish. Surely it must be better to be on friendly terms rather than unfriendly?"

When she thought about it, Joanna was inclined to agree with that point. It was necessary at least to get along with the local people. Better far to be surrounded by friends, even dubious friends, than outright enemies.

Too, she could see that an entertainment at Heart's Folly was an advantageous way of patching things up; far better they all come here to court her than that she go tapping at doors as Alice had done. If there was to be obligation, she wanted it in her favor.

So, to the surprise of everyone but Alice herself, Joanna soon agreed to the idea of a picnic, to be held at the ranch.

"But I have my doubts that anyone will actually attend," Joanna said pessimistically.

"You just leave everything to me," Alice replied, and immediately launched into this new enterprise with an energy and soleness of purpose that forever put to rest in Joanna's mind the image she'd once had of Mrs. Montgomery as vapid and lifeless.

Of the local ladies, two had continued to resist Alice's machinations, for largely the same reasons. Both Doña Sebastiano, Joanna's nearest neighbor, and Melissa, Joanna's own daughter, had fancied for themselves the role of local social arbiter. Toward that goal, both had made some currency with their disapproval of the way things were managed at Heart's Folly. Blood ties had not dissuaded Melissa from her often-voiced opinions regarding the treatment of

blacks as if they were the equal of decent white people, and it was
well known that only familial duty accounted for her token visits
to the ranch. She had balked—and many knew the tale—at Joanna's suggestion that her own son, Ronald, be the second child
christened at the ranch's little chapel. "A nigra chapel," Melissa was
wont to say, in a voice redolent with scorn.

Only Joanna's threat to take the ranch's business elsewhere—
"And how would that look, I ask you," Melissa fairly sobbed, "my
own mother declining to give me her trade?"—had persuaded her
to change her mind; the ranch's share of the store's account books
was considerable.

So when word first reached Melissa of the planned picnic, she
sniffed and made it known that she was certain that date was already
accounted for in her engagement book.

But Melissa had made the mistake, which Alice had not made,
of underestimating the persuasive powers of envy and curiosity. It
was soon evident that those she had expected to applaud her brave
stand were in fact planning on attending in droves. From all in-
dications, Melissa was likely to have the town to herself on the date
in question.

On the other hand, while she was debating how to extricate
herself from her position without embarrassment, Doña Sebastiano, more experienced in such fencing, scored a coup. She was
among the first to accept Joanna's invitation, which surprised many,
since she'd been even more open in her scorn for those Hartes
than Melissa had been. But Doña Sebastiano's acceptance was accompanied by an invitation of her own. She was holding an authentic Texas barbecue, an even month after Joanna's picnic, an
invitation that Joanna, under the circumstances, could hardly decline. So Doña Sebastiano, who ranked high on Joanna's list of most
disliked people, was the first who would play hostess to the Hartes
outside their ranch. In one stroke, Doña Sebastiano had both ac-
knowledged Joanna's new prominence in the community and challenged it.

The stage was set for a confrontation, Old South against New
Texas. Even those who had always disliked Doña Sebastiano quickly
forgot that that lady herself would have preferred to live elsewhere,
and cheered for her side. The dour señora had never enjoyed such
a favorable limelight, and she basked in it, to Melissa's further
dismay.

Melissa, wisely deciding that to hesitate longer could only find her ground more shaky than ever, discovered an error in her engagement log and jubilantly announced that she would be able to enjoy the picnic after all.

Hardly anyone noticed her change of heart, however; by this time everyone was agog at the latest move on Joanna's part.

For some years Doña Sebastiano had employed a cook known only as Angel, a wizened little Mexican man who spoke little English and was much admired locally for the fire of his chili and the lightness of his tortillas. He was known as well for his consumption of the local beer. The disapproval that this might have brought upon the head of another was somewhat mitigated in Angel's case by the fact, much observed, that the more he drank, the better he cooked. Indeed, his cooking when sober was so inferior that even the most ardent teetotalers had been known to assist the quenching of his considerable thirst, the better to assure themselves of enjoyable victuals.

Doña Sebastiano had quarreled often with her cook, enjoying the envy his skills brought her, but deploring his otherwise shameful behavior. Shortly after the issuing of her barbecue invitations, an understandably edgy señora lost her patience on one occasion and declared a torta offered by her cook "inedible."

In response, Angel attempted to hang himself from the barn's rafters, saved only by his drunkenness, which caused him to tie a faulty knot so that when he made an overexuberant leap from the timbers of the loft, the noose he had fashioned slipped easily from about his neck and he landed unceremoniously in a recently deposited cow patty, at the very feet, indeed, of the startled bovine who had so cushioned his fall.

The story was much bandied about, in versions that did nothing to enhance Doña Sebastiano's reputation. Fearing that she was to be made a laughingstock on the very eve of her most important social effort, the enraged señora fired her cook.

Whereupon Joanna, highly amused by this display of quixotic gallantry, promptly hired him.

If she had flung a glove at the feet of her rival, she could not have better fanned the flames of controversy. No one spoke of anything else for days. A breathless Alice Montgomery mentally counted the score: The move had gained Joanna some admirers and lost Doña Sebastiano some. But the one who gained most, and lost nothing, was, of course, the delighted Alice herself, whose efforts now to ensure the success of Joanna's picnic approached the point of hysterical frenzy.

Traveling to town almost daily, she regaled her now avid listeners with one news item after another, until an almost unbearable suspense circulated.

Joanna had dispatched an army of workmen into the mountains, from which they had returned with wagonloads of ice, each massive block buried in straw. A whole new shed had been built for its storage alone.

An entire army of Angel's relatives—sisters, cousins, aunts, nieces—had descended upon the Folly, their housing forming almost an entire village. Dusk to dawn, they were grinding, kneading, mixing, baking.

An entire pavilion had been built in the shade of the pecan grove. A corral. Extra stables. Extra hands, cowboys, though the Folly was almost bereft of cattle.

The surrounding hillsides were all but stripped of their flowers, which, since they could not be expected to keep the necessary length of time, were hung upside down to dry with their colors intact. Those who strolled from pavilion to main house would be spared the rigors of Texas sun, but would walk instead beneath a canopy of bluebonnets.

In one instance, Joanna was quickly proven entirely wrong. She had voiced her opinion all along that they would be lucky if anyone showed up on the day of her picnic. It was soon obvious, however, that scarcely anyone who could make the trip intended to be absent. They came not only from the town itself but from ranches as far away as one hundred miles, some of them blithely assuming they were meant to stay over. That, at least, Joanna had anticipated— it was a custom she was used to from South Carolina—and the main house had been supplied with bedrooms aplenty.

The festivities were slated to begin at noon on the Sunday in question. Ordinarily, some of the guests might be expected to arrive earlier; certainly those coming long distances. But this was virgin territory in a sense, and Joanna, though she'd now been in residence nearly two years, really a stranger. Not until shortly after the sun had reached the middle of the broad sky did the first guests begin to arrive; then, as though they'd waited in a line, they arrived in an almost unbroken stream, on horseback, in carriages and buggies, wagons and carts, by every conceivable means of conveyance, and some on foot as well.

What they found as they passed through the elaborate gates, many of them puzzling over the apparent misspelling overhead, was Joanna herself, waiting beneath a festooned canopy that had been erected for her. Her oldest son was with her; Lewis and Jay Jay were to do honors at the house, with the inestimable aid of Alice Montgomery.

But it was Joanna they had come to meet, and there she was, seated astride a splendid pinto pony—astride, mind you!—in a costume that she had been at some pains to devise for the occasion. She wore one of her now infamous "trousers," these of tooled black leather that actually gave the impression she wore chaps. This skirt was cut unusually short, even for her, to reveal high-calfed boots and the merest flash of bare leg. Her white silk blouse had been exquisitely embroidered in Texas bluebonnets, the work done by one of Angel's many cousins. Over the blouse, she wore a short jacket, in the bolero style, to match her skirt.

Even her hat was a shock to their eyes. Unlike the bonnets and imported chapeaus the other ladies wore, this resembled more than anything else the hats worn by the vaqueros, or Mexican cowhands, except that it was flatter and smaller-brimmed, and as black as her skirt and jacket. A single yellow rose, one perfect blossom, had been attached to its brim, and at her earlobes and throat were the magnificent yellow diamonds that had been her wedding present from Lewis.

As each guest rode through the gate, Joanna rode forward the few feet to extend a gloved hand and welcome them to Heart's Folly.

The effect was stunning; even those who were most disapproving were not immune to its theatricality, and went on, awed, up the drive to the main house, the stage appropriately set for the splendor waiting there.

And splendor there was. In the enormous pavilion set up among the trees, and in the gallery connecting it to the main house—both, as Alice had promised, artfully festooned with flowers—stood table after table of food and drink.

There had been some speculation of fireworks between Lucretia, who certainly saw herself as only slightly less than mistress of the house, and Angel, the usurper. But Lucretia fostered in her heart a burning hatred of Doña Sebastiano, and had welcomed what was seen as an insult to her. What was more, Angel's admiration for her skills had been so quickly apparent and so obviously sincere that they had become almost at once partners rather than competitors. What they each cooked was different from the other, and she soon came to admire his skills as well.

The result was that they had outdone themselves for this occasion. Whole pigs and great slabs of beef sputtered and sizzled over open fires, and Angel's cousins and nieces stirred huge caldrons of his justly famed chili. Entire tables groaned under the weight of game that the men had furnished—roasts of venison; partridge, grouse, and pheasant; rabbit and squirrel; and even, though Lucretia had for a time balked at this, rattlesnake. Smaller birds were baked in pastry; there were pâtés of ham and pheasant adrift on a sea of smoked oysters Joanna had so thoughtfully brought from Galveston. Blocks of ice, carved in the forms of such diverse wildlife as swans and dolphins, held champagne and beer, frozen sorbets and mousses, and fish shimmering in aspics.

While the guests strolled in and out of the house and about the grounds, oohing and ahhing over what they saw, a band of musicians in colorful costumes serenaded them, strumming guitars and singing songs that seemed to turn liquid on the fragrant air.

Joanna had confidently assumed that the house and grounds would suffice to interest the guests for an hour or so. By that time, all but a few stragglers had arrived, and she and Gregory rode up to join their guests.

It was evident, too, by that time, that Joanna had scored a triumph. There was reserve in the attitudes displayed toward her as she circulated among her guests, but there was a new respect as well. In the future, she would have less of a struggle setting her own course for Heart's Folly, she was certain.

In midafternoon, a fanfare played a bit shakily on a brass trumpet by one of the Mexicans drew everybody's attention to the corral that had been set up behind the barns. When they got there, the guests found that a grandstand had been built around the corral. Inside the corral, a number of cowboys recruited from surrounding ranches milled about, tightening cinches, looping lariats, scuffling their boots nervously in the dust.

This had been Jay Jay's inspiration, and it immediately proved another triumph. For the next hour and a half, the assembled cowhands competed with one another to see who could stay on an unbroken horse the longest, rope and tie a calf the fastest, even ride an angry bull.

The assembled guests loved it, and more than a few of the men, finding this part of the afternoon's entertainment far more to their liking than flowers and strolling musicians, shed their coats and ties and joined in the contests.

After this, there was dancing in the pavilion, cleared by now of its food tables.

"I'd like to see her match this," Alice said, catching up with Joanna for one of the few times in the course of the afternoon.

There was no need to ask to whom she referred, nor to embellish upon the remark. Feeling more or less satisfied with herself, Joanna drifted away from her guests, in the direction of the stream. It was nearly dusk.

Her success was not entirely unmitigated. She had very nearly bankrupted them again; thinking that to take this gamble in a halfhearted way would be worse than not taking it at all, she had spared no expense to make the impact she thought most important. It would take them another year, and that necessarily a good one, to make back the money she'd laid out. Nor was she fool enough to ignore the envy she'd aroused in some, not alone Doña Sebastiano. She'd already decided it behooved her to be gracious in that quarter. She would do what she could to ensure the success of Doña Sebastiano's barbecue; she could afford to now.

But, yes, surely, she had made future enemies. There were those who would resent her, and the ranch, all the more deeply; she had merely made certain that their resentment had been tempered with due respect.

A twig snapped. Startled, Joanna whirled about. "Who's there?" she demanded of the shadow among the darkening trees.

"It is only I." Don Sebastiano stepped into the pale light.

"Don Sebastiano, you startled me. Are you not enjoying the party?"

"It has been splendid, though I must leave soon. My wife complains of a headache." His smile was faintly ironic.

"*Que lastima,*" Joanna said. "How sad. But we shall see one another soon again. I look forward to my first authentic Texas outing."

"It would grieve me to wait so long to see you again." His gaze, as he came to stand close before her, was unusually warm. He took one of her hands in his and, bending from the waist, kissed it. Afterward, he did not release it.

"But of course," Joanna said, smiling, "you are always welcome here. We are always happy to see you."

"Not so welcome, not so happy, as I would wish."

"Then you undervalue my delight in our friendship."

"You are the fairest flower in all Texas," he said, and now there was no mistaking the ardor in his eyes.

Joanna attempted to make light of it. "You are kindness itself, Don Sebastiano. I am a grandmother now; I cannot help being charmed by such flattery."

He leaned toward her, meaning to kiss her. For a moment, Joanna was at a loss.

The moment passed. Don Sebastiano stiffened, and looked past her. "Someone's there," he said, and then, "That Indian of yours, skulking about." With an angry scowl, he straightened and took an involuntary step back from her.

"William Horse?" Joanna looked over her shoulder, but the Nasoni was already vanishing back into the shadows. "He likes to keep an eye on me. I think he looks upon me as an incompetent child."

"What is he doing here anyway? Why is he here at all?"

"He came back to San Antonio, he said, to see his mother. It is my understanding, though he almost never speaks of himself, that she was dead and buried when he got here. I suppose, because I was kind to him on our overland journey, he's made me something of a substitute for her."

"Perhaps he's in love with you."

Joanna shrugged. "I can't imagine why."

"Indeed, I can."

"And perhaps you've had too much wine." Joanna laughed lightly to take the sting out of this, and linked her arm through his in comradely fashion. "Come, I must return to my guests—they'll be leaving soon. And we mustn't ignore your wife's headache."

The Sebastianos left soon afterward, and taking that as a cue, others soon followed suit. For a time the carriage lights made a flickering stream down the darkness of the long lane. Still, it was well on to midnight before Joanna had bade goodbye to those guests not staying, paid and thanked all those who had worked to make such a success of the party, and finally joined a weary but exultant Alice Montgomery in the front parlor.

"A victory, an absolute victory!" Alice crowed, for once making her words short.

"And we owe it all to you," Joanna said.

"Yes." Alice fanned herself with a paper fan and looked altogether smug. "Yes, that's true," she agreed.

Joanna was in her room, brushing out her hair, when Lewis tapped at her door and came in. She smiled a little wearily at him.

"You outdid yourself, Joannie," he said.

"You were the perfect host." It was true, in fact. She had scarcely seen him take a drink. He had been, throughout the afternoon and evening, the perfect image of the southern aristocrat. She had been proud of him, and now told him so.

He beamed, and looked around, flustered, before he brought his gaze back to her. "By God, you've done what you said you'd do, haven't you? You've made a grand place here for yourself."

"For both of us," she said.

He put his hands on her shoulders. "I'll say this for you, Joan, you're a woman like no other."

For the second time that evening, Joanna found herself before a man who obviously wanted to kiss her, and was uncertain of her reaction.

She stretched on tiptoe to brush his cheek lightly with her lips. "Goodnight, Lewis," she said. "Thank you for all your help."

She pretended not to see his look of disappointment as he went out.

Aside from Doña Sebastiano, only one other guest had failed to enjoy herself that day. Melissa was miserable.

She could not but think that fate had conspired against her. She'd chosen Peter Hansen's home in preference to scrabbling in the dust to start a ranch, and now found herself going home to a mere hovel in comparison to the grandeur that was Heart's Folly. She had sided with the local people in their prejudice against her mother, and now they were bowing and scraping as if her mother were some sort of queen.

Worst of all, she could most certainly have been the belle of today's ball, with every young swain there at her feet; instead, she was a married woman, a mother, and men in whose eyes gleamed the unmistakable light of desire bowed formally to her and called her "Mrs. Hansen."

She began to sniffle.

"Is something wrong?" her husband asked. They were a part of that parade of vehicles making its way back toward town.

"Wrong? Why, what could I possibly see wrong in the spectacle of my family living in the lap of luxury, while I, I will be once more at your establishment on the morrow, working like the drudge that I am?"

Mr. Hansen was understandably puzzled by this outburst from a wife who had in so short a time virtually usurped his management of their store.

"But it was you who wanted to learn," he said in his defense.

"Yes, indeed, and why should I not," she railed at him, "when the choice was to live in near-poverty or, by applying my own wits, to eke some little profit out of your establishment." She began to sob. "Oh, when I think what I've sacrificed—my beauty...my youth..."

Mr. Hansen gave her a startled look at that, and might have remonstrated with her—the mantle of old age had hardly settled itself on her—but she saw his look and turned on him in a fury.

"Yes, my youth. I was a mere child when you had your way with me, need I remind you? And now...now..."

But the words needed to express her woe failed her at this point, and they drove on in a silence weighted on his part by guilty confusion, and on hers by heartbreaking sobs.

It might have seemed that Joanna's triumph with her picnic, which was the chief topic of conversation locally for days after, had scored a clear-cut and decisive victory over her self-appointed rival.

In its own way, however, Doña Sebastiano's barbecue was a triumph, too.

For one thing, Joanna stuck to her resolve to help make the affair a success. For another, Doña Sebastiano had wisely chosen not to compete head on, but had offered instead an entirely different sort of entertainment, one in which she was experienced and at home, and Joanna, of necessity, the fish out of water.

There were other details, too, that served on Doña Sebastiano's behalf. Lewis and Sulie quarreled. She resented his going, and in truth he himself would have preferred not to, had he dared make such a suggestion to Joanna. He went, and drank too much; not enough to get falling-down drunk, but enough to make himself look a bit silly. This had the contradictory effect of winning a certain amount of sympathy for Joanna, and at the same time somewhat tarnishing the grand image she had achieved.

Then there was the matter of that severed head....

The Sebastianos' barbecue was not at their ranch house but actually on the open prairie itself, beyond the outbuildings and the bunkhouses.

Despite the fact that Rancho Sebastiano was the nearest neighbor of Heart's Folly, it seemed to Joanna that they rode forever to get there. They were going by buggy, she and Lewis, Alice, and the boys; Joanna had had the unpleasant job of explaining to William Horse that, as he was not invited, he could not to accompany them, however much he might keep out of the way.

She had dressed more conservatively on this occasion, in a conventional dress. By the time they had driven for an hour, however, Joanna was missing her wide-brimmed hat, so much more practical than a bonnet for shading from the sun. And she would have been far more comfortable on horseback, in one of her own costumes, rather than hooped and petticoated as she was, jouncing about in a buggy over the rough terrain.

Worse, when they arrived at the barbecue location, already crowded with throngs of people, there was no shade there either, not even a tree for miles. There were a few clumps of the pale green mesquite, looking cool, but offering virtually no protection from the sun. Joanna felt as if she were moving through a haze.

The men and women drifted into separate groups. This was apparently the Texas custom—Joanna had noticed the tendency to do this even at her picnic. Once or twice she moved to join the men; they treated her with a respect they did not usually show their own women, but she could see as well that she was breaching etiquette. On her good behavior, she rejoined the women, though she promised herself that was one custom she would not often share in.

As if divining her thoughts, her hostess said, "In Texas, a man's horse comes first, then his cattle, if he has any. After that come the women, if they're lucky."

"A woman may live by a man's rules, or make her own," Joanna replied.

"It's a man's world," Doña Sebastiano said.

"Mine isn't."

For a moment, the look Doña Sebastiano gave her verged on admiring; but that wayward emotion was quickly quelled.

Alice Montgomery floated by on a cloud of words, difficult to tell for whom they were meant, if anyone in particular.

"I hear the Yankees have withdrawn from Galveston," Doña Sebastiano said. "Yet Mrs. Montgomery lingers on."

"I rather think she's found a home for herself," Joanna said.

"On a ranch? I confess that surprises me. Has she any family?"

"Children, you mean? No, none. I think she's more or less adopted us. All of us, I mean." She made a gesture that took in the entire party. "For all her flightiness, she's really a maternal sort."

"Yes." Doña Sebastiano was thoughtful for a moment. "Maternal women are always ruthless, aren't they?"

"Do you think so?" The remark surprised Joanna. "I've always thought of myself as maternal, you know."

"Exactly," Doña Sebastiano said. "Ah, I see the food is nearly ready. It's been cooking since last night. I hope you enjoy our little barbecue."

All this while, one man, a Mexican, had been working industriously at a red-hot cooking fire, juggling coffeepots and huge urns full of beans and rice.

Not far away, a group of vaqueros in colorful Mexican costumes was struggling to lift something from a deep cooking pit. This apparently was center stage; people had begun to crowd nearer, and there was a shout when they lifted their prize from the ground.

A trio of cowhands brought an enormous burlap-wrapped bundle to the table, deftly cutting away and discarding this wet outer wrapping, to reveal yet another layer of burlap, this one fairly dripping with juices. There were little cries of delight and excited anticipation from the collected Texans.

The last of the burlap was cut away, and Joanna suddenly found herself face-to-face with the entire head of a cow. With its protrudent tongue and its eyes fallen back in their sockets, it seemed to be making a grotesque face at her.

"Smell that aroma!" someone shouted, and someone else, "My mouth's watering so, we could irrigate cotton."

People with dishes in hand pushed closer to the prize, but Doña Sebastiano handled them deftly. "Please," she said, "our guest of honor. Mrs. Harte? May I serve you first?"

"Yes, thank you," Joanna managed to say, but she could not take her gaze from that of the bodiless animal before her.

She had expected that her hostess would cut off some of the juicy shreds of beef hanging from the animal's cheeks—that, at least, off the head, would look much like any other roast beef. Such was not the case, however. One of the serving men had been hacking at the head, cutting the top off and setting it aside. With an enormous ladle, Doña Sebastiano dipped into the cavity and brought out a heaping spoonful of soft, steaming brains. "I daresay, you'll find this different from your South Carolina cooking," she said, handing the plate to Joanna.

One of the eyes had come up with the brains; it stared balefully up at Joanna. Joanna reached to take the dish, and thought better of it. "Please, will you excuse me for a moment?" she murmured, and pushed through a watching throng to make a hurried path toward one of those clumps of cool-looking mesquite.

She reached it barely in time to be loudly, violently ill.

It was generally agreed afterward that though "The Battle of the Ranch Queens" had left Joanna in the preeminent position, Doña Sebastiano had not scored badly.

TWENTY

In the first year or so that Webb Price was gone, Joanna received occasional word from him, brief messages that could hardly be called "love letters," but sufficed to let her know that he was well and alive. In letters from Manassas, Fair Oaks, Shenandoah, he wrote of "the rigors of war" and of how he missed Texas, leaving Joanna to presume that included her as well.

Then the letters stopped. Month after month passed, and spotty news of the war—not going well for the South—arrived in San Antone, but there was no word of Webb Price.

Locals now called the Hartes "high cotton"; the land had proven richly fertile, not only for cotton but for a variety of produce crops that they now cultivated as well. Unlike their neighbors, however, Joanna resisted suggestions that they turn to cattle. Gregory, increasingly in charge of the ranch's management, was unusually set on this. "The Hartes are farmers," he said, "not cattlemen."

"If he could ride or rope," Jay Jay argued, to no avail, "he'd see things a mite different."

He, at least, was the perfect picture of the Texas cowhand. Lean and already handsome, he made up for his lack of height with an exaggerated swagger that Joanna found amusing, though she had begun to notice that the young ladies about town thought it less so.

Gregory—"old sobersides," his brother called him—was handsome, too, but in a less striking way. Alice Montgomery described him as "seventeen going on forty," and it was true, he was altogether too serious for a boy his age. Still, Joanna admitted wistfully, she didn't know how she could manage things without him. He seemed to miss nothing connected with the ranch; for that matter, he seemed to think of nothing but the ranch. At times Joanna felt guilty about not encouraging outside interests on his part, but at present the ranch was the most important thing in her life as well. Later, when things were more firmly established... well, they'd all have time for more-frivolous pursuits, wouldn't they?

"I can't think, Joanna, why you've chosen such a roundabout way of going. I was under the impression when we set out that we were meant for town." Alice Montgomery held to the sides of the trap as if she feared being bounced out of it.

"There's a wateringhole just a little farther along here," Joanna said, keeping her attention fixed on her driving. "Jay Jay says when he last stopped at it, it was fouled. I wanted to take a look for myself."

"Really, Joanna, all the men you employ, I can't understand why you insist on doing this sort of thing yourself."

"I suppose because I enjoy it," Joanna replied. "Here we are." She reined in the horse.

"I wonder who that man is?" Alice mused aloud.

Joanna followed the direction of her gaze to where a solitary rider sat astride his horse, some distance away. The sun was behind him, making it difficult to see more than a mere silhouette. "William Horse, perhaps, keeping his customary eye on me?" Joanna suggested.

"No, no, I don't think so. But he does seem to be following us."

Joanna laughed. "Really, Alice," she scolded. "There are plenty of pretty señoritas about. I hardly think we'd be the two to catch a passing stranger's eye."

"You may laugh..." Alice said, offended.

Joanna got down from the trap and walked toward the wateringhole, keeping her skirts up; on this occasion she'd submitted to Alice's request that she "dress like a woman, for once."

They were lucky, on Heart's Folly, to have plenty of water. A number of streams crisscrossed the land, and here and there were wateringholes that, except in the driest weather, could be counted on for refreshing oneself or one's horse. Still, this was Texas, the plains—if a watering place went dry, or went bad, it was important to know.

She saw at once that Jay Jay had been right—this hole was tainted. The surface of the water was black and shining, and even at a distance its smell was acrid. Joanna bent and put a finger into the water; it came out with a stain she was at some pains to rub off.

Better not to poison a horse, she thought. The water lay in a pool at the bottom of a rocky embankment; it was not difficult to loosen some of the rocks so that they rolled downward, effectively burying the water hole.

That done, Joanna made her way back to the trap. As she did so, she glanced in the direction in which she had seen the distant horseman before, but he was gone. Some vagrant cowboy, she supposed, perhaps looking for the Folly to ask for work.

She thought no more about him until Alice said, some distance later, "Why, there he is again."

"Who?" Joanna asked, but knew even before she was answered who was meant. She looked, and again saw a horseman on a distant ridge. It was impossible to be certain, of course, that it was the same rider; but Alice was right—he did seem to be following them. "We're not far from town," she said, and whipped up the horse a little, just to be safe. Even if the man rode all out, he'd be hard pressed to catch up with them before they reached town, and she could hardly imagine anyone accosting them in broad daylight on the streets of San Antone. Still, better to be safe than sorry.

After a moment or two, she looked in that direction again. Once more the rider had vanished. She wasn't sure whether to feel relieved or worried; it *was* mysterious, to be sure.

"I never cease dreading all this wilderness," Alice said. "And the people are little better than savages, for all that one tries to civilize them. Is he after us?"

"No. Not a sign of him," Joanna assured her, but she did not slow the horse until they were passing that first cluster of cantinas that marked the edge of town. *Alice's foolishness must be catching*, she chided herself, and once more put the vanishing horseman out of her mind.

She stopped at the little shack in which Lucretia's son, Abraham Lincoln Harte, had been born. Alice remained disapprovingly in the trap, but Joanna, ignoring her, alighted and went toward the building. The little girl, Yolanda, and her mother, Maria, came to stand in the doorway.

"*Gracias, señora.*" Maria thanked her for the basket of food Joanna had brought. Yolanda, accepting the basket, made a little curtsy.

"You know," Joanna said, studying the girl, "we have our own little school now at the ranch. Lucretia handles the classes for now, but we're advertising for a full-fledged teacher. I wonder if it isn't time your daughter thought of schooling?"

Maria gave an apologetic smile. "Yolanda? She is very bright, but, begging the señora's pardon, I do not think you will find her sitting still for so long. She is like a butterfly, that one."

As if to prove her mother's words, Yolanda gave a nervous giggle and disappeared through the curtain into the house.

Joanna sighed. "One can't hope to improve one's life without some education. I know whereof I speak."

Maria's smile faded. "Some of us are what we are born to be," she said.

"We are born to be happy, in my estimation. And free. Ignorance is a form of slavery."

"Then we need not worry," Maria said, brightening. "There is no one freer nor happier than my Yolanda."

Joanna gave it up as a bad cause. They exchanged a few pleasantries before she returned to the buggy and she and Alice continued on their way to the *mercado.*

They left the trap at the local stables, and when they had finished their joint shopping, Joanna suggested taking their packages to the buggy before they strolled to Melissa's where they were to have coffee.

"I've a few things I want to look for at the Emporium," Alice said. "Why don't I just meet you at Melissa's? Oh, there's that bothersome Doña Sebastiano. I suppose we dare not pretend—no, she's seen us. Yoo-hoo, Doña Sebastiano, how nice to see you," she called, and rushed forward as if nothing could give her more pleasure than this unscheduled meeting.

The señora was accompanied by her daughter Nancy. The younger daughter, Carrie, was of course not with them; she could scarcely be persuaded to leave her father and their ranch.

Nancy's early promise of beauty had been more than fulfilled.

Secretly, Joanna tended to scoff at Doña Sebastiano's self-styled title, considering that she was Baltimore-born and -bred. Nancy, however, was physically her father's child, revealing in full the aristocratic lineage from which she had sprung. Her hair had grown darker; it now shone like ebony. Her wide, dark eyes, her ivory skin, her proud, even haughty carriage bespoke the old Spanish nobility that had once ruled here as masters.

She was, as well, a coquette, though without that nervous silliness and fluttering of lashes and fans that most girls her age used as flirtation. Nancy had a way of looking at a man, her eyes widened still more, her tiny mouth pursed, so that she seemed to be burning inside with some all-consuming question, the answer to which only this particular male could provide. If a man remained immune to her beauty—and few did—that question was certain to be his undoing.

The look she gave Joanna, however, was not so charming, though it was distantly polite. Joanna paused only long enough to exchange pleasant greetings before telling Alice that she would carry their parcels to the stables and put them in the buggy.

Before she got there, she met the stables' proprietor, Mr. Carey, just on his way into the nearest saloon. He stopped, looking somewhat embarrassed, when he saw her.

"Mrs. Harte. I was just on my way to have a little, ah, bite to eat. Will you be wanting your trap hitched up?"

"No, no, don't bother, thank you," Joanna assured him; she was well aware of Mr. Carey's penchant for frequent "bites" of the liquid sort. "I'm just leaving some packages for now."

She left the packages in the buggy and turned to leave the stable, but paused, looking around as she always did when she was here alone. It was here that she'd last seen Webb Price; in that very corner they had lain and—

She stiffened at a small, furtive sound. A rat, perhaps? Or was there someone here with her? If the latter, it was someone who meant to be secretive, else they would surely be in plain sight.

She listened. Yes, almost certainly there was someone there, behind that half-closed door that led, if memory served, to a storage area. Her thoughts went at once to the mysterious rider they had seen on their way here; had someone followed them after all?

She was alone here; she glanced around, but there was no one visible in the alley outside. Should she turn and run? she wondered.

There was a rifle under the seat in the trap. She decided it would be best to try to reach it, and strolled toward the buggy as casually as she could, feigning an attitude of having forgotten something she meant to do.

The door in question creaked slightly on its hinges. In two more quick steps, Joanna had reached the trap and, bending inside, snatched up the rifle from its hiding place. "You there," she called aloud, "I know you're there, and I have a gun. You'd better come out now."

"Don't shoot, Mrs. Harte, and don't call out again, please."

The door swung open and a man stepped into view. He was dressed in filthy rags, with the sombrero and sarape of the Mexican peasant, and his beard and hair were matted and unkempt. For a moment, Joanna had no idea who he was, or how he knew her name. Then, suddenly, she gasped and all but dropped the rifle. "Why, it's—" she began, but he put a warning finger to his lips.

"Don't say it," Sergeant Burke begged.

"But—what are you doing here? If they found you here..."

"I'd be shot, probably," he said. "I came to see you. I've been following you at a distance, waiting to find you alone."

"So, it was you we saw. But I still don't—oh, you're hurt."

He had swayed drunkenly and taken a few staggering steps toward her. As he did so, the sarape fell open and she saw what she had not seen before: One of his arms was missing; in its place was a mere stump, crudely wrapped in a tattered bandage.

"I lost it at Vicksburg," he said. "That's where I've come from. I'm on my way to Washington, to deliver some letters. Then it's a discharge for me. The army needs men with both arms."

"You've come a bit out of your way—and into enemy territory at that."

"I came for Lieutenant Price. I made him a promise." He hesitated, his eyes on hers, then drifting away, and back again. "We used to talk, him and me, the way soldiers do before a battle. He told me about—well, about how he felt toward you. He asked me, if anything was to happen to him, if I'd come to tell you about it myself."

Joanna caught her breath. She could not bring herself to ask the obvious question. After another moment, the sergeant answered it for her.

"He's dead. At Vicksburg," he said.

It was Joanna's turn to stagger. The sergeant moved to her side, supporting her with his one arm.

"No, it can't be true," Joanna said, shaking her head. "I don't believe it."

"It's true," he said, gently but firmly. "I saw him fall myself, just before the blast that—that did this to me. Later, when I'd got out of the hospital, I went over the dead lists myself. His name was on it. He was already buried by then. But I took some flowers, picked them in the woods, put them where he'd fallen, the graves weren't marked yet."

Joanna fumbled in her reticule for a handkerchief and dabbed at her eyes. It was impossible to believe. Her last memories of him had been of love and strength and passion—of life. And now, like the turning of a page in a book, he was gone.

Beside her, Sergeant Burke shifted his weight wearily, bringing her back to the present. She honked rather unceremoniously into her handkerchief and looked at him through her tears. "That wound is festering, sergeant," she said in a businesslike tone. "And you look entirely exhausted."

"I rode day and night," he said with a sad smile. "This little detour wasn't exactly sanctioned by the army."

"No, I can imagine not. You must come to the ranch with me. We can feed you, at least, and do something with that infection...."

There was a step outside, and Doña Sebastiano appeared in the doorway. "Mrs. Harte?" she called into the dimness within. "Mrs. Montgomery asked if I'd tell you, she's gone on to your daughter's and will—oh, I thought you were alone."

More than likely, Joanna thought with a flash of resentment, the old crow heard voices and came snooping. She took a quick step in front of the sergeant, hoping to shield him from view, but it was too late. Doña Sebastiano had traveled here from Galveston in the sergeant's company, as she herself had; it was too much to hope that she would fail to recognize him.

She stared for a moment, as if questioning whether she could believe what her eyes told her. Then, wordlessly, she set her lips in a thin, grim line and, turning, walked quickly away.

Sergeant Burke moved to take the rifle Joanna still held.

"No," she said sharply. "You can't."

"She'll sound the alarm," he said in an angry, agitated voice.

"Probably. Quick, we'll go to the ranch. Is that your horse? Heavens, he looks worn out. Hitch him to the buggy—you can ride with me."

The sergeant shook his head. "I'll only be putting you in danger," he said.

"I've been there before. Let's not waste precious time. Help me put this top up; if you sit well back, no one will see your face."

"Locking the barn after the horse is gone, isn't it?" he asked, but he helped put the top up on the trap, and hitch up her horse. In only a couple of minutes, Joanna was driving the buggy pell-mell along the alley outside, with the sergeant sitting well back in the passenger seat beside her.

They reached the ranch without incident. Lewis was on the front porch playing with Abraham Lincoln Harte, as he often was. Joanna swept the sergeant by him with only the briefest of explanations. Gregory was on the stairs, on his way down from the office to investigate. She sent him back to the balcony outside her room, where he was to watch the road from town with a spyglass, warn her of any approach.

Of all of them, Lucretia seemed the least surprised to see this northern soldier. She took in his wasted appearance, gave the wounded stump of his arm one quick glance, and set to work. While Sulie prepared food at her direction, she set water to heat on the stove, sent Joanna for clean cloth for bandages.

The sergeant ate first, wolfing down the food. He was still eating while Lucretia cut away the sleeve of his tunic, baring an ugly mass of flesh, red, green, purple. Using one of her razor-sharp kitchen knives, she cut in two places where it was festered. Joanna turned away from the sight of pus, then made herself swallow and put aside her revulsion. The sergeant continued eating the whole time, though for a moment Joanna thought he might lose some of what he'd eaten, when Lucretia put the red-hot poker from the stove to the wound to cauterize it. The smell of burning flesh made Joanna's legs weak.

A poultice was applied over the burns, and a clean bandage over everything. The entire operation had taken less than half an hour.

"I'm obliged," Sergeant Burke said, testing the severed arm gingerly. "I expect I'd better be getting on my way. Wouldn't do for them to find me here if they come looking."

"I'm going with him," Lucretia said.

Every eye in the kitchen turned toward her.

"Well, now, look," the sergeant said, "I don't think that a—"

"It'll be a lot safer for him," Lucretia said, talking to Joanna as if the sergeant weren't even there. "People'll be less likely to think he's a Yankee, traveling with a slave wench. And I can look after that wound for him; it's going to need some attention for a while.

Anyway, he's too weak to look after himself proper."

"Well, now, see, I can travel faster—" the sergeant tried again.

"I can bandage his throat," Lucretia went on. "Say he was wounded there, too, lost his voice. That way I can talk for him—no one'll have to hear that accent of his."

"But I don't understand why..." Joanna said. "Why go at all?"

"There's blacks up north doing things," Lucretia said. "Educating people, giving lectures. Raising money. Encouraging the war effort. I could help. I know I could. Better than staying here cooking. Sulie can do that, and Angel. And you know how I feel about people hereabouts."

"That's true, I do see," Joanna said. She was thoughtful for a moment. "I can't give you permission, of course."

"I wasn't asking it." Lucretia smiled fleetingly. "But—there's one thing. I'd be grateful if you'd look after my boy. I don't know what my life will be like up there. I'd feel better knowing he was looked after."

"I'll treat him as my very own," Joanna promised.

"And I'd like your blessing."

"Which you have. My love and my prayers will go with you every step of the way."

The two women embraced, both fighting back the tears that threatened. The sergeant looked from one to the other of them. It looked as if the matter were settled. He scratched his head with his good hand. "Can you ride?" he asked Lucretia.

"We'll take the cart," she said, not even bothering to ask if Joanna minded. "I can drive that. And I'll ride in back when we go through towns, like a good darky."

He grinned. "Well, then, I guess that's that. We'd best get that cart hitched up, I suppose."

There was another flurry of activity. Jay Jay hitched horses to the lightest of the ranch's carts. Lewis fetched an armload of clean clothes. "Don't imagine they'll fit," he said apologetically, "but they're bound to smell better." Sulie and Angel, under Lucretia's directions, loaded food and water—flour, beef jerky, salt.

Joanna found herself laughing unexpectedly. "When I think," she explained to the others, "of the weeks and weeks we spent preparing to travel from Galveston—if I'd only known it could be done in minutes."

"There was a boy in our company, came from Ohio, had an expression," Sergeant Burke said. "A gun up your butt puts wings on your feet—begging your pardon, ma'am."

Gregory came running down from the balcony; Joanna saw that he carried the rifle that hung on the office wall. "Riders coming from town," he said breathlessly. "A posse, looks like."

"I'll buy you all the time I can," Joanna said. "And, sergeant, thank you. I'll always remember what you did for me.

He looked agonizingly embarrassed. "Ma'am," he managed to say; but Lucretia was already in the cart.

"Get in," she commanded imperiously, and he had no more than scrambled up beside her than she was whipping up the horses, and they were gone, not even time for goodbyes.

The trap was still hitched up, as she'd left it when she arrived. She glanced at Jay Jay; as usual, he was wearing his guns. "I hope those are loaded," she said. "Come with me. Give me the rifle," she told Gregory, but to her surprise, he stepped back from her out-stretched hand.

"I'm coming with you," he said.

"Don't be silly," she started to say; Gregory couldn't hit a barn broadside, everyone knew that; but she looked into his face, and changed her mind. "Very well—but quick, before they reach the gate."

They made it barely in time. The sheriff and the five men riding behind him were nearly at the gate when Joanna jumped down from the still-rolling buggy. She stood directly in their way. "That's far enough, sheriff," she greeted him.

He reined in his horse, studying her thoughtfully for a few seconds. In his mouth was an unlighted cigar, which he chewed from one side to the next.

"Heard a rumor, Mrs. Harte," he said finally. "Heard there might be a Yankee spy here. Came out to take a look."

"You heard wrong," Joanna said. The boys had taken up positions on either side of her.

"Now, you know, the lady as told me, she seemed to know what she was talking about. I reckon maybe, just to be safe, I'd better see for myself." He grinned insolently. "Wouldn't want to think of you folks as being in any danger."

"We're not, I assure you."

"Step aside, Mrs. Harte. I mean to ride up to your house now."

"I'm afraid that won't be permissible," Joanna said firmly.

"I need to remind you, Mrs. Harte, I am the law in these parts."

"Your parts stop at those gateposts. This is my land, and I say who comes on it and who doesn't."

His angry glance went from one to the other, and came back to Joanna. "Who's going to stop me, I wonder," he said with a scornful smile. He swung himself down from his saddle. "You ain't even got a gun, and your oldest boy there, he ain't got sense enough to take the safety off that there rifle he's holding. You think that little pipsqueak there—"

He never finished. Joanna hadn't even seen Jay Jay reach for his pistol. From nowhere, it seemed, there was a gunshot, and the tip had vanished from the cigar in the sheriff's mouth.

They all stared at the smoking gun in her youngest son's hand.

"Why, you little bastard," the sheriff swore, reaching for his own gun; Joanna noticed that the men on horseback behind him looked uncertain whether or not to do the same. "I'll ram that..." Again he left his threat unfinished. He suddenly looked past Joanna.

She glanced over her shoulder, hearing the hoofbeats the same moment he had. What they both saw were Lewis and William Horse approaching in a cloud of dust, William Horse looking every bit as fierce as his forebears must have looked riding down upon some terrified party of settlers, Lewis riding as Joanna had not seen him ride since the fields of South Carolina. Behind these two, in an uneven line, came at least fifteen or twenty others, workmen from the ranch—blacks, whites, Mexicans, some of them born to the saddle, others barely able to ride, all of them with an unmistakable air of purpose.

In another moment Lewis was beside her, William Horse off to one side where, of course, he would have a clear shot with the rifle he held, without endangering Joanna. A moment more and the others began to arrive, forming a rapidly growing line of men ranged behind the Hartes. All of them were armed.

The sheriff chewed, and looked, and chewed some more. "This is serious business, Mrs. Harte," he said finally.

"My people think so," she said.

The sheriff fixed his attention on Lewis. "What kind of man are you, anyway," he demanded, "letting your wife give orders—you got no pride?"

To Joanna's surprise, Lewis laughed aloud. "Pride? Why, man, we are the Hartes, of Heart's Folly, San Antonio. We got more pride here than we know what to do with."

At that, all of them—at least, all of them on one side of the gateposts—laughed with him.

The sheriff clambered back into his saddle. "We just might be back," he said.

"Leave your guns in town, I'll fix fresh coffee for you," Joanna said. She watched them ride back the way they had come, casting an occasional apprehensive glance over their shoulders.

"What'll we do if they come back?" Gregory asked.

"Let them come," Joanna said. "By that time, Lucretia and the sergeant will have enough of a head start, the way she was driving."

In all that had happened, Joanna had completely forgotten Alice Montgomery, until, some time later, a warning once again went up that someone was approaching.

This time it turned out to be a highly disgruntled Alice, driving a buggy she'd had to borrow from Melissa.

"I declare, Joanna, if you aren't the world's single most thought-less person, never an idea in your head of anyone else. Was I supposed to walk clear back from town? I wonder. First you dis-appear, and then Doña Sebastiano, and finally I said to Melissa, "Well, it does seem as if not a single soul even remembers I'm alive." ... What is that, pray tell?"

Joanna and Sulie were burning the bandages and the tunic they'd taken from Sergeant Burke, feeding them a piece at a time into the kitchen stove.

"We had company," Joanna said. "I'll explain after a bit."

"Company? But that looks like—surely that's part of a Yankee uniform, isn't it?"

"A Yankee spy," Jay Jay said, grinning mischievously. "We caught him hiding in the house. In your room, matter of fact."

"Under the bed," Gregory added, getting into the spirit.

"He ran off with Lucretia," Lewis said.

"A Yankee...under my... Oh, Lord, Lord," Alice cried, her eyes going from one face to another before they finally rolled heav-enward and, with a whimpering sigh, she sank in dead swoon.

TWENTY-ONE

I t was ironic that the last shot of the Civil War was fired in Texas, where hardly any action had occurred. This final battle, at Palmito Hill, near the mouth of the Rio Grande, took place more than a month after the surrender at Appomattox; the soldiers had not heard that the war had ended.

On the Fourth of July, General Joseph O. Shelby crossed the Rio Grande with what was left of his army. He paused in midstream to lower the last unsurrendered Confederate flag into the muddy brown water before he rode into Mexico, and the pages of history.

"I was right, wasn't I, Joannie?" Lewis asked from his sickbed. "It did keep us out of it, didn't it, bringing us here?"

"Yes, Lewis, you were right," Joanna agreed with him. She saw no reason to point out that in every other particular—preserving their way of life, Eaton Hall, their slaveholdings—he had been wrong. The important thing was, after all, they were here, and for that she owed him.

Now he was ill; had been, of course, for a great many years—what else could you call his drinking but an illness?

"It's his liver," the doctor had pronounced, with no more than a cursory examination. "You can see that by how yellow he is. It's all that liquor. He'll have to give that up if he wants to live out the year."

So had begun a battle that had occupied Joanna and Sulie, and to a lesser extent nearly everyone on the Folly, for months far more fully than the ending war: the struggle to keep Lewis from liquor, and vice versa.

Lewis tried, she could see that. He would promise, he would weep over his failings and beg forgiveness, and then for some time he was the model of sobriety, and Joanna fancied she could see him getting better.

Then, somewhere, somehow, he'd get his hands on a bottle, the craving would get too strong for him, and just like that, he was back where he'd started, drunk, scarcely able to sit up in bed, let alone leave it, his skin turning as yellow as the huisache blossoms in spring.

Then, when they'd dried him out again—and now Joanna had good reason to be thankful for Sulie—it would start all over again— the tears, the remorse, the self-flagellation, the reform, and, just as inevitably, it came to seem, the relapse, each one growing more serious, taking a more obvious toll.

Until he died, not long after asking his wife if he hadn't shown foresight in bringing them here when he did.

There were some who were surprised by the grief Joanna displayed, and even a few who assumed it must be false, but they, of course, did not know the widow well. Joanna's sadness was not feigned. She was sad not because she missed him but in a sense because she didn't. She couldn't miss the marriage they had never had. She couldn't even remember the events that had led to their children; those might as well have come by stork.

Lewis was like someone left behind when you started on a journey, standing by the road, waving, getting smaller and smaller each time you looked back, until he was gone and you weren't sure if he had vanished or simply left on a journey of his own when you weren't looking.

When he was buried, when the mourners—a surprising crowd of them, it seemed to Joanna—had gone and she could be alone with her own remorse, Joanna went to her room and carefully, one by one, emptied her closets and wardrobes of all their prettily colored outfits—dresses of green and amethyst, yellow and purple, mauve and amber, and put these aside to take into town to give to the Mexican woman, Maria. She had wanted to do something—a gesture, something—in memory of the man who had, however unwillingly, given her all that she had now. She had looked at herself in the mirror, dressed all in black, severe, older than she'd yet realized she was, and had vowed that this was the color she would wear henceforth.

If her choice of mourning black was influenced, too, by the loss of Webb Price, why, that was something private: it would not take away from the public respect she would pay her husband. No one would know—or the few who did would never mention it. Lewis had not been the only one she wedded to herself.

Now where, she wondered, *had that thought come from?*

But she chose not to pursue it. Just now, having just buried her husband, having found it unavoidable to take stock of herself, of her life, her situation, she had decided that there were things about herself that did not look so fine under close scrutiny.

Yet all along she had done what she had to do, for the sake of others as well as her own. Fate had so determinedly flung open those doors through which she had only blindly marched. Who would it have served for her to balk on the threshold? Men made their own destiny; she'd had to snatch frantically at the few shreds that came within reach of her grasp. Women were chained to their pasts, bartered for their futures. Was she to feel guilty for demanding that the present be hers?

Don Sebastiano waited a full six months before he came to propose a marriage.

"It is partly my ranch that brought me here," he said, "my concern for it. Though it is not what Heart's Folly is, to be sure, still, it is my life's work. And I grow old. Someday before too many years have gone by, it will pass into—into whose hands? I ask myself. My wife does not care for it, nor does my oldest daughter."

"But surely Carrie adores it as you do," Joanna said.

"She is but a child."

"A child will become a woman."

"Even so—she is not the one to run a ranch on her own."

"I run Heart's Folly."

"And you are a most remarkable woman," he said, grinning widely.

"Anyway, you're exaggerating the seriousness of the situation. You're not that old."

"I am older by far than the husband you lost. And death sometimes comes unannounced. It is best to be prepared for her visit.
But it is not my wish to be morbid. I have a proposal to make to
you. You have a son. I have a daughter. Our properties adjoin; it
is logical that they should become one."

Joanna was surprised, though she could immediately see the
logic of what he suggested. Gregory and Nancy—he, sober, overly
occupied, perhaps, with the Folly; so far as she knew, he'd had no
time for courting. And she was beautiful; it would be a rare man
indeed who didn't find the prospect of possessing that vixen a
tempting one—though whether any man, particularly one so un-
assuming as Gregory, was ever really likely to possess her, Joanna
had some doubts.

More to the point,, Rancho Sebastiano would in effect become
part of the Folly; that already immense kingdom would have en-
larged its borders without, as most nations did, having to go to war.
And it was a time-honored tradition, wasn't it? How many empires
had grown swollen on the sheets of the marriage bed?

"I shall have to think about that, of course," she said, but her
smile was encouraging. "And certainly I will need to discuss the
matter with my son. No doubt you will want to take it up with your
daughter as well."

"I will decide for my daughter."

"I'm afraid I haven't such unbridled authority to speak for my
son," Joanna said.

Which they both knew was not entirely true.

If Joanna rarely underestimated herself, she had a failing in
often underestimating others, of underestimating men in particular.

She underestimated Don Sebastiano's feelings for her. In that,
Doña Sebastiano was shrewder than Joanna, for she did not share
in that mistake. She was aware of her husband's feelings from the
first; perhaps even sooner, for she often thought she'd had some
premonition of them from the time she herself first laid eyes on
Joanna.

He was awed by Joanna, and intimidated by her; that could be
fatal to any relationship between a man and a woman. But she
exhilarated him, too. When he had been to see her, even for a
brief, formal, visit, he felt as if he had traveled some great distance,
not only a greater distance than what lay between his ranch and

hers but some vast distance beyond himself. He could see that she lacked the faith in men that she had in herself. Weak men would ever fail her, strong men threaten her.

But Joanna had underestimated, too, Don Sebastiano's intentions for their properties. Of course, she was right in supposing, in believing what he said, that he wanted to preserve what he had built. He loved his ranch, despite the fact that it had never really been a success. It was something of himself—in one sense the son he'd never sired. And yet he was entirely aware that in bringing the two ranches together, it was his that would be absorbed into the other.

Just as he had always believed in the destiny of his beloved Texas, through Spanish colonialism, through Mexican rule, and wars, and independence, and finally statehood, he was always sure that Texas would triumph in the end as what she had always been—Texas. And so he perceived some destiny for that ranch, greater than he could grasp, greater even than Joanna herself, or her vision for it.

Rancho Sebastiano would be his gift to that destiny; whatever it became, a part of his blood, his soul, would have flowed into it, merged with it.

That was why he had been so confident of his daughter's doing as he wished. Certainly, what he proposed was not pleasing to her mind.

"Never, never, never" was her reply. "A thousand times never."

His wife sided with their daughter. "You are mad to suggest such a thing. Even if she were to agree, I would not."

"You are mistaken, both of you, if you thought you heard a request," Don Sebastiano told them calmly with the haughty imperiousness of which the Spanish were masters. "It has been decided. You will marry Gregory Harte. What's more, you will go to live with him on Heart's Folly."

For the merest fraction of a second, Nancy's dark eyes flickered with interest. The Folly was grand—far, far grander, certainly, than Rancho Sebastiano. One could live like a queen there....

But, she remembered at once, that world had its queen already, one hardly likely to abdicate. There, she would be but one more subject.

If it were the younger son, after a few more years...but the older one, he was a bore, and so dominated by his mother.

"I will not marry him," she said aloud, defiantly, firmly.

"Then you may find it hard to marry anyone."

She tossed her head, showing her father a cruel smile that few men were permitted to see from her. "You think I have no ad-mirers?" she demanded.

"You will find that a penniless girl has fewer than a girl with a dowry."

"Penniless . . . ?" It took her a moment to grasp his meaning. She gasped, in anger and surprise.

"Yes," he said, and his smile, too, was, briefly, cruel. "Yes, I will disinherit you if you refuse to do as I say. There is another son. And another daughter. And I promise you, if I must wait for them to reach an age to marry, everything I have will be theirs. You will receive nothing. Perhaps you will not like living on your sister's charity."

Nancy's eyes flamed with anger. She despised her sister nearly as much as she despised the prospect of living on anyone's charity.

"You cannot disinherit your own daughter," Doña Sebastiano cried.

"Your daughter," her husband replied. "If she will not obey, she is no longer a daughter of mine."

He turned and started from the room, the signal that the con-versation was over, the subject closed.

Nancy, seeing the lay of the land, made the quick choice of the opportunist. She sobbed aloud. "Very well, papa," she said to his departing back. "I will do as you command me, though it breaks my heart."

Having capitulated, she now threw herself into the role she thought likely to bring her the greatest advantage. Weeping loudly, she threw her hands over her face and dashed around her father, making her exit before him.

Don Sebastiano, stopped in his tracks, looked after her briefly, wondering at the extent of his triumph. He knew his daughter too well; she would take revenge, somewhere, on someone. Privately, he did not envy his future son-in-law.

He felt his wife's eyes on him, and turned with reluctance to meet them.

"So," she said, with a voice like the lash of a lariat, "the fine widow will take our daughter in slavery?"

"I have done what I thought best," he said, suddenly weary.

"For whom?"

"For all of us. For this ranch. Had you thought, wife, what would become of it if I were to die? Would you manage it, make it another Folly?"

"Fool. You think I haven't given that question any thought? You think I haven't already investigated what price I could get for it? I would sell it in a week, if you would but convenience us by dying."

He sighed. He had long since lost any illusions he might have had regarding his wife's affections for him. "Then I have certainly done the right thing," he said.

"We shall see. We shall see."

She, too, went out, leaving Don Sebastiano alone in the room. For some time he stood silently, listening inside himself, feeling tentatively for that quick stab of chest pain that had become, of late, such a familiar companion.

Joanna's interview with Gregory was less stormy, but in some ways just as troublesome.

He sat at his desk the whole while she broached the subject, outlined the possibilities, argued the advantages to be gained by the match she was suggesting.

"Only suggesting," she repeated.

He nodded, and waited for to go on. His face told her nothing. He was weighing what she said in the same way he would weigh her ideas for a change in their crops, a need for more or fewer hands to work the harvest. They might indeed have been discussing some aspect of the ranch's business management.

And in a way, she supposed they were.

It came to her out of the blue, even while she was talking: She really didn't know her son at all. Oh, she knew that business side of him, could more often than not predict his judgment on ranch questions, was accustomed to the way he worked. She took his loyalty, his dedication to the Folly, for granted.

But for perhaps the first time, she saw him as a man, and that side of him was a stranger to her. What feelings, what emotion, what longings and fears coiled within him like snakes waiting to strike? Did the thought of that regal beauty fill him with desire, or trepidation? There was no one else, surely. She had not so much as seen him looking at a girl.

Or would she even have noticed?

She had finished, a trifle lamely, after an enthusiastic beginning. Gregory sat expectantly, as if unaware that she had finished. Joanna made a little gesture, spreading her hands palms upward.

"So," she said. "The decision is up to you, naturally. Your happiness must come first."

"Yes. Of course." He got up from his desk then and went to stand at the window. Joanna did not need to join him to see the view as he saw it; it was one she had memorized long ago.

"And the girl?" he asked without turning. "She is willing?"

"I am assured she is." For only a second or two, Joanna felt a sudden urge to leap up, go to him, urge him to decline, insist after all that the suggestion was a foolish one. This was not some European duchy, with princes and queens deciding borders, staving off wars, enlarging empires; this was a question of two neighboring ranches, one of them already too large to be of practical use to her.

But as if reading her thoughts, he said, "It would add nearly seventy thousand acres to the Folly, wouldn't it?"

She was not surprised that he should know the size of Don Sebastiano's holdings. "Something like that," she said. "Of course, the Folly is already enormous...."

"Size can be intimidating. To others, I mean. Big men often don't even have to fight."

"Often when they do, they prove to be ill suited for it."

"But," he said, "a man both big and clever can have things pretty much his own way."

"Yes. That's true."

He turned abruptly from the window. "What date shall we set for the wedding? Not, I think, until after the picking."

She did not remind him that it was the bride's privilege to choose a date. In that regard, she and her son understood one another well enough. The Hartes made their own rules here.

That was the point, wasn't it?

TWENTY-TWO

S oon after the announcement of her daughter's engagement to Gregory Harte, Doña Sebastiano made an announcement of her own: She would be leaving the ranch and setting up residence in the town of San Antonio itself. This was relatively easy to accomplish, since like many of those living on outlying ranches, the Sebastianos kept a small house in town anyway. In the future, she would remain there.

Furthermore, she informed her husband, while she would attend the wedding itself as the mother of the bride, that was the only concession she intended to make to what she called "this mockery."

It may have been that she expected her husband, or at least her daughter, to plead with her; neither did. And whether Don Sebastiano felt any relief at knowing his wife would not be exercising any future quarrelsome influence, Joanna was certainly grateful.

As for Nancy, she fully intended to have her revenge, as her father had so rightly guessed, but it would not be in the form of niggling arguments over this protocol or that wedding detail— which, she was sure, would have been her mother's way; for that reason, she, too, was glad to have her mother absent herself from the arrangements.

Nancy hated the Hartes, in particular Joanna. She hated them for having so spectacularly eclipsed her socially. Only Melissa could be forgiven, and only because by marrying, and by marrying a man whose fortune was limited within certain boundaries, she had more or less removed herself from the arena.

Now, Nancy was being forced, against her will—an act that in any circumstances was likely to enrage her—to marry a man she despised, the son of a woman she bitterly hated. She would marry Gregory, for her own sake, not theirs; but they would pay for this humiliation, that she had vowed.

Still, no one would have guessed at her feelings from her smiling show of acquiescence. The only one with any inkling of how she really felt was her father, who knew her better than she thought, and liked her less than she imagined.

The wedding took place at the Folly; Joanna politely asked Doña Sebastiano if she objected to its being there instead of at Rancho Sebastiano.

"Why should we pretend this is anything but an acquisition?" Doña Sebastiano had replied coolly.

Despite the señora's coolness and the bride's lack of enthusiasm, Joanna had determined to spare nothing to make the event a success. She even took the liberty of arranging for the groom's wedding gift to his bride: an awesome strand of amethysts, each nearly the size of a robin's egg, each encased in its own delicate web of gold filigree.

To her surprise, Gregory seemed disappointed when he saw the necklace.

"You've no idea what a job it is to get something like that in San Antone," Joanna informed him, annoyed by his failure to be impressed.

"Oh, I can imagine," Gregory said. He did not point out to her that he himself had paid the bill, though he had supposed at the time that it was for something Joanna had bought for herself.

After a moment, he raised his eyes from the necklace and looked directly at her. "She'll be expecting the yellow diamonds," he said.

"She what?" Joanna looked at him as if he had taken leave of his senses.

"She mentioned them."

"And pray why should she presume to do that?"

"You wore them at your picnic. Everyone saw them. Father

bragged about them. He told a great many people, the Sebastianos among them, that they were his wedding gift to you, that they belonged to his mother before that; she wore them on her wedding day and then gave them to him to give to you for your wedding. It's logical for Nancy to expect you to hand them down to your oldest son's wife."

"I don't see what's so logical about it," Joanna snapped. The diamonds were her favorite jewelry and, not coincidentally, her most precious. She had always thought of them as a form of insurance against disaster; they could never really be without resources, so long as she had her diamonds.

Gregory did not argue the point, but as he sat looking at her from his desk, closing the case that held the amethysts with a soft but definite snap, his expression was easy to read. He had cooperated in this merger they had agreed to between them; he was doing his part without cavil.

With a flush of guilty resentment, Joanna strode to her dressing table and yanked open the drawer in which she kept the diamonds. "Here," she said, all but flinging the case at him. "Give them to her. I hope they choke her."

She herself wore the amethysts, their shimmering violet hue a lovely contrast to the red-gold of her hair and the stark black of her dress, a rich brocade embroidered with flowers of gold thread. She was hardly mollified by the compliments she—and the amethysts—received.

Nor did it give her pleasure to have to agree with the many guests who so fervently declared they had never seen a lovelier bride.

Nancy made her appearance at the head of the main stairs, descending slowly on her father's arm, amid a chorus of oohs and ahhs, to the parlor, where the wedding itself took place; subsequently, the bride and groom and their three parents would walk over a red plush carpet to the chapel, where the priest would give the union his blessing before they emerged to greet the waiting throng. Nancy, to Joanna's surprise, had proved entirely agreeable to all of Joanna's arrangements. Only her gown had been chosen by the bride herself, and, seeing it, Joanna could easily guess that it had been chosen all along with the diamonds in mind.

The dress was of watered silk, the color of old ivory, and trimmed in Spanish lace that was more than one hundred years old and had come with the Sebastianos from the mother country. With her dark hair and lashes, her alabaster complexion, and Joanna's diamonds casting near-blinding reflections, Nancy was resplendently beautiful.

Surely, Joanna thought, half listening to the vows being recited, her son could not regret such a prize. What man present was not envying him just at that moment?

His brother was, certainly. Jay Jay, miserably uncomfortable in the stiffly starched shirt and tight fitted suit his mother had demanded he wear, looked at his brother's wife with barely concealed lust.

Lust, unfortunately, seemed to be with him full-time of late; his mind was almost never free of the most lurid, the most tantalizing, fantasies involving virtually every female he knew or happened to see. "I think I'm losing my mind," he had recently confided to his friend William Horse. And William, observing the many and varied sources of the young man's distress, had only smiled tolerantly.

Fidgeting, Jay Jay forced himself to look away from the bride's lush figure—a waist that looked no more than a hand's span around, hips and breasts of maddening fullness. He looked toward the open window, where a crowd of Mexicans were straining together for glimpses of what was happening inside.

And found himself looking straight into a pair of wide, dark eyes, glinting with some mischief of their own.

The girl saw him look at her and smiled, a swift, darting flash of a smile, before she ducked down and out of sight in the throng.

For a few seconds, Jay Jay seemed to see her still there, like one of those lightning-scoured landscapes that linger before your eyes when the darkness has swallowed them up again. Thick, sweeping cascade of dark hair, darker even than Nancy's, made darker still by the single yellow rose pinned in it; scarlet lips, parted, shining wetly. He knew that face, it was familiar, and yet, not familiar— but where...

Joanna nudged him sharply with an elbow and he dragged his eyes back to the now-concluding ceremony, to find that the bride's beauty no longer made his trousers feel a size too small.

Later, with the wedding party in full swing, he made a slow circuit of the grounds, looking for the girl whose face he'd seen at the window.

Not one of their regular people; he would know he had seen her before. Not, certainly, one of the wedding guests. One of the extra workers, then, hired to help out for the day.

As if to confirm his conclusion, he saw her just then, moving lightly, gracefully among the guests with a tray of cold meats. She turned, saw him looking at her, and once again flashed one of those taunting smiles at him before she moved toward another group of wedding guests. He saw her laugh—not at him, nor even at some remark from a guest, but more from the sheer delight of being alive, of being young and beautiful, and noticed by a young man.

All at once, he knew—the girl from town; the little shack where Abraham Lincoln had been born. Maria, that was the mother's name, and the little girl was—he thought for a moment—Yolanda, yes, that was it.

Yolanda. And not so little now, either. She wore a white, puffed blouse pulled down off the shoulders to reveal the merest glimpse of pert young breasts, well ripened now, if he was any judge. And her richly embroidered skirt swayed provocatively as she walked.

A real beauty, he decided, grinning. Maybe after all this wedding party wouldn't be as boring as he'd expected.

Gregory danced the first dance with his bride, aware of the admiring looks they got and of the envy in so many men's eyes. That his new wife was beautiful, there was no question. He was no more immune than any other man present, and he looked forward to the night to come with both desire and trepidation.

Most of the time, it was impossible for him to guess what this beautiful creature in his arms was thinking. He did not think himself so dashing a figure that she had chosen him, though he could understand her choosing to marry the Folly. He'd half expected, had been watching for, some sort of resistance—to him, to the ceremony; he wasn't sure exactly what form it might take. So far, however, she had been the very picture of docility, playing her part with cool reserve, but no indication of resentment.

Which made that one, fleeting glance of implacable hatred so much more unnerving when it came. He lost the music and had to apologize for stepping on her foot. She smiled so placidly that he thought surely he must have imagined that other expression in her eyes. But it lingered, troubling him.

He danced with her mother after that, Doña Sebastiano so stiff and unyielding, the movement of her feet so fully concealed beneath her voluminous skirts, that he might have been wheeling a wooden dummy on casters about the floor.

He was grinning from that thought when he took her back to her chair and claimed the obligatory dance with her younger child, Nancy's sister, Carrie.

She responded by smiling back at him as he led her onto the dance floor. Joanna, looking across the room just then, thought that they looked like a pair of mischievous children. It was peculiar, she had not realized until just that moment how rarely she saw her oldest son smile. It made him look younger, and far more handsome than he usually did.

Carrie was looking up into his face, her head tilted back, and for the first time Gregory looked at ease, as if he were actually enjoying this dance. Something the girl said made him laugh, and Joanna had a troubling thought: Had she made a grave error?

Gregory was, without consciously thinking of it, more at ease than he had ever been. Though they had never shared a great deal of conversation, he and Carrie had been far more in one another's company than he and her sister. For one thing, she had been often to the Folly in her father's company; and whenever business had taken Gregory to Rancho Sebastiano, she had nearly always been there. There was a kindred spirit between them, an unspoken but shared loyalty to their ranches, to their parents, a similarity of duties and responsibilities.

A girl after my own heart, he thought, and as soon as the idea came into his mind, he was astonished by the obvious truth of it.

Something of his surprise must have shown on his face, because when she looked up at him just then, her own smile faded into a worried expression. "Is something wrong?" she asked, looking altogether so concerned that he had a sudden, nearly overwhelming desire to take her in his arms and reassure her.

"No, no, I just—it's close in here, let's get some air, shall we?" he said, and without waiting for her reply, led her deftly through the doors standing open nearby, to the moonlit balcony that ran the full length of the ballroom.

"Oh, smell that air," she said, breathing deeply. She spun away from him into the moonlight, the folds of her skirt whispering. "Texas is my favorite perfume," she said.

He moved without thinking, went swiftly after her, had caught her arm and pulled her around, against him, and kissed her, before either of them even knew quite what was happening.

"Oh" was all she said when his lips left hers, their touch seeming to linger rather longer. If her sister's face throughout this afternoon and evening had been carefully devoid of expression, Carrie's now was all too full of it. Every tremulous, hopeful, fearful, heartsick, and gladsome emotion was there to be read with ease.

"My God," he said, bewildered and astonished; how could he not have known, how could he have been such a fool, not to have seen that light that had been in her eyes all along every time she had looked at him? "I'm sorry," he said, for she still had said nothing, could only continue to look at him with all the yearning adoration of which a young lady was capable. "I'm sorry for everything."

With that, he bolted, all but ran back inside, leaving her alone.

She stared after him, the tears that had been threatening all through this endless day misting her vision so that he seemed to move through water. He vanished finally into the crowd, and she turned away, to stand at the railing, her heart threatening to break.

But the next moment, something glorious and magical happened inside her breast, like a field of flowers bursting into bloom all at the same time.

"Oh," she cried aloud, her hands flying to her suddenly burning cheeks. "He kissed me," she told the night. And the Texas wind, that had come all the way from the Gulf for this occasion, sighed rapturously in the branches of the trees.

TWENTY-THREE

O utside, the workers were having their own party. Field hands, kitchen help, maids and gardeners drank and sang and danced together. While those inside glided decorously about in their waltzes, here there were reels, fandangos, even a spontaneous jig.

Jay Jay was still trailing his Mexican beauty. He watched her dance, surprised at the pang of jealousy when she flirted with the young men who partnered her. But at least she favored no one individual; she was not spoken for.

He could, of course, have gone into their midst and claimed her openly for a dance. No one would stop him, certainly. But aside from the fact that his presence would put a damper on their fun, a public meeting was not what he favored.

So, he waited until she left the group, starting alone toward the house. Jay Jay waited for her near the kitchen door.

"Ah," she gasped lightly when he stepped from the shadows; and then, recognizing him, smiled and said calmly, "It is you."

"You don't sound surprised."

"When the hawk hovers so long, it is not surprising if he finally swoops."

He laughed, flattered rather than disconcerted to know that she had been aware of him, too. "Maybe I hovered because I was shy," he said.

Her smile was mocking, unconvinced. "Of what, pray tell?"

He shrugged. "Of asking you to dance, maybe."

She tilted her head to one side, listening. From inside came the sound of violins; from the yard behind her, the energetic strumming of a guitar, the two rhythms creating a melody of their own.

"Your music and mine, they are far different, señor," she said. "They speak not the same language."

He moved toward her, taking her in his arms. "There is only one language for a man and a woman," he said.

They danced in and out of the shadows, but when he lowered his face to kiss her, she slipped from his arms and would have run by him had he not caught her by the wrist.

"Come here," he said, his voice husky.

"I have things to do, señor," she said.

"I said, come here." He yanked violently, making her fall against him, and tried once again to kiss her, but now she resisted him stubbornly.

"I am not yours to command," she said, her eyes glinting angrily in the moonlight. "Let me go."

His mouth found hers, but no sooner had their lips come together than she bit one of his, hard. He yelped and, in his surprise, let go of her. She was gone before he could catch her again.

"Bitch," he swore softly, wiping blood from his lip.

He did not see her again, except at a distance. It was soon evident that she was deliberately avoiding him, and the one time their eyes met, the look she gave him was angry and accusing. He smiled, hoping to coax one from her in return, but she only tossed her hair and looked away.

"To hell with it," he said angrily, and stomped from the house. Angel, he knew, kept a supply of liquor in his shack. Jay Jay went there, found himself a bottle of fiery tequila, and went to sit on the step outside, drinking morosely and occasionally muttering indistinctly.

Alice insisted on making a ceremony of the wedding couple's retirement for the night, though Joanna felt that perhaps it would be better left unobtrusive. The bride was to be accompanied by several of the women—led, of course, by Alice herself—to the bedroom, where they would help her change into her nightclothes. Then the men would bring the groom.

Joanna had seen Gregory return from the balcony where he had escorted the bride's younger sister, and had read misfortune in his flushed and harried expression. Worse, she had looked around instinctively for the bride, and had surprised one of those malevolent looks upon her face that had so startled Gregory earlier. Nancy, too, was watching her husband return to the festivities, and she most certainly recognized as well as Joanna what had just happened.

To the casual onlooker, however, bride and groom seemed much as before. Gregory's demeanor was restrained, and the bride had been cool and reserved throughout the evening.

Nancy was escorted to her bedchamber. An entire suite of rooms had been prepared for the newlyweds in the wing that Joanna had planned all along for the families of her sons. Alice and the others helped remove the splendid wedding dress, and when they left, Nancy was sitting up in the canopied bed, her magnificent hair fanning across the embroidered pillows, her sheer lace nightgown tied back with ribbons to reveal an expanse of creamy bosom. Alice and the ladies tittered as they passed the groom and his escorts in the hall.

Gregory hesitated at the door. He would have liked to go on to their sitting room, to have some time alone to better compose himself; but the guests were waiting farther along the corridor, watching him and already making whispered jokes among themselves over his "shyness."

He knocked discreetly, and went in. His wife was in bed, as the women had left her; but in the interim, she had gotten out to leave a pillow and a blanket on the horsehair divan for him.

Gregory looked at her, and then at the sofa, and back to her again. Her little mouth was curved in the faintest hint of a smile and her dark eyes watched him without blinking.

"I am tired," she said finally. "I wish not to be disturbed."

He crossed the room wordlessly to stare down at her. From here the cleft of her breasts formed a deep and husky valley. He could see a tiny pulse beating at her throat.

"I will not take long," he said, and, kneeling down, took her shoulders in his large hands and kissed her.

Her mouth was unresponsive, but one hand went up, about his shoulders. He took that for a good sign, until he felt the sharp prick of pain in his back, and realized she had stabbed him.

"Damnation," he swore, and lurched back, grabbing her arm and twisting it until the little dagger she held slipped from her fingers and clattered to the floor.

"I ought to..."

She met his furious gaze without flinching, and her smile had grown a little wider. "If you try to force yourself upon me, I will kill you," she told him in a flat, even voice.

For a moment he nearly struck her; he could see in her eyes that she was expecting it, perhaps even welcomed it.

He shoved her arm away and stood up. "Have no fears, señora," he said, "I will not force myself upon you. I have all that I desire from you already."

He strode quickly across the room and went out, loudly closing the door that connected with their sitting room.

His insult hovered on the air after him. Her eyes flaming, she grabbed a little pottery dish by the bedside and hurled it; it shattered against the door, shards flying about the room.

The sky was already growing opalescent with the coming of dawn when Sulie, the last to quit the kitchen, left the big house and hurried on bare feet across the dusty yard to her own little cottage. She left the door standing open and undressed in the dark, glad to have the festivities ended.

"It don't seem like a wedding, somehow," she had confessed earlier to Angel. "I've seen brides aplenty, but I've never seen one as cold as that one."

Now, picturing the bride's face, she shivered unexpectedly, as if someone had walked on her grave. She made a quick sign, an old-world shield against bad omens.

The step outside her door creaked, and the light was blocked by a silhouetted figure. "Who's that," Sulie demanded, more annoyed than frightened. It had been a long day, and night, and she was in no frame of mind to be disturbed now.

The silhouette took a step into the room. "Sulie?" Jay Jay said in a suddenly boyish voice that belied his manly figure.

"Oh. Mr. Jay. What you want this time of night?"

He came closer, swaying slightly; now she could smell the tequila, and she knew the answer to her question before he said anything.

"What do you think?"

She was not particularly surprised. She had been aware of late that he was growing up; it was a rare woman who wouldn't have noticed it in him. Despite herself, she laughed softly.

He took the laugh for assent. She was still naked, and he began to take off his clothes as well. She stood where she was, watching with interest.

"Well," she said after a while, "looks like you're your daddy's son, all right."

"Because I'm drunk, you mean?"

To his surprise, she slapped him. "Your daddy was a good man," she said.

He grabbed her roughly, pulled her violently against his own hard nakedness.

"Don't do that again," he said, not at all boyish. "I'm different from my daddy in a lot of ways."

He kissed her, and the brief surge of fear she'd felt at his violence dissolved into something warmer and far more pleasant. His hands on her buttocks, he walked her slowly backward toward the bed.

In the distant barnyard, one of the roosters began to celebrate the night's ending.

TWENTY-FOUR

"You're up early this morning."
Greg answered his mother with a shrug, and helped himself from the enormous platter of pancakes Sulie set on the table just then.

It had been agreed between them that a honeymoon trip would wait for a more propitious time. Still, Joanna had not expected to see him at his usual morning hour, just after dawn.

She glanced down the table at her youngest son, Jay Jay, too, looked out-of-sorts. For that matter, only Sulie seemed to have anything to smile about, despite all the work she had been saddled with the day before.

"Well, I'm sure your bride will want to sleep in," Joanna said, thinking that after all she appeared to be holding a conversation with herself.

"She's awake," Sulie said, setting a pot of honey down with a thump. "She wants her breakfast served to her in bed."

The two women raised eyebrows at one another. "Serve it," Joanna said. "This time."

"Yes, ma'am." The brisk closing of the kitchen door indicated Sulie's opinion of that sort of coddling.

•

It was nearly noon when Nancy appeared downstairs. Joanna was waiting for her in the parlor. "My dear," she said, smiling, but in a voice that could not be misinterpreted, "now that you're going to be living with us, I think I should help you to understand a little of the way things are run here. You're perhaps accustomed to a more luxurious way of life at home than we enjoy. Most of us work hard here at Heart's Folly. I don't expect that of you, of course— your time is your own, including your choice of hours for rising. However, we do have a set time and place for breakfast; it makes running the household easier. We eat in the dining room, between six and seven. You may have coffee anytime you wish after that. And if you like, I'll arrange for some bread and butter to be left on the table for you."

For an answer, Nancy merely smiled and nodded, to show that she understood.

The following morning, a disapproving Sulie said, "She wants it again. Her Highness has asked for breakfast in her room."

"You may serve her breakfast here," Joanna said.

"It'll get cold."

"Let it."

While they ate, each studiously avoiding looking at the others, they could hear the tinkling of the servants' bell in the kitchen, ringing a little sooner and a little more fiercely each time. Sulie came back and forth, bringing platters of steaks, eggs, oatmeal, and pancakes, and the Mexican girl who was her assistant trotted in and out with biscuits and fresh pots of coffee. In the kitchen, the bell rang. And rang. And rang.

Finally, the ringing stopped. Gregory, who looked as if he had been holding his breath, excused himself and went out. Jay Jay lingered, until a cool look from his mother helped him decide that he was finished.

Joanna sat on alone, sipping coffee and reading some reports Gregory had left for her. Sulie had just brought fresh coffee when Nancy appeared in the dining-room doorway. She was dressed, but her hair had been left down and it flew about her contorted face so that she looked like some avenging fury.

"There you are," she greeted Sulie, ignoring Joanna altogether. "Have you gone deaf? A strip of hide on your back will teach you a thing or—"

"Sit down," Joanna said without looking up.

"Not till I've taken a whip to this insolent nigger," Nancy said.

"I said, sit down."

"I mean to—"

"Sit down." This time there was no mistaking the warning in Joanna's tone. Nancy hesitated for a moment more; then, having turned to look at Joanna's face, she dropped sullenly into a chair.

Joanna did look at her then. "Make no mistake of this," she said. "I am mistress here, and I shall be so long as I live. I may resort to whipping before we've finished this morning, but I assure you, you will not be happy I did so. Do I make myself clear?"

Nancy glowered at her wordlessly.

"I asked," Joanna repeated, "do I make myself clear?"

"Perfectly."

"Good." Joanna turned to Sulie, who had remained standing by the door. "I'm sure Miss Nancy is hungry," she said. "Will you be so good as to serve her breakfast? In the future, if she wants to eat, she'll be down to eat with the rest of us."

Nancy watched in silent resentment as a plate heaped with food—most of it stone-cold—was set in front of her and coffee poured. She made no move to eat or drink.

"I've been wondering," she said after a while, "about what to call you."

"I'm sure you must have considered some possibilities," Joanna said.

"Mrs. Harte seems so formal. Would you prefer..."—she hesitated, and when she spoke the word, it came out as cold and as venomous as a scorpion slithering from beneath a rock—"...mother?"

"Joanna will do nicely, thank you." She gave her daughter-in-law a sweetly bewitching smile.

If there was any doubt that Nancy intended to be a disruptive force on the ranch, her actions soon dispelled it. Familiar with Angel's cooking, and with his sensitivity, she declined even to taste anything he had prepared. She was churlish with the servants, openly rude to her husband, acidly polite to Joanna. She spent money like it was water.

"No one could be more pleased with this marriage," Joanna had confided to Alice, "than Melissa. She must be the happiest shopkeeper in Texas."

Alice sniffed her disapproval; by this time, she had felt the sting of Nancy's bitter tongue.

"You are only a guest here," Nancy had reminded her, a subject on which Alice remained sensitive.

"*My* guest, need I remind anyone," Joanna had replied for her, but Alice had spent an entire day in her room, nursing wounded feelings.

In fact, Joanna found herself spending a great deal of her time tending to wounded feelings—Angel's, Alice's, Sulie's; hardly anyone on the place was spared.

"She's a regular *gato montés*," Jay Jay said, "a real wildcat, for sure." He did not offer to his mother his own opinion of what his brother's wife needed to tame her.

Only Greg made no comment on his wife's behavior, and as he did not mention it, Joanna did not bring the matter up with him. This had been her idea in the first place; and she could not look at her son's face, stern, set, without feeling a pang of guilt.

They were surprised by a visit from the new territorial governor, Wilkinson, who rode up the drive one day in an elegant brougham, accompanied by a party of horse soldiers.

"I'm here to take charge of the reconstruction of this part of the state," he explained when Joanna and an Alice Montgomery all adither had escorted him into the parlor and seen him served a generous glass of bourbon.

"I'm afraid you'll find there's little reconstruction needed," Joanna said. "There were no battles fought here. As I'm sure you must be informed."

"Yes, that's true. But there is the political structure. The federal government wants to see a future Texas committed to the knitting together of our great nation." He took a sip of bourbon and eyed her shrewdly over the rim of the glass. "I have heard that your sympathies were with the North," he said.

Alice raised a dramatic hand to her bosom. "Then you have been sadly misinformed, sir," she declared.

"Mrs. Montgomery is quite right," Joanna said, in a more conciliatory tone. "I will not pretend that I agreed with all the policies of the South. All of my slaves were freed before the war's outbreak. It may have been this that gave rise to the rumor you heard, but I assure you, that rumor was false. We are Texans. Loyal Texans, I may add. And Texas was a Confederate state. We are as guilty as our neighbors in supporting that cause. Food came from here, and other supplies, to help the armies of the South."

"At one time you harbored an officer of the northern army, did you not?"

"That officer's visit here had nothing to do with the cause of the war. And in giving him aid, I am assured that I did no harm to the Confederacy."

"I see." The governor was thoughtful for a moment. "But with the war ended, you are not unfriendly to the North, may I take it?"

"That at least is true. I did not welcome the war, I was glad to see it end, and I will be grateful when all its wounds are healed."

"Spoken like a diplomat," the governor said. "And a friend of peace. As I consider myself. In that, may I consider you an ally? May I call upon your friendship as needed, for the sake of building a strong future for Texas, and the United States?"

"So long as what you ask does not come at the expense of my neighbors. We've heard stories, from other parts of the South. What some call 'reconstruction,' others have labeled 'revenge.'"

The governor finished his drink and got abruptly to his feet. "That will not happen here—you have my word on it. I, too, am eager to see the wounds healed, Mrs. Harte. And I believe it is through the efforts of people like yourself—Texans, like yourself, if you'll permit me—that such a goal is best to be achieved."

Joanna rose with him, smiling. "Then we surely share a common goal, governor. As Texans, and as Americans."

He took her hand and bowed gallantly. "May I add," he said, touching his lips lightly to the backs of her fingers, "I have never met a lovelier patriot. Till we meet again?"

"*Hasta la vista*. We are at your disposal. If you'd care to stay here, at Heart's Folly..."

"Your offer is tempting—but if I may say so, that might invite a certain amount of resentment toward yourself."

"My conscience is clear," Joanna said, and left it at that.

"In any case, a location in town would no doubt be more convenient. I have heard, however, that your cooks are the best in Texas."

"You seem to have heard a great deal about us—though I would not deny that charge. But perhaps you should investigate the matter for yourself."

"I would be delighted, if you'll but set a date. Until then, Mrs. Harte."

"A Yankee," Alice said scornfully when he had gone.

"An influential one," Joanna reminded her. "And if I'm any judge, likely to become even more so. It can't hurt us, Alice, to have the right kind of friends. Heaven knows, we have no difficulty picking up enemies."

"The way you talk," Alice said, drawing herself up haughtily. "You may speak for yourself; I'm sure I have not an enemy in the whole of Texas."

"Well, then," Joanna said, putting a companionable arm about the older woman's shoulders, "let us agree, can't we, that I have enough for both of us."

Both women laughed at that, and went back into the house.

At last Jay Jay thought he had found the cure for what ailed him.

The disease itself was easy to identify: It came with laughing eyes and long, dark hair, and when its ghostly presence visited him during the night, it wore a yellow rose.

The cure had been harder to come by. Sulie had seemed to help; at least, visiting her in the dark had seemed to relieve that unbearable pressure that mounted within him until he thought he would burst from it. But there seemed to be an endless source of that painful longing, for no sooner had he thought he'd relieved it than it was there again, more intense than ever.

He found himself often thinking that all he needed was just to see Yolanda. This conviction would grow, nagging him, until he'd mount up and ride into town, feeling a fool, sure he looked one, too. But there he'd be, riding conspicuously and slowly past her house, till he'd hear her laugh at discovering him, or see her glance from behind the curtained doorway, disappearing as soon as he looked in her direction—which invariably he did, regardless of the promises he made himself.

Drinking didn't help. Fighting didn't help. Riding his horse to near-exhaustion across the trackless prairie didn't help.

Then one day a cowboy he knew approached him with a proposition. A rancher from near Austin was looking for some good hands who could ride and who could shoot, and who were looking for adventure.

"A cattle drive?" Joanna looked at her son in surprise. They were having dinner, and he had sprung his announcement on her without preamble. "To where?"

"Kansas," Jay Jay said. "To the railhead there. See, there's this man up near Austin, Catling's his name, he's been rounding up longhorns out of the bush; he figures he can get a herd together, ride 'em up to Abilene, and ship 'em east. People back there pay good money for beef, even our tough Texas steers."

"But, Kansas, that means traveling hundreds of miles, through wilderness. Indian country. There's not even any reliable maps...."

"That's the beauty of it," Jay Jay said, warming to the subject. "There's this trader named Chisholm, half Cherokee he was, he made the trip, mapped out a trail. There's no hills and no woods— hard for the Indians to jump you unexpected. And no towns— you can drive the cattle straight through. He says it's the future. He says cattle will be the big thing here in Texas; cotton's dying."

"He's right about cotton," Joanna said. "It's getting so it's hardly worth the planting." She hesitated, studying her son. She did not know exactly what, but she was certainly aware that something had been bothering him of late. Walking around all the time with a chip on his shoulder, drunk more nights than she'd cared to notice— this was the first she'd seen any show of eagerness in him in a long while.

"Well, you're old enough, and God knows you can take care of yourself," she said.

"You know I'm no good around here," he said. "I'm not cut out to be a farmer."

Joanna sighed; that was certainly true enough. "When will you leave?" she asked, and was glad to see the grin spread across his young and handsome face.

"Day after tomorrow," he told her.

The last thing he did was to go see Yolanda. He had never been inside the shack before, never been so far as the door except the time Lucretia's Abraham had been born.

He did not knock, but dismounted, strode straight to the door, and, flinging the dusty curtain aside, stepped in.

The mother was cooking; she turned from the stove, her eyes large with alarm, her mouth open. At one time, a fair number of men had been accustomed to appearing in that doorway, at odd hours; but since she'd been befriended by the señora from the big ranch, Maria had steadfastly turned her back on her old way of life, and no one had come in like that in years. When she saw who it was, she was even more anxious.

He only nodded curtly in her direction, his eyes raking the room and coming to rest on Yolanda. She was seated at the crude table, grinding corn into meal. She looked not at all surprised, though she'd had no reason to expect the visit. He hadn't known himself that he was coming—and for that matter, couldn't imagine why he had, now that he was here.

"I'm leaving," he said in an angry voice. "I'm driving cattle north, to Kansas, over the Chisholm Trail. I'll be gone four months, five maybe."

He paused; she said nothing, and he could not read the expression in her eyes as she regarded him solemnly.

"I just wanted to tell you," he finished lamely, and whipping about, all but ran back to his horse and vaulted into the saddle with such suddenness that the horse reared and might have unseated a lesser rider.

"Buckaroo," she called—the Texas bastardization of the old Mexican vaquero, cowboy.

He looked and saw her standing in the doorway. She smiled, and for the first time there was no mockery in the smile.

"*Vaya con Dios,*" she called, and taking the rose from her hair, tossed it to him.

He caught it, grinning like a fool, and stuck it in the brim of his hat. "I'll be back," he shouted, and with a wave, he was gone, spurring his horse in a wild dash down the dusty street. He lifted his hat once, and his shout came back to her:

"Ahh-haa, San Antone!"

TWENTY-FIVE

I t had begun to seem to Joanna
that an exodus from Heart's Folly
was under way. Some left without announcement. The carpet-
baggers came with the reconstructionists, and some of them talked
to the few blacks in the area, as they had talked in other parts of
the defeated South, about riches, gold, fortunes to be made. Men
from the Folly were tempted, too, and went off on their quests.
Joanna had heard ugly stories about blacks tricked onto ships in
Galveston, only to find themselves in Cuba or South America, working once more as slaves.

But they still left, convinced that their future was assured.

There were others, too, who had left in a different sense: Lewis;
Webb, of course; and Don Sebastiano, who died only a few days
after Jay Jay had ridden away.

"So now," an apparently griefless Nancy had said to Joanna, "you
are mistress of two ranches." Her father's will had been explicit on
that score: Neither wife nor daughter could be dispossessed, but
the actual running of Rancho Sebastiano was securely in Gregory's
hands—which did, in effect, make Joanna its mistress.

"No," Joanna replied coolly. "Only one; that one has just grown a little larger."

To Alice's suggestion, however, that Nancy might under the circumstances want to spend some time with her mother, Nancy had haughtily replied, "My mother and I have little in common."

Sulie, though, was the last person Joanna would have expected to come to her with the news that she was leaving—to travel north with a group and join Lucretia at her school in Boston.

"The trip is a great deal safer these days, of course," Joanna said, "now that so many are making it. But it's still no small undertaking. Are you sure?"

"Yes. I'm sure," Sulie said. "I'd like to go soon. There's a party getting ready, I understand."

An idea occurred to Joanna. She had recently come through the kitchen early one morning to find Sulie outside the back door, heaving. Now, glancing at her, Joanna thought she detected a telltale bulge.

"Sulie, if you're—in trouble, you know I'll do whatever I can to help," Joanna said.

Sulie smiled sadly. "There's some things even Mrs. Harte of the Folly can't manage," she said with a hint of mockery in her voice. Not for anything did she mean to divulge the name of her child's father. Her mistress might have turned a blind eye toward her husband's fooling around, but a bastard son sired by her youngest, a child who might one day be a threat to her own children's security, that was likely to be another matter. And in any case, here her child would be just that—her white "massa's" bastard, at least in everyone else's eyes. Elsewhere, he might have some chance to grow up normally. Besides, she knew her own heart well enough. She'd grown too fond of that young man who came stealing into her shack at night. Men were funny animals; they'd let that thing between their legs do their thinking for them, and then feel guilty when it went wrong. Jay Jay was in love with that little Mexican gal he liked to follow around; and whether it was her or another, one day he'd be married. Who could tell what that would mean for his illegitimate child by a darky cook?

But that didn't stop her feeling grief-stricken when the day came and Gregory was waiting in the buggy to drive her to meet the family she'd be traveling with. Saying goodbye to Joanna was hard enough, and little Abraham was even harder; since Lucretia had gone, he'd been like her own child.

Finally, she was on her way down the drive, dabbing at her eyes with Joanna's own handkerchief and turning every few yards to wave another goodbye.

Joanna remained on the steps until the buggy was out of sight. Though she was holding his hand, she had all but forgotten Abraham until he unexpectedly asked, "Who's going to take care of me now?"

"Why, I will, darling," she cried, kneeling before him; he was six now, an intense, well-mannered boy. "We all are. I love you, you know."

He accepted the noisy smack she gave his cheek, but the worried expression remained on his face. "If you love me," he asked, "does that mean you'll leave me, too?"

"Oh, my dearest!" Joanna exclaimed, and hugged him fiercely. "Of course it doesn't—it doesn't mean that at all."

Yet even as she tried to reassure him, she found herself wondering if there was some vague truth to his idea. So many had left—was leaving perhaps some part of what love was, some final proof?

She looked up, and saw William Horse standing nearby, watching. She smiled tearfully at him. "Think of William Horse. He'd never leave us, would you, William?"

"No," he said, unsmiling. "Never."

The intensity of his reply surprised her, and she looked more closely at him. *Why, he's in love with me,* she told herself, surprised at what should, now that she faced it, have been obvious to her all along.

Suddenly embarrassed by the longing, by the desire that she saw in his eyes, she looked away and buried her face in Abraham's soft, thick hair.

It was not until Jay Jay returned, till she saw his reaction to the news, that Joanna began to suspect the reason for Sulie's departure. She looked at her youngest son's guilty face, realizing a bit belatedly that he had grown from boyhood to manhood while she wasn't looking. She considered whether she should broach the subject with him and decided against it. Sulie was gone; apparently she had decided on her own solution to the problem. Jay Jay had already announced his plans to leave on another cattle run in a few weeks' time. All in all, she thought it would spare them both some embarrassment if she sought advantage in ignorance.

Jay Jay's love life, however, proved harder to ignore than she had expected. It was only a few days before he was to leave again when Alice, returning from a visit to town, complained indignantly of it.

"People are talking of nothing else," she stated. "Carnal knowledge, of a mere Mexican wench. The very daughter, I might point out, of that woman you so generously befriended, and though I'm not one to say I told you so, you'll forgive my mentioning, I said all along you were being too generous, Joanna. You cannot expect people to simply rise above their station just because you wish it."

"This may all be nothing more than malicious gossip," Joanna said, without much conviction. She had noticed a change in Jay Jay's demeanor since his return, and had rightly suspected that perhaps he was engaged in some minor romance. Since being reminded of his increasing years, she had begun to cast an eye about, thinking ahead to another advantageous marriage—this time with someone more suitable than Gregory's wife had proven to be.

But Maria's daughter—offhand, she couldn't even recall her name, and surely she was no more than a child, wasn't she? Though now that she thought of it, perhaps the girl had grown a little beyond that station, too.

"I hope," Alice said, drawing herself up, "you are not meaning to impugn my honesty. I saw them together myself—they rode right by the Methodist church, like she was as good as anybody, and her laughing and flirting all the while, and your son, the youngest son of Heart's Folly, acting no better than a common scalawag. Or do you suggest that my eyesight has failed me as well as my wits?"

"I'm sure they're both what they've always been," Joanna mollified her. "The question is, what am I to do about it?"

"You most certainly will have to have a talk with your son."

Joanna sighed. "Yes, you're right, of course, but that brings me no closer to knowing what to say."

Certainly she was right in expecting that Jay Jay would not welcome her intervention.

"I can't see it's anyone's business who I court," he said sullenly when Joanna broached the subject.

"There I'm afraid I must disagree with you," Joanna replied. "For one thing, the average Texan's prejudice against Mexicans runs as deep as that of the southerner against blacks, however blindly foolish either may be. You cannot expect to 'court,' as you put it, a Mexican girl without raising the dander of the citizens of San Antone."

"I never noticed you cared much for their prejudices when it involved something you wanted," Jay Jay said.

"I'll overlook your rudeness this once, and simply point out that I, on the other hand, have never deliberately sought the town's disfavor, only our right to live our lives as we choose, here on Heart's Folly."

"Then I'll bring her here," he said ingeniously.

"And have her stoned the first time she reappears in town? It's not just the townspeople I'm concerned about, it's the girl as well. A decent young man doesn't take advantage of a naïve young girl."

He grinned, an altogether too roguish grin, Joanna thought, under the circumstances. "She doesn't seem to feel she's being taken advantage of—as if anybody could, her being as feisty as she is."

"I've no doubt of your ability to turn a young girl's head, Jay," Joanna said sharply, growing annoyed at his stubbornness; it reminded her too much of a younger Lewis. "Nevertheless, that does not mean you aren't taking advantage. The girl is poor, Mexican, easy to dazzle. You are, if I may say so without inspiring conceit, a handsome enough young man. More to the point, you are a Harte, of Heart's Folly, one of the town's more prominent citizens, or will be. You are—forgive me for putting it so baldly—what any young lady would consider a catch. The idea is, we want you caught by someone more suitable."

She regretted that choice of words the moment she had spoken it; and she saw in her son's eyes that it hadn't set well with him, either.

"More suitable? Like that firecracker you stuck Greg with?"

"We're not discussing your brother's marriage," Joanna retorted.

"Nor mine, either." Jay Jay got up from the chair opposite her desk, where he'd sat to hear her out. "I'll do my own catching, mother, thanks for your concern just the same."

"I haven't finished," Joanna said angrily as he strode toward the door.

"I have" was his answer.

He left the ranch that day and did not return. Joanna, fully aware of the fact that she had badly handled their interview, considered going to look for him, and decided instead to wait and give him time to cool down on his own. She knew he loved Heart's Folly as much as she and Greg did; that, if not filial devotion, would bring him home eventually, she was certain.

She counted the days, and when the time had come when he was supposed to have left on his cattle drive, she assumed he was gone, and stopped worrying, though she made note as well of the approximate date he was expected to return.

That day was still some while off when a harried-looking Melissa made one of her infrequent visits to the ranch.

"What brings you so far from that store of yours?" Joanna asked, giving her cheek a perfunctory peck. It was obvious from her face that Melissa had come to air some grief; luckily, she did not take her daughter's griefs too seriously.

"It is because of my store that I am here," Melissa declared. "And our family's reputation, of course."

Joanna could not suppress a slight chuckle at that. "If you're meaning to save our reputation in local circles, I'm afraid you're acting too late," she said.

"Some of us have never ceased trying to repair the damage done by others, though we find ourselves outstripped at times. And, I might say, I am the one who suffers. If the meager profits from my business endeavors continue to dwindle as they have, I shall soon be forced to take my son in my arms and resort to the streets, begging for succor."

This time Joanna laughed openly, which did nothing to soften Melissa's aggrieved expression. "Darling," Joanna said, "if your profits are down, it is most definitely not because Alice and Nancy are failing to contribute their share. Perhaps it's that obviously expensive expansion that seems to go on endlessly. I can't imagine why you should need so much additional space."

"I intend to have one day the biggest store in all Texas," Melissa replied, smiling briefly.

"Biggest is not necessarily best, though I fear one would be hard pressed to convince many Texans of that."

"Anyway, I did not come here to discuss my store," Melissa said.

"But I thought that's just what we were discussing."

"Only as it pertains to the misconduct of your youngest son."

"Who is, incidentally, your brother, in case you've forgotten."

"I disown him, entirely and utterly, though my doing so publicly has not stopped my customers from holding his peccadilloes against me."

"I suppose you're referring to the Mexican girl," Joanna said.

"Who is, this very moment, blown up out of all size with Jay Jay's baby."

Joanna blinked, startled out of her bemused attitude. "Are you certain?" she asked.

Melissa looked pleased at having delivered what was obviously news to her mother. "Of which? She is most definitely with child. And since Jay Jay was plainly living with her in that lean-to, people have naturally assumed...though with a girl like that..." She shrugged a trifle hopefully. In fact, she had tried taking the tack publicly that the child wasn't Jay Jay's at all, but no one had been convinced, and her efforts to produce some other culprit had borne no fruit.

"I can't believe that of Jay," Joanna said. "Oh, the baby, yes, he's a man, certainly, those things do happen. But I'd have been more inclined to expect him to marry the girl."

"And who do you expect would perform such a ceremony," Melissa asked, "in obvious defiance of the mistress of Heart's Folly?"

That question surprised Joanna, too; had they grown so big already that others set their course of action according to her approval or disapproval? But, yes, of course. She had begun to acquire not just position but power.

She filed that discovery away mentally, careful not to let herself start savoring it. Power required responsibility, not pleasure, lest the gods punish one's hubris.

"I'll take care of this," Joanna said.

"She should be flogged through the streets. Past the very doors of the store whose business she's ruined with her harlotry."

"Don't be bloodthirsty."

"I? I am only demanding that you do what is right and proper."

"And so I shall," Joanna said. "You have my word on that."

TWENTY-SIX

Feom the first, Yolanda's mother had made plain her disapproval of any relationship between her daughter and Joanna Harte's son.

"She will not welcome such a friendship," she had said all along, and there was no need to specify who "she" was.

"I have not encouraged him" was Yolanda's reply.

"Not with words, no."

So when Joanna finally found her, Yolanda was indeed living in a lean-to (Joanna had supposed that was another of Melissa's exaggerations) behind a stall in the *mercado,* and not in her mother's house.

At first Joanna thought she had come to the wrong place again— this was not the first place she had looked. Though she had seen Yolanda weekly for some years now, she had developed that habit of looking at her without seeing. But, more than that, the girl she had only casually noticed growing had become, overnight, a woman. There was still mischief in her eyes, but it was a provocative, self-confident mischief, and not a child's mere devilishness.

Love had made her sure of herself. She knew Joanna at once, of course, and while Joanna took a moment for recognition, and another to glance around at the merest hovel in which she found herself, the young lady she had come to see waited in serene unconcern.

At length, the two women regarded each other. Joanna admired the courage with which the other met her gaze. She could appreciate spunk.

"Jay Jay will be back soon?" she asked.

"A few more weeks. Within the month, I think."

"Well, it certainly won't take us long to move you from here. Is this all there is?" She indicated the single room's meager furnishings—a crude table, two chairs, a bed with a straw mattress. Quite a change from the way Jay Jay was accustomed to living; what a man would endure for love!

A chicken strolled nonchalantly in through the open door, pecked at the earth near Joanna's feet, and, at a quick stamping motion, squawked her indignation and marched haughtily back outside.

"Why should I move?" The tone was defiant, with just enough petulance to hint at her recent childhood.

Joanna, reminded by it, softened her own manner. "I did not go to all that trouble to build my ranch," she said, smiling to take any sting from her words, "so that my son's child could be born in a stable."

"It was good enough for the Virgin Mary." Yolanda smiled, too. She was grateful Joanna hadn't questioned the child's parentage, as others had.

"If you'll forgive my being a trifle sacrilegious, she did not have to deal with a bunch of hidebound Texans—as you will, married to my son. And there is always the possibility that you may one day be mistress of Heart's Folly, though you needn't expect me to relinquish that privilege for some time. In any case, you'll have a great deal to learn. And the first is when to fight, and when not to fight. Now, where are your things? I think we can leave the furniture behind, can we not?"

As simply as that, Joanna added yet another member to her growing household.

The addition of Yolanda to the family group, however, was not made without some friction. Alice sniffed her disapproval. "In Galveston, a lady would not be expected to share her table with all and sundry" was her murmured aside. Of late, she frequently peppered her conversations with allusions to the good life she had left behind her in Galveston, though Joanna did not notice any effort on her part to return herself there.

Nancy's attitude was predictably more caustic. She came in to dinner that first evening and paused to stare at the newcomer at the table. "Have I come to the servants' table by mistake?" she asked.

Ignoring the sarcasm, Joanna introduced Yolanda as Jay Jay's fiancée.

Nancy cast a meaningful glance in the direction of Yolanda's midsection. "One hopes the wedding will take place before too long."

"In plenty of time for my son to be born the Folly's legitimate heir," Yolanda replied, smiling.

Joanna lifted an eyebrow at this, but said nothing. Nancy gave a dry bark of a laugh, and ignored the Mexican for the rest of the meal.

The remark stayed with her, however. She had not expected her husband's younger brother to marry so soon; now, it was true, his wife's child would be the heir apparent to this vast ranch. As much as she hated the Hartes, she did not mean to be cheated out of their money or land. It was only for these that she had married a man she despised, and for which she suffered daily the affronts inflicted on her by his mother. Do what they would, they could not change the reality, that she was the wife of the oldest son.

Obviously, however, her position was soon to be undermined, unless she acted to shore it up. That she could do in only one way.

Gregory now slept in his own room in the suite they occupied. He was surprised, the following evening, reading in bed, to hear his door open and, looking up, to see his wife standing there. She was in the nightdress she had worn on their wedding night, and her lustrous hair was down, cascading over her shoulders and down her back to below her waist. There was no denying that she was beautiful, though he found himself more intimidated than aroused by her beauty.

"It's been on my mind of late," she said, twining a lock of hair about one finger, "that it is cruel of me to deprive my husband of what is his by right."

She waited, expecting some answer, but her husband only sat propped up against his pillows and stared at her as if he hadn't comprehended what she'd told him.

"I'll leave the door to my bedroom ajar," she said, and to make certain he could not fail to understand, she gave him her smile, the one with the unspoken invitation, before she turned and left him.

In her room, she splashed a final dab of perfume on her throat and blew out her candle. The door was only just ajar; her eyes had to adjust to the darkness before she could discern the faint chink of light that spilled through it. Between her bedroom and his was the sitting room, an arrangement that heretofore had struck her as convenient, but which now stretched like an empty wasteland between them.

The fact was, having made her mind up what she must do, she found herself facing the prospect with less displeasure than she might have expected. Her husband, all in all, was not an unattractive man; looking back to the few brief seconds when he had kissed her on the night of their wedding, she actually remembered his kiss with pleasure, and now she felt a warm glow stir within her as she contemplated what such a kiss might lead to.

The minutes stretched long. She heard a floorboard creak, and glanced toward the door, expecting to see his shadow fill it. Her eyes strained at the gloom—was that him? The light seemed unchanged. She listened, fancying she heard a rustling—or was that merely the house, settling itself in the coolness of the Texas night?

Desire became impatience. What could the fool be doing? Certainly he could not have misinterpreted her meaning? What preparations could delay him so long?

Her fingers began to tap a staccato beat on the sheets beside her. Perhaps after all she would make things a bit less easy for him when he finally did arrive, just to remind him of his place.

But in order for her to do that, he must first arrive, and that had not yet happened.

Finally, impatient and angry, she flung back the bedcovers and glided swiftly across the sitting room to the door of his bedroom. It was closed. She hesitated for a moment and then tapped. There was no reply. She opened it cautiously, wondering if he could possibly have thought she meant that she was coming to him. Did he think by so simple a ruse to establish mastery over her? He would have another think coming, she promised herself.

She waited in the doorway, unable to see anything in the darkness of his room, sure that he would say something now that she was here. But he did not speak, and after a moment she became aware of his deep, steady breathing—the breathing of a man fast asleep.

She stood, incredulous, growing more livid by the second. Surely it was a jest, a pretense. She listened more carefully, trying to find the lie in some unevenness of his breath, willing the darkness to separate itself for her, like the Red Sea parting, so that she could see, across the room, his eyes watching her.

At last, however, it sank into her consciousness: He was really asleep, sound asleep. He had never meant to come to her, nor was he waiting for her to come to him.

She was furious. If she had had her little knife with her at that moment, she might well have leaped across the space that separated them and plunged it into his heart.

What she did was slam the door of his room, with such violence that Joanna, sleeping at the far other end of the house, wondered what her son and his wife were about.

It was a smiling, unconcerned-looking wife who came down to breakfast in the morning, early enough to greet her husband before he set about his day's work.

She had lain awake long into the night, at first imagining the most outrageous ways in which she could repay him for insulting her as he had. As the hours passed, however, she had grown calmer and more thoughtful. Her first goal must necessarily remain what it had been. There would be time enough to have her revenge, on all the Hartes; first, though, she must cement her position so firmly that none could challenge it. One day, she meant to be mistress here. If that meant playing the strumpet for her fool of a husband, so be it. In the end, they would all see who was the cleverest.

The next time, she left nothing to chance. She went to her husband's office that evening, where he was working late, before she went to bed. "I'll come to your room tonight," she whispered, and bending down, brushed his cheek lightly with her lips.

There. There could be no mistaking that!

She waited in her own room until she'd heard him come up, until the light from his room had vanished. Then, once again in her most alluring nightgown, perfumed, her hair a cloud floating about her, she stole across the sitting room to his door.

This time his door was locked. She tried the knob, and tried it again, realization coming to her only gradually. She stared at the door, murderous thoughts crowding into her mind. How dared he? She would never forgive him for this.

Even greater than her anger, though, was her bewilderment. No man had ever failed to succumb to her beauty; she was too fully aware of her effect on the members of that sex to comprehend that one could refuse her, not once but twice. She looked around for some explanation, and had no difficulty finding one.

With their father's death, it had become impossible for her sister, Carrie, to remain on Rancho Sebastiano alone. She had moved into town with her mother, but Carrie preferred ranch life, and more often than not, she was at Heart's Folly. In the past, Nancy had paid no more attention to her younger sister than she had to her husband. When she began to do so, she saw at once the glances from one to the other, the shy embarrassment, the hopeful smiles.

Yes, here was the source of her trouble, of course: These two were in love; even when entire rooms separated them, their awareness of one another was undiminished—they seemed to travel on some current of feeling all their own, unshared by the others around them.

But what was she to do about it? Her first hope was that she might catch the two of them together in a compromising situation that would give her an upper hand and enable her to make whatever demands she chose. It was soon apparent, however, that whatever outlet the two found for their feelings, it was not in physical expression. She haunted them both for days, to her own frustration: They were never alone together.

The fact that her husband loved another woman—loved a woman to the point of declining her own favors—galled even more than his outright rejection. She studied her sister, and was all the more dumbfounded. Plain, she would have called her at best; tomboyish, even. What kind of man would choose a chaste relationship with a woman like that?

She looked at herself for hours at a time in her mirror. No, it was not simply vanity. She was beautiful, she'd always known that. Yet, there was nothing for it—she had been spurned. Her husband plainly and simply did not want her, and still he was too honorable to have her sister. How could she not loathe him?

The knowledge gnawed at her. She experienced a new feeling, of inadequacy; her very womanhood seemed threatened. She grew more irritable, more churlish than ever. Venom dripped from her lips, her eyes grew as dark as onyx, and as cold. Her nerves were taut, like a treed cat waiting for an attack.

Something had to come of the frustration and the bitter anger churning within her. Nothing now could please her, nothing escaped her displeasure. Alice was a "fat old fool," Abraham a "both-

SAN ANTONE

ersome pickaninny," Carrie "mannish," the food "abominable," the ranch itself "not a folly but a farce."

As for William Horse: "I wonder you can tolerate a savage like that coming in and out of the house as he pleases, like he was a member of the family," she complained one evening.

"He is, almost," Gregory said, and Joanna added, "We'd be hard put to run this ranch without him."

Their answers were made so offhandedly, it was impossible to doubt the truth of them.

And Nancy, smiling serenely to herself, wondered that it had taken her so long to recognize an Achilles' heel.

TWENTY-SEVEN

I t was not easy to get close to William Horse, particularly not for someone who, like Nancy, had been openly unfriendly toward Joanna.

Patiently, determinedly, Nancy persisted. She found endless occasions to be where she would encounter him. She took up riding again, which she had neglected of late, and inevitably it had to be the Nasoni who readied her horse for her and took it from her when she rode back. It was he who had to help her into the buggy when she went into town, and he alone could answer the questions with which she expressed her newly discovered interest in the workings of the Folly.

In all these meetings, brief, businesslike, she saw plainly his partisanship; his look was unfriendly, his manner curt to the point of rudeness. But she saw more than that, too. She saw in his eyes that light she was accustomed to discovering in men's eyes when they looked at her. William Horse might ignore, even dislike her as a person; but that part of him common to every man was aware of her as a woman.

Her confidence restored, Nancy spun out the threads of the delicate web she had envisioned.

Now she chanced to meet him outside his own cabin; once, as if confused of her directions, she actually ventured inside the door, feigning surprise at finding herself confronting a shirtless and genuinely surprised Indian.

William Horse splashed himself with cool water at the horses' trough at the end of a hot workday, and looked around to find Nancy on the opposite side of the trough, just coming to water the horse she'd been riding.

William came from Gregory's office at the end of some conference, nearly to collide with Nancy in the gloom of the hallway, where she was just passing.

If he was aware of her machinations, he gave no overt sign; but as she happened to glance into his eyes, it seemed to her that both the contempt and the lust burned gradually brighter.

Finally—and it had taken her weeks—she discovered what she wanted: William Horse had a place, a private place, a sheltered inlet of the creek, hidden by brush and a little ravine, where he went to bathe. Alone. And naked.

She made the discovery by accident. Several times she'd ridden out after him, riding in whatever general direction he had taken, hoping for some chance meeting away from the ranch. She kept losing him, though. And then, one day, she'd been sitting on her horse in the shade of a pecan tree, scanning the horizon for some sight of a rider and horse, and he'd appeared over a little rise only a short distance from her. He didn't see her, and rode off in the direction of the ranch. Her first impulse was to ride across his path, but instinct held her back.

His hair was wet, hanging over his forehead from beneath his hat; his shirt, too, clung damply to his shoulders and chest. Even the dungarees that he wore looked plastered to him.

She waited until he was out of sight. Then she rode in the direction from which he had come, mounted the little rise, and found herself looking down into the ravine, and the bend of the creek where it formed a little pool. She could still see his damp footprints where he'd emerged from the water.

The next time, she left her horse tethered and stole on foot to the hillock overlooking the water. She wanted to confirm what she thought she had found, and she did.

He was standing waist-deep in the water, splashing himself, his back to her. As she watched, deliberating, he dived suddenly under the water's surface. She had a fleeting glimpse of naked buttocks and bare, thickly muscled legs.

An electric shock went through her; she had supposed until then that he was wearing at least his drawers. She had intended to clamber down the hill and surprise him, but now, suddenly, she felt overcome by the hot sunlight; she might have been suffocating.

She slid back down the embankment and fairly ran back to her horse. She was gasping for breath when she regained her saddle.

But she exulted as she rode back to the ranch. She knew now where and how to set her trap for him.

She watched him come and go, no longer needing to shadow him. He went once a week. In the late afternoon, at the end of the workday.

It was surprising how quickly the family grew accustomed to her new habit of riding each day, at the same time—late afternoon. They paid little attention to what she did; they were grateful, no doubt, that she had suddenly become so much less difficult.

"She seems finally to have settled her mind," Alice remarked; and Joanna, who was inclined to distrust her daughter-in-law, agreed thoughtfully, "To something."

William Horse was angry to discover her there on the bank waiting when he emerged from the water.

Angry, and unable to disguise his immediate and powerful reaction to seeing her as naked as he was. He disliked and distrusted this beautiful young wife of Joanna's son. But she was beautiful, and she was naked, and his physical reaction was as instinctive, as natural, as it was impossible to disguise.

Angry with himself as well as her, he turned his back, on the ripe fullness of her breasts, on the dark, silken triangle at her thighs, on the skin of an alabaster whiteness that made his own flesh feel afire.

"Come here," she called to him in an imperious voice.

He ignored her, went to where his clothes were lying in a heap.

Nancy, ready for him in every sense, was enraged at this, yet another rejection—and from a mere primitive, at that. She had been lying upon the blanket she had thoughtfully brought with her. Now she leaped up and ran at him. "So, is an Indian less than a man after all?" she demanded. She struck his bent back with her fists, and when he seemed not even to notice her blows, opened her hands and raked her long nails down his back, drawing rivulets of blood.

He jerked and whirled about, seizing her wrists when she would have clawed his face as well. But the struggle brought their bodies together, and the touch of her flesh upon his was like a scorching flame. In another instant, he had grabbed her violently, flung her over his shoulder like a sack of grain, and carried her swiftly to the waiting blanket.

Joanna and Yolanda had easily become friends. For her part, Joanna admired the courage and tact with which Yolanda handled the touchy situation in which she found herself. It was obvious that there would be prejudice against her. Nor was it only Alice and Nancy who demonstrated this; Gregory, too, though polite, was a bit distant; and the hired help, even the Mexicans who were now in the majority, were initially cool. Only Carrie made any effort to extend a genuine welcome—perhaps, Joanna supposed, because she herself felt something of an interloper.

Still, Yolanda was quick to win people over. She did not allow herself to be cowed, nor was she haughty. She had spirit, and warmth, and her smile was so quick to come, so obviously sincere, that it soon melted many a heart set against her. Even Alice finally came to pronounce her a "sweet child." Only Nancy seemed immune, and she at least seemed to have other matters on her mind of late. Joanna wondered what they were, and was grateful at the same time for them, as it made her more tractable.

Yolanda had long admired "the señora." Texas was man's country, by and large, and the mere fact that Joanna was able to run her own ranch, and such a grand one at that, seemed to Yolanda nothing short of miraculous. She learned quickly, she wanted to learn more, and it was not difficult to learn just from observing Joanna. Indeed, she had done that all along, at every opportunity; merely working at the ranch for Gregory's wedding had been like a finishing-school course for her.

On the other hand, she thought Joanna was making a serious error in judgment, and told her so.

"You are losing your son, señora. To cattle."

"What do you mean?"

"Already Jay speaks of going to work elsewhere, a cattle ranch."

"That is not possible," Joanna replied firmly. "I will forbid it."

Even as she said it, however, and Yolanda smiled at her, Joanna was thinking that forbidding Jay Jay was a futile pastime.

"It's true," she admitted, "he prefers cattle, and the life of the cowboy, to farming. And I've followed the progress of these cattle drives. They say fortunes are being made, but it would cost us a fortune to buy breeding stock, and a long time to breed a sizable herd from that."

"There are cattle for the taking," Yolanda pointed out.

"The longhorns, you mean?"

"That is what many of these men are driving north now."

The Texas longhorn was the descendant of the cattle the original Spanish explorers had brought with them, but since then the cow had gone wild. Narrow-hipped, swaybacked, bony, the longhorn had adapted to the wilderness with a vengeance. They could fight off the wolves and wildcats of the plains—even a bear. They ignored the hardships of blizzard or drought and could travel incredible distances without seeming to tire. They lived now mostly in the "black chaparral, a no-man's-land of mesquite, of prickly-pear cactus, of sharp-thorned paloverde, home to the rattlesnake and the fierce-tempered javelina as well. And no man pretended it was easy to catch the longhorn in such a setting.

On the other hand, any man who could, owned them. And they were the ideal animal for the long, arduous cattle drives to the railroad heads in Kansas and Nebraska.

"You're suggesting we round up our own longhorns?" Joanna asked. Yolanda nodded. "But where would we get men for such an undertaking? Our people here are farmers."

"There are many men out of work, many of them home now from the war. It would not be hard to find men, all the men we needed."

"But who would lead them? Jay Jay won't be back for weeks yet. And if we meant to send off a herd before winter, he'd have to leave soon after he got back."

Yolanda smiled. "You ride as well as any man in San Antone. You handle a gun, a knife, a rope. And men listen to you—I've seen that already." She glanced down and added, more modestly, "And I can ride. I could help."

Joanna was incredulous. "But—you can't mean—two women, lead a roundup? It's unheard of."

"You run a ranch already. The biggest around."

The two women regarded one another for a moment. Then Joanna began to laugh, and after a few seconds, Yolanda laughed with her. They laughed at first with amusement, and with astonishment at their own audacity at even contemplating such a scheme. But their laughter changed, colored by excitement as each realized, without even saying so, that they were, indeed, going to do what they talked about.

And finally, arms about one another, they laughed together at the sheer joy, the wonder, of their own special womanhood.

TWENTY-EIGHT

I t was not as easy as Yolanda had indicated to gather enough men for a roundup. There were many who did not care to ride under a woman—even Joanna Harte, notorious as she was.

Gregory thought she was crazy, and told her so. Nancy declared the plan "unbecoming to a lady." Neither dissuaded Joanna, and despite resistance, she did manage to hire enough riders.

"A motley crew," Gregory pronounced them as the men began to assemble at the Folly. The riders were young and old, experienced and novice, Mexican, Negro, white, and Indian.

"Typical Texas, I'd say" was Joanna's reply. It was one of the things that had first impressed her about the place that was now home to her, in a way that South Carolina, where she'd been born, had never been. America was said to be a melting pot; certainly Texas—San Antone in particular—reflected this. It amazed her that people from such diverse backgrounds, so many different nations and cultures, had managed to find their way to this isolated little town.

Not that you could really call it a little town anymore; it was fair to being a city now. The San Antonio River still flowed on its aimless, leisurely course—the Indian name for it meant "drunken old man going home at night"—and dogs and old men still drowsed in the plaza; but the population had nearly tripled just since Joanna had arrived, and the streets, stretching farther and wider each year, it seemed, were crowded with traffic—coaches and buggies, horsemen and foot travelers, all the bustling commerce of a boom town.

It was cattle had brought the boom. In increasing numbers, Texans were driving their herds northward along a variety of trails. The Chisholm was the most popular; it started near the Mexican border and came right by San Antone, almost the last town it reached in Texas.

A whole new industry had sprung up, catering to the cattlemen. Bet-a-Million Gates had set up a fence of something new he called "barbed wire" in the city plaza, to prove that it would hold back the toughest cattle, and already strands of the new wire were springing up across the open range.

"One thing about being in a mule train," Joanna answered Gregory's objections. "Unless you're the lead mule, the view is pretty much limited." If cattle was the coming thing, she meant to be the lead mule.

"At least you should let me manage this fiasco," he argued.

"That *would* be a fiasco," Joanna said, laughing. "You've got all you can do to stay in a saddle."

They set out at dawn. Joanna, she well knew, had never looked more scandalous. The longhorns hid themselves in the brush country for good reasons: It was hard to spot them, and harder still to catch them. The country dictated clothing and equipment. Even her customary split skirts would not do; they would be too easily caught on branches and thorns. She wore snug-fitting trousers the same as the men, and tough leather chaps over these. Her jacket, too, was closely fitted, her boots sturdy, and further protected by the tapaderos that covered the stirrups of her saddle.

With her gloved hands and hair safely pinned up under a low-crowned Texas hat, she was nearly indistinguishable from the men with whom she rode.

The men, of course, knew the difference, Joanna could see that in their eyes when they looked at her, could hear it in the deference of their voices. She knew if the roundup was to be a success, she would have to make them forget she was a woman.

Toward that goal, she had been secretly practicing with a lariat. From his inexhaustible supply of relatives, Angel had produced one who was near to a magician with a rope, and by now Joanna felt she had mastered most of the essential throws: the *lazo remo-lineàdo;* the *piale;* the *mangana;* and the most critical of them, the *media cabeza,* or half head, the loop thrown behind one ear and horn and in front of the other and the underjaw—this was the throw needed for a really mean cow. A longhorn could weigh eight hundred to a thousand pounds; a badly cast rope could spell disaster for horse and rider.

Since Yolanda did not rope and, in view of her condition, would not take part in actually catching any longhorns, her role was to be chiefly that of "spotter." The variously colored cattle were clever at concealing themselves in the brush; it took a keen eye to discover them.

Joanna, however, felt that she would have to prove herself if she wanted to win the respect of the cowboys riding with them. It would take weeks to collect enough cattle to make a long drive north profitable. Jay Jay would be back before they finished, and with the experience he had gained the past few months, he could take over the job.

Until then, Joanna was running things herself. Curiosity, need of work, the reputation she had already earned for herself here in the neighborhood of San Antone—even amusement—had brought some of these men on the roundup. But she was conscious of a general wait-and-see attitude: If she made a fool of herself, she and the Folly would be a long time paying for her mistake.

They pitched camp at the edge of a vast tract of brush, and a pen was set up for the cattle. They would be branded as they were caught with the Heart's Folly brand, *H* and *F* sharing a middle staff and a common crossbar; simple enough, but hard for any would-be rustlers to change into anything else.

The *marcadores* would do the actual branding, the *ataleros* would come after them and smear lime paste on the fresh brands to see that they scarred properly. A *capador* castrated the males—Joanna had had to conceal a certain squeamishness on learning that the cooked testicles were considered a delicacy among the men—and pieces were nicked from the ears of male and female alike to give them a count of the herd.

By morning they were ready for the first day's riding out. When it came to actually finding the cattle in the brush and roping them, each rider was pretty much on his own, as the brush was too thick and hard to travel through for them to work as one group. Joanna had no doubts, however, that everything she did would be known that same evening throughout the camp; on this day, in particular, even the mesquite would have eyes and ears, she was certain.

They set out at dawn, and by midmorning Joanna's nervousness had turned to genuine apprehension. So far, neither she nor Yolanda had spotted a single cow, though the shouts and whoops from other cowhands in the area told her that the men were being more successful.

Suddenly the palomino she was riding, a horse she had bought just for its cattle experience, paused in its stride and pricked it ears.

"There," Yolanda said in a low voice, and pointed with her riding crop.

At first Joanna saw nothing but a seemingly solid wall of brush. Then, as if a fog had cleared, her eyes spied the twisted horns of a cow, neatly camouflaged by the mesquite. A thrill of excitement went through her and without thinking she let out the cry she'd been hearing from the cowboys all morning: Ahh-haa, San Antone! She spurred her horse and rode at the longhorn.

With a speed and agility belying its size and clumsy appearance, the cow was up and racing through the brush. It looked to Joanna at times as if she were riding straight at impenetrable patches of mesquite, but she was determined to go wherever the cow went. One of the men might philosophically shrug off a cow's escaping the chase, but that was a luxury she knew she couldn't allow herself.

Still, it took all her considerable skill in the saddle to stay on the palomino. Branches were cracking and snapping around her, tearing at her chaps and the tapaderos over the stirrups. One thorny protrusion nearly took her eye out, and left her with a little trail of blood on one cheek. She bent down, flattening herself to the horse's straining neck, dodging as best she could, and taking the blows she couldn't dodge. Ahead of her, the longhorn twisted and darted, vanished and reappeared—but Joanna was gaining, and that realization gave her a surge of exultation.

The longhorn broke into a patch of open ground. It was the opportunity Joanna had prayed for; if she let the cow reach the next thicket of brush, it would be hard to find room to get a rope over her. Heart in throat, Joanna twirled her rope overhead and cast a loop twirling through the air. It seemed to float, like a feather, interminably slow—and then, with an accuracy that astonished even her, it settled neatly about the long, curving horns.

The palomino, trained to this job, tensed to take the strain when the cow reached the end of the rope. Now was the critical time.

Sometimes the longhorns turned and charged the riders. Sometimes a cowhand caught a real *ladino*, a maverick that would fight to the death. Till you actually got your rope on one, there was no knowing what you were in for.

The rope held, and the palomino and the longhorn were in a tug-of-war. The cow bellowed and bucked. Then, abruptly, the fight was over and the longhorn began to obey the pull of the rope.

A loud cheer went up. Joanna, totally engrossed in subduing the cow, had not even been aware of the cowboys riding up to watch her struggle. Now, turning to see them, she couldn't restrain a big grin and a loud yell. A couple of the men threw their hats in the air, and when she rode by them, proudly dragging her catch back to the waiting pen, several of them leaned from their saddles to clap her enthusiastically on the shoulders.

Another cheer went up when she rode into camp, and she could see in the eyes of all the cowhands that she had proved herself.

What initially had been a great thrill for her soon became a job, and a rigorous, bone-wearying one. The days went on, became weeks. Gregory rode out to judge their progress, and could not conceal his surprise and his pride. Scarcely anyone in this area had attempted to round up the longhorns before this. The cattle were plentiful, the pile of ear pieces mounting steadily.

They had better than a thousand head collected, when trouble erupted.

The weather turned hot; the cowhands worked with sweat streaming down their faces. Joanna had earned the respect of all the men by this time, and Yolanda was nearly as well regarded. Both had worked as hard as anyone; neither complained nor expected any special privilege. Joanna had wondered privately about the two of them being the only women out on the prairie with so many rough-riding cowboys, but it was as as if the men had an unspoken agreement among them. Modesty was observed, but in every other sense they were treated no differently from the men.

Of course, as Joanna privately noted, it would have taken a very foolhardy man to make any untoward approach to where she and Yolanda slept beneath the chuck wagon: William Horse slept only a few yards away, his rifle ever at hand, and by now everyone in the camp knew that he slept as lightly as a cat.

Joanna herself was sleeping lightly in the weighted heat that had settled over them, when a light footstep and the sound of her name spoken low brought her awake. She saw William Horse crouching nearby.

There was no need for him to explain why he had awakened her. Just as she opened her eyes, a sheet of lightning lit up the prairie sky.

"You'd better wake everyone," Joanna said, scrambling to her feet, instantly alert. She had been warned of this in particular, and earlier the experienced cowhands had been casting anxious glances at the sky. A good thunderstorm could easily stampede the cattle. The temporary corral they had erected wasn't likely to withstand an onslaught of a thousand or more charging longhorns.

Distant thunder rumbled ominously. In the next flash of lightning, Joanna could see every man in camp was up and hastily saddling his horse. There was no need for her to issue any orders. Everyone here knew the danger, and what they had to do. If the cattle stampeded, the only necessity was to stop them. How, you could never be entirely sure till you'd tried and done it—or failed.

The cowboys riding guard were singing aloud—not very well, any of them, but the crooning of their voices sometimes helped to calm the cattle. Joanna could see now that the cattle were on their feet, testing the air, milling about nervously.

"Looks bad," Joanna said, swinging into her saddle. William Horse said nothing, but his face was grim.

In another flash of light, Joanna turned and saw a rider approaching in the distance, from the direction of the ranch. He was not, she was sure, one of the hands, though he was too far, and the light too brief, for her to recognize him. All she saw was that he was wearing one of those new "slickers" that Melissa carried so proudly now at her store, a coat made of a rubberized fabric that was impervious to rain, though Joanna had thought them extremely ugly to look at.

In the next moment, however, she forgot the approaching rider completely. The cowhands had been singing louder and louder; the air seemed to become denser, heavier, the movements of the cattle more worried.

Then a blinding blue flash set the night afire, and at almost the same moment an earsplitting clap of thunder rent the air. For a moment, in the blackness that followed, Joanna was blinded, but it didn't matter—she didn't have to see to know what was causing the earth to tremble beneath them.

The cattle were stampeding!

TWENTY-NINE

H ardly anyone was aware that the storm had unleashed torrents of rain upon them. It was the thunder and lightning that had spooked the cattle, and each rider cursed as he rode in pursuit of that thundering, bellowing herd.

Joanna rode for all she was worth, the palomino all but leaping out from under her with his charge. You had to get to the front of the herd—that was what everyone had drummed into her; it was the only way to turn a stampede.

She could hardly see in the darkness and rain. Once, twice, the lightning flashed and she could see not only the herd but a rain-slickered rider off to her right, riding with the rest of the boys hell-bent for leather, but she hadn't time now to wonder who he was.

The ground shook beneath pounding hooves, and she could feel the heat of a thousand rangy bodies, smell the cowhide smell filling her wet nostrils. The palomino snorted wildly, his heart fair to bursting with the effort of his speed. She could see nothing of what was before or beneath them; one misstep—a prairie-dog hole, a fallen branch—and the horse and she would both end up with broken necks, but she wouldn't let herself think of that. The bang-

ing of horns together was like the clicking of castanets in one of
those fandangos the Mexicans were fond of dancing, but this was
a deadly dance they were at now, and the thunder-drums and the
alto cries of the cows only made it more eerie. Unreal, even. This
might have been some dreamscape, some heat-engendered fiction
of the mind, racing through the dark like this, the horse's muscles
stretching and straining beneath her.

The sky turned blue-white again and, glancing aside, Joanna saw
that they were alongside the leaders of the herd now, she and one
of the boys, and the stranger, stride for stride with the front-run-
ning bull.

Now was the greatest danger, for they must literally push the
cattle aside, turn them from their headlong flight. To fall now was
to lie beneath those charging hooves, to be pounded into the very
dust of the Texas rangeland.

The palomino was steady—she thanked the day she'd bought
him, and laughed to think she'd cursed how much he cost. A pain
shot up her leg as it was crushed between two massive bodies for
a moment. She clung tight, barely able to stay in the saddle; nothing
she could do but trust the horse, and God, too, of course, though
at the moment the palomino was closer to the heart of things.

They were turning. The cattle were yielding, veering, and once
the leaders had started, the others followed, slowly forming a circle
that wound in and in upon itself, until cattle were bumping into
cattle and none of them knew which way to run, or could find an
open path for it.

The stampede was stopped. The rain had lessened, the thunder
sounded more distant, and it had been several minutes now since
they'd seen more than a far-off flash of light.

Joanna and the palomino were both gasping for breath. She
leaned down, patting his powerful neck, and whispered in his ear
to tell him what a fine fellow he was. The horse tossed his head,
as if disdainfully reminding her that he could certainly be expected
to know his job.

There was no telling till morning how much of the herd they
had lost. Until then, the boys would have to ride a containing circle
about the gradually calming cattle. With daylight, they'd be penned
again, the corral repaired, damage assessed.

Joanna rode about, thanking everyone she met, sharing the relief
and the pride that they all felt in a dangerous job well done. For
all the effort, all the risk, she felt oddly elated. She'd never before

felt so close to the men who worked for her—nor, for that matter, to the land itself, to Texas, and the Folly. It seemed to her as if in the crash and glitter of that night, she and her ranch had been truly wed.

Finally, she rode back to the camp, where by now the cook's campfire could be seen to glimmer—he would be making coffee by the gallon, thick, bitter brew that would keep the men awake the rest of the night.

She was just getting down from the palomino when she heard someone riding up, and glancing in that direction, saw the stranger riding into the light of the campfire. With the long, dark coat that gleamed wetly, and his ten-gallon hat pulled low over his eyes, it was impossible to see his face. It was obvious, though, that he was coming to see her; he jumped down with a quick, lithe movement that struck a chord in her memory, and strode swiftly toward her.

As he neared, he reached up and whipped off his hat. Joanna gasped aloud and felt her heart give a lurch in her breast. "But, it can't be," she cried aloud.

"It sure is," he said, grinning that grin she remembered, that had the power to stun her senses, to numb her to everything else.

"Webb." She could scarcely breathe the name, for fear she'd send this fantasy flying, find herself alone in some empty darkness, having imagined it all.

But this was no dream, this was real, the arms crushing her to him, the lips sweetly smothering her own, the fingers that locked violently in the curls of her hair, yanking her head back for his kiss.

"They told me you were dead," she managed to say at last. "Sergeant Burke, he said..." The rest was lost on a sob.

"Some other poor soul. Though I wasn't far from it. I must have lain for a day or two with part of my head blown off, and wandered in a daze for two or three more. Some rebels found me; figured I was near enough dead, they might as well finish the job; very near did. Took me a year to get halfway well, and most of another one before I could even remember who I was, or I'd have been here a lot sooner."

"You're here now, that's all that matters," Joanna said, and for another long moment they were too occupied for words.

He took a step back, holding her at arm's length, and looked her up and down. She had grown so used to dressing like the rest of the cowhands, she'd forgotten what a peculiar sight she made.

"I feel like I'm kissing a cowboy," he said.

She laughed aloud. "By now, I must about smell like one, too," she said.

"Señora!"

Joanna turned at the call. The cook, a little Mexican protégé of Angel's, was running toward them, waving his arms frantically. "*Venga*—come quick! The young señora!"

In all the excitement, Joanna hadn't even thought of Yolanda. Now, as she ran after the Mexican, she saw Yolanda's horse, saddled and sweating like everyone else's, and guessed at once what had happened: In the heat of danger, Yolanda had responded the same as the others—had saddled up and ridden out with them to help turn the stampede.

She was lying now on the ground, on the opposite side of her pony. The pool of blood spreading between her thighs, melting into the rainwater, evidenced at once the result of that violent riding.

She had miscarried.

It was a cruel twist of fate, Joanna couldn't help thinking, that brought Jay Jay riding into camp only two days later.

She waited at a discreet distance, watching with a heavy heart the grin with which he greeted his bride-to-be fade into a grim, heartsick scowl as he learned what had happened.

He did not even come to greet his mother, but after a few minutes with Yolanda, left her and walked slowly to the edge of the camp. Joanna gave him a brief time to himself before she followed him. His eyes were dry but red-rimmed when she walked up. She put a hand on his shoulder; though he was a man now, with a powerful, hard-muscled figure, he was still no taller than she was.

"I am sorry," she said.

The look he gave her was hard and resentful. "Why'd you let her do it, ma? You should've known better, her bein' the way she was."

"It was her idea. How was I to stop her? You said yourself, before you left, she has a mind of her own."

He smiled, a bitter, accusing smile. "Besides that, it was helpful to the ranch, I suppose?"

Joanna winced. "You make me sound very heartless," she said.

He shook his head, and when he answered, it was in a softer, less angry voice, though no less bitter. "No, not heartless—you got plenty of heart. But you got a blind spot, too, the size and shape of this ranch. Someday that's going to cost you, ma. Someday you'll have to pay."

He turned from her and walked away, leaving her alone with those ominous words hanging on the hot Texas air.

THIRTY

I t had not been Nancy's intention to have the Indian's baby. She had thought simply to seduce him away from his loyalty to Joanna, into a devotion to her, which she could then use against the Hartes.

Considering the savage passion with which he had succumbed to her initial seduction, it came as a great surprise to her when he did not again return to his bathing spot in the river. She was angry, but undaunted. She went to his cabin by night; it was easy enough to steal from the main house, and since she and her husband had separate bedrooms, who was to note her absence?

The first time he took her with the same angry violence as before; but the second time she came, the door was bolted, and after trying vainly for some response from within, she was forced to return in defeat to her own bed.

The roundup interrupted their contest, and while he was away for that, she realized she was carrying his child. At first the discovery filled her with disgust and dismay; but after she'd thought of it awhile, it seemed to her that here, indeed, was the way to strike at the proud Hartes.

There were some difficulties, of course. Gregory could hardly be expected to think the child she was carrying was his when they had yet to share a bed together.

She rode into town, alone, to the *mercado* and rambled about until she found a tiny apothecary shop, manned by a hot-eyed Mexican who smiled with appreciation when he saw her pause outside. She went in, giving him *her* smile, the one no man could resist.

"I want something to make a man sleep," she said, and when the request startled him out of his grin, she only smiled more broadly, and added, "Very soundly."

That night when he went up to bed, Gregory was surprised to find his wife waiting there for him, seated in one of the little armchairs by the window.

"I thought maybe you'd have a glass of port with me before you went to bed," she said in the way of explanation.

"Why?" he asked warily.

She shrugged. "I'm lonesome, frankly. No, that's not it, though it's true enough. I just—well, I felt so bad about the way things have gone between the two of us—it's so foolish. Oh, I know, the fault is more mine than yours. We might as well be honest: Neither one of us really wanted this marriage, except for business purposes. But we *are* married, aren't we? There's no need for us to be enemies. Why, if we tried, I'm betting we could even get to be friends."

She smiled, and her loveliness was such that she was able to project an air of sweet innocence even to one who knew better.

The truth was, Gregory himself was lonesome. He missed his mother; her strong presence was, to him, as integral a part of the ranch as the distant hills or the little river that meandered across it. Anyway, his wife didn't look as if she were up to anything. She was fully dressed, just as she had looked at dinner. And now that he thought of it, she had been a great deal more subdued of late, downright considerate, even. It seemed churlish not at least to have a drink with her. He returned her smile, and took the glass she offered him.

"There, doesn't this seem so much better than snubbing one another?" she asked. She took the merest sip from her glass, and regarded him mischievously over its rim. "Tell the truth now— you're really in love with my sister, aren't you?"

He stiffened and eyed her suspiciously. "What makes you think that?" he asked.

"Oh, tut tut, I'm not blind, you know. And I don't care, honestly. If you'd ask my opinion, I'd say it's a shame you two aren't married;

it would have been a much better arrangement all around, seems to me. But there, it wasn't up to me, any more than I suppose it was to you. Still, we're not lovers, are we? There's absolutely no reason for me to be jealous. What's more, I'll tell you a little secret— I think she feels just the same about you."

Greg drained his glass, uncomfortable with the subject. "She's never taken the slightest impropriety," he said, "and I assure you, I would not so humiliate you in what is now your home."

"Oh, bother that. I don't care, I tell you." She quickly refilled his glass. "All I want is for you and me to get along better than we have."

He sighed, and took another drink. "You're right, of course. And I promise I'll do my best in the future."

"Then let's drink to that," she said. She lifted her glass. "To a happier marriage."

"A happier marriage," he agreed, and drank.

It seemed as if the drowsiness came over him all at once; he was suddenly barely able to stand on his feet.

"You poor dear," Nancy said, leaping up from her chair. "Why, you look all in. You've been working far too hard, of course. I've noticed it, but I hardly wanted to complain."

He brushed the back of his hand across his forehead; it felt hot and sticky. "I am feeling a little peckish," he said. "I think it's time I called it a night."

"Are you all right? You look positively wobbly. Here, let me help you with your things."

She was at his side, helping him undo the buttons of his shirt, and then, somehow—he wasn't quite sure how—she was in his arms, and they seemed to be falling, falling backward, across the bed....

The last thing he remembered before he fell asleep was kissing her.

He woke with a dull, throbbing headache and a sour, venomous taste in his mouth. He turned slightly, and found himself lying alongside his wife. She was naked, the covers pushed down about her feet, and she gave him a smile of sweet gratitude as his eyes opened.

Jay Jay's words of warning lingered in Joanna's mind, particularly when, with nearly ten thousand head of cattle ready to drive north, she and her two sons discussed the future of the ranch.

Gregory, though impressed with their success, held to his position that agriculture was their future; Jay Jay scornfully pointed out that cotton profits had dwindled dramatically since the war, and that tomorrow in Texas belonged to the cattlemen. Listening to them argue, Joanna found herself reflecting that each had his own blind spots when it came to the Folly.

In the end, with a clearness of vision that she thought ought to sufficiently answer Jay's criticism, she decided on something of a middle course. They would build on the success of their roundup. They had kept a stock of longhorns from which to begin breeding a standing herd; and following the examples of others who were venturing into cattle, she had already ordered additional breeding stock from other strains, notably Brahmas from far-off India. Bred with the longhorns, the Brahmas were said to produce better beef and animals that were immune to tick fever.

But she did not mean to give up on farming, either. "The railroads are spreading like wildfire," she pointed out. "They'll reach clear to San Antone in a few more years. That means opening up the whole eastern country to what we grow here. Not just cotton, but food crops as well. Why, we can harvest vegetables here as late as November, long after it's snowing in the North. Someday we may be able to ship beans clear to Boston, and tomatoes, too, not to mention pecans."

"You're a visionary, ma," Greg told her, and she smiled, but it did occur to her that what he called her "vision" was the very same thing Jay Jay called her "blind spot," wasn't it?

Of course, she was delighted to learn that Nancy was expecting. With Yolanda's baby lost, it meant their eventual heir. More than that, Nancy's baby would be the very first Harte born and bred on the ranch, on their land—a true son of the Folly.

She made up her mind that she would get along better with her son's wife. In point of fact, Nancy seemed to be going out of her way to make that possible. Joanna even found herself losing a bit of her sympathy for Carrie. She was the only one, it seemed, who wasn't pleased with Nancy's news, though at times Gregory himself appeared more astonished than pleased. Joanna could still feel sorry for the two of them, Gregory and Carrie. But there was a child to consider now, a child who would one day take over the reins of this steadily growing empire: That was the first thing they must all think of. She had made her sacrifices; others would have to make theirs as well.

At least, she no longer had to sacrifice love. Though nothing could completely distract her from the business of the ranch, Webb Price was for now the chief focus of her attention.

"Surely you don't mean he's just going to live right here, in the house with us?" a shocked Alice Montgomery demanded, but Joanna was quick to pooh-pooh any criticisms on that front.

"He's a hero," she argued firmly, "and after what he's suffered, he deserves to be treated like one. Besides, it's not as if I'm a virginal sixteen-year-old. I'm fast pushing fifty years old, and a widow to boot; it's a little late for anyone to worry about my virtue."

Alice, who was vague to the point of density about her own age, disapproved of any woman's being so frank about the matter. "You shouldn't tell people you're that old," she scolded. "Though I must admit you don't look it."

"Why shouldn't I tell? It's the truth," Joanna said. "And frankly, if I don't mind, why should they?"

She was no sooner alone in her room, however, before she went to study herself critically in her dressing-table mirror.

She *was* getting older—that was something no one could avoid. All the more reason, of course, why Nancy's child was important to them all. When you got right down to it, neither Gregory nor Jay Jay was exactly suited to running the Folly; they both saw things too one-sidedly. She would raise her grandson differently, see that he was eventually equipped to take over. Until then, she would have to simply continue running things herself.

There was Webb; he was glad to do whatever he could. He would, she knew, manage altogether for her if she wanted him to. That, of course, she would never agree to, but she had considered long and hard his proposal of marriage.

"You're free now," he'd pointed out, "and plenty of time has passed. No one could criticize you for marrying again."

"Oh, there's people glad to criticize me just for driving down the street," she said. "Not that I give a hang. It's just that—well, I've gotten used to my independence."

"I for one don't recall that having a husband in the past greatly hampered your independence," Webb said smilingly, but he didn't insist, for which she was grateful.

The truth was, Webb was a different man entirely from what Lewis had been. For all his love and devotion, she had a suspicion that, were they to marry, he would come to think it his right to manage, not just her but the Folly. When a woman married, the law took away most of her rights, pretty nearly all of her authority. And that she just wasn't willing to endure. She'd worked too hard to get where she was.

So she ignored the disapproval of Alice and a few of the women she encountered in San Antone, sure they would get over their dissatisfaction with her this time, just as they had in the past. And when Doña Sebastiano, always her most ardent critic, unbent enough to accept her daughter's invitation to dinner at the Folly, where she was given the news of her grandchild-to-be, Joanna thought the point proved.

Most important of all, notwithstanding the question of marrying, she and Webb were happy. She supposed there was something foolish about a woman of her age engaging in romance. Alice suggested such "girlishness was not becoming," and Nancy made one of her rare reversions to sarcasm when she remarked on "old dogs becoming pups again."

Together, she and Webb rode far out onto the range that was the Folly—largely under cultivation now, thanks to the money raised from cattle. They spent evenings by campfires, watching the slow, glorious sunsets, peculiar, it seemed, to Texas. Webb talked to her, as he could to no one else, of the war.

"It's not like those other things that mark a person's life," he said. "First fights, first loves, your career...you do them, or plan them, and a part of the fun is thinking, Wait until so-and-so hears about this.

"But you can't share a war. All those thousands of places and events, and they're all one event, running together, mercifully blurred. The night you lay in the mud in some Tennessee field and shot at one another—only it wasn't one night, it was ten, or twenty, or a hundred, you can't remember afterward, and later it was another field, or maybe it was the same one, you couldn't really tell. You helped fire a cannon, knowing you were killing not one man but you-don't-know-how-many, and it wasn't one shot, it was another after that, and another, and nobody in his right mind would want to remember how many, or what it was doing.

"I don't even know when I first killed a man," he said, "or how many I killed. They say that makes it easier, not knowing; it seemed like it did for the others, but it didn't for me; it made it worse."

She said, inadequately, "Webb, I'm sorry," but he went on as if he hadn't heard her.

"There was a night, one of the few I can separate from all the other nights. We were in Georgia somewhere—I don't know where exactly. We'd been there for a century, it seemed that long, us and some rebels on the other side of a little rise, shooting at one another. It had been raining the whole time—our clothes were wet and stinking. We slept in the mud and ate in the mud, and relieved ourselves in our trousers—I'm sorry, I'm still not used to polite conversation.... And then, all of a sudden, the shooting stopped—I don't know why. The rebels had backed up, I guess, pulled out. And just like that, it was as quiet as a church, and the rain almost stopped, like it was worn out, too.

"We sat around, the ones who were left—there weren't a whole lot of us—and we built fires. It was the first time we'd been warm in I don't know how long. Nobody talking, nothing to eat, just sitting in little groups around these fires.

"Then, this one fellow—he wasn't even close to me, but it was so quiet, you could hear it like a bell—he started to sing: 'Tenting tonight, tenting tonight, waiting for the war to cease; many's the heart that is looking for the light, waiting for the dawn of peace....'

"I'd been all right up until then," he said, his voice breaking slightly. "I hadn't thought much about it: These weren't some foreign soldiers we had been killing, these were Americans, too, neighbors; some of our boys had relatives on the other side. And there we were, sitting in that damned field.... There was a piece of leg lying on the ground next to me—I could have reached out and touched it.... All those men, those poor, miserable men, and nobody said anything, they just sat and listened ... and then, they began to cry, a couple of them at first, and then more and more of them, and nobody made fun of them, because the ones that weren't crying were too busy holding it back. These boys had been fighting and killing and dying for longer than they could remember, and that song had them blubbering like babies...."

And he began to cry again, at the memory, while Joanna held him and gentled him like a child.

It was a busy winter. They had discovered that it was easier rounding up longhorns when the bushes and trees had shed their leaves and offered fewer hiding places. Jay Jay took to the cattle operation like a duck to water. He had promised a herd of thirty thousand by spring.

The months passed quickly, but for Joanna they were unusually pleasant. At Christmas, she gave Webb a splendid saddle in tooled leather. Her present from him was one that Melissa had selected, and sold him on: an immensely long rope of a necklace that, when she put it on, hung in triple loops nearly to her waist: pale ivory carved into miniature roses, and alternating with each flower, a splendid topaz, its brilliance casting a yellow hue on each pale flower.

On Christmas Eve, Nancy wore the yellow diamonds Joanna had forfeited for her wedding, and for once Joanna felt no resentment.

She had gone out of her way to befriend Nancy, and she had to admit Nancy had been sweeter in return than Joanna had ever imagined she could be, though she was never able to rid herself of a nagging sense of distrust toward her daughter-in-law. She found herself watching Nancy, wondering what she was "up to." Then, when everything she saw proclaimed innocence and sincerity, she would chide herself for her mean-spiritedness, and try all the harder to make amends.

William Horse, too, worried Joanna. He seemed more distant than ever, and his always-rare smiles had become virtually non-existent. She could only suppose that there was an element of jealousy toward Webb, and could see no solution for that but to hope that it would pass in time.

With the approach of spring, however, other considerations began to take priority in her mind. Nancy's time was drawing near. Joanna's first grandson: She was determined it would be a boy. The others chided her, but she continued to insist. Nancy only smiled, and looked quite pleased with herself, Joanna thought.

Her labor began on a rainy night in March. With the first twinge of pain, Webb was dispatched for the midwife, and Joanna prepared herself to wait out the event, too excited to even contemplate sleeping.

The birth, as it turned out, was an easy one. It was soon after midnight when the midwife, Mrs. McCrory, descended the main stairs and appeared in the doorway to the parlor, where Joanna and the others were waiting. Joanna was surprised to see that the midwife had donned her bonnet already and was carrying her traveling bag.

"Oh, Mrs. McCrory, you needn't think of riding clear back to town," Joanna said at once. "I've ordered a room made up for you."

"I'll not be staying," Mrs. McCrory said in an unmistakably frosty voice.

Joanna glanced upward. "Is the—has the child come?"

"He has."

"A boy, then," Joanna said, beaming.

"It is. If you can take any pleasure in the fact."

"Indeed I do. The boy is a Harte. One day he will run—"

"A Harte?" Mrs. McCrory sneered. "Do not think to fool anyone with this passel of lies, Mrs. Harte. I shall see that the entire town knows the truth of this scandal."

Gregory had started from the room, but the exchange had given him pause. He and Joanna exchanged glances.

"What scandal are you speaking of?" Joanna demanded abruptly. "I think you'd best explain yourself."

"Did you think I wouldn't know an Indian baby when I saw one?" Mrs. McCrory demanded, her eyes glinting angrily. "If you please, I should like to be driven home. And do not again call upon my services in such a situation."

At the top of the stairs, Nancy clung weakly to the balustrade, listening. She smiled happily to herself. Let the Hartes live down *this* shame, she thought with grim satisfaction.

She made her way slowly back to the bedroom, supporting herself against the wall. At the crib where the midwife had placed the baby, she paused, looking down. Yes, it was unmistakable; no one could doubt the truth. She smiled again, but the smile faded quickly. The damage was done. The child had served his purpose. But, certainly, she had no intention of rearing an Indian's son. She leaned down and took the embroidered silk pillow from beneath the baby's head.

It was Joanna who came to see the infant. Gregory would have done so, but she insisted on going in first.

She emerged a moment later, her face ashen. Gregory was waiting in the hallway for her. "The child is dead," she announced. She did not add that she had had to resist an almost overwhelming urge to smother with a pillow that smiling woman asleep on her bed.

"Dead?" Gregory echoed numbly.

"Perhaps a merciful deity thought it would be kindest," Joanna said. She would not mention the suspicion that had occurred to her, and that she had thrust aside as unworthy even of that odious creature she now hated with all her heart and soul. Surely not even a woman as vile as that could harm her own baby. And babies did die in their cribs, often none knew why.

"Was it..."

"It's his, beyond a doubt."

THIRTY-ONE

"He'll have to go, Joanna." This was Webb speaking. He had long since driven an indignant Mrs. McCrory into San Antone, and returned. It was nearly dawn by now. He and Joanna, Gregory, and Jay Jay were still in the parlor, arguing what was to be done. Jay Jay had already set some of the hands to digging a grave.

"Not the Indian" was all Gregory had said.

The point was moot. By the time the women had prepared the infant body for burial, the guilty news would have spread throughout the ranch—as, they were all aware, it was no doubt already spreading through San Antone.

"No," Joanna said flatly to Webb's suggestion.

"It'll have to be, ma," Jay Jay said.

"I won't ask William Horse to leave the Folly. I can't."

"If he stays, I'll have to go," Gregory said. His voice was dull and flat, weary-sounding, but the look in his eyes was stubborn.

Joanna turned on him. "Why wasn't it your child, I'd like to know? You're as much to blame as anyone, it seems to me."

"Ma!" Jay Jay said, and Joanna immediately felt ashamed of her outburst.

"I'm sorry," she said. "I suppose, truth to tell, it's my fault more than anyone else's."

"Whose fault it is isn't the point," Webb said conciliatorily. "The point is, he's made a laughingstock of your son, at the very least. A cuckolded husband is a sorry sight under the best of circumstances. The fact that it was an Indian, and people resented his being here anyway—they'll never tolerate his remaining here. No, wait..." Joanna had tossed her head as if to defend her independence, "...Even if Greg leaves—and he's right, he'd have to; he'd never be able to look anyone in the eye here—they still wouldn't put up with that Indian's hanging around like nothing happened. We'd be lucky if he was the only one they lynched."

"I wouldn't mind if it was her," Joanna said with a quick upward glance.

But she knew they were right. To keep William Horse on now was to put a stamp of approval on what had happened. Not even the Hartes of Heart's Folly were that far above public opinion.

She looked around at them with tears threatening in her eyes. Jay Jay, too, looked almost ready to break down; he and the Nasoni had been the best of friends.

"I'll take care of it, if you like," Webb said.

"No, no, that's my job," Joanna said. She got up, for the first time in her life feeling the years that had begun to advance upon her.

"I guess it could as easily wait until morning," Gregory said. "The damage has already been done."

"It won't be any easier then," Joanna said.

It did not occur to her that William Horse might be asleep. Everyone had known when Nancy went into labor, earlier that night. He must at the least have suspected; she did not imagine he would have slept without learning the truth, one way or another.

She was right. There was a dim light glowing at the window of his cottage as she approached. She had thrown a shawl about her shoulders, but her hair was damp from a light rain that was falling; it shone like myriad diamonds in her hair as she stepped into the open doorway.

He turned as she came in. He had been packing; his saddlebags lay on the bed, flaps open, and the drawers to the room's single dresser gaped emptily.

They looked long and hard at one another. "You wouldn't have left without saying goodbye?" she asked.

"No," he said. He did not embellish the answer, and it seemed, now that she was here, now that he was leaving under his own initiative, that she had little to say either. All those things that had remained unsaid between them were too far along the road to bring up now.

"I'm sorry" was what she said.

He made a quick, dismissive gesture, a violent shake of his head, as if to say the fault wasn't hers. He looked at her a moment longer. Then, as if the sight were too painful, he went back to his packing. He finished, and strapped the bags shut, then stood for a while, not moving, staring down at them.

On an impulse, Joanna went to him. She did not embrace him, but only rested one cheek against the rough woolen of his shirt, heedless of whether or not he felt the tears staining the fabric.

It was the most intimate gesture that had ever existed between them. It was hard to credit that his devotion to her should have existed on so little reward.

Finally, abruptly, he moved away, bending to pick up the saddlebags and toss them over his shoulder. She walked outside with him, waiting in the fine mist while he disappeared into the darkness in the direction of the stables.

After a while he came back, walking his horse, walking, she thought, with an old man's gait, shoulders bent, feet scuffling the ground. Dawn was just beginning to edge its way over the far horizon, nudging at the darkness.

Jay Jay appeared from the house, coming with his catlike walk swiftly toward them, pausing a few feet away from his friend, and then taking the final steps more slowly, hand outstretched. They shook, and nodded wordlessly before William Horse put one foot in his stirrup and swung himself onto the horse with the grace of a dancer.

"Adios," he said to both of them, and "*Hasta la vista*," Jay Jay replied.

"*Vaya con Dios,*" Joanna said, and with that he was gone, riding slowly away. After a few yards, when the gray light had nearly swallowed him up, he spurred his horse to a canter; they could hear the hoofbeats long after he'd vanished from sight.

Joanna had supposed he would ride away from San Antone, where he could hardly expect to be welcomed. So she was no little surprised when, the following evening, Jay Jay returned from town riding hard to deliver his unhappy news.

"They've arrested William Horse," he announced, bursting unceremoniously into the office where Joanna and Gregory were going over the receipts. "He got drunk in a cantina, busted up the place, killed one man, broke another man's ribs."

Joanna was on her feet immediately, snatching down the repeating rifle that was kept on the wall just behind her desk.

Webb, who had been reading quietly in one of the room's big leather chairs, jumped up, too, and came at once to grab her arm. "No, you can't," he said firmly.

"I won't let them hang him," she said angrily, and tried to shake his hand off, but he held her fast.

"There's some things even you can't do," Webb said. "You can't start a war, Joanna, between yourself and the whole town. He's killed a man. It's a matter of law now; you'll have to let it take its course."

"I stopped Sheriff Farley once. I can do it again," she said.

"That was here on the ranch," Gregory said, "and it wasn't a killing. The whole town'll be behind the sheriff on this. You can't have a civilized town and let people get away with murder."

For a moment longer Joanna looked at them defiantly; but even Jay Jay, for all the agony in his eyes, nodded his agreement, and at length her shoulders slumped and she let Webb take the rifle from her hands and put it back on its pegs.

Despite the efforts of the attorneys, Joanna hired, the best the city had to offer, the trial took only three days to reach its conclusion: The Indian, William Horse, was to hang.

The hanging was set for a Saturday morning at eight o'clock. "So that no one need miss the show," Joanna remarked bitterly.

On Friday afternoon, Joanna dressed, her funereal black seeming horribly appropriate, and ordered the buggy brought around. "I'm going to be with him," she explained when Webb asked her plans.

"I'll go with you," he volunteered.

"No, I'll go alone" was her reply, and she left it unembroidered as she climbed into the buggy and drove off by herself.

In the days since William's arrest, Webb had been even more

considerate, more patient and helpful, than usual. Despite that fact, and her own knowledge that the others had been right in preventing her from rashly trying to free William after his arrest, she could not help feeling resentment toward all of them, and Webb in particular. It was unfair, she knew, but she harbored a feeling that she had been betrayed.

The sheriff was waiting at the door of the jailhouse to greet her when she arrived. This was the same man with whom she had quarreled over the other William's lynching, and with whom she had had her confrontation at the gates to the Folly. She was well aware that he harbored no goodwill toward her.

She had come with the unformed intention of spending the night with William. Though he had never expressed any fear—had been, indeed, as outwardly emotionless as he had always been—she knew the enormity of his crime, and the fate that awaited him, lay heavy upon him, and she felt that the least she could do for him now was to share what was certain to be a long and sleepless night.

The sheriff heard out her request with a placid smile that held no trace of sympathy. "Sorry," he said when she had finished explaining why she was there, "it's against the rules."

She had expected this, and for William's sake was prepared to humble herself in whatever way necessary to change his mind.

"Surely you can't deny a man the comfort of companionship during his last night on earth?" she argued.

The sheriff switched his cigar from one corner of his mouth to the other and winked lewdly. "Companionship?" he asked. "If you'll pardon me saying so, that there Indian's screwed his last piece. He can spend this night praying."

Joanna bit back the angry retort that was on the tip of her tongue and added instead, "If that's what you're afraid of, I can sit outside his cell, so long as he can see and hear me. You can leave the door that leads to the cells open so you can see everything yourself."

"Sorry," he said. "Rule's rules." He would have turned away from her, but Joanna grabbed the sleeve of his shirt. "Sheriff, I beg of you," she said.

He plucked the cigar from his mouth and grinned. "Are my ears deceiving me? The high-and-mighty Mrs. Harte begging from a mere sheriff? Why, what will I hear next, I wonder? What is she prepared to offer to change my mind?"

"Anything you like," Joanna said. "You want money. How much?"

"That's bribery, isn't it?"

"Call it what you like. Name your price."

He studied her for a moment, his eyes looking her body up and down in an insinuating fashion.

"Anything?"

The direction he was heading in was obvious. Joanna met his gaze evenly, unable to hide her disgust.

He flushed and looked away.

"You can sit there, outside his cell, like you said," the sheriff mumbled.

"May I have a chair?" Joanna asked.

"The floor's good enough," he said.

If William Horse was surprised to see her, he did not show it. From his manner, you might have thought it the most natural thing in the world for him and his former mistress to be sitting on opposite sides of iron bars. She had brought a picnic—cold game birds and a bottle of wine—and they ate, passing the food back and forth between the bars. She had books in her bag, and after they had eaten, she read to him from the poems of Longfellow and the Bible.

They did not talk much. Conversation had always been scarce between them, and when Joanna was not reading, in something near to a monotone, they sat for long stretches of time in silence. Once, when Joanna was temporarily adrift in a reverie of her own, he reached through the bars and took her hand gently in his. On an impulse, she brought his hand up and kissed the backs of his fingers, but he reacted as if he had been stung, snatching his hand away so violently that he gave it an ugly bruise on the bars.

Toward morning, despite her resolve, Joanna dozed. The shuffle of approaching footsteps brought her guiltily awake in time to see the sheriff and his deputies approaching.

A scaffold had been erected in the plaza the previous evening and a crowd of people had already gathered. This was the first hanging in several years, and the identity of the victim and his connection with the illustrious Hartes made it of more than common interest. A carnivallike atmosphere prevailed, but when the Indian emerged from the jailhouse, hands cuffed behind him, and surrounded by a half-dozen armed men, the silence was so keen that the gentle soughing of the wind was like the howl of a hurricane.

Asked if he would ride or walk to the scaffold, William Horse had cast one quick glance in Joanna's direction and said simply, "Walk."

"I'll walk alongside him," Joanna had said at once.

The sheriff looked about to dispute that idea, but changed his mind when he saw her expression.

So when they emerged into the morning light, Joanna was at William Horse's side. Oddly, though this was unprecedented, no one felt any particular surprise at the discovery.

Webb and the others—Gregory, Jay Jay, Yolanda, even Alice Montgomery, in her little trap, refusing to meet the eyes of any of the townswomen present—were already in the plaza. A delegation of hands from the ranch was there, too, ringing the outer fringes of the plaza, and it must have occurred to the sheriff, as he flicked a nervous glance in their direction, that Joanna could, if she wished, launch a virtual revolution with a single gesture. Certainly she had more men immediately at her disposal than he had, and this prompted him to make a show of deference: When she turned to say goodbye to her friend, he looked away and offered no objections.

Conscious of the hundreds of watching eyes, Joanna determined to be as calm and brave as William Horse was. Still, she could not prevent the tears that scalded her eyes as she stretched on tiptoe to kiss his cheek quickly, lightly.

"Till we meet again," he said in English, and nodded to the deputies that he was ready. With a man holding each arm, he was led up the steps to the waiting noose.

Webb came forward and took Joanna's arm, leading her back to where the family waited. When she looked again, the rope was already around his neck; and a scant second or two later, the trap was sprung and he dropped, with a sharp snapping sound. One foot caught at the edge of the opening through which he fell, not enough to break the fall, but it gave an eerie impression that the dead man was trying to climb back up.

There was a low murmur of voices. Now that the deed was done, people felt dissatisfied, and uncertain whether to stay or go. There was much milling about, and few looked directly at their neighbors. For all that people had feared and resented the Indian's presence at the Hartes' ranch, few of them had any real cause for complaint against him, and, belatedly, many of them were now recalling that fact.

But Joanna was recalling all those thoughts and impressions that came unwillingly, uninvited; the unworthy thoughts that shame you, that never grow dim in your memory. Moments of fleeting anger: Only an Indian. Damned redskin. What can you expect? It's in their blood. They're born that way.

The thoughts had lasted no more than an instant and never had one passed without shame for thinking it. Now, they were as sharp as knives, all those sins against his soul that she would never be able to make up for, not to him, not to herself.

"Come on, I'll take you home now," Webb said.

"No." She shook her head, shaking off the morbid thoughts that held her. "I want you to claim the body. Take it to the ranch. I've already marked the grave spot, had the hole dug, but wait for me before you put him in it."

"What are you going to do?"

"I've got business to attend to," she said. When he hesitated, she gave him a look that allowed for no argument. "Don't worry," she said, "I'll be all right. I'm all right now."

"Ma," Gregory said, but she went right by him. The lingering crowd stepped quickly back out of her way, making a path for her as she went.

THIRTY-TWO

V ery nearly the only resident of Heart's Folly who was not present at the hanging of William Horse that Saturday morning was the woman who, in a sense, had placed the rope about his neck.

There was, in fact, a moment when Nancy came close to deciding she would go with the others. Though hardly anyone who knew her would have credited it, she had actually been shocked at what turned out to be the results of her machinations. The truth was, though she certainly scorned and reviled him for his bloodline, and had bitterly resented his place in the bosom of the Harte family, Nancy's hatred of the Hartes had not extended to the now dead Nasoni. He had simply been a necessary part, as she saw it, in her plans for revenge. She could not say she had been fond of the Indian, and his attempts to forestall their relationship had earned her anger; on the other hand, they had inspired some dim sense of respect for him, too, respect for him as a man. And physically, she had keenly appreciated his manly qualities.

Her plans, however, had not gone beyond publicly shaming the Hartes. She had sincerely regretted the necessity of William Horse's leaving the ranch, if for purely selfish reasons. How could she have suspected what would subsequently happen? The blood that he had shed was surely not on her hands. Yet, when the others had gone, each conspicuously avoiding her company, she was assailed by an indescribable restlessness. Abandoning the bed where she had generally remained since the birth of the child, she dressed and spent several hours roaming about a cavernously empty house.

When she heard the others returning, she retreated to her bedroom, from the window of which she saw the plain pine coffin being unloaded from the wagon. The sight gave her a strange and troublesome pang. She suddenly remembered him alive, vibrant and hard, the pant of his breath against her ear, the earthy smell, the violent slap of flesh on flesh....

Feeling weak in the legs, she turned from the sight outside the window.

Later, though, while the others were sharing a conversationless dinner, she stole from the house as stealthily as a thief and made her way to the little cabin where William Horse had lived, and where his body now awaited its burial.

The lid was down upon the coffin, but unfastened. She told herself resolutely that she did not want to look upon him; at the same time, approaching the box, her hands seemed to reach out of their own accord, and gently, lest some sound be overheard (but by whom? He was the only other present), push aside the concealing cover.

No undertaker's art had been practiced upon him. His face was still contorted in the grimace with which he had died, and it gave the morbid impression that he was mocking her.

He did not look dead to her, however, notwithstanding that twisted expression; that might have been some childish tomfoolery, and the burn about his neck was no worse than what was inflicted on the hides of the cows.

One tentative hand reached out, slowly, very slowly, until just the tips of her fingers touched his skin. It was of that coldness indistinguishable from heat, and it struck terror in her heart. She snatched back her hand and, without replacing the lid, bolted from the cabin, ran blindly past stables and barns, wanting only to put distance between herself and that lifeless figure.

Finally, she stopped, breathless, only to discover to her dismay that her heedless dash had brought her to the iron fence that surrounded the burial plot, and there, only a few yards away, gaped the hole into which the coffin would soon be lowered, while here, practically at her feet, was the recent and miniature grave in which the Indian's son lay buried.

Now she felt pursued by some nameless nemesis and, wild-eyed, looked around. Her glance fell on the distant cross that marked the roof of the chapel, and on a thoughtless impulse she hurried there.

The building was of adobe, its walls nearly four feet thick, and inside, it was cool and dim, refreshing after the glare of the late-afternoon sun. She sank onto a bench, struggling to slow her breath, growing gradually once again calm.

After a while, she felt shed of the inexplicable panic that had assailed her, and she became more conscious of her surroundings. She had not been here, inside the chapel, since her wedding day, and then she had paid it no more than cursory attention. It was a pretty place, though—she saw that now—and a singularly peaceful one on a ranch that, even in the dead of night, seemed to thrum with a life all its own.

All at once, she felt the urge to pray. She could not say why— she was still unconscious of any remorse. It was no more than a whim, but she slipped from the bench and dropped dutifully to her knees, closing her eyes. Her lips parted to speak. But no words came. She knelt, struggling, aware of words seething and bubbling up within her, wanting to issue forth, and unable to surmount the dam that held them back. There was a roaring in her ears, a beating like the thrashing of wings, so real that she opened her eyes in alarm and looked overhead.

The chapel was empty, the silence accusing. With a cry of pain, she leaped up and started from the place. At the door, a little plaster virgin stretched one hand over a basin of water. The sightless eyes seemed to beseech and pity her.

With an angry toss of her head, Nancy leaned forward and spit into the cheap plaster face. Then, with a resolute hauteur, she strolled back to the house and ascended the stairs to her room.

She was there when Joanna returned, late in the day, from town. Looking down from her window, Nancy watched Joanna alight from her buggy. As if aware of the watcher above, Joanna glanced upward, and for the first time Nancy felt fear of this woman's powerful personality. She stepped quickly backward, letting the curtain fall into place, but she did not deceive herself that she had been unobserved.

It was only a few minutes later that the bedroom door was flung open and Joanna came unceremoniously into the room. "We're burying him now," she said without preamble. "You will stand beside your husband."

"I'm not coming," Nancy said, and was angry with herself to hear a tremor in her voice.

Joanna gave a fleeting glance at the pale pink dress Nancy was wearing. She went to the massive armoire that stood against one wall and, throwing its doors back, flicked through the hanging garments with one gloved hand. She found a black dress, snatched it from the cupboard, and threw it across the room. It fell on the floor at Nancy's feet.

"Five minutes," Joanna said, and left the room, her heels beating an imperious staccato on the tiled floor.

The service was mercifully brief. Despite the day's warmth, Nancy shivered with a chill, and would, for once have welcomed her husband's arm about her, but he had not glanced in her direction. It might have been she who had gone on to the ghost realm, for all that any of the group noticed her, and she wondered resentfully why her presence had been needed at all. Surely she did not deserve punishment; it was the Hartes who had wronged her to begin with.

When it was over, Nancy led the way back to the house, hurrying toward the shelter of her own rooms. But by the time she reached the front door, Joanna was at her side.

"If you'll come to my office," Joanna said, and did not wait for a reply. She led the way up the stairs. It was evening, and lamps had been lighted in the hall, but the office was dark. Nancy hung back, waiting in the doorway while Joanna struck a match, lighted the lamp, adjusted the wick, replaced the glass chimney. The flame danced and swayed, leading the shadows in a brief ballet before they settled back into their places, expectant, watchful.

Joanna glanced at her, but did not invite her to sit. Determined not to be cowed, Nancy came across the room and sat stiff-backed in one of the chairs facing the desk. "I have a headache," she announced. "Say what you mean to say, please, and get it over with."

"This won't take long," Joanna said. She took up the valise lying on the desktop; Nancy remembered now that Joanna had been carrying it when she arrived home. Joanna rifled through the papers she took from it, and tossed one sheaf of documents on the desk between them. "These papers spell out the terms of your separation," she said. "I won't ask that you divorce my son, but you will see that your future role as his wife will be minimal. These"—

she threw down another bundle of papers—"are for the bank. You'll receive a check monthly, so long as you do not violate the terms of the separation—primarily, that you do not set foot here again. And this is the deed to the house I've purchased for you in town. You'll find it quite adequate. You may have your mother there to live with you, if you like, and servants, subject to my approval. No one else. I've ordered a carriage to drive you there tonight."

Nancy stared at the papers before her, and then at Joanna. "Are you mad?" she asked, too angry at the moment to be frightened.

"Quite possibly. To the extent that grief and rage may drive one so. You'll find the places for your signature are indicated on each of the documents." She pushed a quill pen in its holder across the desk as well.

"I won't sign. You can't make me." Joanna's eyebrows arched upward. "I did not choose to marry your son. That was an idea of yours, to add to your grand Texas ranch. Well, I am married to him, and I shall remain so, in every respect. Do not think you will now cheat me out of any portion of what I'm entitled to. We are stuck with one another. I will remain right here, in residence, until I am an old, old lady, and you shall have to endure my presence all that while."

For a long while Joanna met her defiant gaze wordlessly. Then, calmly, with no sign of haste or even of anger, she turned and went to the wall behind her desk, where her rifle was kept. It was a Beal repeating rifle, a gift from Jay Jay two Christmases before, and it was kept loaded at all times in readiness for any emergency. Methodically, she broke it open and checked to be sure the chambers were filled. It shut with a click, and she came back to prop it against the desk by her chair before she sat gracefully down.

"I assure you," she said finally, as casually as she might have mentioned the last fading glow of the sunset framed by the windows, "if you are still beneath my roof when the sun rises tomorrow, you will never be an old, old lady."

Nancy snatched up the offered pen and began to sign the papers where indicated.

So little notice was taken of Nancy's departure by those remaining at the Folly that one might, in looking back upon her brief tenancy there, have thought her no more than one of those passing ghosts that can be expected to enliven any place so "lived-in."

"The lawyers will do the rest," Joanna said in handing over to Gregory for his inspection the various signed documents his wife had left behind. And though he might have been tempted to remind his mother where that marriage had originated, he read the papers wordlessly and, handing them back, merely nodded his assent before going about his own business.

Jay Jay had more than once found himself tempted in one direction by his sister-in-law's snide and condescending manner toward him, and in another by the lush outline of her figure; and since in his more reasonable moments he felt disinclined to yield to either temptation, he treated it as generally a good thing that the house had one less member.

For largely similar reasons, Yolanda was glad, though she expressed no such opinion to anyone.

Only with Carrie, Nancy's younger sister, did Joanna have any sort of discussion on the subject, if "discussion" it could be called.

She went to Carrie's room on the very evening, at the very time, in fact, that Nancy's carriage was disappearing down the drive, and said, in the way of explanation, "I've booted your sister out of the house."

Carrie made no pretense of surprise—Joanna thought it reasonably certain some such response had been expected of her—but she did make some show of confusion. "Are you asking me to go as well?" was her response.

"Far from it. I should be saddened if you did. And I don't think my son would thank me, either."

Carrie blushed and shyly lowered her lashes, which Joanna took for a good sign.

Alice Montgomery's attitude was more or less that no such creature as Nancy had even existed—indeed, the occasion marked the end of what, for want of any suitable term, had been regarded as the "friendship" between Alice and Nancy's mother, Dõna Sebastiano. Only one oblique reference did she make. "I wonder if Miss Carrie ought to stay on here now," she remarked one day some weeks later. "Regardless, your son is still married."

"Why, she loves the Folly," Joanna replied, innocently enough that she might have fooled someone with a less keen eye for the peccadilloes of others.

"It wasn't her love for the Folly that was bothering me," Alice said.

So it was no secret that "something pregnant" (a phrase Melissa had recently taken up from the lurid romances to which she had become prone and which, in her repeating of it, took on an unmistakably weighty significance) existed between the two. Practically the only two who seemed oblivious to its charm were the two most directly involved: Carrie and Gregory.

Joanna, who felt she had some amends to make in that direction, would have been glad to turn a blind eye to any indiscretion, but neither blind eye nor good could find any. She toyed with the question of what she might do to help. Carrie was shy, after all, and Gregory decidedly "slow-footed" when it came to romance. On the other hand, her matchmaking attempts until now had not been noticeably successful; and anyway, short of roping them together, she didn't see how she could do it.

She tried dropping hints in Carrie's direction: "Happiness, you know, is an attitude, a state of mind, not some future event. Those who wait for it to come along are likely to miss it altogether." And when that provoked no response, she added, "And to miss the happiness is to miss everything."

Another time she went even further: "You know, men are shy creatures sometimes when it comes to love. Even a man as capable and strong-minded as Gregory sometimes has to be shown what it is that he wants."

To these efforts, Carrie responded with shy smiles and blushes; but of what was on her mind, or in her heart, she said nothing.

Gregory's response to Joanna's thinly veiled hints was more to the point. "Perhaps, mother, just this once you'd let me manage things on my own."

Since this was the single rebuke he had directed at her for mismanaging his personal affairs, she let it pass.

Just when or how he did "manage things," Joanna had no idea. It had begun to seem unlikely to her that anything was ever going to come of the obvious feelings the two had for one another. The looks she saw them exchange were tender, loving even; but of heat or passion she saw no evidence, and with a sigh, Joanna turned her attention to Jay Jay and his wife.

She had more or less pried from the doctor the information that future pregnancies might be complicated for the couple. Did that mean the dynasty would end with her sons? After all she had done to build this ranch, was it, within a single generation, to pass to the children of others?

So occupied was she with this troublesome consideration that

Joanna was slow to realize it was on its way to solving itself.

"I'm having Carrie's things moved into Nancy's old room," Gregory informed Joanna one early morning.

"I'm glad," Joanna said after a moment's surprise. "I'm sorry that you can't be married, but at least you are entitled to all the happiness you can find together."

But Gregory had not yet delivered his biggest surprise. "She's going to have a baby," he added in an almost offhand manner.

This time Joanna really was flabbergasted. "But—how on earth did that happen?" she asked.

"I'd say in about the usual way" was Gregory's smiling response.

"Well, at least," Joanna told Alice some while later, when she confided the news to her, "it means I don't have to do everything around here myself."

Joanna was prepared for a public display of disapproval from the local Texans. Gregory was still married, and it could hardly be kept secret for long that his wife's sister was now carrying his child.

Perhaps it was residual guilt that lingered over the hanging of William Horse, or maybe the local citizenry had simply begun to adopt an attitude toward the Hartes significantly different from the way they regarded other people. Whatever the reason, it was soon evident that most people were simply "looking the other way." No one seemed to want to make a scandal out of the occasion. People ignored Carrie's gradually expanding waistline, or took it as a matter of course.

To this, Joanna found they had a rather unexpected ally. Her daughter, Melissa, had been on more or less friendly terms with Nancy in the past—Nancy, for one thing, had been a generous customer. And Melissa, too, was ever on the alert for the sort of bad public image that might offend any would-be shoppers.

Yet here was Melissa, plainly Carrie's champion, walking boldly down the street with her in broad daylight, defying any criticism; holding teas that just bordered on "baby showers," though they were not called that; bringing her town friends with her for ostentatious calls on "the little mother-to-be" at the ranch—more visits, Joanna pointed out, than her daughter had made since the ranch had been founded. It was true, as Alice Montgomery pointed out, that since returning from the ranch to the town, Nancy had taken her business to Melissa's chief mercantile competitor, but Melissa loudly denied that this had had any influence on her behavior. "I'm glad, to tell the truth, that I don't have to cater to that woman's awful taste; it didn't advertise well for my store," she was heard to say.

"They say," Alice mentioned, in the way of a dig, "she's living quite grandly. Quite the lady of manners, I hear."

"Manners?" Melissa scoffed loudly. "I passed within three feet of her the other day on the street and she didn't so much as give a warning rattle. You call that manners?"

It was true, Melissa's store had grown to the point where the opinions of one would-be customer were not likely to make such a difference as they might once have made. The Emporium filled an entire city block and towered three full stories high. Only Neiman-Marcus, in Dallas, challenged the Emporium as Texas's biggest and best store, and in San Antonio the Emporium reigned as the arbiter of taste and fashion.

Still, Melissa never really felt satisfied. It privately galled her that her mother, who made not the slightest effort, or so it seemed— who, it might even be said, did practically everything that she could do against her own best interests socially—remained in fact something of a social figurehead. Whatever she wore was now automatically accepted. Whatever she served at table was duly reported and could be counted upon to appear at tables throughout the city. When a party was thrown, and proved a success, the real compliment was "Couldn't have done it better on the Folly," and to have a house, a horse, even a hat, praised as "Folly grand" was to have arrived at last.

In public, Melissa was unconcerned, and was as wont as anyone to boast of the Folly's grandeur and bask in the reflected glory of her family's status. In private, her husband rarely got through a week without being held personally accountable for the deprivation his family suffered.

"Is it any wonder?" Melissa demanded of her vanity mirror, "I'm old before my time? Look at me—the lines, the wrinkles... why, I can only be grateful my friends have stood by me. They'll soon be mistaking my mother for my sister—for my daughter, even."

"You are still the most beautiful woman in the city," her husband assured her dutifully.

"That's only because she lives on that ranch. When you think of it, they don't even keep a house in town. It's barbaric, living like cowhands, even if it is the biggest house in all... That's it! Why didn't I think of that sooner? We'll build us a house just as big—

bigger, even—right here in San Antone! I'll be the queen of the city—you'll be important, too, naturally. We've suffered long enough in this place, God knows—not enough room to turn around in, though I've never wanted to complain...."

Her husband, lying in bed behind her, had been on the verge of sleep, but now, as his wife prattled on, found sleep fleeing from him as dollar signs began to dance before his eyes.

Carrie's baby was born in the spring, a little more than a year after Nancy's. Of this child's parentage, at least, no one was in doubt, and notwithstanding his illegitimacy, the boy was named Harold Sebastian Harte.

It was an exultant Joanna who received the news. At last, a grandson, an heir to Heart's Folly. It had been a difficult birth, and throughout the long and arduous labor, Joanna had fretted, fearing that fate would somehow once again cheat her.

"Bring the baby to me," she demanded right off, and the nurse hurried to do her bidding.

She waited in the hall and, when at least the child was placed in her arms, she paused to give him a cursory examination of her own—no tricks this time—before she carried him into the parlor where the others were waiting. "A fine, healthy boy," she pronounced, with as much pride as if she herself had had some hand in the event.

They were still making a fuss over the newest member of the household when a grief-stricken Gregory burst into the room, to make his tragic announcement.

"Carrie's dead," he told them. "The boy killed her."

But it was not only the child he accused with his anguished look, it was his mother.

Joanna, trying to meet his gaze, found herself thinking of Jay Jay's ominous prediction: "Someday you'll have to pay...."

She'd paid so much already, and now she was paying with her son's grief as well.

How much, Oh Lord, she wondered, how much?

Even as she thought this, though, she was holding her grandson close, and a part of her was thinking she had not yet found the price she wouldn't pay for the Folly.

PART III

HORIZONS

THIRTY-THREE

It was the horizons, Joanna had decided, that really meant Texas to her. "Where else," she was fond of asking, "could you sit on your porch and watch a storm on one horizon and a peaceful sunset on another?"

Yes, to be sure, there was also that Texas wind, the Gulf wind that seemed to sweep forever and ever into the distance, carrying faint whispers of things the sea tries to warn land-men of. The mountains, blue and vague in their distant grandeur. The bawling longhorn and the trackless prairie. The flat, wide rivers with their muddy waters. San Antone, its streets as twisting and mysterious as the ancient trails they followed.

But it was that wedding of land and sky that never failed to thrill her, that kept Texas forever on her mind, imprinted on her soul. It was why she had never moved into the city. Often ranchers did; they built grand mansions for themselves and visited their ranches once or twice a month as if making pilgrimages.

Joanna didn't even have a house in town. "Not," as she pointed out, "that we've any need for one. Melissa's is big enough to house an army."

There was more to it than that, of course; it was a sort of treaty between herself and her daughter. Here in town she permitted her daughter to reign on her behalf—not only permitted her, but helped her where she could.

Which made it possible for Melissa to play hostess on this particular evening to this particularly glittering assemblage. "Everyone," Melissa had boasted several times to her husband, "who is anyone in San Antone, or Texas either, for that matter."

That may have been an exaggeration, but only a slight one by Texas standards. Senator Wilkinson, once in charge of reconstruction and now an influence in Washington, was there, as was the new governor of Texas, Governor Adams.

There were millionaires aplenty, of course, for what was a Texas party without millionaires? Cattlemen, mostly, for cattle was king now in Texas, cotton little more than an earlier dream despite the railroads that had finally opened up the state to the rich markets of the North and the East.

"If that chandelier fell," Joanna remarked at one point to Webb, "half the cattle money of Texas would be wiped out."

She herself counted as cattle money. Unlike many of the others present, she had not completely forsworn agriculture, and farming still represented a healthy portion of their income, though nothing compared to their cattle profits. Heart's Folly was one of the leaders in the crossbreeding of different strains, in the never-ending effort to produce the best beef. The old longhorn strain was dying out— "Rest in peace," most thought. The days of the cattle drives were over. The eastern markets craved a beefsteak they could cut without a hacksaw, and they got it from the Folly. Along with corn, wheat, oats, some cotton still—even some rice, thirty years after Lewis had first thought of growing it in a far-off place called Texas.

Three or four times a year, when her schedule permitted, Joanna liked to trudge out herself to the graveyard where Lewis lay buried. She weeded and planted new flowers. Silently, she talked to her husband, told him of the progress they had made. She wanted him to share the triumph, that massive ranch, which seemed every year to grow larger, feeding on Texas, sharing the propensity for size that was the state's most obvious characteristic. It was true, she had early taken the reins from his hands, had assumed the responsibility for making Heart's Folly what it had become—but, as he had once bitterly pointed out to her, the very chance to do so had been his gift to her, born of his dependency on her, his need, even his failings.

If the ranch owed its existence to her, she owed it to him.

"Why, there you are, Mrs. Harte. It has been troubling me for some minutes that the light seemed to have gone out of the party."

Joanna turned and watched Senator Wilkinson emerge onto the terrace, crossing toward her a bit ponderously, for he had grown ample on the bounty of serving Texas.

"Forgive me," Joanna said. "One hears so many complain of the hot Texas air, but it never fails to revive me."

"As you revive whatever portion of Texas is graced by your presence."

"An example," Joanna said laughing, "of that Texas hot air I was mentioning."

"Pure Texas," he said, laughing with her. "Why, in Texas what could be more typical than a little bull?"

"I'll wager you won't say that where your voters can hear."

"I stand before my voters—at least, a large percentage of them. It's no secret in political circles, no one in Texas owns more votes than Joanna Harte."

Joanna did not smile at that. "I represent a great many votes," she corrected him. "I do not own them."

"They vote the way you tell them."

"They choose, more often than not, to vote the way I recommend."

Unintimidated, the senator laughed again. "There's not a hand on that ranch would dream of voting otherwise. Nor hardly a member of that ranchers' association you head."

Joanna shrugged. "As it turns out, what's good for the Folly is good for the people living on it—and, by and large, for the people of the other big ranches."

"You should be a politician yourself," the senator said jovially. "I've said it before and I'll say again, right this minute, you should be in Washington, my dear, you belong in the heart of things."

"This is the heart of things, senator." Joanna gestured beyond the terrace, to where San Antonio and its winding river lay in the moonlight. As always when she spoke of Texas, Joanna seemed to look beyond the moment, seemed to see the whole sprawling land in one sweeping glance, its past, its present, even what waited ahead. "Why, do you know, out by the Big Bend, there's a town that's been inhabited for more than ten thousand years? The oldest inhabited town on the continent, they say. The Spanish raised the first cross here in 1691, and no one knows how long the Payayas had their village here before that. The missions were teaching music here— the harp, the violin, the guitar—long before they thought of setting up music schools anywhere else in the country. No, I could never leave San Antone. I don't imagine anyone could who's ever lived here."

"It's that ranch of yours you can't leave, I'd wager."

Joanna did not try to argue that point; she smiled up at the senator. "My husband is buried there," she said, as if that explained everything.

"For whom you still wear black," he said, but his smile was a trifle mocking. No one could honestly describe Joanna's gown on this occasion as mourning garb. It was black, true; but if one believed the lecture Melissa had delivered with the dress, it had taken no fewer than eight women no less than six months to sew on the thousands and thousands of beads, made of Austrian crystal, with which the black silk was embroidered. They cascaded from bodice to floor, a shimmering waterfall that outshone even the pink white diamonds at Joanna's throat. A gasp had gone up when she entered Melissa's spacious foyer, and even the enormous chandelier had seemed for a moment to dim its resplendent light.

"Ah, here you are," Webb said now from the doorway. He came forward smiling. Turning to watch him, Joanna thought, as she often did, that surely he was still the handsomest man in Texas— which, of course, meant in the world as well. "Evening, senator."

"Here I am," the senator said, "in the company of a woman of staggerin' beauty and undeniable charm, and her gentleman friend on discovering us shows no trace of jealousy. I declare, I don't know whether to be insulted or amused."

"Awed, I'd say, by the lady's unimpeachable virtue," Webb said, and to Joanna, "The governor is preparing to leave. He specifically wanted to say goodnight to you."

"And, no doubt, to thank you for that advice you gave him on one or two pending bills," the senator suggested. The two men, one on either side, accompanied Joanna toward the doorway.

"Advice I hope he'll take to heart," Joanna said.

"A man would be foolish to ignore the advice of such a shrewd constituent."

"Particularly one who contributes so generously to his campaigns."

The senator laughed, but there was an edge to his laughter. "Why, Mrs. Harte, I am forever telling my confreres in Austin and in Washington, cold cash is not everything."

"Not so long as the banks accept checks," Joanna said. "Ah, Governor Adams, they tell me you're about to deprive us of your company." She went smiling toward the governor. Melissa was already at his side, clinging a bit too fervently to one arm.

"It is I who will feel deprived," the governor said, bending to kiss her hand. "San Antonio is lucky indeed to count two women of such beauty among its inhabitants."

Doña Sebastiano had come up uninvited on the other side of the governor; though her daughter did not socialize with the Hartes, Doña Sebastiano had not yet retired from the social field of battle. Melissa had been against having her to the party; it was Joanna who had argued for her old adversary.

"She represents the Old Guard," Joanna had pointed out.

"I remember when they came here," Doña Sebastiano said to the governor, "and now look how they live. I still say they did something crooked."

The governor looked a trifle askance at this, but when he saw nothing but amusement on Joanna's face, he joined in the general laughter. "Well, Texas is a land of opportunity," he said. "Goodnight, ladies, senator, Mr. Price."

The senator went with him toward the door; and Webb, with a wink in Joanna's direction, asked Doña Sebastiano if she cared to dance.

"You could waltz me over to that punch bowl," the señora replied coolly, "The way those waiters are guarding it, you'd think it was the Alamo."

Melissa and Joanna were left momentarily alone. "What a charming man that governor is," Melissa said.

"As crooked as they come" was Joanna's assessment.

"Oh, pooh, crooked politician. That's the nature of the beast, isn't it? So long as there's steak enough to go around, why should I care if the governor's got a dab of gravy on his?"

"I think I like you better being silly than cynical."

"If, instead of lollygagging about in the country, you had to drudge for a living as I have had to do since the day you foisted

me on that shopkeeper I married, you would know more about
the ways of the world. I for one have seen businesses run to no
profit by honest fools, whereas the man who has one hand in the
till is likely to keep the register ringing with the other, to everyone's
advantage."

Joanna, who still had not learned to take her daughter very
seriously, laughed. "Perhaps you're right," she said. "In view of
your management policies, I might be better off giving up my ranch
and taking a job at the Emporium."

"Working for a living would open your eyes to things, I promise
you. Ronnie John, come here."

Melissa's son—and heir apparent to the Emporium—left the
blowsy-looking woman to whom he was speaking nearby and came
obediently to join his mother. "What is it, mama? Hello, grandma."
Melissa's son, Ronald, was the only person who had ever called
Joanna by that title, and she was certain he knew how much it
displeased her. She did not, in fact, derive any pride from the fact
that he was her grandson. He was Texan through and through,
she'd grant him that, and good-looking, in a flashy sort of way. But
though she had never seen him armed, he reminded her too much
of the old train stops in Cotulla, where as the train slowed, the
conductor would yell, "Cotulla, get your guns ready!"

For all the elegance of his dress, Ronnie John was unmistakably
an outlaw.

"Alissa Ayers is a married woman, and her husband an important
man locally," Melissa was saying. "It does not look respectable for
you and her to be tee-heeing together behind a palm tree. What
were you talking about, anyway?"

"Why, I was telling her about that new shipment you got in,
mama, of that fine French underwear. I expect I've about talked
her into a large order."

"Well, the way her husband's looking over here, I expect he's
about ready to see you get paid."

They were still arguing as Joanna drifted away. She was looking
for Gregory, and at last she found him, standing by himself in a
far corner. Joanna paused some distance away, regarding him sadly.
Since Carrie's death, her son had aged badly; he looked older now
than she did. Not just old, but grim; she couldn't recall when last
she'd seen him smile.

He looked around and saw her staring at him. Joanna smiled at him, and came to where he was standing. "I really think I'm getting tired," she said. "I'm sure no one will mind if we leave. Are Jay and Yolanda around?"

"They've already gone. Alexandra had a cough earlier; Yolanda wanted to look in on her."

"Alice is still holding court," Joanna said. "I'll see if I can get her eye. You look around for Webb, why don't you."

Alice was where Joanna had left her two hours before, in the withdrawing room. She herself declared that she was "no longer fit for dancing," but the real reason, Joanna discerned, was that on the dance floor Alice could hardly help being eclipsed by all the young, beautiful women whirling about. And despite advancing years, Alice was no more fond of being upstaged than she had ever been.

In the past few years, Alice had taken, without specific announcement, to nearly always wearing white, in contrast to Joanna's black. "Salt and pepper," Melissa declared them derisively, though not in her mother's presence. But the trick had its effect, for the more stunning Joanna's appearance, the more reflected glory Alice accrued.

Of late, however, her voice had begun to weaken (overuse, Joanna thought privately); for Alice, a real calamity. Undaunted, she had risen to the difficulty by means of a little crystal bell that she carried in her reticule and, wherever she ensconced herself, was to be seen at her side. Whenever she had something she wanted to say, which she wished heard by more than just those at her elbow, she rang her bell and, into the surprised hush that followed, dropped her bit of gossip, an epigram, a dot of unasked-for advice. Another ring of the bell was the signal for others to take up their conversation where it had broken off. Since Joanna herself had been the first to show respect for the custom, others had been obligated to do likewise, and by now it had become a thing generally accepted. The individualist had become a commonplace in Texas.

Later, on their way home in the brougham, through night air so balmy and soft you felt you could float away on it, Joanna found herself thinking of the senator's remarks about her owning votes.

The Folly had grown enormously. The simple hands living on their own little plots of grounds—how naïve that seemed now— had become rancheros, each family with its own ranch, or *ranchito,* many of them quite distant from the main ranch. Mockingly, Jay Jay compared it to a feudal principality, or one of those English estates with its tenant farmers.

Where the hands had once lived, there was now something very like a town—they even called it Heartsville, though it was not actually incorporated. Mostly it was occupied by the migrant workers who came and went seasonally from Mexico. There was a little general store, run by Mexicans but actually owned by Melissa; an apothecary; and the school, run by Abraham Lincoln Harte himself—despite those who disapproved of Mexican and even white children being taught by a Negro.

"There's a man in Alabama, name of Washington, has opened an all-Negro college," Abraham had informed her recently, but he had declined her suggestion that he might want to do the same in Texas. "All mixed up together, that's the best way," he insisted, in defiance of custom.

Aside from the considerable number of people who now made up the population of Heart's Folly, there were others who presumably felt Joanna's influence as well; she now headed a ranchers' association that stretched over a goodly portion of the state. No doubt her advice was listened to; people tended to listen to those who were successful.

At least, she hadn't done as a great many other ranchers were said to do: It was said that some actually locked the gates of their ranches at election time, in effect holding their workers prisoner until they'd voted as their masters wanted them to vote.

At the Folly, Joanna actively worked to see that her people understood the candidates and the issues, and she even tried to persuade them to vote according to their own judgments and not hers. She went out and around the *ranchitos,* sent Greg and Jay and Yolanda as well. The end result, however, was nearly always the same: The people voted exactly as they divined she wanted them to vote, sometimes astonishing her with their perception.

Well, she hadn't courted that sort of power, had she? It was as she had told the senator: What was good for her, for the ranch, was likely to be what was good for the people on it as well, and for other ranches, too.

Still, the thought nagged, that perhaps no one person was entitled to wield that much influence—or, for that matter, was competent to do so. Heaven knew, she was capable of making mistakes, and the thought of all those thousands of people compounding them in her name was a bit disquieting.

Gregory interrupted her thoughts. "I heard from Harold," he said, in the carefully noncommittal voice he always used regarding his son.

"Oh?" was all Joanna said; she had learned to tread warily where that relationship was concerned. Fathers and sons; mothers and daughters; the quagmires, she thought, of human relations. Was anything else so hard to get right? Or so important?

"He's on his way home. He's stopping in South Carolina. Wanted to see, I gather, the place we came from."

For a moment, for the first time in years, Joanna's thoughts went back, to South Carolina. Lord, it seemed like a foreign country to her now, like someplace she had read about in a book. So far had she come since then, and not in miles only—why, they covered the miles now in no time at all; by train, it took—what?—two, three days to travel the distance that had taken them months. Everything had shrunk so—her memories, distances...No, that wasn't true, not everything had shrunk. Not San Antone. Not the Folly. Not Texas. They had grown. She had grown, and she smiled into the darkness, relieved once more to discover that she had been right all along.

"He's changed his name."

The remark brought her head snapping around. "Not from Harte?" she demanded sharply.

"No. He's still Harte, but he calls himself Sebastian now instead of Harold."

So, in a sense, she thought, it was yet another rejection. A rejection of the name his father had given him, and, in some measure, of the Harte name, too; Sebastian was clearly derived from his mother's name. Just as he'd seemed to reject Texas when he had insisted on going east to school. She'd half expected, when he went, that he wouldn't come back.

Well, so he was coming back, and bringing with him the problems that had existed since the misfortune of his birth. It was more than just the strain that existed between him and his father. Yolanda and Jay had children now; her miscarriage had not repeated itself. The twins, Lewis and Mathew, and their youngest, Alexandra, had all been born without mishap. Legitimate heirs to the ranch.

That was something, of course, that could not be rectified.

Though he bore the Harte name, Harold (she would have to try to remember, Sebastian now; he had so many resentments already, she didn't want to add to them) would always be Gregory's illegitimate son—the bastard; even his cousins called him that, despite having their seats warmed for it.

After all, the birth of that first heir, for which she had waited and hoped so fervently, had only complicated matters, and not solved anything.

It was up to her, of course, to settle the succession. Gregory was the obvious heir apparent, but though he managed the business of the ranch well, she suspected his heart was no longer in it—and certainly he was no cattleman.

Jay and Yolanda were cattle people, and nothing else; neither had the business head needed for an enterprise as vast as the Folly. Who, of the younger generation, should take over when the time came, as it must, for her to step down? No one asked her that question directly, but she knew it was on their minds, as it was on hers.

She sighed; they were nearly home. Well, she would wait and see what effect if any an eastern education had had on the prickly youngster she had once thought the obvious heir.

THIRTY-FOUR

"It must have stood just there, by that bend in the river."

Sebastian Harte—named Harold at birth—looked in the direction indicated by his cousin's pointing finger. There was nothing to see but a slight rise in the land and a grove of magnolia trees, thick now with white blossoms. In his imagination, however, he thought he could see Eaton Hall as he had seen it since first hearing, as a little boy, of that magnificent home he had never known. His aunt Melissa had been fond of describing it to him, and once in a while he had pried some little reminiscence from his uncle Jay. Aunt Alice, who was of course no aunt at all and had never seen Eaton Hall, had never been reluctant to embroider what he had gleaned with details of her own.

The house thus raised for him by imagination was, surprisingly, not so far from what its reality had been: immense, festooned with wrought iron and bougainvillaea, with countless columns and verandas, shaded by the trees, in sight of the Ashley River. Exactly the sort of place he'd have liked to grow up in. And why anyone should want to go from here to Texas was beyond his comprehension.

His cousin, Beauregard, fidgeted beside him; his fifth cousin, if he counted right, or maybe sixth. If some ardent swain had whispered in a girl's ear on a moonlit night thirty years earlier, it counted as bloodline to these Carolinians, or so it seemed to him.

Well, for that he could be grateful; otherwise, it was unlikely his cousin, who clearly was none too fond of him, would have troubled to make this trip with him.

People often didn't like him. He rarely let that trouble him; indeed, there were times when he seemed to go out of his way to cultivate the dislike of others.

"Shall we go?" he said, turning to his cousin. "I am grateful to you for bringing me here."

"Not at all," Beau said, starting for the carriage without hesitation. "Though why you should want to bother, I can't imagine. The property was sold out of the family long ago." He made something of an accusation out of this fact, as if the deed were a crime against him personally.

"I know," Sebastian said, and made no effort to explain himself further; he wasn't entirely sure he could have anyway.

They rode back to town, where Sebastian was staying with his cousin's family. There was little conversation along the way, each of them more interested in his own thoughts than in the company of the other.

Sebastian Harte was tall and thin, with narrow shoulders and chest. His eyes were his most arresting feature, large and wide, with nearly fanatic brilliance. His pale, thin lips were curved in an almost perpetual smile, but it was a smile that bordered very closely upon a sneer. As a boy in Texas, he had grown up the butt of jokes. It seemed as if everyone who had a grudge against the Hartes— and to some degree or another, practically everyone in San Antonio had—regarded this bastard son of Gregory's as the perfect outlet for it.

A thin, nervous child, he had early developed as his defense a sort of contemptuous arrogance—he could dismiss one entirely with nothing more than the raising of his eyebrows, a habit that, as he grew older, only aggravated the antagonism of others toward him.

Year by year, he had grown more inward-turning, more openly defiant toward the world at large. By the time he was ready to pursue his schooling, he had no friends, and no love for his native Texas. Going away to school had been an obvious choice for him.

When at last the train bearing him eastward had left Texas behind, he had felt for the first time in his life as if he breathed freely, without the necessity of justifying in some way each lungful of air.

Yet his life in Boston, as a student, had not been conspicuously happier. Nor, for that matter, any more filled with friends. His name was right—it was known, as it turned out, even here in far-off Massachusetts—and no one gave any indication of awareness that he was only an illegitimate member of the clan. He found that among the wealthy young men who were his fellow students, he was far from the poorest. He was at best an indifferent athlete, but so were many others, and certainly he was among the better students.

None of which availed him in the least when it came to making friends.

For one thing, it was soon accepted as fact that he was a liar. He was quite offhand about it. Most of his life heretofore had been spent in fantasy realms of his own devising, and now, far from home and from those who knew him as he really was, it came to him naturally to offer his fantasies in place of the grim realities of his life. He spun one yarn after another, many of them in blatant contradiction, and with no apologies for the fact that they were often patently preposterous.

From surprise and embarrassment, his listeners soon advanced to scorn and eventually ridicule, the same sort of ridicule that he had come east—and invented his stories—to escape.

If he had been more good-natured, possessed of the charm that makes many a rake more enjoyable company than his virtuous brethren, this vice of his might have been looked upon and tolerated as a mere eccentricity. There was something about him, however, that grated on the sensibilities of others and interfered with the natural forgiveness of youth.

The four-in-hand necktie had only recently assumed ascendancy over the cravat and the string tie in popularity. That fashionable item, however, had not yet come to Texas. Soon after his arrival in Boston, observing that the new tie was de rigueur, Sebastian purchased one, and quickly found himself stymied when it came to tying it. Too proud to ask assistance, too disdainful to conceal his ignorance, he had stood before the mirror in his room for some minutes, struggling, until his roommate took pity on him and came alongside him before the mirror to guide his hands. At the first touch, however, Sebastian jerked away with a violent shudder, yanking his hands from the contact as if he feared some contamination.

The insult to his roommate was unforgivable, and he was not the first nor the last to discover Sebastian's aversion to physical contact, nor the only one to begrudge it. The young man from Texas found himself as alone in Boston as he had been before he came. And so accustomed was he to being alone that he fell into this state as if it were simply the natural order of things, and rather than trying to remedy it, did pretty well all that he could to foster it, not from preference so much as from a lack of any hope that things would be different. His sneering smile became more pronounced, his eyebrows rarely settled to their natural level, and in a matter of weeks he found himself almost universally ignored by those around him.

This, at least, was an improvement over the badgering and bullying he had known as a boy; so that in comparison, his life in Boston seemed happy to him.

He often went to the symphony and the opera, and if his fellow students had seen him then, transported by the music to sunny Spain, to Mantua, to druid England, they would have discovered him singularly at his ease, smiling a smile more natural than any they had seen on his face, at one with those people on the stage, whose make-believe world was more real to him than the one he knew in Boston or had known in Texas.

He was in the habit of standing about outside the stage entrance afterward, watching the performers as they left. He did not accost them, nor ask for their autographs, and when one or the other of them happened to notice him, he went at once into some ridiculous pantomime or other, scuffling about on the sidewalk in search of some imaginary article he pretended to have lost, looking up and down the street for some fictitious friend he was waiting to meet, until the performer, glancing a little askance in his direction, had entered into the waiting carriage and driven off.

He had discovered the nearby hotel in which the performers were likely to stay, and sometimes, instead of the stage door, he lingered about outside there, watching the guests come and go, observing the quick smoothness of the doorman as he rushed to open doors, stealing glimpses of the gilt-and-velvet lobby. He was entirely aware as he did so that he could have afforded to stay at the hotel himself anytime he chose; indeed, could quite probably have purchased it. So far as money could supply, he had at hand the means for that elegance he admired with such passion in those he observed. His grandmother was nothing if not generous, and if there was a bottom to the Harte wealth, it was too deep for him to discover.

Yet, there was something in him that kept him outside, just as he had always been—outside the circle of his family, outside the larger circle that seemed to bind together all those others in the name of Texas, outside even that still larger family circle of mankind. He seemed to stand just outside the lighted windows, imagining a life for himself within.

They were entering the city of Charleston. "I have some business to attend to," Sebastian said quite abruptly. "If you'll ask your driver to put me down where it's convenient..."

"We'll be glad to take you wherever you wish to go," his cousin Beau said, without any great enthusiasm.

"Not at all. A walk will do me good, particularly with a ball to look forward to." The cousin's family was throwing a party for their guest that same evening.

"And deuced hard it is to know whom to invite," had been Beau's private complaint, "to meet such an odd one, and a Texan to boot."

Sebastian got down at the next corner, with assurances that he would be back at the house in plenty of time.

He waited without moving until the carriage was out of sight before he began to stroll. As he went, he looked up and down the streets at each corner he passed. He was looking for a particular street without knowing its name or even its exact location. He certainly knew, however, that every city of any appreciable size had such a street, almost surely in the meaner section and, in a seaport such as Charleston, probably convenient to the docks.

He found soon enough what he was looking for. A trio of sailors from one of the ships in the not distant harbor were supporting one another down the street, so much the worse for drinking, though it was only midafternoon. The bars were seedy-looking and odorous; music drifted from open doors and windows, and a crudely painted woman leaned down from one balcony to invite him for a drink. He ignored her, and got himself called something less pleasant than the *chérie* with which she had first greeted him.

Only a block farther along, he found a girl more suited to his tastes. She was not particularly pretty, though she was undeniably young, little more than a child. The cheap dress she wore did not disguise a thinness almost certainly owing to hunger, which no doubt accounted for that look of desperation stamped on her gaunt face.

He approached her with a confidence and an air of authority conspicuously lacking in his relations with most. The price he offered her was niggardly, so much so that despite her straits, he could see indecision in her eyes briefly, before she nodded a hasty, embarrassed assent. Why he was so tightfisted in these matters when otherwise he had no qualms in flinging money about, he could not say. Certainly he knew, even as he followed her down a side alley and up a rickety staircase, that it was within his means to bring the limited imaginings that were her wildest dreams to reality; he even went so far as to picture how she would look if he were to open his wallet and scatter at her feet more money than she had ever seen at one time in her life, a fortune to her, a pittance to himself.

But the picture gave him only a fleeting and insignificant amusement, without tempting him to action, and when their business was concluded—she lying exhausted on the bed, already showing the welts that his violent caning would leave her—he put not a cent more on the table than they had agreed upon, and left without a word of parting.

In the alley below, he paused, shivering with disgust as a rat raced across his feet. He was terrified of such vermin, despised with the keenest passion of which he was capable the sort of poverty existent in the room he had just left—the filth, the baby crying from the corner of the floor where he'd been placed to vacate the bed, the broken window from which, no doubt, her neighbors had heard the jade whimpering: All these sickened his stomach and stank in his nostrils.

And yet, strolling back toward the more civilized quarter of the town, he walked with a lightness of foot, he breathed more freely, smiled more easily, than before. He felt strong and powerful, his self-respect restored.

He was ready now to face his cousins' party.

THIRTY-FIVE

"C ourse, these days, you can't expect the real people," Cousin Beau was saying. "Most of them are too old or too poor to leave their houses." And, he was thinking, not much inclined to, to meet an upstart Texan, however rich.

"Really?" Sebastian's haughty gaze was raking the room; several sweet blossoms withered under its passing.

"And that one? Is she real people?" he asked unexpectedly.

His cousin, surprised, followed the direction of his glance. "Emily Cates? Yes, she's real people all right, but you can forget her, I assure you. She's poor as a church mouse, for one thing. Not that that would signify particularly; most of the good families are poor since the war, though they do their best to uphold. The real problem is, too long walking beneath the magnolias, if you catch my meaning. Seems she had herself a sweetheart, till he came up and found himself another little filly with some gold in her teeth. Left Miss Emily standing practically at the church door, he did."

"She's pretty," Sebastian said.

"Umm, yes, if you like another man's castoffs." He looked at his cousin, and again at Emily Cates. "I expect she's not as uppity as she used to be, anyway. It's an ill wind, they say."

They went on, Cousin Beau introducing Sebastian around the room. Sebastian, however, found his glance returning now and again to the young woman they had been discussing. It was easy to pick her out, even from across the room. She had pale yellow hair that stood out like a light—hair, he found himself thinking, the color of a palomino's mane, and was immediately annoyed at himself for the idea; it was the sort of thought a Texan would come up with.

She was pretty, too; but more than that, it was her graceful, aristocratic manner that intrigued him, particularly knowing that there stood against her the sort of prejudice that might easily intimidate one less self-possessed. If Emily Cates minded, or even noticed, the little snubs he saw her receiving from other women present, she showed no sign of it. Expert at ignoring such things himself, he felt a kinship with another who could do so.

Unlike his cousin, he felt no distaste at her loss of reputation. Aristocratic ladies in general put him off, and brought out the worst in his disdainful manner. The knowledge that Miss Emily was what his cousin would call "soiled goods," far from diminishing her appeal, rather enhanced it for him. He, a bastard, had no need to feel inferior to her, a fallen woman.

Emily Cates, on the other hand, refused to think of herself as a fallen woman. She had been foolish—she could acknowledge that with a tinge of bitter self-reproach. But she would not continue to flail herself for that, nor give up all her respect for herself. She had been foolish for love, and what woman in love had not at least been tempted to the same weakness? If she still suffered pain, it had more to do with the depth of her feelings for that heartless man who had jilted her than it did with the rudeness of those women who ignored her this evening, or the men who left her sitting by her aunt while every other woman in the room danced.

"I believe," Emily said, getting to her feet, "I'll get myself some punch. It doesn't look as if anyone else is going to bring me any."

"I'll come with you," her aunt said with a melancholy sigh, but Emily shook her back into her chair.

"Never mind, I don't think at this late date we need worry about my reputation being compromised," she said, and went off, ignoring her aunt's disapproving look.

She couldn't have been more surprised when the young visitor from Texas approached her by the punch table and asked her to dance. Thus far he had danced only one dance this evening, with his hostess, and already the information had circled the room that he was haughty and vain, a peculiar criticism from a collection of people who wore their own hauteur with such ease, Emily thought.

But when he had led her into a waltz, she discovered that his hand on her back trembled slightly. Surprised, she glanced up, and caught an off-guard anxiousness in his eyes. Why, he's shy, she thought, that's why he asked me.

The knowledge made her feel more kindly toward him, and she subtly and firmly set about helping him with the dance, marking the beat heavily with her foot and swaying her body decidedly to provide the rhythm he all too obviously lacked. After a moment he realized what she was about and let her, in effect, lead them, though he appeared to be doing so, with the result that, from stumbling awkwardly about the floor, they began to waltz creditably. She was rewarded with a brief smile that was, from him, far rarer than she could know.

He escorted her back to her aunt, leaving her with a small bow, but was back two dances later to claim her again. After that, he made a rather dismal effort with her aunt Julia, and followed this with two straight turns with (it was obvious by this time) his favorite partner.

"You live with your aunt, I believe?" Oddly, it was very nearly his first effort thus far at conversation with her.

"Yes," she answered plainly. If he did not already know that her father had turned her out of his house, she felt no compulsion to tell him what a hundred others were probably dying to inform him of at the earliest opportunity.

"Would you think it forward if I asked her permission to call on you?" he asked.

She looked up, surprised, half thinking he was making fun of her, but could find no amusement in his eyes. He was not a handsome man, though there was something in that tortured look she fancied she saw in his eyes occasionally that touched a responsive chord within her. She had a notion that the vanity others were already criticizing was a defensive action.

"I shall save you the trouble," she said, smiling at him, "and give you permission myself. I have the unusual advantage of being less burdened by the demands of decorum than many others present."

He came to call the following afternoon. "He's very rich" was all
her aunt Julia had to say of him when he had departed.

He was back again the following day. And the day after that,
when he'd been there an hour or so, he asked Emily to come for
a stroll with him in the garden behind her aunt's house.

"I mean to go into politics," he said soon after they began to
walk. "In Texas. Of course, there'll have to be a period of time in
law, but my family connections will render that easy enough."

She could not think what answer might be expected of her, or
even why he was telling her these things, so she continued at his
side in respectful silence.

"A politician needs not only a wife," he went on after a pause,
in the tone of one delivering a well-rehearsed speech, "but a wife
of a particular sort—someone who can be gracious, who knows
how to entertain, to make at ease a wide variety of people. She
needn't be intelligent—that can be a drawback in the political
arena—but she needs a certain sense, shrewdness if you will. She
must be able to handle herself adroitly in all kinds of..."

He paused; she had come to an abrupt halt beside him on the
path, and when he looked at her, he found her regarding him in
some confusion.

"Is this—are you proposing to me?" she asked.

"Yes," he said. "Yes, of course. What did you think?"

"Why, I don't—you must know, surely, I have a reputation?"
Which was not at all what she had meant to say; she was grateful
that at least he did not pretend ignorance.

"You won't have, in Texas," he said. "There's Texas itself, of
course. Texans are a bullying, loathsome bunch. I won't try to
deceive you—you won't find the sort of people you're used to
here."

"I don't know that I have any great love for the people I'm used
to here," she said. "But if you dislike Texas so, why do you mean
to go back?"

He looked genuinely puzzled by the question. "I don't understand," he said. "You can't just *leave* Texas."

"But San Antonio must be, why, a thousand miles from here.
You *have* left, as far as that goes."

"Oh, no, no, not at all. That's just going away, that's not leaving.
Texas is like—what's that thing you get from mosquitoes? Malaria,
that's it. Once you get it in your blood, it's there forever, like it or
not. Besides"—he paused, and something dark, like a cloud, passed

over his countenance—"there's people there I owe. I could never be free till I had paid my debts."

She shook her head. "Now it's my turn not to understand," she said.

"You will when you've been in Texas awhile. That is, if you mean to accept my proposal."

"Why, I suppose I'll have to, if only to see Texas, now that you've piqued my curiosity.

He looked a trifle uncertain. "Is it settled then?" he asked. "Shall I talk to your family?"

"I think we may assume them willing. But what of your people? Will your mother—"

"My mother is dead," he said quickly, sharply, so that she knew to be cautious on that subject in the future.

"Your father, then?"

"We may assume he'll be as willing as your own, if he notices at all. I'll be here for another eight days. It would be simplest if we returned as man and wife. I don't wish, however, to hurry you into anything."

She hesitated no more than a second or two. "I've got no reason to wait," she said.

And with that, it was decided. They were wed a week later, simply, in her aunt's parlor, and the day after that, as Mrs. Sebastian Harte, Emily was on her way to Texas.

"You mustn't expect much in the way of welcome," he said, though he had sent a telegram to his father before the wedding ceremony. "My family's attention is little diverted from their ranching activities."

She had not traveled ten miles into Texas, however, before she discovered how mistaken her husband was on that score.

THIRTY-SIX

"**O**ur train is being attacked."

"What?" Sebastian shot his wife a startled glance and turned toward the window. By that time they could already hear the gunshots of the masked riders Emily had seen galloping toward the train. Iron wheels groaned in protest as the train began to slow to a stop.

"They're ours," Sebastian said.

"Ours?"

"Those are the vaqueros from the Folly. Someone's idea of a welcome, apparently."

"A welcome? But surely we're not there yet. I thought San Antonio was some distance from the border?"

"Three hundred miles or so."

"And they came all this way to meet us?"

"Texans do things in a big way" was all he said.

The train had stopped fully now. Emily, staring out the window, had observed the riders firing into the air all along. They surrounded the train, pulling down the bandannas that had half covered their faces. Many of them were grinning hugely at their little surprise.

The door of the car opened and a brown-skinned girl with shining black hair down to her waist came in, followed by a short, strikingly handsome cowboy. "There he is," the girl cried, and ran down the aisle to greet them. "You must be Emily—we're your new family, or part of it. That's Jay Jay, and I'm Yolanda."

Emily found herself swept up in exuberant hugs by both of them. She could not help noticing that the greetings they exchanged with Sebastian were far more restrained. So far, she could not detect any sign that her new husband was even pleased by the meeting.

"Come on," Yolanda said, taking Emily's arm possessively. "We've already made arrangements for your baggage."

"But—come where?" Beyond the train's windows, Emily could not even see a town, nothing but Texas prairie, the horizon broken here by distant stands of pine trees.

"We're traveling to San Antone in style," Jay Jay said.

The newlyweds were swept along the aisle to the unloading platform. At the door, Yolanda turned back grinning to say to the other passengers, "Sorry for the interruption, folks. Have a nice trip." To Emily's astonishment, no one had lodged a protest, or even seemed terribly surprised; were Texans really accustomed to such behavior?

They were no sooner outside than the train began slowly to move again. Several passengers leaned out windows to wave and shout goodbyes and congratulations.

The vaqueros had formed a long, unbroken line along the tracks. They made an impressive sight, their costumes colorfully embroidered, their bridles and stirrups trimmed in hammered silver. Now, as if on signal, though Emily had not discerned one, they swept their enormous hats from their heads in a gracious salute.

Spontaneously, Emily grinned and waved her hand in reply. That brought her a chorus of shouts: "Ahh-haaa," in a high, nasal whine, "San Antone!" Then, whirling about in a cloud of dust, they began to ride a huge circle about the foursome.

"This way," Jay Jay said. Emily looked where he indicated and saw another train sitting off by itself on a siding. The engineer grinned from his window in the locomotive, and a big cloud of steam exploded from the stack, apparently another greeting.

"We figured it was too long to wait till we got to San Antone to start partying," Jay Jay explained as he led them toward the train. "So we got up our own train, got a few friends together..." He shrugged, as if the rest were self-evident.

"Our own train?" Emily could hardly credit her ears; she had heard of a few people so wealthy as to have their own private cars—but an entire train was surely beyond possibility.

"Well, just for this occasion," Yolanda said. "And you can't imagine the trouble it took to round up this much equipment on such short notice. There's four more of these crossing Texas in different directions, picking up guests along the way. When Joanna sets her mind to something, she doesn't let anything stop her."

That name, at least, meant something to Emily; she had heard mention of Sebastian's grandmother. "Queen Joanna," he had called her once, dryly, and even his reluctance to talk of her at all had added to the impression of awe that Emily had gotten.

"Is she here?" she asked now.

"Joanna?" Yolanda laughed. "You might as well expect the Alamo to leave San Antone. No, she's waiting for you there, and I expect by now she's got the whole town in a dither getting ready for you."

Emily, who had known her husband was rich but had never before been exposed to the legendary extravagance of Texas millionaires, could not help being impressed. The train was some twenty cars long, and it seemed as if half of them had been set up as bars. The rest, except one, were divided between seating cars and sleeping cars. At the very rear was a private car for herself and Sebastian—though as it turned out, it was anything but private.

"You have to go through the horse car to get to it," Yolanda explained. "I thought that would put you off a little more by yourselves. I figured you two would want time to talk."

Jay Jay snickered at that, and Emily blushed. "The horses have their own car?" she asked.

"Honey, this is Texas," Yolanda said. "If there wasn't room for us and the horses on this train, you can be sure these cowboys would let you and me walk to San Antone." She said this with such sincerity, Emily really couldn't be sure if she was joking or not.

The "party" was already in full swing by the time the private train began to move onto the main track. Emily felt awash on a sea of strange names, strange faces. People were introduced as neighbors who, she discovered, lived clear across the state from the Folly, and yet, despite the distances that separated them, they all seemed to know one another intimately. The men drank, and smoked cigars, and slapped one another on the back; the women were hardly less exuberant.

"You'll have to forgive all this huggin' and hollerin'," Jay Jay said over the din in the car intended to be their private one, now filled to overflowing with loud-voiced Texans. "Texans are an ornery and independent bunch, but you won't find friendlier people anywhere in the world."

It was all a bit overpowering. Emily looked around and finally found her husband, sitting in one corner. Of all the people in the room, he was the only one who didn't appear to be enjoying himself. He was seated between two beefy ranchers, and they were leaning back to talk past him, almost as if he weren't there. Sebastian was smiling, but it was that cold, distant smile she had already come to recognize as a defensive maneuver. She had the impression that, just at the moment, no one and nothing in the car even existed for him.

It was only in the few days since they had been married that her marriage and her husband had begun to appear so strange to her. At the time of Sebastian's proposal, she had been surprised and yet, at the same time, not surprised. Like a piano that has been tuned and already awaits the melody, she had been charged with some expectancy. From the time she was jilted by her former lover, she had seemed to mark time, waiting for the escape from her life's pain and shame, the escape she had been convinced all along was impending.

Some instinct within her seemed to know from the first that Sebastian represented that escape. She could not pretend she loved the man to whom she was wedded, was not even sure she liked him. And she was sure his feelings were no more personal nor pronounced than her own. In fact, she could think of no reason why he had chosen to marry her, beyond the entirely practical one he had given her in Aunt Julia's garden on the occasion of his proposal. Certainly sexual passion must not be one of them. There had been only one occasion, on their wedding night, when that had entered into it at all, and then not with any success.

It had seemed, so far as her limited experience informed her, to be starting off well enough, though she knew that her husband was quite nervous. Perhaps he thought her more experienced than she was; perhaps if she had taken the initiative ... But, no, even when, overcoming her own embarrassment, she had tried—when his fumblings and shovings had failed in their intent to gain him entrance and he had rolled from her with a sound like someone choking on his food, and she had, after a moment or so, reached for him—he had shoved her hand rudely away before he scrambled, nearly leaped, from the bed.

That had been their sole attempt at lovemaking, and no discussion of its merits or failings had been held.

Well, so be it; she herself certainly felt no particular need or desire for that part of their marriage. It had not been especially for his money that she had married him, though that was welcome to one who had lived in aristocratic poverty all her life. She had married him as much because he offered Texas, and South Carolina had become unbearable to her; and, even more simply, because he offered marriage, and where she was and what she was, no other prospects were likely to come along, certainly none as advantageous.

If he had married her only for the contributions she could make to the political career he proposed, why, then, she would make her contributions the best she had to give; she would fulfill to the best of her abilities the debt she owed him for rescuing her.

She would be loyal; and at the moment, that loyalty prevented her from asking his relatives about what seemed to her the rather peculiar relations between himself and his family and friends.

It was noon on the next day before the noisy train finally reached San Antonio. By then, Emily was nearly dazed by the nonstop din and confusion that had reigned from car to car, not excluding their "private" one.

Emily had somehow had the impression that, with so many of its hands halfway across the state to welcome them at the borders, Heart's Folly must be denuded of workers. She was quickly dispossessed of that notion by the sight of an even larger—and more boisterous—group that greeted them on their arrival. She stepped onto the platform between Yolanda and Jay Jay to witness very nearly a full-scale rodeo taking place on the street before her. Even the "Wild West Show" that had visited Charleston a few years before was nothing in comparison to the sight of what must be a hundred or more Texas cowboys, in full regalia, riding at a gallop in both directions up and down the street, the two lines seeming certain to collide, the riders passing within inches of one another without mishap. They rode hanging from their saddles, heads inches from the ground, to retrieve bandannas they had previously dropped; one rode standing up in his saddle, and scores of them twirled lassos in such perfect circles you could almost believe they were solid objects and not mere loops of rope.

Neither the local citizenry nor the other passengers at the train station seemed to mind the inconvenience caused by the free show. "Who'd they complain to anyway?" Jay Jay asked when Emily pointed this out. "The new sheriff is a good friend of ours; he'd know better than to kick up a fuss."

Finally a band of the cowboys rode straight at the station platform; it looked to Emily as if they meant to ride right over those standing there. At the last moment, the leader reined in his horse hard, and before the animal came to a halt, he leaped to the ground and was running forward. Behind him the other riders, too, stopped and jumped to the ground.

Not until the rider was already jumping onto the platform, sweeping off the big Stetson hat to reveal a shock of red-gold hair, did she realize it was not a young man at all, but a woman. In an instant, she knew who it must be, and for all that she thought she'd known what to expect, Emily was astonished at the reality of the mistress of Heart's Folly.

For one thing, no one had thought to describe Joanna's beauty, though she supposed now, seeing her, that would have been impossible.

She was dressed in a man's clothes, and that all black—boots and trousers, shirt and vest, even her hat and gloves. Only a single emerald hung pendant from a simple gold chain to soften the severity of her costume, the stone reflecting its green from her shining eyes. Age had tempered the gold of her hair with threads of silver, but neither age nor her outfit could hide her incredible presence.

"You're Emily," she said, coming straight to her. "Why, you're beautiful. I can see now why Sebastian was too impatient to let his family give him a proper wedding."

They embraced quickly, and Emily attempted, over the din of cheering cowboys, to deliver the little speech she had prepared. "I'm so happy to be here," was as far as she was able to get.

"And worn out, I'll wager, from all these bellowing Texans," Joanna said, laughing. "Come along, there's the carriage now, and everyone's dying to get back to the ranch—you'd think they never ate except when we had a party. Sebastian, my pet, how well you look! I shall want to hear everything about South Carolina when we've got a chance to talk."

Emily saw that his grandmother did not embrace Sebastian, nor did he seem to expect it. Joanna took Emily's arm and fairly dragged her toward the carriage that was waiting. Sebastian trailed rather awkwardly behind. Emily would have liked to drop back and walk at his side—he seemed rather forlorn, and all the more set apart from this bustling activity—but nothing could hold back her imperious hostess.

It was all unreal, dreamlike. She had supposed that once in the carriage they might finally be able to talk, but that proved only another of her misconceptions. The welcoming band of cowboys rode alongside and all around the carriage, shouting and whooping as they went, and frequently firing their guns. Others—townspeople, perhaps, or for all she knew, more employees of the ranch—stood in groups along the streets and the road out of town, cheering as they passed. Joanna frequently leaned to wave out the window, and indicated for Emily likewise to show herself.

She felt like some visiting queen greeting the populace. Across from her, Sebastian sat grinning ferociously, looking like a French duke on his way to the guillotine.

Her impressions blurred and ran together. A handsome black man approached them at the ranch, and was introduced as Abraham Lincoln Harte, which rather startled her. She met Sebastian's father, Gregory Harte, but when she tried to thank him for their reception, he looked at her blankly. "That's Joanna's doing," he said, looking neither pleased nor displeased to see his son, with whom he nonchalantly shook hands.

Her sister-in-law, Melissa, came running up with the news that "Angel is killing himself."

Far from looking disturbed by this intelligence, Joanna only laughed. "It's over the chili powder," she said. Seeing Emily's alarmed expression, she explained, "Angel is the cook. And the chili powder is a dried combination bottled by a Mr. Gebhardt. He's around here somewhere. Anyway, I'm thinking of investing in his product and we agreed to try it in some of the chili here today, to see if anyone could tell the difference. Oh, and don't worry about Angel—he's not going to kill himself and leave his nieces to finish the barbecue."

"Well, I have tasted the chili," Melissa declared, "and I shouldn't wonder at a rash of suicides. As if you could bottle up the taste of real chili."

"I predict," Joanna said, "that within a few years, people will be eating Texas chili all over the country, thanks to Mr. Gebhardt."

"They may be eating something hot and spicy, but it won't be Texas chili," Melissa argued. "And I will never see that poisonous imitation sold from the counter of my store."

"You may lose a healthy profit," Joanna said.

"Greedy. Greedy and ambitious, that is your vice, mother," Melissa said, and turned her attention at last to the newcomer in their midst. "I declare, if that silly Sebastian hasn't done himself proud. Why, you must be a perfect size seven. Ronnie John, come here and look at your new cousin's figure."

A tall, lanky young man came up and did just that, to Emily's discomfort. Mother and son alike seemed to be taking inventory.

"We've got the largest selection of ready-made dresses in all Texas," Melissa was saying. "My mother excepted, Texas women dress well, and I like to think here in San Antone, part of the credit falls to myself."

It was peculiar, Emily thought, that the daughter's barbs directed so blatantly at her own mother seemed to be as much admiration as disapproval. Melissa seemed to hold Joanna as much in awe as everyone else did, and to resent it more.

But she had little time to ponder this, or any other of the tangled relations that existed among the Hartes, for in another moment she had been whisked away to meet someone else—this a plump ghost of a woman dressed all in white and carrying wherever she went a little crystal bell.

It was well after midnight when at last Emily fell exhausted into bed beside her husband.

"So at last," he said, "you have been made acquainted with the Hartes of Texas."

"They're very nice, aren't they?" She smiled wearily at him.

"Nice?" He seemed astonished at her choice of words. Throughout what had been for him an ordeal, he had been comparing his family to those standards of elegance that he had seen elsewhere, in South Carolina, in Boston—even more, in the make-believe world of the theater, which was still more real to him; in his judgment, the Texans had been found wanting.

"Why, they're so friendly, so eager to please," Emily said, unaware that her defense of the people she had recently met grated on his feelings, and added to the distance that existed between herself and him. "I must admit they'll take some getting used to—but I didn't come here to hold myself apart. When in Rome, as they say. I hope they liked me. Joanna, especially."

"And why shouldn't they, when you come so ready to be likable?" The hint of sarcasm in his voice escaped her weary notice; she was already drifting into sleep.

Sebastian took rather longer to get to sleep. For a long while he sat propped against his pillows, smoking the slim, elegant cigars he had brought from Charleston, so unlike those smoked by the men of Texas, and nursing his long-standing resentments.

THIRTY-SEVEN

H e was up very early, to present himself at the door of the office where his grandmother was already at work, despite the rigors of the previous day.

He waited for her to notice him and invite him in. When she did, he took, not the chair she had indicated, alongside her own, but one at some distance.

She pretended not to notice. "I hope you enjoyed yesterday's festivities," she said, smiling.

"It was boisterous," he said. "Typically Texas. Typical, indeed, of the Folly. One Folly perpetrating another."

Joanna, who had engineered the entire reception, was stung by his ill-concealed disdain. "I'm sorry if it embarrassed you," she said. "It was meant to give you pleasure. And to make you proud, in the eyes of your new bride. I liked her, by the way."

"Proud?" His eyebrows lifted still higher than their usual lofty elevation. "By making us look like a bunch of noisy cowboys?"

"This is a cattle ranch, in large part."

"And by underscoring in every way possible the difference in my family status? If it had been any other member of the family who had married, would you have staged such a spectacle?"

"No, perhaps not. I—we all, it seems to me—have always done a great deal to try to convince you that you have no status different from anyone else."

"And only make it more obvious with every effort."

"I think it unfortunate, Harold—forgive me, Sebastian—that you have an image of yourself as this family's victim, rather than as the beloved son you really are."

"A beloved son, who is not even entitled to the family name?"

"It is the name on your birth certificate. You are as entitled to it as any other member of the family."

"As entitled as, say, Abraham Lincoln?"

Joanna's eyes flashed angrily. "He was given it by choice. You were given it because it is your father's name."

"Not, however, my mother's."

"That is unfortunately true. It is also in the past; I have no way of going back and changing that fact."

"And no doubt wouldn't if you could," Sebastian said. "From all that I have gathered, it was you who arranged my father's marriage, and his separation, without divorce—making it impossible for him to marry my mother."

Joanna sighed. Even as a child, it had not been easy to please this young man. He had grown up, it seemed, at war with the world, though she had hoped that spending some time away from the bosom of his family might have made him appreciate it the more.

"Since you know so much," she said, "yes, it is true, I am the one who decided against that divorce. A divorced woman is something of a pariah in society. And Texans are a hidebound lot. They will forgive a woman many a sin, but even today you don't see divorced women treated much better than outcasts. I thought that too harsh to inflict on your father's wife."

"So you chose to punish my mother instead—and ultimately me as well."

"You have peculiar ideas about punishment. Your mother was happy. For a brief time, that's true, but I believe that during that time she was happier than at any other in her life. She loved your father. As for yourself, you have a father who loves you, and a grandmother as well, if I may say so. For that matter, an entire family, who lavish upon you every sign of devotion and generosity. If you choose to see that as some form of punishment, well..."

Joanna shrugged. She could see, however, that her words had had no discernible effect on the young man staring at her—*sneering* at her, she could almost say. At length, since he made no further comment, she asked, "Was there something in particular you wanted to see me about this morning?"

"Yes. I wanted to discuss my future. Since my family's generosity to me is so unlimited, I'm sure I can count on all the assistance I might need."

"That goes without saying."

"I want to go into law. Eventually, politics. Your connections should prove useful there."

"I have friends. Not connections, as you term them."

He ignored the correction and went on. "I'll need an office. Something befitting a beloved member of the family Harte. And a house in town."

"There's no need for that. You can live here, as all our family does."

"Melissa does not."

"Melissa has a husband."

"And I have a wife."

"There is absolutely no reason for you to live anywhere but the Folly," Joanna said firmly.

"There is one excellent reason. I do not wish to live here."

Of all the unpleasant things he had said on this occasion, nothing could have been more certain to distance himself from his grandmother than this statement, delivered in an unequivocal tone.

"I see" was all that Joanna said. "Very well, you shall have your office, and your house in town. We keep no prisoners here. Is there anything else?"

He got up, smiling his humorless smile. "No, I believe that covers everything," he said. But at the door he paused to turn back briefly. "By the way, grandmother," he said, "who decided that you were the one to run peoples' lives—my father's, my mother's, everyone here at the Folly?"

Joanna's eyes flashed again. "I decided," she said angrily. "I *am* the Folly."

Despite her quarrel with her grandson, Joanna found that she quickly became friends with his new bride.

She spied Emily, that very same morning, standing looking at the graves in the family graveyard, and walked across the grassy field to join her.

"I hope I'm not intruding," Emily said when Joanna walked up.

"You're family now," Joanna said. "In time, this will become a part of your history, too. If you care about such things."

"I want to fit in here. I want to become a part of—of this. Texas. The Folly, especially. Your family—my husband's family, I mean to say. But it is all a bit bewildering."

"No one can get a handle on Texas in a single day, or a single month, for that matter," Joanna agreed.

"San Antonio seems, well, like a foreign country," Emily said.

Joanna was genuinely surprised. "Does it?" she asked. "I would have thought it just the opposite; every place else seems foreign to me when I think of them now."

She looked back, across the years—where had they all flown to? Like birds seeming to hover so lazily, so permanently against the white-blue sky, and then, just like that, they were gone. It seemed as if she had always been here, always been a part of the Folly, of San Antone, of Texas, born of this earth and sky, daughter of those magical horizons that knew no ending.

"Here," she said abruptly, "this is my husband's grave. He brought us here. All of this belongs, really, to him. And this, this was a very dear friend, an Indian. He told me one time one of the legends of his people, of an Indian brave who walked into the forest, and while he was walking he heard a mockingbird begin to sing on the branch of a tree. The brave stopped to listen, he stayed just to hear the song through. When the song was finished, he turned and left the forest, and went back to his village. But when he came there, he found no one he knew, or who recognized him. Finally, one old squaw came forward who remembered him from many, many years ago, when he had, as a young man, vanished into the forest.

"I came to Texas many years ago," Joanna said, "and I, too, heard the mockingbird sing, and since then the years have been like moments, and the days seem no more than the flash of sunlight on the wings of that hawk soaring above us."

They were silent for a long moment, Emily glancing upward at the swooping, soaring hawk Joanna had pointed out to her.

"I think, perhaps," she said at last, "it was that song that brought me here, a melody heard in the far distance. I think that's why I married your grandson."

Joanna reached and took her arm companionably, and they started back toward the house. "I suppose, as a grandmother, I would rather that you had married him for himself. But speaking as Joanna Harte, I can't pretend that your explanation displeases me."

It was several days before Sebastian found just the house that he wanted. During that time, though Joanna saw little of him, she and Emily spent much of their time together. She enjoyed and shared in the delight with which Emily explored San Antone, exclaiming over the sharp scent of peppers that pervaded the air (Joanna had long since gotten over noticing that), oohing and ahhing over the missions (the color, she said, of vanilla ice cream), walking in reverential silence through the Alamo.

There were things she didn't like: for one thing, the separate outbuildings for the Mexican *damas* and *caballeros*. They were too like the inequities she had left behind in South Carolina.

"But," Joanna pointed out, "Abraham Lincoln's classes include as many Mexicans as whites, and even a few blacks."

"That's only on the Folly."

"As the Folly goes, so goes Texas, in time," Joanna said.

For the most part, though, Emily was enchanted, and by nothing more than by the Folly itself, which could not fail to delight Joanna.

"I love it here," Emily exclaimed more than once, hands outswept to indicate all of the enormous ranch.

"You must come as often as you wish once you've moved into town," Joanna insisted. "Your rooms will remain just for you. This will be your second home."

"Someday I would like to ride the entire ranch, to see every inch of it," Emily said. She had already taken to riding astride, wearing one of Joanna's old split skirts, to Melissa's outspoken horror.

"That's a tall order," Joanna replied. "I can't say that I've seen every inch myself, and it's grown tremendously since we first came here. For that matter, it's not even all here. Webb's spread, which technically is now a part of the Folly too, is out near the Big Bend— that's twelve thousand acres that came down to him from his family. And we have another fifteen up in the Panhandle, where we're growing wheat. Really, trying to see all of the Folly is about as impossible as seeing all of Texas; it would take a couple of lifetimes."

It seemed to Joanna, though, that of all her family, Emily came the closest to sharing that special, almost mystical, love that she herself felt for this sprawling empire she had built for them all.

Certainly, Sebastian did not. Now that it was settled that he would live elsewhere, he was more open than he had been in his scorn for the ranch and everything connected with it.

The idea that anyone might not love the Folly and prefer living on it to living anywhere else had never so much as crossed Joanna's mind. Even Nancy, who had hated them, had had to be driven off the place, virtually at gunpoint. In Sebastian's case, no doubt her prejudice had blinded her, Joanna supposed. Surely there must have been signs all along that her grandson was so unhappy, if only the idea hadn't been so incomprehensible to her. Or was she, she wondered, in a damned-if-I-do-damned-if-I-don't situation? To show him special consideration, special generosity, only pointed up, as he had said, the difference in his status in the family, and became for him a mark of condescension. But would he have been any the more pleased had she simply ignored the difference? Of course, if his father had been more demonstrative, more affectionate... She couldn't call Gregory a bad father, but since Sebastian's birth there had been an unbreachable wall between father and son.

It was difficult to see, though, how she was to blame for that. Everything she had done, she had done for the Folly—which meant, certainly, for all of them, not just for herself. After all, Sebastian might mock and scorn the family's money and position, but she hadn't seen him turning down its benefits. Her grandson called her a tyrant; Jay Jay accused her of a blind spot the size and shape of the ranch; even Gregory's grimly silent devotion was a sort of accusation: Hadn't he, it said, sacrificed all to her demands? But which of them had ever disdained the benefits reaped from her labors?

And which of them would pick up the reins when she could no longer hold them?

Except for Emily, everyone breathed a sigh of relief when Sebastian finally moved into his new house in town.

Having set his mind on cataloging offenses against himself, Sebastian had managed to find them wherever he looked. It was surprising to him, then, to discover how much at loose ends he felt when he was settled at last in the big three-story house on the quiet, shaded street he had selected. Across the country, in Boston, in South Carolina, he had loathed the Folly and all its business—the cattle; the wheat and cotton and rice and sorghum and lumber; and the people, too—crude, loud, inelegant brutes, no more polished than the wind-carved rocks that topped the distant mesas.

Here, the Folly was just down the road. He could neither escape nor ignore it, and it continually rankled. It seemed as if there were no conversations in San Antonio that did not somehow circle around to the subject of that ranch. He conducted no business that was without reference to it; the behavior of others, their attitude toward him, changed at once and noticeably when his name, Harte, became known.

Frustration grew. If he had loved his wife, or even desired her sexually, that might have given him some outlet; but the more Emily, trying to do what was right, learned to love Texas, San Antonio, the Folly in particular, the more he despised her as well.

He visited one of the local whorehouses. But when he tried to cane the girl he'd selected, a simpleminded youngster from the Mexican quarter, she bolted from the room and disappeared into some other part of the house. When he descended the stairs, dressed and chagrined, the madam was waiting to see him. "This is where you want to go," she said, and handed him a folded slip of paper. "They will cater to your whims." Her grin was sly, as if she had some secret amusement at his expense. He would have liked to crumple the paper and fling it at her feet, but the knowledge that there was such a place, where whims such as his would be catered to, was too great a revelation. He settled for crushing the paper in his hand, where he kept it until he was safely in his carriage. Then he unwadded it, and held the crumpled paper to the window to read what was upon it.

The handwriting was poor, just past the point of illegible. He squinted, thinking at first that he had misread it, went back over it time and time again, as if to memorize it.

He had no need to do that, however. He knew the address, could have described the house in detail. Since he had been a child, he had gone there often, never inside, and never catching more than a glimpse of its chief occupant.

He knew her, too, without ever seeing her. How could he not know her, when her name was the same as his? What son would not know his father's wife?

THIRTY-EIGHT

"**Y**ou." A finger tapped loudly on the window of the big black carriage. "Over here."

Sebastian hesitated briefly; then, assuming his usual haughty indifference, he strolled across the sidewalk to the waiting vehicle. The door opened as he approached, and an imperious voice commanded, "Get in."

"Why should I?" Sebastian wanted to know. The carriage's windows were curtained; it was impossible to see who was inside. He saw a trouser-clad leg and one booted foot, nothing more. The hand that had summoned him sported an enormous diamond on one finger and clasped an ash-ended cigar.

For a reply, Sebastian felt something prod him unexpectedly in the ribs, and glancing over his shoulder, he was surprised to see that two men had approached without his hearing them. Even had not one of them had a knife at his ribs, he would have known the two for thugs.

Frightened despite the hauteur he tried to maintain, Sebastian managed a casual shrug—but he got obediently into the carriage. The two men crowded in with him, one on either side. The door shut, but the carriage did not move. Sebastian blinked, his eyes accustoming themselves to the gloom. "Judge Harding," he said, surprised. "What are you doing here?"

"The very question, young man, I was about to ask you." The judge fixed him with a steely, measuring gaze, a gaze that had been known to break the will of the toughest, stubbornest criminals brought before him. A "hanging judge" they called him, and there was no question that the justice he meted out was swift and fierce. There were some, however, who questioned whether it was really justice. "You know who lives in that house?" the judge asked, indicating the stately mansion with the shuttered windows.

"Yes. My father's wife," Sebastian said.

"Exactly. You've been hanging around here now for several days, haven't you?" The question was asked in such a way as to make it clear the answer was already known to the judge.

"It's a public street, isn't it?" The attempt to brazen it out, however, melted before that hard gaze. "I wanted to see her, that's all," he finished lamely.

"Why? What exactly has Nancy Harte to do with you? Surely you suffer no illusions regarding your parentage. I can assure you, she had nothing to do with that, if that's what's on your mind."

Sebastian hesitated; then he reached for his pocket. At once the knife was at his ribs again, but the judge gave his head a quick shake, and the knife was gone.

Sebastian brought out the crumpled scrap of paper with Nancy's name and address written on it. He had carried it like a talisman for days, changing it from pocket to pocket as he varied his costume, often reaching into his pocket just to touch it, with a morbid sense of fascination.

The judge took the note from him, smoothed it out, and read it, his thick lips forming the words silently.

"Yes, I recognize the handwriting," he said. "But what does it mean?" He looked across at Sebastian.

"If you know who wrote it, you should know what it means," Sebastian said.

The hooded eyes studied him intensely for a moment. Finally, the judge smiled. "So, it's that, is it?" he asked.

"That. And a certain curiosity, born of my surprise. I had no idea..." He finished the statement with another shrug.

"Mrs. Harte is very discreet. The people with whom she is acquainted represent a cross section of the state's best and most influential families. Naturally, care must be taken to avoid any unpleasantness. You were noticed. She thought perhaps you were an emissary—her relations with her in-laws have not always been pleasant, you understand."

"My own relations with them are nothing to brag about," Sebastian said.

"I see." The judge's smile grew broader, friendlier, "Well, perhaps we might go inside." He reached to open his door, but paused, and leaned to tap Sebastian's knee with one large finger. "Let me warn you, however—you'll make a fool of me to your eternal regret." Once more he looked at Sebastian in a way to make the blood run cold. Apparently he was satisfied with what he saw, for the smile returned and he emerged from the carriage into the sunlight.

Sebastian followed, looking back once to see that the other two had again disappeared, as quietly as they had first appeared.

The front door opened before they quite reached it, and when they had stepped into a dimly lit hall, closed as quickly behind them. The Mexican standing behind the door looked more like a companion to the two outside than a servant.

"Wait here," the judge said, and went along the hall to tap at a closed door. After a minute he opened it and vanished within. He was back shortly, crooking a finger to summon Sebastian along the hall.

His throat unaccountably dry, Sebastian came to the door and stepped into the room as indicated. For the first time in his life, he found himself face-to-face with his mother's sister—the woman to whom his father was still married.

His first thought was that she was the most beautiful woman he'd ever seen, far more stunning than he had realized glimpsing her at a distance. Even when he stepped closer and the reality of her age was more apparent, it scarcely dimmed her luster.

"So," she said, forming a smile with her tiny lips while her eyes gave the impression of ferreting out his innermost secrets—as, in fact, they were entirely used to doing—"you are my nephew?"

"Yes." Sebastian felt tongue-tied and childish. He disliked being at a disadvantage, and it gave him a churlish manner. "I—I've heard of you."

She laughed then, and held up the piece of paper the judge had given her. "Apparently," she said. "But tell me, was this the first hint you had of my activities? No family whisperings, no sly hints?"

"None that I heard."

"I see." She appeared easier after that. "Well, I'm glad. Joanna might take it upon herself—she has important friends. Not," she added, with a nod in the judge's direction, "that I am without influence myself. You know, we'll check this reference of yours, just to be safe."

"Go ahead. It came unsolicited."

"But not unwelcome, hmm? Come, don't look so agonized. There's no reason we can't get better acquainted in the meanwhile—no reason, so far as that goes, you and I shouldn't be friends. You're not all that close, I understand, with your relatives—with the mighty Hartes, of the Folly?"

"I loathe them," Sebastian said, surprising even himself with the quickness and the fervor of his reply.

"There, then, you see," Nancy said, taking his hand in both of hers and leading him to sit beside her on an elaborate horsehair divan. The judge had gone wordlessly; when Sebastian looked, the door was closed and they were alone in the room. "We do have things in common. But let us not dwell overly long on unpleasant matters when there are things far more pleasant that have brought us together.

"You see, that is the difference between myself and my illustrious mother-in-law: She understands ranches; I understand men—the things that drive them, their needs, their wants. And sometimes there are very special wants. And that is where I have found my own very special niche in life, making men happy. Special men. Men like yourself, for instance. Now"—and her voice became a purr, lulling, tranquilizing, coaxing—"suppose you tell me, where none but us can hear, all the special things that you have dreamed of, that would make you happy. And afterward, perhaps I will have the pleasure of making your dreams come true."

"It's genuine," the judge said when he returned; he had gone, as prearranged, to confirm the authenticity of the referral that had brought her nephew here. Sebastian, in the meanwhile, was now on the upper floor of the house, in a room designed expressly to cater to those who shared his tastes. Tastes that Nancy was expert at prying from embarrassed and guilt-ridden men, men of all sorts, with only immense wealth in common—her talents did not come cheaply.

"I was sure it would be," she said. "He's upstairs already."

The judge lifted his eyes upward, head cocked as though listening. There was, however, nothing to be heard; the rooms had been designed with that in mind as well. "Caning?" he asked with a smirk.

"Among other things." She never discussed the details of her clients' visits; discretion was the cornerstone of her success. "You may go now."

He looked not particularly pleased with her manner of dismissal; there was probably not another in all Texas who would have dared be so offhand with him.

"With, presumably, your deepest gratitude," he said a bit caustically.

Unintimidated, she faced him squarely. "You have enjoyed my gratitude on many occasions," she reminded him.

"Yes, it has been a mutually advantageous friendship," he agreed. "Our mutual indebtedness is considerable. What better basis than that for a friendship?"

It was the judge to whom she was indebted for the nature of her "business," which had over the years made her a wealthy woman. She had first invited the judge to her home to discuss with him the legality of the terms of her separation from her husband. The judge was not in the habit of making such house calls, but Nancy could be persuasive. She could also, she discovered then, read with shrewd insight the more lascivious impulses as they crossed men's minds.

She had in her employ at that time a widowed Mexican woman whose daughter, a pretty ten-year-old child, sometimes helped with the housework. On the occasion of the judge's first visit, while he was explaining to Nancy that her situation, galling though it might be, was nonetheless binding, the girl, Juanita, was in and out to serve drinks and the little canapés that her mother had prepared for their illustrious guest.

At first, noting the judge's glance as it followed the girl around, Nancy had assumed that something was being done incorrectly, some breach of social etiquette. In time, however, she, who had always been so finely attuned to them, became aware of the signs of the judge's sexual arousal—the hard gleam in the eyes, the flaring of nostrils, the hungry salivating that necessitated frequent swallowing movements of his Adam's apple.

Perhaps at first the judge had not consciously been aware of exactly what Nancy was about—though with his shrewd legal mind, he must have suspected that the charges Nancy brought against the child's mother were trumped up. What would that woman have needed with the jewels she was alleged to have stolen? Where, in San Antonio, could she have hoped to dispose of them?

If those questions troubled the judge, they did not prevent his sending that hapless woman to prison for the maximum time allowed by the law; nor did he hesitate to grant Nancy the custody she so charitably requested for the daughter.

So it was no wonder—having seen how the law worked in the interests of some and against others—that the child, when threatened with the same fate as her mother's, acquiesced to Nancy's bidding. Nancy had her first "client," an important one, for he knew many men, in the city, throughout the state. From them, rich, powerful, perverted, Nancy built her clientele, and a business so discreet that not even her mother, who lived only a few blocks away, suspected its existence.

The girls Nancy hired were mostly Mexican, though little prejudice entered into it; there had been at various times Chinese, black, and even white girls. What mattered was that they were uniformly young, and exploitable. There were the poorest of the poor, usually orphans, though out of the kindness of her heart, Nancy had in the house at this very moment the Mongoloid mother of one of her girls, despite the woman's inability to perform more than the simplest of chores.

Among her clients, Sebastian was unique. Certainly he was the youngest who had ever climbed the stairs to the closely guarded third floor. And, though certainly his connection with Heart's Folly was not to be lightly dismissed, in his own right he had neither the wealth nor power that the others had in common.

Why, then, had she accepted him? She wondered that herself, and knew that the judge, too, wondered. Her risk, to some extent, was his as well.

She felt a kinship with Sebastian that went beyond their shared dislike of the others in his family, their disdain for the Folly. What exactly that kinship was, she couldn't say; maybe, she thought with grim humor, hatred was thicker than blood.

Sebastian was disappointed to find his wife waiting for him when he arrived home. He would have liked to savor alone the contemplation of what the afternoon had wrought, and had hoped that Emily might be at the ranch, as she so often was, or out exploring the dusty, winding streets of San Antonio.

But here she was, coming into the hall to meet him before he was even quite inside, her eyes as alarmed as if she knew all along what he had been about.

Sebastian was annoyed, and still largely preoccupied, so that it was a full minute before he grasped what she blurted out so unceremoniously. He stood blinking, digesting the information.

"It's your father," she said. "They sent one of the servants from the Folly for you. He's dying."

THIRTY-NINE

Among the other problems that Gregory's death precipitated for Joanna, it brought to a head the argument that had been building between herself and Webb since they had learned of Sebastian's marriage.

Webb, too, wanted to marry.

At first, Joanna hedged. They had been all through this in the past, she pointed out; *she* thought it was settled.

"That was a long time ago," he argued. "I could see then that your previous marriage had left you wary. But we sure as the devil have had time since then to get to know one another. You can't think I'm another Lewis."

Which was exactly the problem, though she couldn't say so. Instead, she said, "I promised Lewis I would never marry again."

"What?" He was incredulous. "When did you make that promise, Joanna?"

"I made it over his grave," she said defensively.

He laughed, not without a certain acidity. "When you vowed to wear eternal mourning, I suppose? Don't fence with me, Joanna. It's the ranch, isn't it? You're afraid if I'm its legal master, it will take something away from you, from your position here, aren't you?"

"I am afraid, yes," she admitted. "A woman loses her rights when she marries. With Lewis, I got back what he couldn't hold on to. But, as you yourself have pointed out, you are no Lewis."

"So there's no way a man can win with you at all? A weak man earns your scorn, and a strong one is too great a threat?"

"Webb, don't, please, don't be bitter. We've been good together, you have been a great comfort—"

"While you've been running your empire, you mean? And I sit on my butt doing the busywork you toss my way to create the illusion I'm contributing something?"

"You've done a great deal. But don't you see? This ranch has been my life, building it, running it—"

"What makes you think we couldn't run it together?"

"What makes you think we could, without constantly clashing—just as we are now. You speak of marriage, but here we are, arguing about running the Folly. From the moment we married, you would be its owner, and I would be simply your wife. When I gave a command, would they jump the way they do now, or would they wait to see what the master had to say? Particularly when he was as independent and strong-willed a man as you are, my dearest."

"There are women perfectly happy to be the wives of the men they love."

"There are women who have no choice."

Webb ended that argument by downing three strong drinks in quick succession, before it occurred to him that this was the same refuge to which her first husband had turned. He wondered, with fleeting disloyalty, if he hadn't gained some insight into a man he'd always felt contempt for.

The quarrel, and the subject of marriage, was put aside for the present; but it gnawed, like an intrusive rodent, at the fiber of their relationship.

As the year passed, events caused it to weigh ever more heavily on Joanna's mind. In the fall, Melissa's hapless husband, Peter Hansen, died, without ever understanding his wife. A few months after that, very soon after the New Year began, Doña Sebastiano passed away as well.

Of the two, it seemed to Joanna that she felt the loss of her high-starched rival more than she did her son-in-law, who had remained nearly a stranger to her—and, she suspected, to his wife. More to the point, however, they were both nearly her contemporaries, Peter somewhat younger, Dõna Sebastiano a bit older, but in neither case was the spread of years particularly great. Their deaths, and that of her oldest son, could not but remind her of her own mortality.

Once reminded, she began to feel her own years more and more. An occasional stiffness became a chronic complaint; she became periodically absentminded, and when she tripped going up the stairs, as anyone might, she took it as another reminder that the years would not stand still for her any more than for anyone else.

With Gregory gone, she more than had her hands full running the Folly, and it seemed to her the job became daily more difficult. The time must come when she would have to share the responsibility with someone, or hand it over altogether.

In time, perhaps Jay's sons, Lewis and Mathew, would be ready. They were both bright, if a little too fond of play. She had already approached her son and daughter-in-law with the idea of sending them east for schooling.

"I don't see why Texas schools shouldn't be good enough" had been Yolanda's response to that, but Joanna was confident she would be brought around; she had an idea that, in years to come, Texas would be less isolated from the rest of the country—the trains were already accomplishing that, weren't they? The broader one's education, the better equipped one would be to run an enterprise as vast at the Folly. Even now, they had interests outside of Texas; inevitably, those would grow.

But the boys were only fourteen, too early yet to tell. Their sister, Alexandra, was Texas—and the Folly—through and through; she, however, was a mere eleven. Jay Jay and Yolanda had never been serious candidates, and Sebastian had taken himself out of the running.

So she was back where she had been, managing it herself, and feeling the burden ever more onerously. What she wanted, she told herself with wry self-perception, was someone to run the ranch whom in return *she* could run—and that, in one part or another, eliminated all of the prospects so far, including Webb Price.

Early in the summer, Alice Montgomery took ill and went to bed for three days. Everyone—even, to her surprise, Jay Jay—hovered and fussed, and Alice gave every indication of remaining in the room she had had redone entirely in white and shades of off-white. Joanna, however, had her own ideas. "You are not to think of leaving me," she declared flatly, standing at the foot of Alice's bed. "I have had enough of funerals for a long while."

Alice declared herself offended to the core at being spoken to in such a manner; but the suggestion that perhaps she really might be as bad off as she pretended frightened her, and the following day she was up and about, none the worse for a rest. Her voice now had sunk to a whisper, however, and her little bell rang incessantly.

"Nothing wrong with her voice," Joanna said, "except she just plain wore it out with overuse."

Emily, to whom she made this remark, laughed with her; they were both unashamedly fond of their "aunt."

Emily's time was divided nearly in half, between the Folly and the house she shared with her husband in town. True to her promise, though, she never failed in her duty to Sebastian's career. She was exactly what he had said he needed, a perfect hostess.

Sebastian, in fact, needed a wife like her more than most in pursuit of a political career, since despite his astuteness, and the influence Nancy had brought to bear on his behalf, he himself was neither sociable nor, in the opinion of most, likable. "A cold fish" was among the kinder opinions expressed about him.

So sincere and gracious were Emily's efforts on his behalf, however, that they did much to offset his handicaps. Despite the churlishness of their host, few were reluctant to accept invitations from one so lovely and charming as his wife.

Still, his success was not entirely due to Emily's contributions. His first term as city councilman had been marked by a somewhat ruthless shrewdness, a quick grasp of problems, and a small genius for inventing solutions where apparently none existed. There was talk now of his becoming mayor, and others were looking forward to senator.

Despite their quarrel, Joanna did whatever she could to help, and that was considerable. Had she known of Nancy's efforts, she might have been a little less generous; as it was, she publicly praised her grandson for making it on his own, and privately rather enjoyed thinking of herself as the power behind the throne she was sure would soon enough be his.

There were few secrets between Joanna and Emily. They shared their pride in Sebastian's accomplishments—and they shared their doubts.

"I really know him no better now than I did when we married,"
Emily confessed; "which is to say, hardly at all."

When Joanna hinted at the prospect of children, Emily somewhat embarrassedly told her the truth: Since that one abortive try
on their wedding night, Sebastian had made no further claims on
her marital duties. "Yet he seems happy," she added; happier, it
seemed to her, than he had when they married.

"You say he's away from the house a great deal," Joanna said.
"And you're often here at the ranch. Maybe he has a mistress."

"Perhaps." She, too, had wondered guiltily if her husband might
have a mistress; guiltily because it seemed to imply some failing on
her part. Did he, after all, hold that original mistake against her,
despite his assurances that it didn't matter? Or was there something
about her that put him off? It was true, she spent a great deal of
her time at the Folly, and she had been in San Antonio long enough
to understand that there was a deep-seated resentment on Sebastian's
part toward the ranch and those on it. Had it led him to resent
her as well?

Certainly it could not be said that she neglected their house; on
the contrary, she took pride in how well it ran, considering that
there were only two servants—a cook and a housekeeper.

Well, three, she amended, with the girl that Sebastian had brought
home a few weeks before, though she was really too young to be
of much use, and not, apparently, awfully bright. "She's an orphan,"
Sebastian had explained, "living on the street." His charitable impulse surprised her, and made her feel rather selfish for objecting,
and she had generously tried to make the best of it, though it often
appeared to her that the child added more work than she per-
formed.

"Really, there's no need for you to stint on help," Joanna said
when the subject came up. "Sebastian is well provided for."

"But I like doing things myself," Emily had explained. "It makes
me feel a bit more useful. Sometimes I wonder if Sebastian wouldn't
have done just as well with a secretary and a good housekeeper
instead of a wife."

"But then," Joanna said, and leaned forward to pat her hand
affectionately, "the rest of us would have been deprived."

On her way home on that occasion, Emily decided that she would
make the effort, though it made her cheeks redden just to think
of it, to broach the subject with Sebastian of their marital relations.

Perhaps she could introduce it by mentioning children. Sebastian might well be afraid of a repetition of the failure of their wedding night. If he knew that she was not only willing, but wanted to make it as easy as possible for him... And, she promised herself, I will start staying home more. It couldn't help a husband's ego to know that his wife preferred another home to the one he provided for her.

It was in this state of penitence that she stumbled upon her husband's secret.

FORTY

The outlet that Sebastian chose was easier, safer, than directly facing the private guilts with which he was burdened. In some mysterious way, surely, the neurotic side of his nature assured him, he was to blame for his illegitimacy.

Likewise, wasn't he at fault for not only accepting but actually relishing the very wealth and power that he scorned in the Folly, in his grandmother in particular? For he did enjoy it—that much he could not pretend to himself; but how could he both despise and welcome the same things?

In a sense he had enjoyed the contest that existed, though only in his mind, between his grandmother and himself; his father didn't count, or at least Sebastian refused to let him count, any more than *she* did. She, after all, was the Folly, just as she had said. There, too, he both hated and loved, scorned and admired.

So, though it was another of those truths he looked at only indirectly, like glancing over one's shoulder at one's mirrored reflection, he had been pleased, and disappointed, when she capitulated so quickly to his demands. The fact was, he missed their clash of wills.

His victims paid the price. Before, he had always had to search, to pay, sometimes to experience the humiliation of choosing wrongly, of being rejected by persons of the lowest station, who thus in that manner proved their superiority to him at least.

His intimacy with Nancy—sexless, yet as passionate and as cozy as the love affair he had never experienced—was a revelation to him. No more need he tremble inside as he approached some huddled, hungry looking waif on the streets. No more the rising of his gorge while he haggled to reach a price. Never again the mocking laughter to follow him as he stumbled down dark, dirty stairwells. He was miserable in his freedom. His success only proved that men were fools. Yet, weren't they better off than he?

"Sebastian!"

He stared, for a long moment scarcely able to comprehend who was there, and why. Finally, his wife came into focus—her mouth agape, her eyes wide with horror and, yes, just as he had seen it in a hundred, a thousand, nightmare fantasies, disgust.

He blinked, breathing like a near-drowning man breaking the water's surface. He could see it all as if through her eyes: the little servant wench on her knees, naked, crying, the marks of his beating livid and bloody across her shoulders and buttocks; himself in a state such as his wife had never seen him, aroused, boiling over with angry passion. He saw it all with her, shared her disgust, and hated her for it.

He was not even aware that she had gone until he blinked again and saw that the doorway where she had been standing was empty. There were footsteps on the stairs in the hall. He would have run after her, but even in that moment his haughty pride would not be ignored; he could not race after his wife clad in nothing more than cowboy boots, his erection jostling before him like a general leading a charge.

"Get up," he told the girl, and when, terrified, she remained kneeling, he booted her viciously. "Get out of here," he said. "Go back to Mrs. Harte—tell her I won't have you in my house another minute."

He took time to dress and have a drink before he followed his wife up the stairs, to the bedroom where she slept alone. She was standing by the window; outside, the girl was just running down the path that led from the kitchen door to the alley behind, still buttoning her dress as she ran. Emily heard the door, heard, with her highly charged senses, the sound even of his breathing, but she did not turn.

"Why should you care?" he asked after a while.

"How could one not care?" she asked in return.

"Sex was no part of our marriage agreement; not even love. You married me because I was rich, and because I could take you away from where you were. What I do for pleasure—"

She turned at that. "For pleasure?" she repeated, incredulous but he ignored her interruption.

"—Or with whom should be of no concern to you, in my estimation."

"Tell me, Sebastian, why did you marry me?"

He seemed surprised. "For the very reasons I gave you in South Carolina. Because I needed a wife. I wanted one whom other men would find beautiful, and they find you beautiful. I wanted one who was well born, as you were."

"And," she said when he paused, "because no one here in your own hometown would have dreamed of marrying you."

For the first time, he realized how completely he had come to hate her; realized, too, with rare self-discovery, exactly why: jealousy. She, a stranger, from what was nearly another land altogether, had come here, to Texas, to San Antonio, to his home, and had walked without hesitation into the very circle of love that had never been untaintedly his. She adored Joanna Harte, and Joanna Harte as unreservedly adored her. It was the proof of what he had always known in his heart: The world was unjust.

"And," he added, for once holding aside the mask behind which he was accustomed to hiding, "because I was told you were a trollop."

She came across the room without haste, moving with the ladylike grace that was typical of southern women of her class—a grace that all her years of ranch living had not stolen from his grandmother. When she was directly in front of him, Emily stopped and brought up one hand to slap him smartly.

In the seconds that passed, while neither moved nor spoke, he heard the ticking of the clock on the mantel, smelled the scent of roses in a vase on the table, seemed to feel the blood rushing to the spot her hand had struck.

He hit her back, with such force that she staggered, bumping against the table with the vase of roses. They, and she, fell to the floor.

He had not even been aware that he had brought his cane with him; had he been, he might have wondered why. Now, though, the reason was clear. He lifted it and, before she could even cry out or put up a hand to protect herself, brought it across one bare shoulder.

Eerily, she did not once scream, though at first she fought with him, tried to crawl away, even managed to claw at his face sufficiently to bring blood. In the end, though, she lay passive, submissive, only the hatred leaping from her open eyes assuring him that she was conscious, that she knew he was upon her, within her, giving her for the first time the seed whose absence had so recently puzzled her.

"Emily—what on earth..." Joanna stared at the already purpling bruise on her daughter-in-law's cheekbone, at the disheveled clothes and the hair all awry. "What's happened?"

With a sob, Emily fell forward into her arms. It was several minutes before she could tell Joanna of the circumstances that had led to her fleeing her husband's house for the sanctuary of the Folly. As she listened, almost without comment, Joanna's face took on a grim set.

"I can't go back there," Emily cried, "I can't bear to face him."

"There's no need," Joanna said firmly. "I told you before, you always have a home here. Come along. What you need now is some rest. We'll deal with Sebastian tomorrow."

With a little of Alice's laudanum, Emily was soon asleep. Not until she was breathing deeply and steadily did Joanna quit her bedroom, and then it was to have a bed made for herself in the dressing alcove off Emily's room. Had she not been so reluctant to leave the battered and frightened woman alone, she would have ridden into town then and there to confront Sebastian. But as she had told Emily, tomorrow would be soon enough for that.

By morning, Sebastian had come to bring his wife home.

He disliked coming here at any time, and on this occasion his nervousness was increased one hundredfold. Only his conviction that permitting his wife to remain here could not but add to the damage that was already done had made it possible for him to steel himself sufficiently to make the journey. It was possible that Emily had not yet told her story—or at the very least, had told it only to Joanna, who for her own reasons, might be expected to keep his secret. There were others at the Folly, however—Alice Montgomery came to mind in an instant—who could hardly be counted discreet. The longer Emily remained here, the greater the danger, as he saw it. It was this, and not any matrimonial devotion, that brought him.

Still, he was not completely unaware of the peculiar satisfaction his actions of the day before had given him. It had been as if he were assaulting not only his wife but her mentor, his grandmother, as well. He had never been aware of that particular lust before, and he did not even now care to examine it in its fullest; but in that final moment of agonized ecstasy, the woman he had been assaulting had seemed to vanish, and another take her place.

He let himself into the house without knocking, and found his wife in the parlor. It surprised him to find her so calm and collected; he had supposed that a still-overwrought state would work to his advantage. Instead, she displayed neither fear nor distress when she turned and saw him before her.

"I've come to take you home," he said.

"Then you have wasted a trip," she replied.

"I am your husband. The law gives me certain rights."

Her laugh was one he had never heard from her before; it had the sound of shattering crystal in it. "You have forfeited those," she told him.

"When you married me, you became my property."

"You may have thought so," she agreed. "I assure you, *that* I never have been, and never will be."

"Are you refusing to fulfill your marital obligations?" He took a threatening step toward her, but she stood her ground, her chin thrust obstinately forward.

"Not entirely," she said. "It may surprise you to know, Sebastian, that I am grateful to you for marrying me. Otherwise, I would not now be here, where it so pleases me to be. For that, I am obligated to you, and that debt I will attempt to repay. I will be the wife I promised to be. As you reminded me yesterday, there was no commitment on either part to love the other, nor any regarding sexual obligations, so I feel no debt to you in those regards. I will be your wife—in public. I will entertain for you, publicly. I will attend public functions with you. I will endeavor not to embarrass you, in public. That is as much as I will do for you, if you agree to that. Otherwise, I will live here, entirely independent of you."

"And everyone will know, and laugh behind my back," he said. "You would make a fool of me?"

"I do not take credit for that accomplishment," she said.

"Have you forgotten," he demanded, his sneer becoming an angry snarl, "how I dealt yesterday with your impertinence?"

He stepped swiftly toward her and lifted his cane to strike her, but there was at that instant a loud report, and when he brought his upraised hand down, it was empty save for the broken handle of his stick; the rest clattered harmlessly to the floor at his feet. Startled, he looked over his shoulder, at his grandmother, standing in the doorway, the pistol with which she'd shot away his cane still smoking in her hand.

"You had best remember where you are," Joanna said coldly. "This is the Folly. Harte women do not take well to being beaten."

In his rage, Sebastian moved as if he would attack her, but the pistol, which she raised to level at his midsection, stopped him.

"I have shot men before," she said, "in defense of those under my protection."

"If I go under those circumstances," he told her, "our break will be permanent."

"It already is."

He waited to see if she would embellish, mitigate that judgment. Her face remained implacable. His banishment had already been decided.

"I see." It was all, in defeat, he could think of. What really troubled him the most at the moment was not the seriousness of what had just transpired between the two of them but the pitiful question of how, with any dignity, he was to leave the room when she blocked the doorway. It was unthinkable to ask her to let him by; and even if she hadn't had a gun aimed at him, he would never have found the courage to simply push his way past her. He waited, feeling more foolish than offended.

It seemed an eternity before she moved aside and he was able, walking quickly, to leave the room. He tried to look her down, summon up his usual defenses, but they failed him, and he could not avoid the impression, as he went along the hall and out the front door, of a ghostly tail hanging between his legs.

In the parlor, Joanna looked at Emily and saw how actually shaken up she was despite the stern front she had put up. Her color was ghastly, accentuating the mark of the previous day's beating, and her lower lip had a threatening tremble.

"There's still time to go after him, if you want," Joanna said.

"No, that was decided already—don't blame yourself for that.

But there *is* something I would like." She surprised Joanna with a pale suggestion of a smile.

"What is that?"

"I really wish you would teach me to shoot like that."

"Yes, I shall," Joanna said with a laugh. "You should know, if you're going to live on a ranch. Why, that's it—that's exactly the thing! It will do us both wonders. You've always said you wanted to see more of the Folly—let's do it. The two of us. We can't see it all, of course, but I can give you a good idea of what it includes."

When Alice Montgomery came into the room a few minutes later, tinkling her bell to ask, "Was that Sebastian leaving just now?" she was surprised to find the two of them giggling like schoolgirls, planning their outing. Sebastian was already forgotten.

FORTY-ONE

"I still don't like it," Webb said. "Two women, alone, living off the land for weeks."

"Living off *my* land," Joanna said, and was sorry at once, seeing his quick frown, that she hadn't phrased it "our land." To cover, she went on quickly, "And it's not weeks and weeks, and weeks, it's only for a month. And I'd invite you along, but the whole point of this is girl talk. Emily has had an emotional battering. Getting away from a man's world altogether is exactly what she needs."

"A man's world? You certainly can't mean the Folly, can you?"

"It would take very little counting, my dearest, to see that the members of my sex are badly outnumbered here."

"If not outranked." He was in her room. They made a habit of having a nightcap together in the evenings. Most times, that led to other diversions before he retired to the bedroom adjoining hers. Joanna slept better alone. This evening, however, he drained his glass and started toward the door to his room.

"Going already?" she asked, surprised.

"Was there something else?"

"Well, I am leaving in the morning, for a month," she said, smiling a provocative smile.

"I imagine the ranch can run itself for that long," he said dryly. "Or did you have some last-minute instructions? The payroll? Checks to be signed?"

Her smile faded. "I've already signed all the necessary checks," she said.

"Yes. I know you have. Even if you hadn't, I don't have that authority, do I?" He paused unnecessarily, since the question was rhetorical. "Damn you anyway," he added, and stomped out.

His mood was not helped by the fact that he, too, had been in the mood for lovemaking. He sought consolation in assuring himself that he could not have made love with her tonight had she been Juliet, and he Romeo, panting, and not from climbing up to her balcony. The consolation was minor at best.

Worse yet was the nagging suspicion that, for all his quarreling and resentment of their situation, Joanna might be entirely right. Marrying her would soothe his ego, but would it satisfy him? Or would her more authoritative position only rankle all the more if she were his wife? He was strong-willed, he had always been accustomed to being in command. If they were married, wouldn't the temptation to assume command only lead to an even greater clash of wills?

But there was even more to it than that. Joanna had been dealt a good hand by life, but he was as aware as anyone that she had played it well. Suppose they played the hand out together, and he turned out to be less than the best at the table? He could run a ranch, he was good with the hands who were the daily functioning of an operation like Heart's Folly; but Joanna was the very heartbeat of the Folly. It was more than a job to her, which was all it could ever be to him; to her, it was life itself. No amount of hard work or ability could compensate for a passion like that.

In the end, more angry now with himself than with her, he returned to Joanna's bedroom, pleased to discover that she, too, was still awake. They made love.

The two women had scarcely ridden out in the morning, both dressed in the sort of costume that made a secret of their sex, when Melissa arrived. She was dismayed to find that her mother was to be gone for a month.

"But I counted on her being here for my tea next week," she

wailed. "And it's for the war effort, too. Oh, this dreadful mourn-ing, wearing nothing but black. It's all right for her—with the jewelry she wears, you couldn't tell if she had a dress on at all—but it makes me look sallow, and I can't have a decent ball, not for months yet, and then, when I try to do something patriotic, which is the only kind of entertainment I dare plan, she spoils it all by riding off into the sunset."

She burst into tears, which necessitated Webb's holding her in consulation. "And I had so counted on being called a national heroine by Mr. Roosevelt," she interrupted her sobs to declare.

This was the very epithet that Teddy Roosevelt had recently applied to Joanna when he had been her guest at the Folly only a few months before. He had been in Texas, where he was popular for being a rancher himself, recruiting members for an elite cavalry unit to be known as the Roughriders. Joanna's influence had helped boost recruitment by an even two dozen, most of them from the Folly itself. Under his leadership, they were even now on their way to Cuba, the war with Spain having finally been declared by President McKinley.

Melissa had harbored no particular friendship for the former assistant secretary of the navy, whose oft-professed disapproval of big business seemed to her at odds with the Emporium, if not the Folly. For that reason, she had been opposed to the idea of war with Spain over Cuba, since Mr. Roosevelt supported it.

The blowing up of the battleship *Maine*, however, in Havana harbor, had galvanized American—and Texan—opinion on the side of war. Seeing how the wind was now blowing—and hearing her mother nationally acclaimed a heroine—had fired Melissa's own patriotic fervor and she had quickly become an ardent sup-porter of the war.

It was difficult, however, to do one's duty without the coopera-tion of others. First, Mr. Roosevelt had written to explain—altogether curtly, she thought—that it was too late now to re-turn to Texas for the purpose of being guest of honor at her entertainment—which was, after all, on his behalf, since every-body agreed that this was *his* war.

And now, this. "You'd think if she cared nothing for her daugh-ter, she'd have some consideration for her country" was her com-plaint.

After a time, however, her contemplation of life's injustices was somewhat superseded by a growing awareness of the arms that held her and the broad chest against which her cheek lay. To her list of things that seemed to her grossly unfair, she had only recently added the fact that while her own marriage had come to so untimely and tragic an end, her mother, having buried one man, was not the least bereft of male companionship; indeed, had the benefits without even the necessity of marrying, which seemed to her daughter the smallest price she might have paid.

Melissa was not unconscious of the fact that the years had added to, rather than diminished Webb Price's good looks. The gray at his temples gave his rugged features a distinguished air, that went well with his still military bearing.

Sniffling, she looked up at him through fluttering lashes. "I declare," she said, giving him all at once a dazzling smile, "there is nothing like a pair of strong arms to make a girl forget her woes."

At the moment, Webb, whose ego had been of late a bit bruised, was managing to forget a few of his own.

Joanna and Emily traveled at a leisurely pace. Joanna had made several similar trips in the years she had been in Texas, and far from minding the rigors of such a journey, she enjoyed the days spent in the saddle, the nights sleeping on the hard ground with the countless stars blinking down from the soft Texas sky. She had, however, entertained some doubts about her companion, who, though she possessed grit, was obviously used to a more gracious life-style.

Her doubts were soon put to rest. Far from holding them back, Emily was soon impatiently urging them on, eager to see as much of the Folly as their allotted month permitted.

"I confess it," she said, laughing, "I'm as greedy for this land as you always say you are, Joanna. It seems to nourish me somehow."

There were large tracts of land within the first few days' ride that were still devoted to agriculture, despite the massive cattle operations that Jay Jay ran for them.

"This land is too good for growing, not to farm some of it," Joanna explained. "They say you could plant a crowbar and grow ten-penny nails. Anyway, I like to think of it as building a house on pilings. You put a place up on one or two columns, and anything happens to those, the whole thing comes tumbling down. But you build plenty of supports and the structure can survive the loss of one or two without real catastrophe."

Emily was eager to learn all that she could and it was a joy for Joanna to find someone as interested in every aspect of the Folly as she was.

Emily was as quick, too, to learn the use of a gun. From their first day out, Joanna, mindful that this was something she had promised to teach her, had started the younger woman practicing— first with the rifle, then with a six-shooter. Her first effort had them both laughing—the loud report and the rifle's kick had caused her to let go of it altogether; the rifle had fairly jumped from her hands and landed on the ground.

She soon overcame that reaction, however, and proved that she had a steady hand and a good eye. By the fifth day, she'd brought down a jackrabbit, shooting from the saddle.

"If I could only see the faces of folks back home when they heard about a woman riding the range and shooting rabbits," Emily said, plainly proud of her achievement.

"You're a Texan now," Joanna said. "Texas women have to be a little more. I like to think we're all woman *and* all Texan."

Later, she was thankful she had started Emily's shooting lessons right away.

They had brought some food with them—hardtack and jerky, plenty of beans, and flour for biscuits. But there was no shortage of food to be found; the range abounded with game: antelope, the color of smoky sunlight as they ran; wild turkeys and peccaries, the pigs that could slice through a leather boot with one sweep of razor-sharp tusks; armadillos; and even, as they climbed up into the mountains, bighorn sheep. They saw a few longhorns, now grown rare as the Texas ranchers turned more and more to imported and crossbred strains of cattle; and they saw some cattlo, funny-faced results of crossbreeding with cattle and buffalo.

"What about the buffalo themselves?" Emily wanted to know.

"They're gone, for the most part," Joanna said. "They used to be plentiful. Amarillo up north, that was the headquarters for the buffalo hunters. They used to call it Ragtown—the whole town was nothing but hide huts. Now it's yellow houses—that's what *armarillo* means, yellow—and the hide huts and the buffalo have vanished."

There were other animals, too. One night they heard the howling of a wolf pack in the not too far distance, and took turns tending their fire all night to discourage the animals from coming closer.

Once they saw a bear and her cubs fishing in a stream, and gave them a wide berth.

They had been out a week and a half when they brought down a deer, both of them shooting simultaneously.

"Which of us got him?" Emily asked.

"Does it matter?" was Joanna's reply.

They were in the foothills of the mountains. There was a clear running stream nearby and plenty of firewood. Joanna decided they would camp there for a day or two. "That venison needs to hang anyway," she said. They skinned and dressed it, saving the hide to take home with them, and hung the carcass from a branch of a cottonwood tree.

Joanna was cutting a roast from one of the haunches late the following day when a pebble rattled down from a rocky ledge above her. She looked up to find herself staring into the fierce green-yellow eyes of a *gato montés*—a wildcat. In the seconds before the cat bared its fangs in a hissing, spitting snarl, Joanna remembered that she had left her gun by the campfire—thirty feet away, at least. She was unarmed except for the knife in her hand, little better than nothing matched against the claws and teeth of a wildcat, already crouching to spring.

"Joanna, jump!" Emily shouted from behind her.

As the cat leaped into the air, Joanna threw herself sideways. At the same instant, she heard the crack of a rifle. She rolled, sharp rocks tearing her clothes; the cat struck her shoulder and rolled with her down a slope until they both came to rest at the bottom, the animal lying across one of her arms. It was dead, a bullet hole gaping in its forehead, directly between the two eyes that had gleamed such ferocity at her.

Emily was already running up, rifle in hand, when Joanna got up. "Am I glad you asked to learn how to shoot!" Joanna said with a nervous laugh.

"Are you all right?" Emily helped her back up the slope.

"Yes. Yes, I'm fine." She paused to look down at the dead cat. "Looks like you've got your first trophy."

She wasn't fine, though. She had wrenched her hip when she jumped, and by evening was walking with a painful limp, using a piece of cottonwood for a makeshift cane. To Joanna, however, more serious than the pain, which lingered on over the ensuing days, was the contemplation of how foolish she had been. She had made the sort of mistakes a tenderfoot might make. She had enough

experience of the range to know the fresh meat might bring pred-
ators about. It had been nothing short of stupid to leave her gun
behind by the fire.

The journey out into the vast wilderness that made up much of
the Folly had rejuvenated her. Now, however, her carelessness had
reminded her of the years that were inexorably catching up to her,
and she began to consider her quarrel with Webb in a somewhat
altered light.

FORTY-TWO

Joanna had been back less than a week when she discovered Webb was having an affair with Melissa.

The problem with her hip had continued, and she had decided to see their doctor in San Antone. His diagnosis was discouraging. "I'd say you chipped a bone in that fall. More than likely it's going to continue giving you trouble off and on."

"And I'll continue needing this?" she asked, indicating the walking stick she had brought with her.

"Not all the time. But some of the times, yes," he said with a shrug.

She left in a dispirited frame of mind, and decided she would stop at Melissa's store and buy herself some sort of present, something to cheer herself up.

She was surprised as she came near the store to see Webb's horse tied up outside. He had been at the ranch when she left, and had said nothing of coming into town.

He was not, however, in the Emporium; nor, for that matter, was Melissa. "She's at the house," Ronnie John told her, with what seemed to Joanna a sly smile. "Why don't you stop by there and visit a spell with her? She was just sayin' she hasn't seen a thing of you since you got back from rounding up the cows, or whatever it was you were doin'."

She had been about to ask him if he had seen Webb, but something in his manner stopped her. With things as touchy as they had been lately between her and Webb, she certainly didn't want him thinking she was keeping tabs on him. She decided after all she would go see Melissa, and perhaps by the time she came back, Webb would be around.

It was Melissa's maid's day off, and Joanna let herself in the unlatched screen door, calling "Hello?" as she did so. There was no reply, and she went down the hallway to the kitchen in the rear, expecting to find Melissa there. Finding that room empty, she untied her bandanna to pat the perspiration from her brow, and came back along the hall toward the stairs that led to the second story. She glanced up at the landing, and froze—Webb and Melissa were standing there, kissing.

They had not heard her come in. Moving quickly and lightly, Joanna turned and ran back to the kitchen, letting herself out the back door and the back gate.

She was in her buggy, on the way home, before she began to consciously think about what she had seen. The thought occurred to her that perhaps she had overreacted in running off as she had. There must be dozens of reasons why Webb should be there, even upstairs, where the bedrooms were, and not every kiss had a sexual connotation.

She dismissed these ideas, however, as quickly as they came: This kiss certainly had.

Well, what of it? she asked herself angrily. He was a single man, wasn't he, at her insistence, not his own? If she refused to accept the bonds he offered her, she could hardly complain when he chose to exercise his freedom. But Melissa?

She vowed that she would say nothing about what she had seen.

As it turned out, she did not have to bring the subject up. Webb did, soon after he arrived home. He came into the parlor, where she was rereading for the fourth time a page of the book open in her hands, and dropped her bandanna on her lap. "You left this at Melissa's," he said. "I found it on the floor."

She stared at the monogram, so neatly embroidered for her the

Christmas before by Alice, as if she had never seen it. Finally, she lifted her eyes to his.

"I won't be going back," he said. "I went there today to be sure she understood that. It was one of those things. I won't make excuses. It just happened. Now it's over."

"And Melissa? How does she feel about its ending?"

A ghost of a smile flirted with the corners of his mouth. "I think before it began, the idea of putting something over on you was very appealing to her. And I think since then she's lived in mortal terror of what you would do when you found out. So she's probably as relieved as I am."

"I see."

"Envy is a sort of admiration, you know."

"Then I must certainly be the apple of my daughter's eye," Joanna said, a shade dryly.

It was left at that until later that evening, when they were alone in Joanna's room. "I have been thinking," Joanna said, broaching the subject that had been on her mind since before she had returned. "Maybe you're right, Webb. Maybe it is time I made an honest man of you."

"You mean marriage?" he asked, surprised. She nodded. "This isn't because of Melissa, is it?"

"No. Truly, it isn't. I think I've been unfair. And I've acted like a petty tyrant—not even so petty, at that. There is more to life than just the Folly, though I won't deny its importance to me. And if marrying you means losing a little of my authority here, surely I couldn't share it with anyone better."

"You needn't worry on that score," Webb said. "I've had time to do some thinking, too. I've decided the last thing I want is to run this place."

Joanna looked a question at him. "You see," he went on, "it's a no-win proposition for me if I do. If I did a great job and the place continued successful, the credit would still all go to you for making it so great to begin with; everyone would think I was just riding on your apron tails. On the other hand, if anything went wrong and I was in the driver's seat, why, I'd get the whole blame; everyone would say, 'Things like that didn't happen when Joanna was running the place.' Either way, I'd just be Mr. Joanna Harte. So I'll accept the offer of your hand, lady, but not your ranch, okay?"

After a moment, Joanna laughed and, jumping up from where

she sat on the divan, came happily into his waiting arms. "You mean," she said, smiling up at him, "it turns out all our arguing was over nothing?"

"Isn't that more often than not the case? We were just lucky enough to find it out before it really did become something."

As weddings at the Folly went, theirs turned out to be conspicuously quiet, a simple service in the chapel, attended by the family and their closest friends. Under the circumstances, Joanna felt, however, that she could not refuse Melissa's insistent offer of a reception at her house, a gala event that made up for—among other things—the tameness of the wedding itself.

Joanna eschewed the typical bridal white, but her black gown was profusely trimmed in Spanish lace of an eggshell shade, and the severity of her appearance was further softened by Webb's wedding present—a perfectly matched strand of "black" pearls, actually a luminous dark gray. It did occur to Joanna that Melissa, whose store procured the pearls for Webb, had in one stroke paid for her party and made a pretty penny besides, but she could feel no resentment of that fact. After all, she consoled herself, taking a lighter grip on Webb's arm as they greeted their well-wishers, the greater profit by far was hers.

At Webb's insistence, their lawyers had drawn up an agreement between them stating that Webb made no claim to Heart's Folly and assumed no authority for its despite marrying its owner.

"It's not necessary, you know," Joanna had assured him before signing, but he had grinned, and argued that it was, for his peace of mind. "This way, when you finally find that place too big to handle, it'll be your headache and not mine," he said, and scratched his name to the contract.

Joanna laughed with him, but the remark was not entirely without foundation: The ranch *was* becoming too big for her to handle alone.

Not, she admitted privately, that the problem was entirely the ranch; partly, it was her. Her love for the Folly continued undiminished, but the enthusiasm and the energy she brought to the job were less than what they once had been. She found herself more wearied at the end of the day, and working harder through the day to keep track of the hundreds of details involved in such a massive operation as the ranch had become.

And the time—where did it go? It seemed she barely turned around and summer had become fall; she blinked and the winter, when she was used to having a little leisure, was gone, and it was spring again.

"Thank heaven for Emily," she said time and time again.

To a great extent, Emily had begun to slip into that place once occupied by Gregory; but her love for the Folly, which was akin to Joanna's own, gave her a passion for the job that his dutiful attention had always lacked. It seemed as if she couldn't learn, or do, enough.

Which caused Joanna to begin to look at her in a new light. She liked Emily immensely, but her feeling for the Folly was an even stronger bond between them than mere friendship. More and more Joanna found it necessary to delegate responsibility; Emily was glad to take it, while at the same time utterly respecting Joanna's authority. Surely, Joanna thought, she had found the heir she had been seeking.

Would the others sit still for that, though? Emily was nearly an outsider; even Alice, who had been there so many years now, seemed more like a family member. Emily was wife to the one person in the family who actively scorned the ranch (though not its profits, Joanna noted); and she was, at that, wife in name only.

If there was one thing those remaining had in common, it was a passionate devotion to the Folly. Even the youngsters—and it was they, after all, who were most likely to think of the ranch as one day rightfully theirs. The twins, Lewis and Mathew, had had to be driven, practically at gunpoint, from the ranch, to attend school back east; of course, for that, Joanna partly blamed their mother, whose own stubbornness had encouraged the boys'.

"I don't see why a plain Texas education shouldn't be good enough for them," Yolanda had argued to the end.

"It seems to me those two have had more than aplenty of 'good Texas education'" had been Joanna's reply to that, "majoring in carousing."

Not that she could hold the youths entirely to blame. The Folly was really a "man's world," excepting the fact that she ran it. Yolanda was practically one of the cowhands herself, unwilling to be separated any more than necessary from her husband, and as enamored as he of punching cattle; she took what Joanna considered a disproportionate credit for the fact that the Folly was a cattle ranch at all.

The boys could hardly be expected to spend much of their time with Alice, and she herself and Emily were far too busy to provide that softening influence so important to a young gentleman's upbringing. From their earliest years, the twins had been in the habit of spending most of their time with the cowboys. Not that the men who worked the Folly weren't fine men—honest, hardworking, God-fearing. Joanna never had the trouble that sometimes plagued other ranchers with their hands. She paid for the best; she demanded—and got—the best. It was as simple as that.

Still, men will be men, "And never truer than in Texas," as she had pointed out to Yolanda. If the boys were going to one day make a real contribution to the Folly, they needed a far different education than what they had been getting at home—and sending them a mere riding distance away wasn't going to keep them from making the ride. So back east it had been, and Yolanda had had to concede the point.

Their positions had coincided, however, when it came to the question of schooling for Alexandra, the boys' younger sister: Yolanda had been all for sending her away to one of those fancy finishing schools in Boston or New York. "It's different with a girl," she had said, and Joanna had been inclined to agree.

It was Zan herself who vetoed the proposition. "I won't go," she had put it flatly, and while Joanna disliked having someone balk at her suggestions, she had privately admired Zan's fervent attachment to the ranch. The girl had cried and stormed, run away and been gone for three full days, living in a cave like some creature of the wilds.

They got her on a train; she got off at the next station and came back. Webb offered to accompany her all the way to New York; Zan locked herself in her room and the door had to be removed to get her out.

"Oh, well, let her stay," Joanna had said finally, settling the argument. "The education she needs to be a lady, she can get from Alice."

It was decided that Zan would spend two hours each afternoon with Alice, and an equal time twice a week with Emily, who would work on her scholastic shortcomings. Grateful, Zan actually stuck to the schedule for a full month; after that, it was a never-ending battle.

Which only tied up more of Joanna's increasingly limited time. So when a short, stocky man came riding up one day, asking to see her and wanting to know if she needed an experienced foreman, she thought maybe her prayers had been answered. He was brutally ugly, there was no denying that, but she didn't suppose that mattered to the men. On the other hand, he couldn't have been more polite or respectful to her, and he was uniquely qualified for an operation such as theirs, combining both agriculture and cattle; he had experience with both kinds of ranches.

"I was foreman for a time right near here," he added when she questioned him on that point. "At the Rancho Sebastiano, back in the days when the don himself ran it."

"That explains why I thought you looked familiar," Joanna said. "Well, it means you'll have an easier time learning your way around."

"Does that mean I'm hired?"

"Yes, I guess it does. Come up to the office and we'll talk salary. By the way, what is your name?"

"Braxton," he said. "Lafe Braxton."

FORTY-THREE

It was soon apparent that Lafe Braxton was not altogether an unmixed blessing.

His work, certainly, was not a problem. It was quickly obvious that he knew his business, and what he didn't know about the Folly, he set himself to learn. He pored over maps, read reports and correspondence until the wee hours of the morning, and in whatever spare time he could find, he was invariably out riding the range, seeing the ranch at first hand. He worked hard, and drove those working under him to work harder.

Perhaps, the question arose early on, a little too hard. At first Joanna ignored the grumblings; Jay Jay, she knew, could sometimes be lax with the men; she supposed the hands had just gotten unused to having a real foreman around. The complaints, however, did not diminish in time as she expected them to; on the contrary, they seemed to increase. Finally, Jay Jay himself came to complain. "Two of my best men are quitting," he informed her angrily. "They just won't work for him."

"That's the whole point of having a foreman, isn't it?" Joanna countered. "You need someone to push the men. This is no operation for softies."

"It's no place for a slave driver, either. I thought we left that behind in South Carolina." With that, he stomped out of her office, leaving Joanna and Emily to exchange uneasy glances.

When a fourth and fifth and then a sixth man left—one who had been with them almost from the ranch's start—Joanna's uneasiness became downright anxiety. Normally, she would have checked a man's references before taking him on for so important a job as foreman, but there was no one locally to ask about Braxton. Of those who had been on Rancho Sebastiano, only Nancy remained, and Joanna couldn't have depended on any information she might have gotten from her. She supposed that some of the hands from that time had been absorbed into the Folly, but if there was any record of who they were, it must have been in Gregory's memory.

Her dilemma only pointed up what had become uncomfortably obvious: that she had grown increasingly out of touch with the actual workings of the Folly. Already she found herself asking Emily questions about specific matters, information she once would have had at her own fingertips. "Well, even Joanna Harte isn't immortal," she chided herself ruefully.

At least, however, she could resolve the Lafe Braxton question herself, by observing firsthand how he was running her ranch.

It did not take her long to discover that Braxton was more than a difficult taskmaster—he was nothing less than a bully and a brute. The tongue-lashings that befell the men for the slightest infraction were vicious enough—"no-account spics" and "lousy greasers" were among the kinder labels he applied to them—but the violence was not only verbal. Braxton's fists fell no less quickly and no more gently than his curses. Nor did he draw the line at using only his fists.

Braxton was inordinately proud of the knife he wore on his belt. He had won it in a card game in Pennyslvania, and long before that it had come from far-off India. Its handle was teak, inlaid with bronze and mother-of-pearl, and even its razor-sharp blade was etched with fanciful designs of vines and leaves and floral blossoms.

He used it one day, in one of his rages, to slice the ear off one of the Folly's cowpokes.

Jay Jay brought the cowboy to Joanna's office. This was a young man, not much more than a boy, who had hired on just a month earlier when his parents lost a small ranch of their own. He had needed the job badly.

"I want you to see this," Jay Jay said, and brought in the young man who had been waiting in the hall. His head was bandaged with a strip torn from a dirty shirt. "Take that off," Jay Jay said, indicating the bandage.

Looking embarrassed, the boy did so, wincing as the cloth pulled loose.

Joanna stared in silence for a long moment, though Emily could not restrain a gasp.

"What was that punishment for?" Joanna asked finally.

"Does it matter?" Jay Jay asked, but as she was clearly waiting for an answer, he said, "He let a cow bolt from the herd."

To the young cowboy, Joanna said, "Ride into town and have a doctor take a look at that. Forget about coming back to work— you'll be paid your pay every week just the same, and I'll see that you get a spread of your own." To Jay Jay, she said simply, "I'll handle this."

She found Braxton in his cabin, studying yet another map of the Folly. She came straight to the point.

"There'll be no more physical violence," she said. "If you can't keep the men in line without that, send them to me. I've never had any problems with discipline."

He had not gotten up when she came in. Now he leaned back in his chair, balancing it on two legs, and looked long and hard at her. "When I run a place, Mrs. Harte," he said finally, "I run it my own way."

"I'm afraid perhaps you've misunderstood your position here," Joanna replied. "At the Folly, things are run my way."

"You're a woman. There are things a woman can't be expected to understand."

"I understand that when I give an order, I expect it to be obeyed."

"So do I," he agreed. He got up and came around the table to stand directly before her. He was not much taller than she was, but powerfully built, with a massive chest and arms bulging with muscle. "I think the problem with you, Mrs. Harte, is you need to learn to take orders from a man. That's the natural state for a woman."

"And are you fancying, Mr. Braxton, that you are man enough to make me obey you?" Joanna asked.

"I think I just might be." He grinned and reached to take her in his arms. Joanna did not even try to evade his embrace. Instead, she brought the pointed toe of one boot up and kicked him, hard, in the shins. He yelped and jumped backward.

"And that, Mr. Braxton, is the last act of violence in which you will participate on this ranch," Joanna told him. "Pack up your things. You're through here."

"They're already packed," he told her. "I was finished here anyway."

He turned from her and went toward his bunk. Joanna was surprised to see that he was telling the truth—his saddlebags were already packed.

Within the hour, Lafe Braxton had collected the pay he had coming, and had ridden off. He had been there little more than a month.

"But why did he come here at all, then," Joanna asked Emily, "if he meant to leave so soon anyway?"

"Obviously he wanted to learn something, something about the Folly," Emily said.

What, though, neither of them could guess.

Lafe Braxton went no farther than San Antone. He took a room for a week at the city's best hotel, paying in advance for it a goodly portion of the salary he had just collected from Joanna. With much of the rest, he hired a closed carriage and driver. During the next few days, he spent more of his time in the carriage than in his room, most of it sitting still, observing through the curtained window of the carriage without the attendant risk of in turn being observed.

On his fifth day in town, he went to see Sebastian Harte in his office near the courthouse.

"And what can I do for you, Mr., uh, Braxton?" Sebastian asked when the burly cowboy was shown into his office. The name had meant nothing to him, but he knew better than to judge entirely by appearances.

"It's what we can do for each other," Braxton said. He sat down opposite Sebastian and helped himself, without asking, to a cigar from the box on the desk. "I have a business proposition. It means a lot of money. A whole lot." He struck a match on the sole of one boot and puffed appreciatively on the expensive smoke.

Sebastian smiled wryly. "This is Texas," he said. "There's always someone's got a scheme to make a fortune. I don't think a week goes by someone doesn't offer to take me on as a partner in one or other of them—usually meaning I'm to put up the money."

"Not this time."

"You plan on financing whatever this idea of yours is yourself?"

"No. Joanna Harte is going to finance it for us." Braxton smiled at the other's surprised expression. "You know her, I believe?"

"I know her well enough to know she's a shrewd investor. Many have tried to get money from her pocket; few have succeeded."

"I will. We will.".

Sebastian leaned back in his own chair, too curious now to pretend disinterest. "Go on," he said. "I'm listening."

"I figured you would be when you heard it involved Heart's Folly." Braxton paused to smoke in silence for a moment; Sebastian chose not to press him. "I want to see Miss Nancy Harte. Mrs. Harte, that is. She married the older boy, as I remember."

Again Sebastian was surprised. "As it happens, I can give you her address, if you wish," he said.

Braxton shook his head. "That wouldn't do—she wouldn't see me if I was just to walk up to her door, though she knows me, all right. You'll have to take me to her."

"And what makes you think she'll see you just because I accompany you?"

"You're friends. I've seen you going in and out of her place the past few days. Pretty often, too." His leer indicated that he had some idea of the nature of that friendship.

Sebastian glanced away from that mocking grin, embarrassed that his secrets might be suspected by such a man as this. But curiosity brought his eyes back. "I'm afraid you'll have to tell me a little more," he said.

"A little more? Sure, I'll tell you. There's a fortune waiting right this minute under the ground on Heart's Folly. I know what it is, and where it is, and I know just how you can get it for us. For the three of us. You, me, and Miss Nancy."

FORTY-FOUR

"Mr. Braxton. Yes, I remember you," Nancy said.

"I expected you would, Miss Nancy. Call me Lafe." Braxton looked her over boldly, warmly, as if he were judging a prize heifer. His expression said very plainly that he remembered her well, too. "You're looking good," he concluded.

"The years have been kind."

"They can be kinder."

"Mr. Harte"—she smiled, inevitably amused by the common name she and Sebastian shared, through the same man, though there was no relation between them—"mentioned something about a fortune waiting for us on Heart's Folly, a buried treasure, something of that sort."

"Not a buried treasure, Miss Nancy. Oil," Braxton said.

"Oil?" she repeated, a little vaguely.

"Petroleum. It's the coming thing. There's a couple of men, names of Higgins and Lucas, expecting to bring in a gusher out of the Big Thicket, near the town of Beaumont. And there's others think there's oil scattered all over Texas, just waiting for someone to bring it up from under the ground. Some of it is under that ranch. I know where."

"And how would you know that?" Nancy asked.

"It's how I spent most of those years you talked about as being so kind to you. Some of them weren't so nice for me. After I left Rancho Sebastiano, I drifted north, ended up finally in Pennsylvania, where I heard they needed men to work the oil fields there. I spent ten years there. I got to know a lot about oil. But I got to missing Texas, too. So I came back, did some ranching—till I started running into oil people here as well. I was even with Higgins and Lucas for a time, trying to coax that oil out of Spindletop—that's the hill where they're trying to bring it up. But all the while I was thinking about San Antone. I remembered the land, one parcel of it in particular, and the more I remembered, the more sure I was that it was oil land.

"So I came back here and got a job on the Folly, so I'd have an excuse to look around all I wanted. I found that land again. It's oil land, all right."

"How can you be so sure?" Nancy asked.

"I'm sure."

"Even so," Sebastian said, "if it's on the Folly, it might have been better if we were talking about buried treasure—*that* we could pick up and move. But oil...Joanna's not going to hand it over to us, you know."

"She might," Braxton said. "That's where you two come in—it'll be up to you to persuade her."

"I don't see—"

"It's on the property that used to be Rancho Sebastiano," Braxton said with a grin. "Miss Nancy's old homestead, to which she's bound to feel sentimentally attached. Now, I've been asking around. Joanna Harte pays you—if you'll excuse me, Miss Nancy—a pretty penny each and every month, though I don't suppose any amount of money is ever enough for a woman of your elegant tastes. The way I see it is, if you"—he nodded toward Sebastian, though he continued to look at Nancy—"as the old lady's grandson, went to her with the proposition—if you tell her she can settle the whole business with Miss Nancy completely by giving back the old family holding, which ain't worth very much; it never was much of a ranch—she oughta be grateful just to have Miss Nancy out of her hair, once and for all."

He sat back. Nancy and Sebastian exchanged glances. He lifted an eyebrow; she shrugged.

"It might work," she said. "But if these other men can't bring up the oil where they are..."

344

"I know just where to look. And just how to get it out of the ground. You leave that part of it to me. You get us the land, I'll get us the oil, I guarantee it. There's just one thing, though...."

"Which is?" Sebastian asked.

"Don't you two get any ideas about cutting me out. I'm in this full. Without me, you could go to your graves hunting for that greasy black stuff."

"We'll form a partnership," Sebastian said. "Everything completely legal. You'll get your money. Assuming, of course, there's any money to be gotten."

"There'll be more than the three of us can spend," Braxton assured him. "But I won't settle for just money; there's something more that I want out of the bargain."

"What is that?" Sebastian asked.

Braxton leered at Nancy, showing yellowed and blackened teeth with his wide grin.

Sebastian's face colored; it was ridiculous, but he had never been able to deal comfortably with the thought of any sexual experience on Nancy's part. It was all right for her to arrange it for others— for himself, even; but on those few occasions when he knew that it was she, and not one of the girls, who entertained one of her visitors, he invariably felt as if he had been cuckolded.

"If you think to force yourself upon Mrs. Harte..." he began, but Nancy waved him to silence.

"Mr. Braxton and I are old friends," she said. "And what are old friends for? I'm sure we can come to some agreement between us, he and I."

"What I'm thinking towards," Braxton said, "is that I'm not getting any younger. Neither of us is, for that matter."

"Not very gallant of you," Nancy said, smiling.

He ignored that. "I reckon it's time I had a wife."

"And you expect me to marry you?"

He took his elaborately carved and inlaid knife from his belt and began to clean under his fingernails with its tip. "Course, I wouldn't expect you to go quite that far until the money was in the bank. Just a little show of intentions, to prove everyone's sincerity." He glanced up at Nancy and laughed. "You," he said, pointing the knife in Sebastian's direction, "can see about getting those papers together, like you described. And start persuading your grandma to cooperate. The sooner we get the ball rolling, the sooner we all get rich."

Sebastian said to Nancy, "Perhaps you and I should discuss this proposition between ourselves."

"I like Mr. Braxton's plan," Nancy said. "Don't you?"

He reddened, chagrined. "Parts of it."

"Well, then, let's put those parts into effect, shall we not? Why don't you pay a visit to your grandmother, and let me know the results."

Sebastian's earlobes felt as if they were aflame. "Very well," he said. "I'll call later."

He went out, feeling betrayed. As he went along the hallway, he heard the lock on her door click loudly.

"I don't like it," Jay Jay was saying.

"It's a bargain," Joanna said. "A steal, practically. We add a hundred thousand acres to the Folly in one fell swoop—prime grazing land, too."

"If the Platt ranch is so fine for cattle, how come Platt is going bankrupt?"

"Overgrazing, plain and simple. He got too big a herd for the land he had."

"Which is exactly what'll happen to us. With his herd, we'll be running better than a million head. It's too big for us to handle— even the Folly's not that great. Besides which, if I understand what Emily's saying, we'll have to go into debt to pick up the Platt. I don't like the idea of the Folly being mortgaged."

"It's only a temporary loan," Joanna insisted. "We'll have no problem getting all the money we need from the bank, on the best terms. As for the cattle, we can manage them for a short while. It won't take us six, eight months to weed out the weakest and the least desirable cows. We'll unload them, even selling cheap, we'll be able to pay off the loan and bring the herd down to a manageable size—though I daresay it'll still be the biggest in Texas."

Webb coughed discreetly, thus far his only contribution to the quarrel that had been going on for some time already.

Joanna blushed faintly, and added, "Which is not exactly the point. The point is, we've got to keep growing, we can't just stand still. And there are no little holdings for us to pick up anymore; Texas is too big. The only way for us to expand these days is by doing things in a big way. A chance like this comes along rarely. If we don't snatch up Platt's place, someone else will—and make a pretty profit by doing so."

"Or follow in his tracks and fall on their face," Jay Jay warned.

"We made half a million dollars last year off of farming," Joanna said. "And half again that much off lumber. If you'd had your way, we wouldn't have seen a penny of that money."

"If we'd concentrated on cattle, we might have made still more."

"Then," she said, "you should have no quarrel with my decision to go ahead with this purchase. It will give you all the cattle you could possibly want. I have decided. I'm going to wire Platt today."

Jay Jay got up and jammed his hat down hard on his head. "All I got to say," he said, "is don't blame me if we end up cattle-poor." He went out, his boots clattering loudly on the tile floor.

Joanna turned to Webb, but he raised a hand defensively and laughed. "Count me out," he said, and got up to follow Jay Jay. "This is your baby."

Joanna and Emily were left alone in the office. "I suppose you think I'm being foolishly greedy too," Joanna said.

"So far," Emily said, "you've done all right, I'd say. This sounds like an ambitious move, certainly, but I can't find anything to quarrel with. You're right, there's probably no one who could get the needed cash as easily as you can. And certainly the terms sound favorable enough. Of course, I can't judge the cattle end of it. I'm really a newcomer to all this ranching business."

"You know as much right now about the operation of the Folly as anyone," Joanna said. "You've learned well, and fast."

"I've had a good teacher, and it's been a labor of love. But it's one thing to learn how to run a desk, which is what I've learned. It's another thing entirely to run a ranch."

Joanna got up and walked thoughtfully back and forth. "You're going to, you know, one of these days," she said. "Eventually someone's going to have to take over the Folly. The way I see it is, you're the logical choice."

"Me?" Emily was obviously surprised. "But you must be joking."

"I think you know, I rarely joke about the Folly."

"But I'm not even part of the family."

"You have the name. And you've got the Folly in your blood— I saw that right off. That's family enough for me."

"Besides, I'm a woman. Oh, I know, but you're Joanna Harte, there's only one of you. And you've lived your whole life here, on this ranch."

"Not all of it. I started out in South Carolina, same as you, and I knew less about ranching when I began this place than you know

347

right now—far less. As for being a woman, I've said before, there are women, and there are Texas women. Even in this man's country, a woman can make a place for herself, do whatever she sets out to do. The only secret, and it's the same for a man or a woman, here or anywhere, is to resist the temptation to regret. Yes, Delfina?"

The maid appeared in the open doorway. "It's Señor Sebastian," she said. "He's downstairs; he would like to see you, *por favor.*"

It was the first face-to-face visit between the two since their confrontation over Emily's move to the ranch, though there had been glimpses back and forth at a distance.

Sebastian was unexpectedly dismayed to discover that the years Joanna had so long outrun had begun to gain on her. The fact that she was walking with a cane seemed to accentuate the tiny lines at the corners of her eyes and mouth, and the little brown spots that flecked the backs of her hands. It gave him an indefinable pang, and made his manner even more brusque than it would otherwise have been, yet what he really wanted to do was run to her and fling himself into her arms as he had once done as a child.

"Sebastian, what an unexpected pleasure," she said, greeting him with no trace of irony.

"I've come on business," he said. "I'm here to represent Mrs. Nancy Harte." Her smile vanished; Sebastian added, "My father's wife."

"I recall who she is," Joanna said.

"She's asked me to broach with you the question of a settlement against her late husband's estate."

"She has no claim against Gregory's estate," Joanna said quickly.

"But there you are wrong. There is, you see, the monthly stipend she receives from your bank. A very generous stipend," he added hastily before Joanna could comment. "However, Mrs. Harte is hopeful that you may be willing to agree to a trade—the termination of her monthly allowance for a final settlement."

"And what figure has she in mind for a settlement?"

"No figure at all. Not, that is, in money. Mrs. Harte would like to have back her former home, Rancho Sebastiano."

Joanna could hardly have been more surprised. "Nancy? Rancho Sebastiano? But what on earth for?"

Sebastian looked away from her questioning gaze and shrugged. "Sentiment, I suppose."

"I've never imagined Nancy as a sentimental person, nor as a rancher."

"Does it matter why she wants the land? Perhaps she simply wants a place in the country. San Antonio has grown so much larger, all that noise and bustle."

"No, I suppose you're right, it really shouldn't matter why." Joanna, now that she was over the initial surprise, was more than a little intrigued by the idea. Rancho Sebastiano was not a profitable piece of land. It was not entirely Don Sebastiano's fault that he had been unable to make the ranch work. It was neither good farming nor grazing land, and unlike most of the Folly, it was water-short; there were no more than half a dozen wateringholes on the whole property, and she knew that at least two of those were fouled, the water undrinkable. Besides this, with her decision to go ahead with the absorption of the Platt ranch, it would be helpful to be freed from those monthly payments the bank sent Nancy.

There was Don Sebastiano's express wish that the identity of Rancho Sebastiano be preserved; but his fear had been that Nancy and his wife would want to sell out. As things stood now, the ranch was only a portion of the Folly to everyone's mind but her own. Surely his wishes would be better served under Nancy's plan than as things were.

"Does she really mean to own the place itself?" she asked aloud. "It's not for the purpose of selling it elsewhere?"

"I don't know who would want to buy it," Sebastian said.

"Yes, I agree with you there." She couldn't think of any reasons, other than the ones Sebastian had stated, why anyone should want that particular property. She thought a moment longer, but the scheme seemed to her advantage as much as anyone's, and she could think of no reason to object.

"Very well," she said aloud. "I'll instruct my attorneys to meet with you and Mrs. Harte. She'll receive Rancho Sebastiano, free and clear, and in return she will forfeit any and all future claims of any sort against me or the Folly."

"Agreed," Sebastian said.

She walked with him out to the front porch. When he had gone, however, she had another brief period of puzzlement. The bargain they had just struck seemed so out of character for Nancy.

Well, she thought, going back into the house, I suppose worrying unnecessarily is just another sign of advancing years. After all, what had she just done but free herself of a long-standing debt, and unload a nearly worthless piece of land?

FORTY-FIVE

T hat winter, Texas and the world welcomed a new century, the twentieth. On New Year's Eve, while the others cheered in the year 1900, Joanna found herself looking back with a certain satisfaction on what she had accomplished, and ahead with a certain complacency.

She had made her decision to turn over the responsibility for the Folly to Emily, as quickly as Emily could be trained in those areas where she still remained ignorant. Joanna had not yet apprised the others of her intentions, but she meant to carry them out while she was still in a position to enforce them, and while she was still able to help guide the ranch's course for the future.

That summer, Alice surprised them all by announcing that she planned on visiting Galveston. "The Moodys have invited me" was the only explanation she offered, "and I have accepted."

Alice was old, and Joanna had her own opinion as to why her friend should choose, now, to visit her former home. She kept those thoughts to herself, however, and arranged for a nurse and Zan to accompany her. The trip now, by train, was hardly arduous, particularly as the trio would travel in their own car, with every comfort provided. Still, when she stood on the platform and faced that moment of kissing her longtime companion goodbye, she could hardly restrain herself from crying.

"Till we meet again," Alice said in way of farewell, as if she, too, suspected that meeting would not occur this side of the veil.

The feeling proved prophetic. Alice had been gone no more than a month when Yolanda returned one afternoon from San Antonio with news that had just reached the city. "They said Galveston's been wiped out by a hurricane," she reported. "Thousands dead and homeless."

"Zan? Alice?" Joanna asked.

Yolanda shook her head. "There's no word. People are saying it'll be weeks before all the casualties are known."

Joanna wasted no time in deliberation. "Have the carriage brought around," she said, already on her way toward the stairs.

"What are you going to do?" Webb asked, following her into the hallway.

"Do? Why, we're going to Galveston, of course," she said, not even slowing her steps.

"Joanna, you can't," he argued. "The place will be a madhouse. How would we get around? Where would we sleep?"

She was halfway up the stairs already. "I have gotten around the whole state of Texas, one way or another, and always managed to get my sleep," she said. "If it's beds you're worrying about, bring one with you."

In the end, they did just as she said she would.

Getting there proved to be the easy part—astonishingly easy, in her eyes, considering that this was the first time she had made this journey since traveling the same ground in a covered wagon. "Why, it takes your breath away," she said, staring out the train's window at the landscape rushing by, almost too quickly to see it.

Not even the influence of the Hartes, however, could get them past the confusion and rubble that awaited them as they neared Galveston. The storm had carried its devastation far inland—they passed a four-thousand-ton ship twenty-two miles inland, where the wind and water had left it, and they were still miles away when the train was forced to halt.

Despite the haste of their departure, Webb had foreseen this difficulty and made provision for it. A carriage was waiting, with a change of horses tethered behind since Joanna would certainly be in a hurry. At the mainland's end, a boat would carry them to Galveston Island.

There, Mr. Roosevelt's assistance took them directly to the one in charge of the lifesaving efforts—Clara Barton herself, the legendary Angel of the Battlefield. It was now many years since the Civil War had ended, and Miss Barton had served as a nurse in two wars since, while heading the relief efforts in such emergencies as the flood in Johnstown and the yellow-fever epidemic in Florida. Along the way, she had managed to found the American Red Cross. She was now nearly eighty, but that fact was belied by the briskness of her manner.

"I've already located your granddaughter, Mrs. Harte," she said immediately after their introduction. "She's quite safe."

"And Mrs. Montgomery?"

Clara Barton sighed and shook her head. "Nothing yet. She and her nurse were visiting some old friends and were caught there, I gather. But," she added, seeing Joanna's dismay, "you mustn't give up hope."

That was easier to say than to do. Galveston, the city that had remained in Joanna's mind as a unique and lovely blend of Texas and the Old South, had virtually ceased to exist. The damage was mind-boggling: At least six thousand were dead, and half again that many homeless in a city that had been all but leveled.

It was typical, Joanna thought, that while others fled the city, Alice had refused to be intimidated by a mere storm, and had remained.

They were reunited with Zan, who blamed herself for not being with her aunt when the worst of the hurricane struck.

"We should only have had the additional problem of worrying about what had become of you," Joanna assured her.

Not even Clara Barton's own intervention, however, was enough to reunite Joanna with her longtime friend. "We simply cannot wait for all these to be identified," Miss Barton said, indicating row upon row of cloth-wrapped bodies that filled the remaining shell of a warehouse like so many bundles of hemp. "In this heat, we'll have an epidemic of catastrophic proportions if we do."

"But what will be done with them?" Joanna asked, aghast.

"There's only one burial ground large enough and fast enough for these numbers," Miss Barton said, and nodded in the direction of the ocean.

•

It was a burial unlike any known to the history of man, a macabre armada of ships moving out into the vast plain of the ocean to unload their grisly cargoes. The beach was lined with spectators, some openly mourning, others there out of grim curiosity to see such an unlikely event.

"We may never know," Webb said, taking Joanna and Zan back to the home of Alice's friends, the Moodys, where they, too, were now staying.

"I just can't imagine Alice's going without leaving me some sort of sign," Joanna said, though she had resigned herself to Alice's probable death.

The windows were barely turning light with the next morning's dawn when Zan was at the door of their bedroom, rapping excitedly and flinging open the door without waiting for an invitation. "The beach!" she cried. "Everyone's going—you must come quick!"

"But tell us..." Joanna said, sitting up and blinking herself awake.

"I can't," Zan replied, and dashed away.

The entire house seemed deserted, they discovered when they had dressed and come downstairs; even the servants were nowhere to be seen, and the doors stood open.

"What can it mean?" Joanna asked, and Webb only shook his head.

"We're never going to get any of them to tell us." He indicated the throngs of people rushing along the street outside, toward the beach, many of them still buttoning the clothes they had obviously donned in haste.

Webb and Joanna hurried along with them; it was eerie to see these mobs of people all rushing in the same direction, hardly a word being exchanged, all with the same air of horrified expectancy.

At first, as they neared the beach, Joanna wondered at the excitement. What she saw was the white sand littered with an unusual tide of kelp and seaweed, and the water's surface greasy brown with heaps of the ocean's refuse. But then she grasped the truth, and stopped so short that a man running behind her collided with her and would have knocked her to the ground had Webb not been holding her arm firmly. The man rushed on with no more than a mumbled apology.

It was not seaweed at all, but the bodies of the hurricane victims being returned to the site of their tragedy by a capricious sea.

For hours a stunned and ghostly-silent crowd watched body after cloth-wrapped body floating gracefully inward, catching gradually on the sand, remaining as their chauffeuring waters abandoned them there.

Clara Barton approached Joanna and Webb. Already a crew had been organized to collect the corpses; this time they would be burned on massive pyres, the smoke from which would darken the sky even more thoroughly than had the storm that had necessitated them.

"It's horrible, isn't it?" Miss Barton said, for once showing every one of her seventy-nine years. "I thought I'd seen every kind of tragedy there was, but never anything like this."

"How many have come back?" Joanna asked.

"Nearly all. I suppose a few—well, the fish aren't particular."

"I wonder..." Joanna began, and paused.

"Yes?"

Joanna smiled in an odd way. "Oh, it was just a fancy. I was thinking of something.... I thought I heard, just a moment ago, someone tinkling a little glass bell. It's nothing. You must have so much to do. Please won't you let us help?"

FORTY-SIX

On the tenth of January the following year, the men drilling on Spindletop Dome finally struck their oil, a green-black gusher that roared some hundred feet into the air, a hundred thousand barrels a day. It would take nine days to cap the first Texas well.

One day short of a month later, the soon to be world-famous Rancho Sebastiano gusher came in.

"I can't believe it," Joanna said. "Oh, of Nancy, yes, and that Braxton animal. But surely Sebastian couldn't have known when he talked to me."

"Ha!" was Jay Jay's response to that. "The three of them signed a partnership agreement the same day you signed over the title, from what I've heard. And they didn't just start drilling there yesterday, let me tell you."

"Well, why didn't you tell me if you knew this was going on?" Joanna wanted to know. She looked around, and to her surprise saw that everyone—they had all gathered in her office when they'd gotten the news—avoided her eyes. The message was clear: They were embarrassed by her mistake in judgment.

Which was ridiculous. How could she have suspected? Why, she didn't even know exactly what "oil" was, for that matter, or just why it was so valuable. It seemed to her, from what she'd heard, that it was something noxious that ruined the land and made it unfit for any other purpose, either growing things or raising cattle. But Texas *was* growing things, and ranching, and cattle. Why would anyone want to destroy that?

"It wasn't your fault," Emily said, and sounded as if she meant it; but though they quickly voiced the same sentiments, Joanna felt the others still blamed her in some way.

There was one of the family, however, who placed the blame elsewhere, and later that evening, on the pretext of "getting some air," Webb rode into San Antone to see Sebastian.

All three of the partners in the Rancho Sebastiano Oil Company were at Sebastian's house. His invitation had surprised both the others; it was the first time Nancy had been invited to the house, and it was no secret that Sebastian had an aversion to his male partner.

The truth was, it had clearly been an occasion to celebrate, and Sebastian disliked being together with the other two at Nancy's, where their meetings almost invariably ended with Braxton staying behind, for an unmistakable purpose. Here, Sebastian reasoned, they were not likely to steal away together until the time came to depart; then, at least, he could not be certain they weren't going their separate ways.

He had been plagued of late by the difference between matters as one imagined they would be and the reality when they came to pass. His grandmother, for instance. He told himself that he loathed her, and had always waited to see her vanquished. Yet he could not get over the shock of seeing her as he had that last time, walking with a cane, showing the unmistakable effect of her years—years that had since been magnified in his imagination until he pictured her as virtually an old crone.

Even the success of their oil venture, the wealth that was guaranteed them from it—that, too, was unfree from taint. How often had he dreamed of his own fortune, not one that came from Joanna Harte but one that he had achieved on his own? Even more, since meeting Nancy, he had imagined being able to bring her a fortune, which had almost literally been the case. But to do so had meant a partnership with the one man he despised more than any other in the world.

He could not even say what it was about Lafe Braxton that was so utterly repugnant to him. The man was coarse, yes, and a bully, but he had known such people before, all his life. Even the very odor of Braxton's body—that primitive animal scent that permeated his presence and lingered in a room long after he left it— made him ill; there were times when it actually threatened to bring him to his knees, he could almost feel his legs melting away beneath him. He longed, sometimes with a longing that was a physical pain, to strike the other man. He had never struck a man in his life, yet he would look at Braxton and find his fists clenching of their own accord. He wanted to strike not just his jutting chin, but that immense chest, his broad shoulders even, the bulging muscles of his arms, raining blows...blows...blows...

He blinked, feeling suddenly dazed, and realized the other two were watching him, waiting for something, some remark, some action.

"Aren't you going to toast with us?" Nancy asked.

"Yes, yes, certainly," Sebastian said, and lifted his glass, drinking quickly. Over its rim, he saw Lafe smiling at him, as if his thoughts had been spoken aloud, spoken, and greeted with derision.

It was soon after this that the Mexican woman, Ramona, came to inform Sebastian that Señor Price was waiting to speak with him.

That worried Sebastian. He had wondered what the reaction would be from the Folly to the news of their oil discovery. He had both dreaded and hoped that Joanna would come to see him, something she had not done since he had moved into this house. Webb Price was a different matter, however. Price was everything Sebastian was not, and had always wanted to be.

"You think this Price means trouble?" Braxton asked, again seeming to read Sebastian's thoughts.

"He might."

Nancy seemed unconcerned. "Everything we've done has been legal. Even if they try to claim otherwise, the judge is a friend, he'll see that things go the way we wish."

"You think Joanna isn't without powerful friends?" Sebastian asked sharply.

The question gave Nancy a pause. She had other friends, more powerful even than the judge, but there were built-in limits to influence such as she exerted; it could be stretched so far, no farther.

"Maybe Joanna doesn't know he's here," she said.

Sebastian considered that. "It's possible. She's not the sort to send someone else to do her errands. If she wanted to confront us, she'd do it herself."

"We'd better find out," Braxton said.

"Is there someplace we can wait? Where we can hear and not be seen?"

"In there." Sebastian gestured toward an adjoining room. They went into it, closing the door, but not completely. Sebastian sent to have Price brought to his study.

He realized as soon as Price came into the room that they had made an error. The half-emptied champagne bottle still stood on the desk, two glasses alongside; one of the others had taken a glass along into the next room. Sebastian saw Webb's glance go to the bottle and glasses, and swept swiftly about the room. Had he noticed the door, opened a crack, or not? Sebastian couldn't tell. He moved so that Webb's back was to it as they spoke.

"Webb, this is an unexpected pleasure. What brings you here, of all places?"

"Just what you think," Webb answered, not returning Sebastian's attempted smile. "Your—what do you call it? Rancho Sebastiano Oil Company. Quite a surprise to all of us at the Folly."

"To myself as well. When I was first approached about investing money in the venture, I thought it was just nonsense—"

"But that didn't stop you from becoming a partner."

"Really, I had some extra cash—"

"Which came from the Folly, of course. From Joanna."

"I can't see how that concerns you," Sebastian said, bristling.

"I'll tell you how. You tricked Joanna; you used your connection with her, her family regard for you, to swindle her out of the fortune you mean to share now with those snakes you have for partners. Only I'm not going to let you do it."

"And how, may I ask, do you mean to stop it—even assuming what you say is true?"

"Very simply. You're going to write up an agreement, tonight, while I'm here, making Joanna a partner in your oil business."

"You're mad," Sebastian almost shouted. "I won't do any such thing—you can't make me."

"Then I'm going to break your neck," Webb said, with such quiet sincerity that it was easy to believe he meant it. "You're not going to make a fool out of Joanna. Not after all she's done—for this state, for San Antone, for you most of all."

"All she's done!" Sebastian's sneer was grotesque; he might have been wearing a mask. "Connived to have me born a bastard, you mean?"

"You were born a Harte, which is better than you deserve."

The door behind Webb was now several inches ajar. Sebastian took a deep breath to steady himself. "So, she sent you here, her messenger boy—"

"She doesn't know I've come. And you're not going to inform her."

"Yes, that's certainly right," Sebastian agreed. Over one of Webb's wide shoulders, he saw Braxton advance into the room. The gun in his hand he held by the barrel, the butt upraised.

Webb saw, at the last minute, something in Sebastian's expression that warned him, but it was too late. Even as he started to turn, the gun butt cracked against his head with, to Sebastian's ears, a horribly loud sound. To his further dismay, when Price pitched forward, Sebastian instinctively opened his arms, so that the man fell into them. He gave a cry, womanish, and dropped him. Price fell across one corner of the desk, then sank to the carpeted floor.

"My God," Sebastian said, putting a hand over his mouth for fear he would be ill.

Nancy, rushing into the room after Braxton, said sharply, "Be still." She and Braxton both knelt by the inert figure. It was Nancy who said, a moment later, "He's dead."

"My God," Sebastian cried again. "She'll kill us. We'll hang."

Nancy stood up and slapped him, hard enough to make his eyes water. "Be quiet, you fool. Do you want the whole neighborhood to know?"

Braxton had been fumbling through the dead man's pockets. He brought out a wallet and extracted a thick sheaf of bills from it. "There's greasers by the dozen would crack a man's skull for a wad like this," he said.

"Everyone knew he was rich," Nancy said.

"What do you mean?" Sebastian asked.

She gave him a withering look. "We'll put him somewhere—in an alley. There'll be nothing to connect him to us. Everyone will think someone attacked him for his money."

"We'll need someone to blame," Braxton said, picking up the theme. "That judge of yours, he'll help us set someone up."

Nancy thought a moment. "Yes. That's perfect."

"How'll we get him out of here without being seen?" asked Braxton.

Sebastian looked around the room as if seeing it for the first time. "The window?"

"That'll do. Give me a hand with him." Braxton was already tugging the body up from the floor.

"I can't," Sebastian said.

"Do as he says," Nancy ordered. "There's no time to waste."

Sebastian swallowed hard and, stooping, helped drag the dead man to the window. Nancy had already opened it, sticking her head outside to be sure no one could see.

"Put out the light," Braxton said.

She hurried to the desk and blew out the lamp's flame. For a few seconds they all stood in motionless silence, their eyes adjusting to the dark. There was nothing but the ragged sound of their breathing, Sebastian's breath coming in choking gulps, Nancy's the calmest of all.

Finally, Braxton crawled out the window, standing in the bushes outside while Sebastian and Nancy between them shoved and tugged at the body until it toppled over the sill into Braxton's waiting arms.

"I'll take care of him," Braxton said.

"We'll come with you."

"Do we have to?" Sebastian asked.

"If worse comes to worst, we're one another's alibis," Nancy said. "It's best if we stay together."

"Besides, you don't trust anyone, do you?" Braxton asked, the moonlight turning his toothy grin into a wolfish leer.

"No," she said.

"Neither do I."

Sebastian's carriage house was to the rear of the property. They put the body in the back of his buggy, under a canvas sheet, and brought Price's horse from the front, where it was tethered, to tie it behind the buggy.

"Wait here," Braxton said, and disappeared into the darkness toward the house.

Sebastian's nerves were at a feverish pitch. The minutes dragged by, each of them an eternity. Each nighttime sound, each clack-clack of cricket, each rustle of leaf in the wind, seemed to him some disaster rushing down upon them.

At last they heard quick footsteps and Braxton came into view, carrying something over his shoulder. It looked like a sack of flour. He dumped it into the rear with Price.

"The Mexican woman," he said, climbing in over the bodies. "She knew he was here. Let's go."

Sebastian drove, Nancy directed. They crossed the town to the poorer, Mexican section. The streets and alleys here were mostly unpaved dirt trails that wound among little shacks and noisy bars. They found a dark spot close to one of the cantinas and let Price's horse loose, to wander. Braxton rolled Price's body out the back; it fell into the dirt with a thud.

Ramona's body they took farther, to the very edge of town and not far distant from a shabby whorehouse. When Braxton threw her out, without even telling Sebastian to stop, he saw in one brief glimpse that Braxton had taken her clothes off. No one would question what had happened to her.

Back at the house, Nancy and Braxton refilled their glasses with the now stale champagne and drank greedily. Sebastian had lost his thirst.

Braxton and Nancy left together soon afterward, but she was back scarcely more than an hour later; she gave Sebastian a start of terror by rapping on the very window through which only a short time earlier they had moved the body of Webb Price.

"Open the front door yourself and let me in," she hissed when he came nervously to the window. "Don't disturb the servants."

He fairly ran to unbolt the front door. She came in, casting a quick look over her shoulder to be sure she was unobserved. It was after midnight by now; the street was dark and empty.

"What is it?" Sebastian asked in a frightened whisper. "Where's Braxton?"

"I'll tell you in a moment," she said, out of breath as though she had been running. "Get the cards, set up the table in your parlor. If anyone asks, we sat up all night playing."

He moved as if sleepwalking, getting the table set up as she directed, finding cards, even dealing out two hands facedown on the felt cover. The clock in the hall struck one. Sebastian dropped the deck at its first chime and had to stoop to pick up cards from the floor.

"Braxton's being arrested about now," Nancy said while he was on his knees.

Sebastian's fingers refused to hold on to the cards and he dropped again the ones he had already recovered. "What can you mean?" he demanded, wide-eyed. "How can you know...?"

"His knife was found in the body," she said. "Buried between the shoulder blades. There's not another one like it in Texas."

"His knife?" Sebastian's brain was working no better than his fingers.

"He kept the wallet, you know. Stuck it in his own pocket. Thought we'd forget all about it in the excitement and he'd have all that money for himself. Ten to one, he'll still have it when they arrest him. That's what'll convict him."

Sebastian leaped to his feet, his expression frantic, terrified. "We've got to run," he said. "They'll be here to arrest us any minute—"

"Stop it." She blocked his path when he would have run into the hall, holding his arms in a surprisingly strong grip for so small a woman. "They won't be coming here. It's him they're arresting, not us." She paused, and added, in a disdainful voice, but he couldn't be certain to whom she referred, "Men are such fools."

"But—he'll know, he'll incriminate both of us—"

"No. The judge will see to that. He'll offer a bargain. If Braxton talks, we'll all three hang. He'll promise that if Braxton keeps his mouth shut, he'll get the lightest possible sentence. It was the result of a quarrel, he'll say—they'll make it look like a fight between the two. Manslaughter, that's what they call it. He'll promise Braxton a token sentence."

"Then he'll come after us when he gets out."

She gave him a cold look that seemed to chill the very marrow in his bones. "He'll never get out of prison—stop thinking like a child. The judge will see that he hangs for murder. It's just to keep him from talking, until it's too late."

They stared into one another's eyes. It occurred to Sebastian all at once that his own life was hanging in the balance now. If she thought he was a danger...

He managed somehow to laugh. "Well," he said, and was astonished to find he could speak at all, "if you hate a man, he's as good as in hell."

They both laughed.

Their laughter had barely subsided when a crash at the window spun them around. It was Braxton, torn and bleeding but with an unmistakable light of hatred shining from his eyes.

"Whore!" he lashed at Nancy. "Whoreson!"

He was holding on to the damask draperies and it was obvious he'd been shot, perhaps several times. Spittles of blood came from his contorted mouth as he lurched toward them.

Sebastian ran to the door but stopped frozen in horror as Lafe fell on Nancy, his hands on her throat. She might have fought him off, but his sheer bulk was too much for her. He pinioned her body to the floor and Sebastian watched her hands grope for some purchase to break Braxton's hold. Her right hand flashed, and Sebastian saw she'd drawn a small dagger from beneath her skirt. Again and again she plunged it into Lafe's meaty back, but his grip held even as her arm dropped lifeless to the carpet.

Lafe, his face contorted in pain and hate, looked toward Sebastian and began to crawl toward him. Sebastian found himself unable to move. Perhaps he felt it would have to end this way: He would be punished as he had punished; his sin would finally be atoned.

But Lafe's strength was fading; there was a dark trail of blood behind him. Inch by inch he moved toward Sebastian, and with one last vestige of animal strength, he pulled himself upright using a heavy marble-topped table as support.

Braxton stood there, weaving. He was dying, virtually before Sebastian's eyes. Yet Sebastian could not move. Braxton did not have strength left to attack him—he simply let his bearlike body fall forward, knocking over a table on which stood a coal-oil lamp. The lamp shattered, spilling orange fingers of flame across the room. Braxton's hands hit Sebastian on the shoulders and raked down his body, leaving bloody tracks on Sebastian's fawn coat.

Sebastian, his face in a ghastly relief, stood transfixed as the fire reached the draperies and licked at the wood paneling of the room. He could only stare: at the body of Nancy lying with the bloody dagger still clenched in her hand; at the hulk that was Lafe Braxton sprawled at his feet. The heat from the fire began to sear his face as the flames roared out of any hope of control. He was still standing there when the rose medallion ceiling fell. He had soiled his trousers, but those who would find the blackened bodies the next day would never know.

"Mrs. Harte?"

Joanna turned to peer through her veil at the sheriff. She had seen him before, beyond the ring of mourners, and supposed that he was there on some business or other.

"Yes, sheriff?"

"I've got to talk to you."

"Not now, dammit," Jay Jay said. He was on one side of his mother, Emily on the other, supporting her. Joanna had moved through the entire funeral business in a daze, hardly seeming to comprehend.

There was much she couldn't comprehend: how Webb could have been where they said he was; why, of all the people in the world, Lafe Braxton had chosen him to rob. It made no sense to her. The only person who might have answered all her questions was Lafe Braxton, and he was beyond that now. They were all beyond it: Braxton, Nancy, and the pitiable Sebastian. Maybe it was better not knowing, Joanna thought, but she disliked loose ends, even if these particular ends proved more painful than she wanted.

It was this thought—that perhaps the sheriff had brought her some new information—that prompted her to wave aside Jay Jay's objection.

"Yes, sheriff, what is it?"

He looked embarrassed. "We could go inside if you'd rather," he said, but no one answered him, and finally, shifting his hat from one hand to another, he said, "You sold some cows a few months ago, to the Olmsteds, over by Fort Worth."

"Yes." She could not keep the disappointment from her voice. Cows. What did she care for all the cows in Texas at a time like this? "I hope they're not trying to say I cheated them. They got the cows at a bargain price, frankly."

"Not enough of a bargain, I'm afraid." The hat went back the other way. "One of those cows has hoof-and-mouth."

Joanna staggered backward as if she'd been struck, and Jay Jay turned white beside her. "That can't be," he said.

"I got a telegram just today from Fort Worth. It's hoof-and-mouth all right, they're sure of it."

Emily, whose knowledge of cattle was still sketchy, asked, "Will the cow die?"

"Their whole herd will die," Joanna said, speaking in a weary voice. "Every piece of livestock they own will have to be shot and buried underground. It's the only way to keep it from spreading."

"An epidemic could wipe out the whole Texas cattle industry," the sheriff said.

"And the Folly herd will have to be quarantined, of course," Joanna said.

"Until we know," he agreed.

"But that's impossible," Jay Jay said. "There's too many head. We can't—"

"We can," Joanna said decisively. "And we will. If there's an epidemic, no one gets to say it came from here. You have my word, sheriff, the herd will be quarantined."

"It's the Platt cattle," Jay Jay said bitterly. "It must have come with them."

He didn't realize until he'd said it that it became an accusation: It was his mother who had insisted, over his objections, on buying those cattle.

"It doesn't matter where it came from," Joanna said. "What matters is that it goes no further." She turned to Emily. "You're to go into town at once. You're to wire the Olmsteds and every other ranch we sold a single head of those cattle to—everyone we've sold to in the last year. The Folly will underwrite every loss, down to the last penny."

Emily's eyes went wide; better than anyone else, she knew what sort of money they were talking about. One look at Joanna's face, however, convinced her not to argue. She nodded, and left them at once, hurrying in the direction of the house.

"Joanna, I'm sorry," the sheriff said.

"We all will be, I expect, before this is over," Joanna said.

By morning, the worst had been confirmed. The Folly herd was infected, and so were those on six other ranches, with several more still to be heard from. A grim-faced Jay Jay brought the news to Joanna in her bedroom; since Webb's death, she had not set foot in her office, leaving Emily, in effect, to run the ranch.

"Hire every cowpoke you can get," Joanna said when Jay Jay had told her of the outbreak in their herd; the others had been sending wires throughout the morning. "And every field hand, too. All those cows will have to be buried as fast as they're shot."

"That's almost a million head," he said, hardly able to comprehend the totality of the disaster. "Not even mentioning all those other herds."

"I'd guess another million in them, all told," she said.

"We're wiped out, aren't we?"

She had been gazing out the window, at the wide, rolling prairie she knew so well. Now her head snapped around. "What are you talking about?" she demanded in an angry voice.

"Not even the Folly can absorb losses like that, ma, without going under."

To his amazement, she slapped him. "I won't hear a son of mine talking that way," she said, "like some sort of quitter. We've been hurt, yes, hurt bad, but we're not done yet. You don't lose the fight when they knock you down, you lose when you don't get back up. Now get out of here. You've got work to do, and plenty of it."

PART IV

THE SONG OF
A BIRD

FORTY-SEVEN

Joanna blinked and opened her eyes, surprised to discover she had actually been dozing. The hot afternoon sun had faded from the terrace, leaving long, cooling shadows in its wake. It was sunset already, one of those majestic scarlet and purple sunsets she had always loved so.

The shooting and the braying of cattle, however, went on, as it would all night, as it had for a week, as it would until the roundup was finished.

What a roundup! With all the grim reality of it, one could still not help being awed. There had never been one like it. Better than two thousand cowboys, hired and borrowed from ranches as far away as Oklahoma and Kansas, fanning out over the immeasurable acreage of the Folly. Every cow, every steer, every calf had to be rounded up, driven to one of those locations where another army of laborers was digging huge trenches in which to bury the carcasses.

Meanwhile, throughout the state and as far away as New York and Washington, people were shaking their heads, discussing the situation in hushed and solemn voices: Joanna Harte, brought to her knees; the Folly, teetering on the brink. A few ran speculative tongues over their lips, watched their neighbors, and wondered who would be the first to grab for the prize. The Queen of Ranches, waiting for a king bold enough, strong enough—*rich* enough.

The thoughts came back like flies buzzing over dying cattle, hovering, circling. Her mistakes, hers alone. Bad enough to have misjudged Sebastian and Nancy—she ought to have known better than to believe in a suddenly sentimental impulse from that corner. But that was only money they didn't have now, much as they could have used it. The cattle, there was where she had fallen flat on her face. To herself, she couldn't even use the excuse that she hadn't known; she *had* known, something at least. The cattle had looked sickly from the very beginning. Jay Jay noticed it; she had noticed it herself, and had put it down to the overgrazing that had led Platt into ruin. Overgrazing. She had been looking for an excuse to do what she had set her mind on doing. Pure stubbornness, and nothing else. That blind spot again.

Well, she didn't mind admitting her mistakes, nor even paying for them, but it wasn't just she who was paying.

At any rate, the Folly wouldn't pay for any more of her mistakes, assuming they made it through this one. She was ready to retire, should have done so sooner, obviously.

Surprisingly, that bothered her less than she had always thought it would. She was old—overnight, it seemed. Not just old, either; she was old-fashioned—she had begun of late to perceive this. That trip to Galveston had opened her eyes to some degree—the speed and ease with which they had traveled had both exhilarated and saddened her. She was beginning to see those newfangled horseless carriages even on the streets of San Antone, and electric lights, and now these telephones. Emily had just recently brought up the idea of having one installed here at the ranch.

Of course, they were wonderful—it was hard to imagine the convenience that they would bring to life on a ranch such as the Folly. Just think, to talk with someone clear in town without even having to saddle up a horse and ride the distance.

On the other hand, it seemed to her that the blessings were not entirely unmixed. Wasn't there an advantage, too, in that blanket of time and distance that surrounded them here? Why, that was part of why they had come here to begin with. A great explosion elsewhere was no less great, but it reached you, finally, as minor reverberations. A great quarrel? How could it not benefit from being given time to cool down? Decisions to consider? How better to consider them than over the days and weeks of journeying across a trackless plain? And if you could be anywhere else you chose in the blink of an eye, didn't that somehow lessen, cheapen, where you were? Just as waiting weeks, months, for something as simple as, say, a bolt of special dress goods turned that simple pleasure into something of a treasure, something miraculous to be celebrated.

"Joanna? Oh, there you are. I wondered..." Emily came out onto the balcony. "Melissa's here. She's on her way up."

"Oh, Lord, am I going to have to listen to *her* bray, too?" Joanna said. She sighed. "Well, you'd better help me into the office; she always found that room intimidating."

They had barely reached there when Melissa came in, her new hobbled skirt revealing trim ankles. Joanna looked at her with renewed insight, and was actually pleased to see what a handsome woman her daughter really was, hardly less beautiful than when they had set out for Texas originally. Of course, she supposed in a mother's eyes every daughter remained young and pretty, even one as pesty as Melissa could be.

"I have come to save the Folly," Melissa declared with a triumphant gesture.

"I can think of no one more likely to discover a cure for hoof in mouth," Joanna said.

"Now, mother, you know I know nothing about cattle. I have come to purchase your jewelry."

"My jewelry?"

"Oh, not at full price, mind you. I shall have to turn a profit if I am to save us all from the price of your greed. I'll be lucky to manage as it is."

"Then I'm glad to be able to tell you you're too late," Joanna said. "I pledged every last piece of it to the bank, to cover our loans. Of course, if you'd like to put up your store..."

"My store?" Melissa's eyes went wide with indignation. "And see myself and my son on the streets to save this place? No, thank you."

"Well, then..." Joanna shrugged and turned toward her desk, but stopped. "What is that?" she asked, pointing at a bucket sitting on the floor at one end of Emily's desk.

"Oil," Emily said, a little sheepishly. "I was dying of curiosity, I'd never seen the stuff, so I asked Sebastian if he wouldn't send me a sample. Ugly, isn't it?"

"So that's what it is," Joanna said, taking a step closer to stare down at the bucket's contents.

It was ugly; yet there was something fascinating, too. It was like onyx, polished to a green-black shine on its surface. She could not help thinking that there was the stuff of which the earth was once made—the plants, the animals, the life that had once roamed perhaps this very spot where they now stood—reduced to its primeval ooze.

Melissa's reaction to the bucket was predictably more dramatic. "There," she said, pointing a finger. "There is the fortune that might have been ours."

"Really, Melissa," Joanna said, "if I didn't need this stick for walking, I believe I'd crack your head with it."

Melissa, who knew better than to take a threat of her mother's lightly, actually leaped backward a step. "You see!" she cried to no one in particular. "You see!"

Emily was paying no mind to her, however, for at that moment Joanna had swayed as if she might faint, and Emily was immediately at her side. "Delfina!" she cried, helping Joanna to a chair. "Maria, come quick, the señora is ill!"

The two maids came running in at once; it seemed as if these days they were never more than a few feet away from wherever Joanna was in the house. The three women half led, half carried Joanna toward her bedroom.

With a gasp, Melissa sank into the chair Joanna had just left, crying, "Oh, my stars, I think I'm about to expire. Help, someone, please!" to no avail.

The last Emily saw of Joanna that evening, Joanna was abed, sleeping soundly; so she was astonished when the opening of her bedroom door woke her at dawn the next morning and she looked to discover Joanna standing there, already dressed in her riding clothes, holding a lamp.

"Joanna, what..."

Joanna put a finger to her lips. "Ssh, I don't want to rouse the whole household. Get dressed. I want you to come for a ride with me."

"A ride? At this hour? Do you think you should?"

"I can still ride. Better than I can walk, truth to tell. Quick now, it's important."

No one cared more wholeheartedly, nor was more concerned,

for Joanna than Emily, but Emily also knew her friend and mentor well enough to know when her mind was set on something to the point where argument was useless.

"I'll only take a minute," she said, scrambling out of bed.

In fewer than ten, the two of them were stealing from the house. In the stables, Joanna let Emily saddle up two horses for them, and even help her onto her mount, but once they had walked the horses far enough from the house to avoid waking the others, Joanna took the lead, riding out with a confidence and ease that belied the difficulty she now had on foot. They spoke hardly at all. Joanna seemed to know exactly where she was going, only once or twice slowing her horse a little as she looked around to get her bearings.

Little more than half an hour later, Joanna reined in her mount. "Here," she said, pointing toward a little hillock dotted with boulders. The area was only a couple of miles beyond the makeshift town known as Heartsville, though it had once been unbroken range. "We'll walk the horses the rest of the way. You'll have to help me. I didn't bother bringing my stick."

It was slow going, what with leading horses and Joanna's having to lean on Emily's arm. As they reached the top of the rise, however, Joanna's eyes glinted with excitement, and pushing herself free of Emily, she practically ran forward on her own. "Yes, this is it!" she cried.

Emily, coming alongside her, saw nothing but a minor indentation, mostly filled with rocks—the sort of place, she found herself thinking, favored by rattlesnakes and not much else. "I don't..." she started to say, but Joanna was already scrambling down, balancing herself on the rocks.

"There—that stick there," Joanna said, pointing to a weather-beaten piece of cottonwood. "Bring that here. Help me move one of these rocks with it."

Emily got the stick and propped one end under a rock to use it for a lever. "I'll do it," she said, but Joanna ignored her and leaned forward to help tug at the rock. It lifted and rolled aside, and at once Joanna dropped to her knees by where it had been. She yanked off one glove and prodded the wet soil with her finger. "I was right," she said. "Here, look for yourself."

Emily bent, too, but saw nothing except wet, black soil, and an equally black wetness on the tip of Joanna's finger.

"It's oil," Joanna said in a jubilant whisper. "The same as yesterday, the same as Sebastian sent you in that bucket."

Emily stared. She put a finger of her own to the ground; it was muddy wet, and when she took her finger away, the indentation began to fill slowly with a shiny, green-black ooze. Joanna was right—it was oil.

"This used to be a wateringhole," Joanna said, "till it got fouled. I filled it in myself years ago, with Alice Montgomery waiting right over there in the buggy. There's a half-dozen more holes just like this within a few miles of here, all fouled just like this. I didn't know what it was fouling them until yesterday."

Emily looked into her brightly shining eyes, hardly able to believe what this signified. "Do you—do you think there's enough?" she asked.

"More than enough, I'd say. I've been reading up on it half the night—I didn't want to give anybody an inkling till I was more certain. It lies beneath the ground in enormous lakes. This whole ranch must be sitting on top of an ocean of that stuff."

"Oh, Joanna!" They fell into one another's arms across the muddy puddle of oil, hugging each other happily.

"It's something else you'll have to learn about," Joanna said finally, "something I can't even help you with. You'll have to do it on your own. Only, I want you to promise me something: I don't want all this spoiled." She looked out over the rocks to where the sun was even now coloring a distant sky the pink of fresh salmon. "Promise me that you won't let the oil destroy all this beauty."

"I promise," Emily said, and then gave a muffled sob. "Oh, Joanna, I don't see how... Are you sure I'm the one? The only one?"

"I'm sure," Joanna said, smiling. "Don't be frightened by it. You've seen the men who run things; you know you've got just as many brains as some of them, and more than a few have."

"There's so much I don't know."

"You'll never know it all. Learn as much as you can. Guess the rest. That's all anybody can do. Don't ask too many questions—queens aren't supposed to ask questions; they're to answer them for other people. In return for which they'll fear you, and distrust you, and resent you, even the ones who love you best."

"Is it worth it?"

Joanna's smile was tinged with a certain melancholy. "For you? Only you can answer that. And by the time you're able to, it'll be too late to matter."

"Was it..." Emily hesitated.

"Was it worth it for me? Yes. Yes, it was," Joanna said. They were silent for a moment; then she said, "Now, I want you to leave me here. I'd like to be alone for a little while, if you don't mind."

"Will you be all right?"

Joanna laughed. "Here? If not here, where? Go along, and don't worry. I'll be in shortly."

Emily hesitated for a moment more; then, with a final kiss on Joanna's cheek, she scrambled back over the rocks and, mounting her own horse, rode back toward the Folly.

Joanna sat for a long while, watching the sky turn to its usual blue-gray color, feeling the heat begin to rise from the rocks around her.

The Folly was saved, she was sure of that; and if she hadn't worked any miracles to manage that, she was grateful at least that her love for this land had led her to know it so well, had made it possible for her to remember something as seemingly insignificant as the look and smell of a fouled water hole.

So, she hadn't lost the fight after all: To try, to fail, and having failed, to try again, why, that was a kind of winning, wasn't it?

She got up and made her way cautiously over the boulders to where her horse was waiting. Holding his reins, she led him toward one of the larger rocks; it would be easier to get into the stirrup standing on that. She raised a booted foot to step onto the rock, and just as she did so, heard the warning rattle and saw a flicker of movement from the corner of her eye.

Too late! The horse had heard it, too. Her grip on the rein was too light; in an instant he had bolted, and she had lost her precarious balance. She fell, and as she fell, for only a heartbeat's space in time, she found herself looking into the very eyes of death: The rattler, startled and angered to see this creature he had warned plunged toward him, struck out in all his fury. She felt what might have been twin pinpricks; she was lying upon the rattler, she could feel his squirming to free himself, and the pricks came again, and again, and once again, before the rattler was gone from beneath her. She fancied she could hear him slithering over the rocks, and— it seemed ever so far away—the thudding of her horse's hooves as he ran homeward, his saddle empty.

Finally, stillness. They'd come to look, of course, as soon as the horse rode in; but she was no fool—she knew already they'd be too late.

She supposed she should have been frightened, or angry. Oddly, she felt neither. Here she lay, on the land she had loved so well, for so long, and above her, no matter which way she turned her eyes, a shining, endless sky. When had she last felt so content, so at peace?

How long she lay, thinking of scarcely anything, she had no idea. And then, finally, she thought she heard—was that...yes, surely it was, a mockingbird, singing somewhere nearby, the notes of his song cascading like one of those little brooks in the distant mountains, clear and pure, plucking the heartstrings as they went.

She closed her eyes. Through the lids she could still see the brilliant Texas sun overhead, and a shadow passing before it that might have been a cloud, or a bird, or even her soul rushing upward to merge with the warm Texas wind.